ALL
JOE
KNIGHT

Also by Kevin Morris
White Man's Problems

ALL JOE KNIGHT

KEVIN MORRIS

Grove Press
New York

First Grove Atlantic hardcover edition: December 2016

Published simultaneously in Canada
Printed in the United States of America

FIRST EDITION

Library of Congress Cataloging-in-Publication Data

Names: Morris, Kevin (Lawyer), author.
Title: All Joe Knight : a novel / Kevin Morris.
Description: First hardcover edition. | New York, NY : Grove Press, 2016.
Identifiers: LCCN 2016023949 (print) | LCCN 2016032247 (ebook) |
ISBN 9780802125781 (hardback) | ISBN 9780802189677 (eBook)
Subjects: LCSH: Divorced men—Fiction. | Life change events—Fiction. |
Loss (Psychology)—Fiction. | Self-evaluation—Fiction. | Philadelphia (Pa.)—
Fiction. | Psychological fiction. | BISAC: FICTION / Literary.
Classification: LCC PS3613.O7737 A35 2016 (print) |
LCC PS3613.O7737 (ebook)

ISBN 978-0-8021-2578-1
eISBN 978-0-8021-8967-7

Grove Press
an imprint of Grove Atlantic
154 West 14th Street
New York, NY 10011

Distributed by Publishers Group West

groveatlantic.com

16 17 18 19   10 9 8 7 6 5 4 3 2 1

This book is for my brothers,
Dennis and Brian.

America does not repel the past or what it has produced under its forms or amid other politics or the idea of castes or the old religions . . . accepts the lesson with calmness . . . is not so impatient as has been supposed that the slough still sticks to opinions and manners and literature while the life which served its requirements has passed into the new life of the new forms . . . perceives that the corpse is slowly borne from the eating and sleeping rooms of the house . . . perceives that it waits a little while in the door . . . that it was fittest for its days . . . that its action has descended to the stalwart and well shaped heir who approaches . . . and that he shall be fittest for his days.

—Walt Whitman, *Leaves of Grass*

No one knew her religion when they found my mother dead outside of Gettysburg in a smashed-up T-bird with a man named Royal Brown, so they cremated her. The guy who hit them must have stolen her purse and Royal Brown's wallet, the only explanation for two unidentifiable people lying dead in a ditch by a county road.

I had her ashes. They were in a container that looked like the thing Barbara Eden came out of in *I Dream of Jeannie*. I hated that show, especially the way it was set on a military base while they acted like it was a suburban neighborhood. Such classic TV: an obvious deceit on top of a subtle lie. I couldn't believe anyone went for something that ridiculous. I wasn't angry; I just thought a little more respect should be given to reality. You can't rub a bottle and get what you want.

I was six months old. I have black-and-white pictures of her in a bathing suit in Ocean City and an eight-millimeter movie from when she was pregnant, slapping my father's hand as he tried to take food off a platter. There's another one of her playing solitaire. She's alone at a table setting up the game, playing it as it lays. But they weren't so domesticated, even in the home movies. They looked a little like greasers from old TV shows and magazines, dark and shadowy, my mother in pants and a scarf and fake eyelashes and my father with blue-black hair and sunken eyes.

Nine months before the Royal Brown mess, three months before I was born, my father drove shitfaced out of the Lobster Pot on Barren Road and ran into a telephone pole a quarter mile south, by the Dairy Queen. He was on a nonstop bender once my mother told him she was pregnant. He was black Irish, an ass-chaser, a biter of the apple. He looked like a doctor from a doctor show, like Chad Everett, or maybe a crooner, like Roger Miller, hair parted on the side, charming. They were very young to get married, like everybody in those days, my mother not out of high school. It all went fast, wedding, baby on the way. They rallied and had a reception at the Stuckley Firehouse and she got to wear the white dress.

My mother was from the orphanage in Glen Mills, her beginnings a dead secret. All that ever made its way to me were vague accounts of an underage Irish scullery cook and the master of a Main Line mansion. According to my aunt Dottie, she was a pretty girl, not too good in the head on her best days, and after my father's accident she was unbearable: fat-pregnant, crazy, and alone. As soon as she got out of bed, she started going out with men and planning her getaway. She said she was going to North Carolina to become a nurse, but that was bullshit. She disappeared with Royal two weeks early and they weren't headed to North Carolina.

No one wanted me but Dottie and Artie, but I suppose you could turn that around to say those two wanted me like no one else. The story goes that Artie—who was sort of a mystery to what little family and friends there were to say good-bye to my mother—changed my diaper in the last pew of the church while the priest gave the eulogy in whatever kind of cockeyed ceremony they do when it turns out an accidental cremation has occurred. My mother had girlfriends and other acquaintances from the apartment where we lived, and Dottie had a quiet reception for everyone after church. I imagine Dottie just took over, she and Artie picking up cups and glasses and emptying ashtrays, signaling that it was okay to leave, and all the others gladly putting their cigarettes out and fading away.

I was an accident. I was so much an accident that two emphasizing accidents followed—like two more bullets to the head of a mark already dead down on the ground. It is not incorrect to say that I am the only thing my parents put into the world, and because of what happened to them, I am a cleaner slate than most, a more trustworthy accountant of the truth. Having nothing—starting from zero, being the only thing—is not a thing of value or a thing of hurt. It is a natural state. I make of things what I can, trying not to let illusions carry each day, trying not to make mistakes about the hard truth. The effect has been to focus me on fact, to see blades of grass, leaves on trees, trees in forest.

    . . . In the morning I help pick up the dead and lay them in rows in the barn.

This much is fact: 36,285 people died in car crashes in America in 1961 and my parents were two of them. They both were headed north. My father was driving and my mother was a passenger; he was coming home and she was leaving; he was drunk and she got hit by a drunk. Over nine months, same amount of time it takes to have a kid, they were dead. For all I knew, they both did not want to die.

ROSTER—1977–78 FALLCREST H.S. QUAKERS

BOYS BASKETBALL VARSITY

Coach: Jim Casale

No.	Name	Pos.	Ht.	Yr.
11	Scully, Chris	G	6'0"	Sr.
24	Garrison, Jeremy	G	6'0"	Sr.
44	Ford, Phillip	F	6'3"	Sr.
42	Stokes, David	F	6'5"	Sr.
55	LeFeber, Steven	C	6'9"	Sr.

Reserves

No.	Name	Pos.	Ht.	Yr.
22	Polk, Leonard	G/F	6'2"	Sr.
10	Knight, Joe	G	6'0"	Sr.
23	Dunn, Mike	F	6'4"	Sr.
32	Dunn, Sean	F	6'4"	Sr.
45	Coverdale, Henry	F	6'3"	Sr.
4	Butcher, Ethrdge	G	5'8"	Sr.
13	Beatty, Terry	F	6'3"	Jr.
5	Marlowe, Harvey	F/C	6'5"	Jr.

I

FOUNDINGS

What you build is best done with bricks. The man I sent can make them.

—letter from Wm. Penn, 1685

1

First they won the clay. They knew how to choose it. They knew clay with high iron content produced a deep red brick after firing. They dug in the autumn, exposing the soil to the wind and ice and snow from the rivers, from the Atlantic, from the sky. They knew the freeze-thaw cycle made everything softer in the spring, that it rid the soil of oxides: science not yet in books but known to the immigrants who came here. They knew how to get rid of impurities that ruined bricks. They knew the steps.

Pennsylvanians. These are my people who built the brick buildings. These are my people who won the wars. Stone-hard people. The English, Welshmen, Irish, Dutch, Swedes, and Scots. Quakers and Catholics, Lutherans, Presbyterians, Calvinists, Adventists, Abolitionists. Slaves. We are ended here in the Mid-Atlantic, all of us. We are not brash New York or briny New England; not aristocratic Virginian or separatist, agrarian South; not toothless, semi-animal, frontier Western. We are the people who finally ejected the British. We burned the South when the rest were too tired or too dead to finish the Civil War. We have been here. Someone has stood by the cradle. We are underrated by history and underestimated by the rest. Come see the Bell, motherfuckers.

We are a cold weather–ready people, white skinned, hard-hardened in that deep pale white. The blacks are blacksmith black, anvil black. We were mule skinners, tanners, smiths and forge men, fishmongers, horsemen and cavalrymen, union men and masons. We are the bankers of the Revolution. We are the best lawyers there are. The middle soldier raising the flag on Iwo Jima was Pennsylvanian. We came back from the wars. We built houses and churches and courthouses and schools from red brick and stone. We drank ale and whiskey and followed priests and bishops and ministers. We are the people of John Reynolds and Thaddeus Stevens and Winfield Scott Hancock. Come see the Bell.

And we are the hard redbrick people of the ever-since. We are the southernmost north but we are the North, don't forget it. Long nasal oo's. "Are you hooome?" Friday is Fridey. Tuesday is Tuesdey. We drink wudder and touch our farheads. You might not think so, but we call people niggers, we call people harps, we call them kikes and wops. Pick a category. You want the writers, take Jeffers, take Updike. You want the ballplayers, take Honus Wagner and Red Grange. You want quarterbacks named Joe, take Namath and Montana. Try Wilt Chamberlain and Arnold Palmer. You want the music, the real music, the too-true-to-face-it music, you got Coltrane. In this red brick we are the song. Come see the Bell.

2

If you really get down to it, the Indians were first. The Lenape—the Sankhikan, Atsayanck, Remkoke, Armewarmex, Mantaes, Naranti-conck, Little Siconese, Sewapolis, the Big Siconese—lost to the Susquehannocks in 1634 and took south. They had it first, before William Penn got here.

I'll take Penn over any of the others. He's my founding father. The *P* encyclopedia had a long entry on him. He was a serious guy, religious and rebellious—rebellious because he was religious. He said:

I had no relations that inclined to so solitary and spiritual way; I was a child alone. A child given to musing, occasionally feeling the divine presence.

Such were his beliefs that he left his cushy life to become a Quaker, to join the Religious Society of Friends, haters of symbols, silent meditators. They were persecuted throughout England. As a young man, Penn was jailed in the Tower of London, where he wrote a pamphlet called *No Cross, No Crown*, which had sixty-eight citations from memory. Sixty-eight fucking citations from memory. C'mon. Hum babe.

Pennsylvania was actually named after his father, the old admiral, William Penn Sr., who helped the Stuarts retake the throne after Oliver Cromwell. To repay the old man, William Penn Jr. was deeded everything between New York and Baltimore. All he had to do was give the king three beaver pelts a year and 20 percent of any gold. Twenty percent of all the gold in Pennsylvania for anything is a good deal.

The city, Philadelphia, was his great idea. Having had the shit kicked out of him for being a Quaker, he wanted a place for tolerance.

A greene country town, which will never be burnt, and always wholesome.

He chose twelve hundred acres between the Delaware and the Schuylkill and planned a rectangular city with four main streets, four quadrants. He planted trees. He wrote *The Frame of Government*, which predated the Declaration and Constitution. The only white man of the time who tried to be square, he made a treaty with Chief Tamanend of the Lenape. The Quaker schools were open to everybody.

He was obsessed with the Great London Fire of 1666. He wanted people to build on the middle of their lots, so fire couldn't spread. By the 1680s, Philadelphia was a hopping place with shops and merchants and newspapers and all forms of religion. Redbrick buildings were everywhere. Three hundred and thirty years ago it was fully formed. *A greene country town, which will never be burnt, and always wholesome.*

Sad part is that is all gone. Reality is stark. The city might have been an invention, but now it's soft pretzel wrappers flying in the wind. It's broken glass, cigarette butts, cummed-in rubbers, and other shit on the ground. I don't think it's a *greene country town*. I think it's detritus; I think it's what's left after the show.

3

This is my Philadelphia story.

When people ask me how I got so smart, I say television. When people ask me what I love, I say music. When people ask me what made me so successful, I say basketball. When people ask me my plans for the future, I say getting out of here.

I came close to being a real guy. I had chances, good breaks gone to waste. I know I fucked up—with Dottie, with Janice, with Tia. When I was young, I had promise and hope. I thought my makeshift family, my friends, and basketball were God's way of giving me things—sparks, extra bread crumbs—to make up for having dead folks. Almost as though he was saying, "Jump in. It all happens for a reason." But all that was simply a story I was telling myself. Those things were only slots to drop through on the way to being alone.

I might be scattered, but that's okay. At least I'm not one of those guys who just talk about themselves, hyperarticulate, so clever, writing footnotes about their own names. They look at prisms through prisms, reinventors reinventing. Really now, is that all the fuck you can do, talk about yourself, preening in front of the irony?

I'd like to see you tell me your story without lies.

I will tell you what I can, but I will tell you this: you with your thirties story you had the Depression; your forties story you had the War; your fifties story you had the Russians; your sixties story you had Vietnam. You had the wars and Ozzie Nelson and the Generation Gap, blah blah. But it was all clear-cut. You never had to pick over dead bodies through empty popcorn boxes covered with Afros and leg warmers and Jane

Fonda commercialized. You never had to wander with masked wrestlers through the postmodern bullshit of this Postmodern to find a new song.

I remember every face of every man who put me here.

I am Joe, sometimes Joey. Ordinary Joe. Average Joe. Joe Blow. Joseph Michael Knight Jr. Joe Knight. All night long. All Knight Long. All Knight.

I am a great player. The music of basketball was part of me, like my skin, like my big jimmy. I won hundreds of trophies, one-on-one tourneys, summer league championships, all-star medals, and foul-shooting contests. I made all-tournament, all-league, all small-college, all you-name-it teams. I played every day, like water, like blood, even when I didn't want to, like piano scales, like tooth fillings, until I fouled out of my last game in my last year of college. Even when I didn't start, even when I wasn't the star, there was never a doubt of my special ability to play the game. You want me on your squad. I am a gym rat. I will school you. Game, faggots. I'll light you up all night long. All Knight Long.

My favorite moment in all of basketball is when a guy goes to the foul line after time has run out. The refs clear the players off the court and the shooter gets the ball. This happened to me twice. First time, I was ten, playing for Optimists against Rotary at the Penwood Boys Club Championship game. We were losing 49-48 and I got fouled as the buzzer went off. Two shots. The paint of the square above the rim was faded red, worn from thousands of bank shots, the nylon net gone gray.

I made them both. I could have missed them both. Or made one. The point is I made them. Despite what people say, you know if you are going to make it or not. It is a discovery, not a skill. I didn't know it before that day, before I got fouled by a guy on a twelve-and-under team wearing jerseys bought by the Optimist Club of Penwood, guys who drank at Len's Place on 352 and had spaghetti dinners for the Heart Association. But from there on I knew.

There are windmills at the Dairy Queen on Barren Road and some in Dutch Country. You want to talk about the worst vacation possible, consider hauling a pack of brats around Pennsylvania Dutch Country. I had to go there three times when I was a kid and I honestly don't know what the fuck people think is tourist-worthy about that place. Not the Amish. They want to be left alone. It's like going to a zoo. Or a make-believe world. There they are with their own rules, living in a magic universe.

And even with all the time that's gone by, I still go to the Dairy Queen on Barren Road where my father crashed. Still think there is something about a Dairy Queen that is fantastic, like an illusion, like the windmill that is part of the sign. Dottie took me there and we sat under that windmill. She got me a Dilly Bar with nuts. She ordered a hot fudge sundae. I've relived it a hundred times—getting mad about that. It was the only time I was shitty to her. I said, "You shouldn't have that. You don't need that, look at you." When I pulled it away, she tried to shovel the black-and-white mixture really fast into her mouth, three more quick spoonfuls. She loved the fudgy topping.

All she said was, "I wish you would be sweet." Dottie never said anything else but that when it came to me. She saw I had a black streak like the shoe polish in my father's hair. Truth is by the time I came around, I'm not so sure old players recognized young players through some eternal bond, basking in the light of the passed torch. That meant little to us, the sad and plain enduring beauty of connection. I hate to say it, but that's too hopeful. It is old-fashioned and it imbues the whole thing with too much meaning. Life as I see it is more dire, less romantic. Like our asses are flat-out hanging over a cliff, over the abyss, out in the air, with us here wondering what, if anything, we can do about it.

4

My aunt Dottie loved to talk about the first time she took me to church. We walked into St. Ignatius and the priest said, "Christ is the one." I was a really little kid. She'd promised we were coming to see Jesus. I was excited. The priest was at the altar in the modern building, part of the new church, the New Word. There was a tapestry of Him on the cross.

Before she could sit me down, I said, "Where's Jesus?" I kept saying it to her, "Where is he? Where's Jesus?"

"He's up there."

"It's a rug."

It became uncomfortable and after she took Communion, we left. That's the thing: I've always felt that I was the one. That it's on me.

Not I, not anyone else can travel that road for you, you must travel it for yourself.

Might be the circumstances or it might just be me, but I don't think so. I have not met many people who didn't think they were the one. Dottie, maybe, and the ladies like her, the selfless ones who raise children and believe in God, believe that Christ is the one. But if you ask me, you walk the last mile alone.

You must travel it for yourself.

Dottie met Uncle Artie on the train. Her face was a perfect circle with big eyes. She wore a Santa hat to work at the post office at Christmastime. She was ten years older than my father, Joseph M. Knight Sr. Their parents died of cancer within a year of each other when he was in grade school and their two brothers were killed in World War II. With everyone else dead, she took care of him. He got big and wild but they were connected at the heart; Dottie defended him to the bone. She was Irish like that, loyal and forgiving, especially of men. And she did not gloss over the fact that I had dead parents, nor did she pretend that she was my mother. That absence was not hidden, the hole in that place lived with us in plain and blatant truth.

Artie was a conductor for Amtrak, running the D.C.-to-Boston route for twenty-five years. Dottie took the big train into town because it passed through Penwood, where she boarded every morning after driving from Stuckley. Artie was quite a bit older. When they met, he lived in Baltimore with a wife and kids. He left it all to be with her.

She was five foot two, pudgy, with peach-colored hair about the consistency of cotton candy, the result of once-a-month trips to Betty's Beauty Salon on Pennell Road, where she sat under a hair dryer for twenty-five minutes and read *Redbook*. Her holiday verve did not end with Santa hats. She wore a sweatshirt with a turkey at Thanksgiving and she got mad if you didn't wear green on St. Patrick's Day. She was way into the Bicentennial in 1976. The worst thing she bought was a macramé red-white-and-blue Uncle Sam hat. She loved Reese's Peanut Butter Cups so much that she sneaked them when no one was looking. When she made me chocolate milk with Hershey's syrup, she made herself a glass, too.

Dottie graduated from Sacred Heart Catholic School for Girls in Nether Providence in 1948 with twelve years of perfect attendance. Then she went to work for Bell Telephone in Philadelphia and didn't miss a day for another ten. Artie used to say, "She's steady, that's for sure." He was already pretty old when they took me. He had to go to the old folks' home, Woodlawn Acres, when I was ten. But he was around long enough for me to see that he loved Dottie. I haven't really seen anything like the two of them since.

We lived on Mount Road, which was a quarter-mile strip at the top of a hill in Stuckley. At the other end was St. Ignatius, looking out over the town. Stuckley Road was perpendicular to Mount Road, running from St. Ignatius down the big hill, breaking into three smaller streets, each of which led to an industrial facility, each of which had been a textile mill 150 years before. The mills were gone, but industrial plants remained: two container manufacturers, CRI and Stuckley Container Products; and the headquarters of Karl Buttmann Handyman Services and Lawn Mowing.

Rusty cars on cinder blocks, redbrick and cracked, broken concrete steps and landings made Stuckley. Dirt and stone mixed in the yards of houses: black-brown soil with green weeds growing through cement and rocky hillsides with stones and blue glass shards from old-time medicine bottles. The winters were cold and full of trash fires. If you were a Stuckley kid, you walked. Down roads and through back porches and under clotheslines; through gravel parking lots and churchyards; in rain and snow and in the summertime, when it was so hot and bonkers-humid you wished to God for the end-of-the-day thunderstorm that brought steam off the roads and lightning so loud it scared the dogs inside.

Our house had two bedrooms, a living room with a sofa and two chairs, a kitchen the size of a jail cell, and a bathroom with a toilet, sink, and stand-up shower. It breaks my heart these days to think Dottie never got to take a bath. There was one special thing about the place, an extra space off the side of the living room. She called it "the parlor." When she wanted me to sit and talk with her, she put on the English accent and said, "Meet me in the parlor for tea," trying to make me laugh. Laughing because she was so silly when I was little and laughing because I loved her when I was not little anymore. If I whined, she said, "Heavens be . . ."

Dottie and Artie looked out for each other. Artie was an Eschatologist and to keep him happy Dottie pretended to be one, too. But she sneaked off to Mass once a month and then all the time after he went to pieces. It was pretty bizarre of him to take up Eschatology. The things I read said it was a break-off from Christian Science, a system of beliefs developed by William Walter, a store clerk from Aurora, Illinois. It's somewhere between Old-Time Religion and the New Age. They say it deals with Last Days, which sounds like federal-agents-are-coming-to-the-compound kind of shit. They also say it involves telekinesis, which sounds like the Amazing Kreskin. Artie didn't really seem as crazy as all that. He was nice to me.

He did not pretend to be my father, and that hole, too, lived in plain and blatant truth. He told me things to remember and he played me music.

For extra money, Dottie worked at Pinelli's on Baltimore Pike on Wednesdays and Fridays and whenever anyone needed a substitute. When she was gone, I watched TV. Anytime I was not playing basketball or listening to music, I watched TV. In from the cold, rain, cold rain, humidity, thunder, heat lightning, after school, after practice, on Saturdays. I made tomato soup, using milk instead of water when we had it. I crackled up saltines, sometimes oyster crackers when Dottie remembered to get them, and brought the bowl to a stew that was red and orange and pink at the same time, with the ends of crackers darkened like toast crusts sticking out like icebergs above the tomato sea.

I got myself set up. I left a few crackers out to put peanut butter on, put ice in a glass, grabbed a Coke, put it all on a TV tray. In 1974—I think that year was the bottom of everything, with the ten years on either side of it serving as feeder roads of insanity—I must have watched five hours a day.

The shows were about families: *All in the Family*, *Sanford and Son*, *Chico and the Man*, *The Waltons*, *The Jeffersons*. There was an hour-long show on ABC called *Family*. There was a half-hour show called *That's My Mama*. I wondered who had bigger jugs, Mama from *That's My Mama* or Weezy from *The Jeffersons*. Her name was Louise but George called her Weezy. She looked like she had a card table under her dress.

Or they were about belonging to something. I wanted to be on *The A-Team*, on a *S.W.A.T.* team. I wanted to be a prisoner on *Hogan's Heroes*, a reporter for *Lou Grant*, a student in *Room 222*, a *Rookie*, one of Ben Cartwright's boys. I wanted to be in *F Troop*.

I spent more time in front of the television than the mirror. I wanted to be a smart, old crime solver, someone distinct from the dumb normal cops. A detective, or a lawyer, or a private eye, or a coroner. Preferably with a cigar, or a hat, or a limp, or a cane, or a lollipop. I wanted to have special insight. Like Cannon, or Mannix, or Baretta, or Kojak, or

Ironsides, or Barnaby Jones, or Kolshak, or Columbo, or Harry O, or the guys from *Dragnet*, or Petrocelli, or Delvecchio, or Quincy. I wanted to be Perry Mason and jump up and say to the whole world, "Objection, lack of foundation."

I knew *Captain Kangaroo* was a national show. It had good production values: the sets were nice, kind of *Mister Rogers*–ish, kind of post–*Kukla, Fran and Ollie*. Where we lived, after *Captain Kangaroo* you got this other nut, Captain Noah. He was more local, and taller, uglier, weirder, and cheaper than the fat Captain Kangaroo. He wasn't as good, the way *Action News* wasn't as good as the *CBS Evening News* or *World News Tonight*, like Larry Kane and Big Al Meltzer were lamer and cheaper and dopier and cheaper and less remote and cheaper than Walter Cronkite and Harry Reasoner. Same way they were less important than Barbara Walters. There was the weirdest show in reruns called *Family Affair*. It had these two faggoty little kids, Buffy and Jody. They were orphans like me, living with their uncle Bill and a butler, Mr. French, on Fifth Avenue in New York. Their parents got killed in a car crash I think, but it wasn't like my life.

I watched commercials, endless commercials, which they tell you is bad. There's some vague notion you should look back at this like a smoker, that the damage from the secondhand poison will show up later. Movies are more passive than books, TV is more passive than movies, and commercials are the most passive of all. Once conditioned to commercials at an early age, the mind relaxes a notch and ingests the information in a more automated fashion. Like everyone, I was waiting for *Mannix* to come back, or to get back to *Hawaii Five-0*, to figure out who the fuck Dano was.

I remember the ads as much as I remember the shows, maybe more. Alpo, Alka-Seltzer, State Farm. Guys putting shaving cream on half their face, or shampoo on one side of their head. Madge, Mrs. Butterworth, Mr. Whipple. Some asshole sticking both arms into a tank filled with mosquitoes, but spraying only one side with Raid. The Indian crying about the trash on the highway.

They were delivered the same way as TV shows, but were cheaper, shorter, different. A replicated world, bastardized. Commercial. But they also told stories. Like they were on the same field but different, like a new and improved virus, a secondary narrative seeping in while the world was still trying to figure out what to make of TV. I wondered who was behind it all. It was obvious that while they were playing with my head on one level with the programs, there was a more serious thing going on underneath, in sixty-second chunks.

TV shows were like scheduled visits from friends. On Friday nights, Dottie left early to go see Artie before going to the restaurant. *The Brady Bunch* was on at eight and *The Partridge Family* was on at eight thirty. An hour of household fun. Two ragamuffin families, just getting by. The Partridge Family drove around in a van with a guy named Ruben Kincaid and, to this day, I can't figure out if he was fucking the mom.

I watched wrestling on Saturdays at noon. Every week the card ended with a guy called Chief Jay Strongbow applying the sleeper hold, a double-armed headlock from the back, which cut off the oxygen flow to his opponent's head enough to knock him out but not enough, apparently, to kill him. If Chief Jay really hated an opponent, he left him asleep on the mat while he gave a post-match interview to the announcers, which was a problem in and of itself because Chief Jay didn't really speak English. The refs could never wake the poor bastards—they didn't have the secret. Chief Jay had to go back to the ring where he did some ridiculous tomahawk move with his hand and the guy spasmed awake.

The more batshit-crazy thing was that there was another wrestling show right after: *Wrestling from Florida*. These guys wore only the tights—no costumes—and they did a few more legit wrestling moves. But if a Martian came down, he wouldn't have seen too much difference. A few of the guys wore masks, and the guys who didn't wear masks tried to pull them off. That was the ultimate humiliation—getting de-masked.

Gorgeous George and Mil Mascaras were before my time, but I did see Dusty Rhodes a.k.a. the American Dream. In truth, he was a real fat guy with bleached blond hair. He was like the white, fake Cassius Clay.

He went around saying, "I am the American Dream. Don't touch me, I'm beautiful." He carried a mirror into the ring. "Don't touch me, I'm beautiful."

Bruno Sammartino was the Champ. A closed-circuit event was planned for Bruno to fight a cat named Antonio Inoki, a Japanese guy who supposedly had never lost. It was at Madison Square Garden and I wanted to see it more than anything. But there was no way. If it were *The Flintstones*, I could just ride with Fred and Barney to Joe Rockhead's house—he got all the fights.

They advertised and built up the match for six months on the wrestling shows. It was supposed to be the Match of the Century. I was at home alone when they had it, so no one saw me cry. I couldn't even get it on the radio.

5

I live alone now, divorced five years ago, in an apartment on Locust Street high above Center City at the end of one decade and the beginning of the next. Truth is I like it, being alone. I like to put on a curated Van Morrison streaming channel and smoke cigars. I kill the smoke with open windows and an air-sanitizing machine. The place gets cleaned every day by a housekeeper from Ecuador named Nancy. She washes and puts away my clothes and does my dishes, too. I like having food brought to me by delivery guys and I like that there are restaurants right outside my door. Occasionally, I go out for the chase of women, but as I inch along in age, I don't like putting the effort in for the new ones, the time variable working against me in the sense of what is left on the clock. Like the lion's share of men, when they are honest, I prefer transactional sex, the kind where you pay to get off and they go away happy. The old-fashioned way leads me to either dangerously young girls or women with mileage trying to be fresh, meaning free of referents of old cocks they are used to and therefore forever in the way.

I have weights and a rower in here to exercise enough to keep the night sweats away, the worst time being around noon when I try to get myself up for the day. Truth is I've made enough money and cut off enough strings that I don't have to do anything and I like it. Coming up the way I did, from where I did, I am not burdened by a sense of sympathy or the guilt of a free pass. Truth is the math is simple: I don't care enough about changing the general state of things to do anything. If you tuck enough away and are just carrying yourself, there is really not much anyone can do to you, especially if you are not pushing into anyone else's world. That's the great thing about America—the freedom to succeed and the freedom to be let alone once you do.

I think about kids once in a while, like who is the kid out there who is me, just forty years later. That passes unanswered. My own kid, she'll be okay, I have her fixed up, and she doesn't really want much from me anyway. Truth is there's nothing about the status quo that on balance makes me want to do anything other than live life in this nice-ass apartment, above what's left of the *greene country towne which will never be burnt, and always wholesome*. Truth is I have ridden a wave generated by a miracle wind-machine born in this brick city five lifetimes ago. All this freedom. Truth is I will probably die like this, another American man who got what he wanted.

Each semester, I draw an erasable black square on the whiteboard, dividing it into quadrants. I tell my students the life of a business can be broken down into four parts, four quarters, four segments, four lives, call it any of those things.

The first is the beginning, the start-up phase when the identity is found and things come together.

The second is when it gets concrete, when the operational aspect begins to gel.

The third is the prime, the season, when it all happens, when championships are won: the right product at the right price; the right clients paying top fees; the right chemistry creating wind at your back.

And the fourth is what happens after the peak, when the business deteriorates, things fray, discipline is lost, other opportunities arise, stasis sets in, markets change. You want to move on. I draw a little circle inside the square. The circle starts in quadrant one and ends with the point of an arrow in quadrant four. The cycle of business. The cycle of life. From nothing, through the crucible, to harmony, to nothing. It happens everywhere, all the time. Select a time from memory and it was happening then. It is happening now. Everything's in a place on the cycle. We are in one part or another. We are trying to get out of the first, move through the second, stay in the third, stop from falling into the fourth quarter of things, where life intercedes and brings our business and our families and ourselves toward the unavoidable, unforgiving end.

I am authorized to tell them this by Kane College, where I am somehow a teacher of economics and entrepreneurship. I am a reluctant academic, here through an indirect route. The dean of the business school found me and asked me to come up with a course for the kids trying to kill it on the Internet. He wanted an alternative perspective in addition to the academic's. He wanted me to drill fundamentals, give the practical viewpoint. I had been thinking I would play the start-up thing again, but teaching seemed right since my head was becoming lost in books. My ex-wife told me I'd be good at it, probably because she wanted me to get structured.

That was more than ten years ago. On paper, I am a nontenured instructor (no PhD) and a semiretired investor. The entry in the Kane Business School Course Selection Guide says:

ENTREPENEURSHIP IN THE INTERNET AGE—Joseph Knight, Jr.—Adjunct Professor, B.A. Lattimore College, 1983.

Adjunct Professor Knight is the founder and former chairman and CEO of JK Disintegrated Media Solutions, which today is a division of Credit MBOA Omni Media. After founding JKD in the mid-eighties, Professor Knight built it into the premiere independent advertising agency in the Northeast. JKD was acquired in 1995 by the French advertising conglomerate Publicité Rouge.

Professor Knight provides firsthand experience to the complex issue facing today's start-up companies in the fast-changing Internet landscape. The enormous success of JKD as a start-up in the local suburban Philadelphia market is both a great accomplishment and a valuable demonstration of the potential to operate in a nontraditional situs for an industry base. Readings and lectures will center on the entrepreneurial experience in the Internet age.

The course will focus on initial capitalization, hiring, team building, and sales strategies. It will involve strategizing sessions regarding the

> *opportunities presented by modern equity markets and the importance*
> *of the creation of value for long-term investors.*
> *The course is not open to undergraduates.*

The business school students come and go. They wear Main Line preppy shit like alligator shirts and docksiders, or crewneck sweaters over turtle-necks, or Philadelphia Phillies red pin-striped button-downs. All of this is contemporized by flip-flops and Abercrombie & Fitch—traditional and modern at once. They have cropped hair, wire-rimmed glasses, are on time, and take notes on their laptops. They stay after class and ask me what I mean by this or that. They are serious. They are into money. They smell it on the Internet. That's why they're here: to make a shit-pile of money. They want to know how I did it, how anyone did it before the Internet. They are, by and large, spoiled rich pussies.

B-School is the place where there's not much difference between the students and the teachers, at least when it comes to greed. The sales and marketing teachers have high-priced consulting gigs; the quant guys are all creating risk models for the banks. If this is academia, then I am the academic's academic.

When I need a break, I walk or take a cab over to the Penn campus. I stand outside the Palestra. It is rectangular, with arched windows and a five-column structure like the knuckles of a fisted hand. It is the holiest of the redbrick buildings, set back from the street, the way it should be. At game time, the kids from campus walk fast in the cold over the cement courtyard to get there. It seems a lot smaller now than when I was a kid. When it's open, I walk inside. It's so simple: North, South, East, West. Banners in the rafters; horizontal floorboards in the court. It's a new floor but a replica of the old floor—replica of a replica, really.

I know that everybody lets off steam through sports. But it's more intense in this town, where you can't avoid it, where they have sports radio on in every cab and every bar, where you can't believe it's possible for another person to have another opinion about the Eagles, or the Phillies, or Penn State, or even Notre Dame, which is in fucking Indiana.

The faculty fields a team in the University Softball league and the University Basketball league. Our kids play T-ball and Little League and the dads fight over foul balls. When basketball season comes, the grad students and statistics instructors get all fired up for intramural games. They play against the law firms or medical schools, fight with the refs, and elbow each other, hack, and walk and sit in the lane. They will analyze the other squad's defense and set up a play, and then nobody can put it in the bucket. I don't play anymore. I can't even watch, not even on TV.

Then there are the fantasy leagues: fantasy baseball, fantasy football, fantasy basketball. I throw in once in a while for fantasy football because I like a certain player, but I'm not a fan like them. When I make an observation during the draft or over lunch, they cluck at me, feeling sorry for me, feeling bad that I don't have a supple understanding of the game. I keep quiet. I let them think they know so much. I sit back and watch them try to work out being caught in this Volvo-based, cossetted life.

They never played.

6

I grew up with guys who could play.

I can still see them as they were. I can hear them, smell them, hear what it sounds like to be stripped, feel what the body feels when it is smacked, feel the slap of it being taken. Things got taken. When I see it, we are young, our bodies are bendy. We were all the same. I do not remember being scared when I was with them. There was nothing before or after basketball. The way we played together was what we owned, as real as rain, tangible like a family Bible or a Sears photo of the kids. It was the thing.

Our game was never that white suburban bullshit, with the bounce passes and the two-three zones and kids named Brandon shooting jump shots from the wing, with the peeled orange sections at halftime from a rotating group of mothers—or, worse, a team mother—and sugary snacks after the game. Neither was it the black game of the playground where they dress like they're in the fucking Mummers Parade and mouth each other and play no D because they are releasing so early, cherry-picking, hoping to get a break-away or a two-on-one against the white guy, the token moron, usually a little off in the head, the kind that doesn't understand boundaries, who comes to the court and sits out four games, till he says "next" enough times that one of the brothers lets him play, but some days it doesn't happen, because they don't care, that's a cold place, trying to get in a game like that, because the brothers don't fuck around when it comes to playing ball.

It only gets worse. The white game becomes intramurals and then Lawyers League or a steady Saturday morning league with knee braces, bandannas, squeaking sneakers and fat guts, elbows, stock tips. The blacks don't get so pathetic when they get old. They play the regular games and the guys just fade, hanging back and rebounding, kicking outlets, organizing the team more, keeping score, once in a while telling the trashy motherfuckers to shut the fuck up and bring the rock.

I have a life, not a story. I talk about everybody—Catholics, blacks, Main Liners, Jews—the way I learned. None of them are 100 percent nice. They usually hate each other just to hate each other. The Catholics where I came from would much rather hang out with blacks than Jews. Same for the Protestants, although they hate everybody in private. The few Jews I knew were mistrustful of everyone and they were right, because most people talked about Jews when they weren't around. Like they say, just because you're paranoid doesn't mean there's not someone out to get you.

I can say it was a symphony without fear of boastfulness because it wasn't me in the lead, ever. I spent most of the time on the bench, helping the coaches. We played against type. The rich white kids were not lazy on defense. The Stuckley guys played smart, not like white trash from other towns who can't run once they get to high school because they're smoking pot. Our black guys played like blacks when they had to, but they also knew reads, set screens, passed, played defense, and made foul shots, all the things they say blacks can't do.

Glentop Elementary School was on Route 352 between Stuckley and developments like Hidden Hills and Havenswood. It was your basic school for little kids, but it had a great outdoor court. It was a little small, which made it fun to run. The baskets were ten foot and had chain nets that never broke. The blacktop held up, it had good painted lines. It didn't run right up to the grass like most of the courts at elementary schools, too close to the baby merry-go-rounds and swing sets.

In the seventies, you were from wherever your local TV news told you you were from. That meant we were from Philadelphia, even though we weren't from the city, which is the holy land of basketball. Ask anyone who really knows basketball or Philadelphia. More people live just outside Philly than within. It created a dilemma for me: I wasn't really from there, but I wasn't from anywhere else, either. We lived in lower Dover

County, near Chester, highest murder rate in the nation. Chester was a black shithole city surrounded by white shithole areas, like Stuckley, and a few towns that were mixed, like Penwood. Farther into the suburbs, into the thick, twisty country roads, the places got richer, whiter, and nicer. Way out they even got really nice.

I love the Palestra. It is a cathedral—they call it that. Officially, it's the University of Pennsylvania's home court, on its campus in West Philadelphia. But it belongs to the basketball nuts and gym rats of the town. When I was a kid, I watched games on Channel 17 late into the night. Big Al Meltzer from *Action News* went over to do the play-by-play after he did the sports at six thirty. I wondered how he worked for Channel 6 and Channel 17 at the same time. When I was twelve, I figured out how to get there by myself. I took the trolley to Sixty-Ninth Street, grabbed a bus down to Walnut, and was there by the first game at five. I lived to go there on Saturdays. The best night of each year was a triple-header in February: St. Joe against La Salle at five, Villanova-Temple at seven, and the big Penn-Princeton game at nine. The first four schools plus Penn are the Big Five, the intercity league. All Big Five games were played at the Palestra. When seats were tight, I squeezed into the college sections, moving down between games when the students left for parties. I liked to get tucked in deep. The Villanova kids passed plastic cups of vodka and orange juice; La Salle guys made me do long pulls of keg beer out of gallon milk jugs.

But usually I sat alone behind the basket high in the West Stands. I saw it all from up there. I learned to process the game pictorially, dynamically, nonsequentially. The players were real live x's and o's. I went inside myself. I covered my ears and watched them move, closed my eyes and saw the diagrams. It was ABCs, addition and subtraction. I learned about patterns. I knew when the coaches had to go to a new defense, when they needed to work the refs. After four minutes of the first half I could tell you who was going to win.

Villanova and St. Joe had more discipline than La Salle or Temple. Most of the guys grew up playing together on playgrounds and in high school. They knew each other completely—so, win-loss records, point spreads, none of that mattered. They just got it on, like dogs fucking and fighting. The gym was hot, the crowd was drunk and berserk, and the game was played right. Nine thousand rocking and waving flags. A stage for the Owl and the Explorer, the Hawk and the Wildcat. For the Quakers.

After the first basket, in keeping with the long tradition, each school's fans rained streamers in its colors down on the floor. So, when St. Joe scored, the air erupted with maroon and gold crepe paper. The refs would have to call time while the cheerleaders ran out to clear the mess. Villanova made a bucket and the place turned blue and white. For La Salle it was blue and gold; Temple, red and white. Since it was their gym, the Penn Quakers were always at home, sharing that one special house in the neighborhood where the kids love to hang out. On nights at the Palestra, as one game ended and the guys walked off, the players from the next game ran past them to warm up. The noise and energy lifted you and, if basketball was your thing, transported you to another place, another feeling. It was like being high. If I could live in one place and time it would be nine fifteen on a Saturday night in West Philadelphia between games two and three of a triple-header, alongside thousands of kids from five colleges, watching basketball.

I waited all year for the Penn-Princeton game at the Palestra. It was always the last game of the night, always for the Ivy League title. No matter how exciting the first two games might get, I knew the best was coming. It was like watching football in the afternoon on Thanksgiving Day, smelling dinner getting ready, eating something here or there, like celery stuffed with Lebanon bologna and cream cheese. No event—no trip, no concert, no movie, nothing—built up to a crescendo like those triple-headers.

I remember the 1974 game—it was on February 16. I hated Princeton but I loved the way they played, lots of long, lanky white guys with moppy hair in perpetual motion. They made seventeen straight passes without a dribble. They were scientific. They ran weaves, screened down, and went backdoor in a constant flow, like one of their physicists working out a problem no one else understood. But Penn still won, because in basketball, magic beats science. And the Palestra was magic. There was no hope for a team from New Jersey. Not in that gym, not on that night.

7

There might have been a question who was smarter—me or Chris Scully—but there was no question we had a problem over the issue. I met him for breakfast at the Lenape Diner, his favorite place, where he's been eating his whole life. I wouldn't go there on a bet, but I went there when I had to see him.

He spent five minutes shaking hands between the door and the booth where I sat. "Counselor," I said, standing up when he finally made it to me. Coffee was waiting for him the way he liked it, with lots of milk, the color of soft-serve chocolate ice cream.

"Hey, there he is. All Knight. Were you standing here the whole time? I didn't see you." We clasped palms around the thumbs, in what we called the Black Power shake when it first came around. Funny for me and Scully—two white boys from Stuckley. I only did the old shake with people from the team, from memory, from a place buried in the cortex. The clench was followed by each of our left arms coming around for a brief hug, not too much, masculine and quick.

The waitress was smoking hot, unspeakably odd for the Lenape Diner. Her roots were black and grown out, but the body was a rocket ship. "The rack's not real, trust me," Scully said. We sat down and he smiled at me. "Professor Joe, the Millionaire."

Scully had done well, more Turow than Grisham. He was the district attorney of Dover County. Forty-nine, still young, a Republican. You could just see him jumping up: "Objection. Lack of foundation." He had played it very smart, which was not surprising—raising a war chest for a run for Congress, maybe even the Senate if and when the plates shifted. His annual fundraiser, "The Friends of Chris Scully Dinner," was coming up at the Sheraton Valley Forge. I went to the first one. It must have been ten years ago. The ballroom had been full of lawyers, cops, and judges. Irish. Catholics. A few blacks, a few Jews, a few of the Italians. Lots of gray slacks and blue blazers, J. C. Penney dress shirts and striped ties. Everyone shaking hands the regular way, the white way, as they say in Stuckley. Lots of gold class rings from St. James, St. Joe's Prep, Archbishop Ryan. They drank Heinekens from the cash bar—at a fancy event on the weekends those guys will drink imported—or whiskey and water in the little thin hotel highball glasses. The wives all had cutoff hair, even the ones I knew from high school—pretty girls—old biddies before their time. They had cut their hair off happily, those girls, as if they were joining something.

"James J. Ramp," Scully had said from the podium. "I'm sad to say not too many people remember the name. Well, I do. Officer Ramp was killed on August 8, 1978, during the Philadelphia Police Department's eviction of the members of the radical separatist movement MOVE from their rat- and lice-infested headquarters in Powelton Village." He paused for effect. Heads had nodded. Those guys love that shit. Get a little booze in them and it is unbearable. "Jimmy Ramp was a friend of my father's. They were in the Marines together in Korea. Jimmy had already served in combat in World War II and had reenlisted, something pretty much unthinkable today. My father said he was one of the finest men he ever knew. I hope that we will never forget the sacrifice of Officer Ramp and the other men who have given their lives in service of us all. To that end, if I may, I'd like to impose on you all to have a brief moment of silence." Back at the diner, I wanted to cut Scully off at the pass: "I sent my check, so don't even start on me."

"Thanks. You're coming, right?"

"Yeah, sure."

The waitress was there. "Go ahead and order," he said. "She knows what I want." They exchanged looks.

"Just some scrambled eggs and toast," I said. She smiled at me as she wrote it on a little green-and-white order book. When she was done, she touched the point of her pen to the pad with a pop, like waitresses do, still not looking down. It was show-offy—an instantaneous thing for my sake, as though she was ignoring Scully.

"How's the teaching?"

"Good. I like it," I lied.

"What's it like having all that money?"

When I smiled, he said, "No, seriously, tell me. Can I come over and look at it one time? Just to see it?"

"Very funny."

Scully had stayed in good shape. He was lean; his was a cagey body. He had that cop feel to him that DAs have, somewhere between a detective and a corporate lawyer, with the gray suit and the thick, heavy, spit-shined wing tips. His shoes were better than the dog shit ones at the malls, not New York nice, not Italian nice, but nice enough to make a solid click on the marble floors of courthouses.

After she walked away, he said, "You know, they say those who can't do, teach. But I don't believe that. I think I admire teachers more than almost anyone. And some teachers do a lot. Look at you."

"Why'd you call me?"

He paused. "Hubert Betours." He pronounced it "Hugh Burt," rather than "U Bear."

"What about him?"

"The AUSAs are about to pin him."

"What's that mean?"

"Assistant United States attorneys. Means federal prosecutors are about to indict him." His food came: toast with peanut butter on the side and a glass of orange juice. Kid food. The food of a guy who gets everything he ever sets out to get.

"So? Tough shit for him."

At that, Scully sat back. "Joey boy. So tough. You work on that at all? The anger? Or no?"

I ignored him. "I sold my company to the guy a long time ago. I haven't seen him since." I hesitated about whether to say it, then did anyway: "You should know that. You were the only one who didn't take me up on it."

"I know, rub it in."

"Oh please, Scully." I was suddenly a little nervous. "What do I care about this? What do you care?"

"You should care, trust me."

"Is that why you called me? To give me some secret tip?"

"You've got a lot of nerve, you know that?"

I didn't say anything. He was pissed.

"I'm trying to give you a heads-up, which I shouldn't be doing." He took a bite. "And you just jump down my throat." He sipped his orange juice. "What's going on with you?"

"My life is complicated."

"How?"

"I am getting divorced." Now I wasn't nervous. I was pissed off, too. "C'mon. Don't pretend you don't know that."

"Yeah, I heard. I hope you're taking care of your family."

"I am. My kid is fine, if that's what you're asking."

"And using some of that money on a shrink."

"You know what? Spare me. Spare me this part, the sanctimony part. Don't worry about what I need to do."

He leaned in, "Okay, Joey. Watch your tone with me. We're not in high school. This is me talking to you and risking my position to help you—get that through your fucked-up head." It hadn't gotten hot like this between us in many years. "You need to call your lawyer."

"Wow, Chris. So that's it. It's like that?" I wanted to taunt him. "Or are you wearing a wire? Is that it? Is that how it works?"

"Fuck off." I thought he was about to go further, until he saw an old-timer coming toward him. Scully's eyes brightened, all phony politician. "There he is. Mr. Carney, how are ya?" He jumped up to shake hands.

I should have stayed, should have asked for his help, but I didn't. Couldn't. I motioned to the waitress and she gave me the green-and-white check. She smiled. A real whore. I smiled back at her. She looked at my crotch. I smiled again. I said, "Can I get a blank one?"

I wrote two words on the flimsy paper, folded it, and wrote "READ," on top. I put a twenty with it. Scully sat back down.

The politician was now in gear, so his demeanor was changed. "I'm just telling you to be ready. This thing seems real and it could get hairy. Don't be a tough guy. You need to get ready for this."

I took the olive branch. "I get it," I said. "Say hi to your mother. This is on me." I pointed to the twenty and the folded check and left. I bumped into the waitress as I turned for the door. I grabbed her waist to keep her from falling.

"Excuse me," I said. We traded more smiles, and I walked out.

I had written two words inside the blank check for Scully: "I KNOW."

8

Some girls remind you of songs and some girls remind you of bands. Janice O'Malley was a song. I met her—on the phone only—when my business was going strong. We were two years apart in high school but I didn't know her then. She said she came to basketball games, but she didn't remember me. She had a crush on Phillip Ford. She was working at a PR company or some shit like that and she cold-called me.

"I've been assigned to you," she said.

"Then you better come over here so I can show you everything." She sounded cute. But I didn't need what I thought I needed, or at least it wasn't such a rush. I got distracted and didn't see her for a year.

I wanted a family after I sold to Betours. I kept thinking of her voice. We had our first date the night I got the call that the last of the funds transferred into my account. The money made me feel different. It wasn't rich so much as unafraid: of any client or deadline or test or requirement or taxes or banks or Gods of the preachers. I could pursue when I wanted and get pursued when I needed.

Even so, I thought better to impress, so I took her to the Lafayette Inn, a colonial restaurant with a fireplace. It was dressed up the way all those places are: three-cornered hats and white wigs on waiters. A lamb chop, two fishes, two steaks, and the obligatory special with crab from Maryland, a nod to Lord Baltimore. Revolutionary War food. Which is stupid because they didn't have any food during the Revolutionary War, at least the revolutionaries didn't.

The waiter tried to explain the menu, pour water, and open a bottle of red wine at the same time. As his left hand swept up to describe the lamb chop, it hit my drinking glass, which flew off the table to my immediate right. I stabbed the glass and hardly any water spilled. Click. I set it back on the table. They all stared at me like I did a magic trick.

Janice had the big steak, the New York, and she had big firm breasts. She knew how to put the chest right there, enough flaunt to be completely unmistakable but not slutty. A girl has those tits all her life, she should know how to use them. Not many do, so busy hiding them or pushing them up, never keeping them well positioned right in the middle, where you can see them, judge them, evaluate them.

She went directly at me. "What's your story, anyway?"

I deflected, but I liked her way. It was easy to see Janice was a cool girl, as victimized by the sundial as me, maybe more. Lots of boyfriends, always a bridesmaid, never a bride. She was huge into music, which I loved. She was a DJ in college and we hit a groove right away, quizzing each other, testing range, depth, and taste. She knew the difference between the Pixies and the Posies and the Pogues. She was funny and no pushover. She had that little bit of feminism smart girls have before they get married and have kids, when the harangue of women's studies lectures is still in their heads. But it was already in retreat, just enough there to reassure me that she wasn't a moron out hunting for a husband. I got it right away that though she hadn't found the right guy yet, it wasn't for lack of interest or that she was holding out. Or nuts, which happens.

All romantic relationships begin with sexual attraction, period. "I was not attracted at first," is a sentence spoken only by women. Janice and I had it and we both knew it. She was cute as hell, about five five with black hair, like I loved. We closed the restaurant and went out for a drink. It was snowing. She smelled nice. We touched a little: I guided the small of her back through held doors. When she took my arm walking to the car, her chest rubbed against me through her navy peacoat. She had round and pillowy flesh, not the kind that is taut and competitive. It was receptive, inviting, cushiony. Lots of layers. That's my thing, the soft girls. She made me comfortable. When I told her about my parents, she said, "Oh my God. My father's father died before he was born, too." I didn't really make much of it, since any couple anywhere, at any time, ever, will discover uncanny things they have in common that snowball into connection. But she was moved by it.

She loved her dad. "He's the best person I've ever met." He was from Philly—Germantown. "That's why he wanted me to go to school down here. And I never left."

I said, "Why?"

She held her hand up, as in, "Don't ask."

"What?"

"He's tough on everybody, but he wants the best, you know?"

"You two are close?"

"Yeah, we are. Me and Ray. We fight, but we're close." She drifted away for a second, and then she was back.

After dinner, I took Janice to a bar with a piano. She ordered an old-fashioned when we walked in, and that cracked me up. I liked things that broke patterns. "Tell me about the business, big shot," she said. "How did you do it?"

"Well, basically, the story goes that when I graduated from Lattimore, I was kicking around Stuckley and Penwood, playing pickup games and not doing much else. The man who owned the local paper was named Walter Hudson. He was sort of famous back then. He wore a straw hat and khaki suits. He knew my aunt Dottie. He was a hard bird, but he was nice to me. He hung around in the bars and I was doing a lot of that. You know, hanging around in bars. We used to watch football at the Plumstead. He talked me into selling ads." I looked at her glass. "How's your drink, slugger?"

"Fine," she said. "Don't change the subject."

"Okay. Okay." She was funny. "It began as mostly helping him in the classified section, but he was like seventy, and he was over it. His wife had died and he had no kids. Pretty soon he had me talking to everyone. He had six papers—all the little pipsqueak papers you see in towns around here, the *Penwood Saver*, the *Springfield Sentinel*. Another two in Delaware. They all had the same advertising insert for used cars and furniture, that stuff."

"Like a 'Recycler'?"

"Exactly. He made tons on that. I was still kind of a fuckup, but I got interested. I set my own hours and, you know, I made a little commission. I got a taste of what that felt like."

"Sure," she said. She liked business stuff, not yet having the house-wife's lost confidence about such things.

"Anyway, the lightbulb went on when I was on the phone with the guy who bought ads for Buy-Rite. Jerry something. I'll never forget it. I was twenty-three. He had this, like, *deep* South Philly accent. He goes to me, 'How much for a two-month ad buy across all your papers?'"

I imitated his voice and she giggled. "'I'm going to Bermuda next month and I don't want to have to fuck around with this again in three weeks. So, just buy me through two months.'" She giggled some more.

"So I said, 'All right, Jerry, hold on.' I had the rate sheet for all of the papers in front of me and I read him the cost. And bam, it hit me.' I smacked my hand down on the bar in front of her. "I realized I was only charging him the whole rate because he was a big out-of-town account. But anyone in the area got it from Walter for half the price. The big guys, like this guy, paid the full rack rate. So, I go, 'Hey, Jer, can I call you tomorrow?' And he says, 'What? Why?' And I said, 'Just let me call you tomorrow,' and I hang up."

I took a drink of my beer. "Then I walked in and told Walter I quit. He says, 'For crissakes, what for?' I said, 'I don't know, Walter. I'm not cut out for this.'"

She opened her mouth wide like she was horrified, but she was smil-ing underneath, the way a first date or your new girlfriend looks at you and pretends to be astonished, but really at the same time she's showing she's impressed, so much so that you don't really even know what to think of her, like when a chick acts like you're screwing her better than she's ever been screwed, when you're in that new, hot, excited stage you immediately take it to be true and genuine—because it is, in some ways—and you're so aglow with the newness and the sweaty fucking and how really *good* it feels to be feeling like that you go with it.

"Yup. Then I called Jerry the next day and I said, 'How much do you spend on local ads in a year?' and he says, 'Like a hunnerd thousand bucks?'—I don't know where he got that accent from—so I said, 'What would you do if I told you I can cut that by twenty-five percent?'"

Janice slapped me on the arm. "You did not."

"And he goes, 'I'd kiss you on the mouth.'"

"Nooo. You are kidding me."

"That's how it started," I said. I was nonchalant. "I mapped it all out—Pennsylvania, Delaware, and Jersey. Even looked down in Maryland. There were forty-five local papers within a two-hour drive. I made a list of every major ad buyer—cars, discount stores, pharmaceuticals, whatever—food companies, lots of supermarkets. I went at all of them. I told them all I'd cut their budgets and take my piece and they'd never feel it. I knew I could get all these guys. And that's what I did. It was awesome."

"What about Walter?"

I shrugged. "I don't know. I was, like, fuck Walter. He was already rich. He was more lonely than anything. He got pissed at me for a couple months. Then I found him at the Plumstead. We worked it out. What could he do? I had him."

She shook her head. "Amazing. Wow. So you're a smart cookie?" But before she said another word, she changed gears. She knew she was being too gaga, too over-the-moon, too easy. It was a boy-girl thing, a cool-girl thing, a good thing, because she knew to go slow when it mattered. She turned sarcastic. She stroked my arm like a groupie. "It's *sooo* cool."

I laughed. "Okay, wiseass."

"I have to pee." She got up and I watched her walk through the dark bar to the ladies' room. So jiggly soft, so sexy.

9

Leonard Polk. That's my boy, right there. Say the name to anyone in Penwood and you'll get a smile. We were eight years old when we met. He was the first black kid I knew and he took me to the Penwood Boys Club. It was kind of a blind date. Dottie worked with Paulette Polk at the post office. Paulette noticed I was coming by after school and on Saturdays to wait for Dottie to finish. She told Leonard to take me to the club.

It had pool and Ping-Pong tables, and there was even a floor-level boxing ring in the back. But the place was for basketball, the place black kids played. It was a long, one-story, redbrick building. The court was great: hardwood, polished, waxed, swept after every game. The games were serious. I spent more time at the Boys Club than any other white kid. I brought some of the other white guys over. The guys from the developments came more readily than guys from Stuckley. Their parents dropped them off but didn't come inside because they were never quite comfortable. The crowds weren't quiet. It was like a mix between a Baptist service and a pep rally. On nights Dottie didn't waitress, she went to the State Street Diner for a chicken potpie, and then she came to the club to watch me play.

Back in the day, Leonard sat down anywhere he could to watch girls walk by, in malls, in the stands, in the library during study hall. He looked them over, evaluated them, let them know how he felt. He'd hang out on a bench in the SilverRun Mall by the high school. "You looking *good* today, girl. You put that together. *That's what I'm talkin' about*, right there. Ya damn skippy. That's what *I'm* talkin' about." They tried or pretended to ignore him, but they loved it—there were girls in our high school who got dressed in the morning just for Leonard.

Sitting with him in the mall, you got his philosophy. "I like the way they put it to-*gether*. That's my thing. Look at you, right? I bet you got some scraggly-ass undies—what kind of draws you got?"

"Boxers."

"Ha, figures. Okay, you got boxers. Then, look here: you got on beat-up old Levi's and a raggedy T-shirt. How long it take you to get dressed?"

"Two minutes."

"Brush your teeth? Comb you hair? What else?"

"Of course I brushed my teeth. Deodorant."

"Old Spice stick?"

"Yes."

He closed his eyes and put his head down and stomped his feet a little, enjoying the fact that I used Old Spice stick. "And you done in what, ten minutes? Out the shower, and you done?"

Then he grabbed my head and turned it toward a girl coming up the escalator. "Now, look here. Look at this. Start at the hair—that's at least an hour with shampoo and brushing and all that shit."

"An hour?"

"Then look at the outfit: slacks, sweater, little white top. She got on a little white watch that match, little biddy white earrings. There's a little bra in there, she got powder on, creams, all kind of stuff. All that shit is put together, man."

"Leonard, I get it."

"Look at the shoes. Girls walk around all damn day on Saturday just to buy a pair shoes. And you so out of it that she can walk by and you won't even notice."

The girl walked by.

"Hi, Lisa," I said.

"Hi, Joe," she said. Then she put her hands on her hips, in mock seriousness, but with a smile. "Hello, Leonard."

"I love the shoes, Lisa . . . *I love the shoes*," Leonard said. "Where you come up with those shoes, girl? Awww, you went shopping, didnja?

C'mon, don't lie, now. Where you get them? Do they hurt walking like that?"

She blushed. "Leo-nard, you're too funny . . ."

After she moved on, he sat back down and leaned back and talked out the side of his mouth.

"Now, look at that, boy. *Ungh ungh.* You see that? That's what gets me. Put to-*gether.* Nice and *clean.* I bet when you throw your draws in the hamper you got skid marks and everything right?"

"Huh . . . ?"

"Don't lie to me, you gross-ass motherfucker. You got skid marks like every other guy got skid marks. But girls ain't like that." He leaned forward and put his hands up like he was holding something very fragile. "They got it all up there nice, all perfumed and stuff, then the little panties get pulled on just over it." He stood up. "DAMN BOY. That's what I like. You know what I'm saying?" Now he was yelling, people in the mall were looking at us. *"Do . . . you . . . know . . . what . . . I'm . . . sayin'?"*

He was swinging his hands at me, punching me and looking for a hand slap of some form or another. I gave in and laughed and held my hand out straight. He slapped it and grabbed my forearm and kept slapping it.

It was time for us to leave. As we walked away, he was still going. "Uggh." He crossed his arms real fast, like he was mad, like he just missed an easy shot. *"Damn.* I got to get *on* something. This mall will drive you *crazy."*

10

Dottie put it all in boxes the day Artie went to Woodlawn, but she left the record player. "More room to play," she said, "and you can listen to music." She put my plastic guns, baseball glove, and basketball in a toy chest and set up a light blue Formica table with one edge against the wall. This became her spot and the place we talked each night when we got home, no matter the time. There had to be a few minutes of talk, over dinner, or coffee for her and ice cream for me, before she put me to bed.

And I was scared to go to bed every night. It was always there, the thing that happened to me in the middle of the night. First, I had the fear of the thing clobbering, hitting me so hard I went black. That would lead to a panic attack. As I lay there, I thought, "It's me, here, me. I'm going to die. I'm going to evaporate and go and be gone. And I will never come back. This will end. I will be dead. Me. I will be dead. It is real, I will be dead." The awakening to the point that it was not abstract, that it was not happening to some person in a movie or character in a book, that's what got me. It was real and I was real. For all the world's science and medicine, nothing had been done about dying and we were all headed for that wall. I grabbed my head and shouted. "La la la la la la la, no no no!"

Dottie came running. "Hey, hey, hey," she said. "What's this? What's wrong? Stop, it's okay, it's okay. Calm down, calm down." After a second, "What is it?

"I can't stop thinking about dying."

"Oh, honey," she said. Her face relaxed and she got her arms around me. "I know."

She didn't try to talk me out of it, didn't go waving babyish notions of the afterlife, like a nursery school teacher holding up a finger painting or a nun giving out ancient prayers with all that shit like he that knoweth none knoweth all and his glory shall never end.

"I've been around longer than you so I know something about this. Here's what I do: First, I will tell you I think that there's God up there. I do. And I think he knows what we are doing. And that he keeps an eye on us. When we die, if we've been good, he decides whether to let us live with him or not."

"How do you think I'm doing?"

"What do you mean?"

"With God and what you talked about. What would he say about me?"

When you have a special chubby aunt who takes you in because your parents are dead and she tells you it's okay to die, you see the sparkle and shine of her eye. "Well," she said, "I think he would say that for a boy your age, you're doing very, very well."

After I settled down, she ushered me back to bed and lay with me on that cold, quiet night. "Tell me a story," she said. "Use your imagination. Tell me any story at all."

The low-slung ceiling was like the stars. I said,

This is a story about The Lost Boy. He lives in a forest with lots of trees and vines and jungle around it. He got lost from his parents at the A&P, and when he tried to walk home, he ended up in the Jungle Forest. He could never, ever get back. He never saw his Mommy or Daddy again.

"Goodness," Dottie said.

He had to sleep in the Jungle Forest, so he made a house out of sticks and mud and leaves. It was a pretty good house once he worked on it for a couple of weeks. He had the same kind of day every day; he woke up and tried to walk out of the Jungle Forest. When it started to get dark, he headed back for his stick house and tried to build it some more before he went to sleep.

Right to Dottie, I said, "If you ever tell a story about the Lost Boy, he can never ever get out of the Jungle Forest. Promise?"

"Promise."

It was a pretty good house after he worked on it for a while, so he got it so he could spend more time looking for a way out. Then one day, he met a boy out walking. His name was Henry. He was lost, too. Henry and him decided to walk together and they saw a big, scaly green dragon. It could talk and it said, "Only one of you two will be allowed to pass to the road behind me and out of the Jungle Forest. The other will stay in the Jungle Forest forever and ever." And he spit fire out his mouth.

The Lost Boy stood up and said, "My friend Henry really misses his mommy and daddy and I want him to go home." And the dragon let Henry through and the Lost Boy went back to the Stick House. He was still alone but he helped his friend. The End.

"Boy, that's an excellent story." I could tell she was upset. She lay very still and said, "Is the Lost Boy you?"

"He is, kind of. But he is bigger and he is very strong. Stronger than me." I liked making up the rules, inventing a world that had to accept them. I felt like we were in sleeping bags in a field, like how it probably feels to go camping with your dad, or even in the Jungle Forest. "He's superstrong and he can run faster than me, too."

We took turns with "The Lost Boy." My stories usually had fast endings after sword fights, or foul-shooting contests at the Jungle Forest Basketball Courts. Dottie made up two friends for the Lost Boy: Candy and Ronnie, who fought with him on magic carpets. She made up a bear named Horatio who protected him from wild man-eating bats. The Scullys had bats in their attic all summer; I think that's where she got that from.

11

In the telling of this story—of me; of Scully; of the big Dunn twins; of the influence of Stuckley, the town full of white-skinned, yellow-toothed, racist, and anti-Semitic workingmen and their kids; of the Irish Catholic fury that the four of us, in different roles and in different ways, instilled in the heart of our team—in the telling of all of it, here's what you have to start by saying: Roll up three hundred years of Irish finding their way to Philadelphia, working for nothing, drinking themselves to death, building the city and everything around it, hating all those who hated them, starting with the English and all the way through. Roll up the uneducated, blarney-sweet, mellifluous stories and songs of braggarts and the prattle of washerwomen searching for a world of order, following the Church in Rome and building its outpost schools and rectories, feeling that all were lifted and some were rising so far that the mothers would cackle and the sons would burn with envy, being set back but proud of their boys in all the wars, all the wars, the broken and dying boys in the great struggles and the boys who made it through and sons moving to the police forces, perfect they were for cops to keep hold of this grand new world. Keep those things in mind and you can start to understand it. And even when it long since stopped being new, even when the old country recipes were eroded from memory and real Irish butter and unprocessed corned beef and celery with cream cheese were no longer proper, and kids had no sense of horseshit on me boots as something that made sense, long after these memories faded, the people, the Irish people of this assimilated colony each still keep in their hearts an imprinted sense memory emotion of where they came from, their identity fired by Celtic dragon DNA-flavored blood, the skeletal whiteness of their bodies undisguised, the intensity of their poetic minds, the density of their wild-eyed anger, and their propensity for life at the extreme, dangerous edges of passion, rendered ironic because they are so often the ones enforcing it, in religion, in law, in writing. I am of this world but not in it, same as Knight is perfectly Irish but not thought of as such. I am set off by the black hair of my father.

i.

Stuckley was Catholic and so were the Scullys. I waited for Chris outside St. Ignatius, on a sidewalk between the church and the rectory where the priests lived. I brought the ball when he had to do early Mass. Actually, I brought his ball, which he left with me the night before, because Chris Scully didn't like to play with someone else's ball.

Scully was always number one. He was the point guard and I was his backup. He wouldn't play at the Boys Club. None of the Stuckley guys would. They played for St. Ignatius in the church league for kids, in ratty gyms in basements or in multipurpose rooms that doubled as the school auditorium. It was pretty disorganized. When they were short on players, Scully got me to fill in. He gave me a jersey in the car and told me to use the name of whichever moron was out smoking bowls in the parking lot because he didn't give a shit about basketball like we did. We ran it up on the fancy new churches with courts inside rec centers that had air-conditioning and carpeting.

We were happiest when there was no school, especially on snow days and over Christmas. In eighth grade, we did the same thing nine days straight during the holidays. Scully left his gown in the changing room off the side of the altar and met me outside, where he took the ball and started walking. I followed, happy to let him lead because he cut the wind. His boots stepped in the black ice, snow, and salt mixed on the side of the county roads, leading from Stuckley up to Indian Pass Junior High. We stood on the cement islands at intersections and waited for the cars to pass before heading through the next stretch of highway in the frozen rain. We had winter coats with the Eskimo hoods and knit hats with eyeholes and mouth holes that made us look like bank robbers. Scrappy little bank robbers.

We had to go around back to a janitor's door, which had a bad lock. We didn't exactly pick it; it jarred open when Scully smashed it with a rock. Inside, we took off our wet stuff and pulled our sneakers from under our jackets. He had a trick for keeping his shoes dry: he stuck the toes down the back of his jeans, wedged under all of his other garments. We kept the ball as dry as we could, but it took about ten minutes for it to heat up and bounce right.

The baskets were up, which meant we had to crank them down with the long metal rod that hooked to the side rigging. The rod had a hook on the end, which turned the center rod of the apparatus, raising and lowering the basket. But the rod was in the office and the door was locked. We saw the side window was not shut all the way, so Scully shoved it down until the gap was about three feet, then I held him up while he squeezed through the opening. He got the rod from next to the filing cabinet and climbed out.

We shot around for a while, getting warm. Then we ran drills. He started under the basket and I was at the top of the key. He popped out and I hit him on the left wing for a jumper. Twenty-five times. For the next twenty-five, he drove right, stopped, and hit a six-foot bank shot. Then the same thing on the other side: twenty-five jumpers, twenty-five stop-and-pops. Then it was my turn.

In everything we did, ever, Scully went first. It wasn't so much me, it was just Scully. We were the point guards. We led everybody and he led me. We were the same size, six foot, good sized for the point. He was better. He was wiry, strong, smart, and really, really tricky. He had brains and an edge I can only put on how crazy his mother was. He had three brothers. The oldest, Jack, was a douche bag five years older than us who was kicked off the varsity for fighting and smoking cigarettes his senior year. When we were nine, Chris and I followed Jack around, watching him pick on people, like the Black Hand in *The Godfather: Part II*. The one who says, "Wet my beak." Chris was never as bad as Jack because he knew Jack was a loser.

Next, we played full court one-on-one to a hundred. The school was quiet, no running between the halls, no teachers smoking in the lounge, no reading, no kickball, no white cardboard cartons of pint-size Vitamin D homogenized white milk being sold in the lunchroom. Just Scully taking a rebound sprinting up court, the ball part of his hand and me trying to catch him, finally catching up and him crossing over to his left just as I flew by, him laughing at me, saying "Bye," and laying it in. I grabbed it out of the net and he was on me, slapping at me till he stripped it and laid it in again. Three times in a row, till I got by him—but then he caught me at half-court, and touched my hip with his hand, and I had to get by him all over again. When he put his hand on your hip, he had you. He might have been somewhere else, behind you, wherever. But when you got that hip check, he was in your jock.

Most days he beat me about 100-65. I judged how I was doing by how much above or below 65 I was. That day, I played him tough. I was ahead 90-86. He brought the ball up and pulled back from eighteen feet and I put a hand in his face. He missed.

"Foul."

"What?"

"You heard me."

I checked it to him up front and he went by me to the right, planting an elbow in the middle of my rib cage. I let it go. I took it out underneath and started up the right side. He forced me left so I put it behind my back, crossing over to the side he was giving me. He smashed his forearm right between my eyes.

When I looked up, he was finishing a left-handed layup. He slapped the backboard, as he did when he was mad. He grabbed the ball, came over, and handed it to me on the ground.

"Get up."

I tried, but the gym was spinning and I saw little flashes of white light around the corners of my eyelids. He slapped the ball out of my hands, turned, and hit it from the foul line. He gave it back.

"Ninety, eighty-nine, you."

I was feeling the first drops of blood from the bridge of my nose. "Hold on a second."

"Nope." He threw a chest pass and the ball hit my shoulder and rolled back toward him. He turned and made another one from the foul line. "Ninety all."

"Cut it out. I'm hurt."

He threw it off me. "You," he said, "are a pussy." He drove hard at the bucket. "And you don't beat me." He slapped the board again. "Ever."

Each time he scored, he came back and threw it off me. After he got to 100, he put his stuff on and headed for the door. I managed to get up on an elbow and used my shirt for the blood. "I'm leaving," he said.

"Wait up."

ii.

The two-man is your sniper. When Jeremy Garrison squared to the bucket, the toe of the top of the line Adidas black-and-white basketball sneaker was a little more beige than the white-white leather of the shoe. A rubber hemisphere with vertical ridges ran from the arch across the tip of the toes to the flat line at its base. Eighty-six bones in the foot engaged, releasing fifty-seven others, as tendons brought forward his ankle, heavily fortified by, in order of application, antiseptic spray; a spongy Ace bandage product also used on the blood-blotched forearms of geriatrics; and two rolls of traditional one-inch Johnson & Johnson athletic tape, which were wound around a leg shaved ninety minutes before game time from the calf down by a Schick razor run through Gillette shaving cream.

The filaments of the Achilles and soleus locked together causing a contraction that started the lift. No matter how many times the other guy had been smoked, the elevation was faster, snappier, higher than anticipated. Veins showed in the thigh and the quadriceps that overlapped the top of the kneecap, and carried first the center, then the rest of the core upward. The shorts were fire-engine red with yellow gold trim; underneath was the elastic Spalding athletic supporter with the same hemispheric shape and symmetrical lines as the rubber-ribbed toe of the Adidas shoe. The semicircle of the jock started at the waist and ran down, covering his package, keeping it together, and ended by the anus, where the material intersected with the two elastic leg straps, forming the whole system.

The rhythm was identical each time: it carried up through the solar plexus and into the pecs as the triceps lifted the biceps of the left arm. He was, he must have been, left-handed, this kid, because he was of that tradition, the Musial, the Williams, the Stabler, the Koufax type. The fabric of that jersey did not breathe; it was the time before mesh and Nike. The letters were sewn on, as were the numbers, 2 and 4, 24, the correct number for the two guard. Their trim was the color of a Roman helmet, like a melted gold Crayola, around the neck and shoulder starting at the scapula and going up and around the deltoid. The strap rose over the trapezius. Up to a sweat line under the chin around creases, making, again, a semicircle, in this case around the neck. The eyes, dead black, saw not just the whole of the rim but the very closest part to him, the front, where he knew to put it. He learned this on his own, not from anyone, you can't teach that, it's too secret. But once he knew it, he knew like he knew to swallow, to put it just there, over the front.

There are eight lines around the circumference of the ball. His hand was perpendicular to the lines. From the base of his palm to the finger-tips, his hand touched three of those lines perpetually. It was how he caught it, handled it, held it. It was never different, it was a rule, like a given in geometry, a natural law. The wrist and palm and hand bent as the machine-body reached the apex of the lift and he kick-levered the stroke straightforward. The ball rolled off the palm like a tire on the highway or a steamroller on the ground. He made sure the last part that touched it every time, every single time, was the tip of the middle finger. As he put it forward, the last cell of the tip of the epidermis—the part even beyond the fingernail, another little half-moon, more of the pattern—disconnected from the last brown ridge of the circular grain of the leather, the last bit of touch. It flew away, a cycle of semicircles cast out, a sequence of spinning rainbows forming yet another semicircle between his hand and the ground that it hit after easing through the cords like a car going through the slotted hanging-down chamois cloths at the end of the carwash, taking its motion back the other way before it touched down on the painted, oiled, shellacked, varnished, and mopped wooden floor.

I think I will do nothing for a long time but listen . . .

They say the great backcourts, the Fraziers and Monroes, complemented each other. Scully never would have been what he was without Jeremy Garrison. Garrison was left-handed. He was skinny and a little bigger than Chris. And he was just so money. At Glentop, he'd float around outside and wait for you to take your eye off him, then bang, lightning-fast left-hand stroke, chain-shred. Coaches taught guys to give weak side help but Garrison buried them for it.

He hated school. His dad was a big doctor and they had money, but Garrison wasn't like that. He was quiet. He was bored whenever he wasn't playing ball, and at Fallcrest, he got away with murder. He was smart and did okay in classes, and with all of the derelicts and drugs in the midseventies, the school had bigger problems than a rich white kid with a jump shot like Garrison's. There was a guy named Stuey, who must have been like thirty, who came to our games. Stuey gambled and Garrison and a couple of his buddies fell in with him. Garrison skipped school a lot to go to Stuey's house or the track at Brandywine. I used to see Garrison going into the locker room a half hour before practice and I knew he'd been at the races.

Garrison had a great way with the brothers, too. He didn't try to mix or be black, which black people appreciate in the very white. He had an ear, and picked up new expressions Etheridge or Leonard used. He parroted things back long before anyone else caught on. Since he didn't talk much it made it funnier. The black guys started calling a jump shot a "J" when we were kids, as in "shoot the J." There were variations. If Leonard was open, for example, he said, "J-land," which meant, "Give it to me." If someone else or I was open, the black guys said "J-land," as in "He's open, give it to him." So, when Garrison, the wiseass, got open he said, "I'm in J-land." It was sarcastic, mocking his own whiteness. He also pretended to fall asleep when someone was coming at him, waiting till the last second to drain it, rubbing it in.

I did not know why—still don't—but the brothers called each other "Cutty." It might have had something to do with Cutty Sark whiskey, I guess. But whatever it was, Garrison caught on to it. When he got on the bus he walked by Stokes or Etheridge and said, "What's up, Cutty?" They laughed their asses off.

He was just so goddamn money. Smooth where the rest of us—except Phillip—were all elbows and stains. Quick and slick. Bang bang. Over. Your ball, faggots. Off the court, he wore casual Adidas, low top with the red lines. He was not a pussy like a lot of shooters. He did not put his collar up; he did not wear shoes with no socks like the rest of those rich kids. He winked at girls when he walked down the halls. They went nuts for him—all in all I'd say he got the most out of any of us.

Scully and Garrison were magic. They weren't best friends; they didn't really even hang out. They played together in seventh grade at Indian Pass and it never changed after that. Scully was in charge: he brought it up, ran the offense, called the defense, yelled at everyone. Garrison was the two guard. His thing was getting open, being where they couldn't find him, rubbing off picks, finding seams in zones. He released early to start the break; he looked for steals when Scully was all over some guy. Garrison was the one who shot technicals. On that team, that was saying something.

iii.

Three is five split down the middle. A hundred years into the game, the three-man is all things to all people. He is the sweet creamy center of every team. He is guard and forward, little man and big man, swing man, small forward, third guard.

The Boys Club was six blocks from the courthouse. Etheridge and Coverdale lived in the bad part of South Penwood, the "run-down" section as they said on *Action News*. Stokes and Leonard lived closer to the courthouse, in the well-kept Negro section of town. Back then, Dottie said, "The Polks are a nice colored family," and there was never anyone less prejudiced than Dottie.

I remember sitting in the stands at the Boys Club when I was in seventh grade, eavesdropping on two guys talking in front of me.

"When you going, then?" said the first man.

"I'm not sure I want to go," said the second.

"You don't want the job?"

"I just don't want to go. My job's okay."

"What the hell you want to stay around here for?"

The second man leaned back. "Lot of things." He pointed at a player squaring up at the top of the key, number 44, tow-headed and strong. Phillip Ford. He shredded the jumper. The second man shook his head. "I want to watch that kid play, for one."

That kind of shit happened all the time growing up with Phillip Ford. He made black guys who barely knew him want to stick around town to see him play. He was great-looking, a kind of young Redford, almost unreal. "The Hope," that's what Stokes called him. Put it this way, he was the leading scorer in every league he ever played in from the time he was eight until he graduated from high school. He was one of those guys, like a Jerry West. He was something special but he was always one of us. So half the time we didn't notice, and he didn't push it. He was a star who didn't have to try; he was the reluctant kind, the shy and retiring kind, happy to be with the guys. I saw a documentary on HBO about the Baltimore Colts in the sixties. The way they described Johnny Unitas made me think about Phillip. The old-time Colts guys said they just loved playing with Johnny. They said they just wanted to be in the huddle with him. That was Phil, too. He wasn't a floor general—Scully took care of that. Phillip was a different kind of genius. He played as if he was older than every-body else. And then when it got to where age didn't matter, he was just better. He made space where it didn't exist. He hit shots no one thought he could make. When it was tight, he got the rebound over five guys each five inches bigger than him. Play with a guy like Phillip once and you know what I'm talking about. It sounds queer, but I'm thankful I got to play with him all the time. I know what those guys from the Colts mean.

He moved up and down the court like everyone else was running around in a full-court bowl of lemon Jell-O. He was always a bit bigger than Scully and Garrison, but not as big as the twins or Stokes. He was completely ripped from head to toe. Little teenage girls brought signs to games saying I WANT TO MARRY PHILLIP FORD'S THIGHS.

He shot better than anyone except Garrison, who shot better than anyone anywhere. But that was only part of Phillip's game. He also did what all threes have to do: he took it to the cup. From the left side, he dipped his shoulder enough to turn the corner, any amount, got it in there, in the chest, and got his triceps across the guy. Then he brought it through, smacking his left hand to join his right as he went down the lane. He looked for contact, trying to make someone stop him, thinking of three. I never saw another guy try to draw fouls like that, like he wanted three the hard way every time. I imitated Phillip anytime I touched the ball.

They put Phillip on varsity when we were in tenth grade. He was a phenom, always in the papers, led the league on scoring as a sophomore. By our junior year Scully, Garrison, and Stokes were playing a lot on the varsity as well. Leonard and I made it, too, but we rode the bench.

The great Phillip moment from that year came against Ridley, which had a player named John Donaly, who they said was as good as Phillip. I could tell in warm-ups that Phillip was feeling something different. After a sloppy first minute, Donaly juiced a twenty-six-footer. Phillip took the ball from Stokes on the inbounds, which ordinarily never happened because no one but Scully ever brought it up. He took it right at Donaly, jumped into him, and shot as he fell to the floor. The whistle blew for the foul and the ball went in. And one. Phil made the final shot to complete the three.

They brought it back down and Scully pressured the ball, but they got it to Donaly again and he pulled up from the same spot. As he released it, Phillip flicked his right hand down on Donaly's shooting elbow. Air ball. No whistle. The refs saw nothing.

The next time you try to shoot a basketball, have someone flick your elbow as you release it. You will see what happened to John Donaly. Only the players, I mean the real players of the world, know how to do what Phillip did. "Watch," Casale said to me on the bench, "he's done."

Except for the front end of a one-and-one in the third quarter, Donaly didn't score any more. He finished with three points, one-for-twelve from the field, one-for-three from the line. Phillip had twenty-eight.

iv.

Glentop was our home every day it didn't rain. A group of us white kids who could play started meeting up on our own. Scully and I walked there with the Dunns, Mike and Sean, big, scrappy identical twins. They were Stuckley boys like us; we'd known them since we were born. Garrison and Ford came together, getting a ride from Garrison's brother, who got the car only if he brought them to Glentop. Those guys lived in Hollow Hills and brought big leather Adidas tennis bags for their basketball stuff: socks, sweatbands, tape, and towels. Mike Dunn called them faggots for bringing those bags. We played three-on-three or fours, and as we came together we had full runs.

The summer we were fourteen, a guy with a mustache showed up out of the blue. He asked Scully how often we played.

"Every day."

"That's good," he said. He took the ball. "I'm Jim Casale." We knew he was the new coach at the high school, north, about four miles away. "I'm sending some guys over here tomorrow from Springton." He was talking about the other junior high school that fed Fallcrest. "Do you know the guys over there?"

"They're not great," said Scully.

"The guys I'm sending are. They don't play for their school because of the coach."

"What, the black guys?" I said.

He looked at me. "That's right."

I liked those guys. Along with Leonard, it was David Stokes, Etheridge Butcher, and Henry Coverdale Jr. Leonard was the leader; Stokes was the biggest; Coverdale was the strongest; and Etheridge was the quickest. They came over with Stokes's mom, who worked at

Woodlawn Acres, the old folks' home where Artie lived. They got a ride back to South Penwood any way they could, sometimes with Garrison's brother, then later with Garrison when he started driving.

Before Casale sent the black guys over to Glentop, we sometimes talked about them, about getting them to play once we got to high school. Scully liked to scheme about it. "Who do you think can do it? Any of them?"

The other guys didn't know.

"Stokes," I said.

"He's getting big," said Phillip.

"There's your four man, Chris," I said.

Phillip was right, David Stokes *was* getting big, and as he grew, you could just see he was going to be stronger and faster and possessed of more ups than anyone around. More important, he felt it. Stokes lived in a little house on Center Street. His dad was gone and his mother was secretary at the AME Church of East Parkside.

Walk the side of the lane from the baseline to the foul line. That's where the power forward eats, that's his house. The first thing a good team will do is pound it down low to see if you can stop their four man. Coaches wonder what the other coach has down on the box. If you don't own that, you can't win. Stokes owned it like you want to own the best piece of pussy. He made us legit. He moved up and down and pounced on anything that came his way. His turnaround from the low part was so sweet, Casale called it "Carolina."

It was an inside joke. Every team in the county had an offensive set called "Carolina," the same thing every time, a motion play. Always the same thing: some punk brought it up yelling "Carolina," then they swung it to the weak side, brought it back, set a double screen for their shooter in the corner. It never worked on us. Scully usually stripped the guard before they got started. Or Stokes and Phillip were so on the guys they were guarding, the point guard had to stop his dribble; or Leonard was so on top of the shooter, he couldn't let it go and had to kick it back out front and they were screwed, no set left.

Our play was not named after something as gay as that, something learned at expensive camps in the Poconos with college counselors wearing TARHEELS T-shirts, and high school coaches in coaching shorts, three-quarter-leg polyester. Our play was named after a girl. It came about because Casale was in a good mood one day and said, "Damn, Stokes, that is a sweet move. It's like a girl at my college, Caroline, rhymes with wine. You know what I said to my boys? 'Carolina got that vagina, you know what I'm saying?'" And we fell out. The brothers loved Casale. Stokes doubled over. Leonard laughed so hard, he lay on the ground saying, "NOOO coach . . . stoooop."

Casale would not name a play after another team. He wasn't like that. It was our play when we needed a bucket. Scully yelled "Carolina" one time only, not some dramatic announcement that gave the thing away. The right side was cleared. Stokes posted in low on the box and Chris got it to him. Stokes gave a quick feint left, pivoted on his right foot, squared, and rose and, with a soft flick at the top of the jump, let it go. The ball always kissed the top right corner of the box on the glass and went into the hole.

v.

Funny, Swarthmore College is one of the great schools in America and it wasn't twenty miles from Stuckley. We had no idea. We heard about it once in a while and never gave it a second thought. Dottie told me I was smart enough to go there, but I'd have to watch out because, as Artie said, "There's a lot of communists over there." Didn't rule it out for her, but she wanted me to know.

That's how I went through school thinking about Swarthmore. That and their basketball team always sucked. In fairness, there were a lot of great little college teams in our area like Cheyney, Widener, and Drexel. Swarthmore didn't have a chance against any of them, let alone Temple or St. Joe. The only other thing I knew about Swarthmore was that our big man, our center, five man, Steven (we called him Herman), his father taught there. Don LeFeber was six foot nine and had a PhD in microbiology. They lived between Stuckley and the developments. Professor LeFeber had some kind of genetic pituitary gland thing because his kids were all gigantic, too. Two boys, thank God—any girl that big would have been in trouble.

Steven was Herman's real name. He went to practices the way most kids go to piano lessons. He was huge, about six six in eighth grade and six nine by the time he got to high school. And he was solid, not a string bean like most kids who get tall young. He was awkward and shy. He never talked and the kids tortured him. He took it, and over time he got a little better. It also was clear he wouldn't quit.

But he was terrible, and no one thought about him much. So, it was a surprise when, a week after Casale's visit, Scully ran to meet a Plymouth station wagon pulling into the Glentop parking lot. Doctor LeFeber and the big kid got out. Scully chatted with the professor for a minute and then brought the kid over to us. We all saw what Scully was doing.

Who knows why some things stick? As soon as they walked on the court, Stokes said, "Let's play." First time down, I gave it to the big kid at the foul line and he turned, backed in with two dribbles, spun, and put it in over Stokes. It was butt-ugly ball, but it got in. We all kind of just stood there, not knowing what to do. Then Leonard said, "Nice move, Herman. Where's Lily?"

We cracked up at the reference to *The Munsters*. Scully ignored Leonard and just started up toward the other bucket and said, "Let's go." From then on, in the way of boys the world over, Steven LeFeber was called Herman.

A lot of the adjustment of having such a big dorky kid on the team was on Stokes, who really had to play with him, had to be his partner up front. Every basketball team has two groups: the guards and the big men. At the start of practice, the two groups split up. Everything was different for the big men. Drills, stats, assignments. Coaches yelled at them for different things. If your big guys didn't get along, if they didn't physically handle the other team, everything, all the savvy of a point guard like Scully, all the nothing-but-net of a shooter like Garrison, all of the full-court spider work of a star like Ford, did not matter. You needed buckets from inside, you needed boards.

During practice, I liked to look down at our big guys. Casale's favorite drill was putting them all in the lane, bricking a shot, and telling them to fight for it. Stokes, Coverdale, and Mike Dunn pounded on Herman. If he got an easy rebound, Stokes yelled at him. "Don't let me do that, man. Don't let me take it. What's wrong with you?"

Herman stayed late at Glentop and at practice and did the George Mikan drills: layup from the right, catch it without letting it bounce, layup from the left. Back and forth a hundred times. Stokes stayed with him most days, playing back-to-the-bucket one-on-one. They were both quiet guys and they got used to each other. They weren't like call-you-on-the-phone friends, but they got tight. That's what busting your ass together every day does. Sometimes I stuck around with Herman to lob it or bounce it into the low post, where he worked on his pivot moves. He even messed around with a baby hook.

vi.

When we were kids, Leonard and I didn't think about getting to know each other, it just happened. Even at eight years old, he had a good-size Afro and was long and lanky. We lived for basketball, yet neither me nor Leonard was on the starting squad in high school. Leonard would have started on any other team in the county, but on our squad he had to settle for being the sixth man, the first one off the bench.

The sixth man is mostly a work of fiction. Like Bigfoot. To me, it probably doesn't exist. They talk about Tommy Heinsohn and Michael Cooper and Dick Barnett, but I don't buy it. In my book, the real sixth man is one who can come in and play two, three, or four. There have been sightings, but it is hard to prove.

As a practical matter, aside from your regular subs, you need one really spectacular guy coming off the bench if you want to win. A guy who might be better than most of the starters, like John Havlicek. For us that was Leonard. He was dead from twenty-two feet in. He put it high above his head with his long left arm stretched way back. He elevated more than anyone and he let it go from a good three feet over his head. But his ball wasn't flat; it was still sweet as hell, great backspin, got home.

He could also mix it up inside. With his big wingspan, he played down low when we went to the two-three. He broke up a lot of shit from down there and he grabbed a lot of rebounds. When we played man-to-man, Leonard stuck the other team's best player. It was a real weapon to bring a guy in off the bench who could pick up the pressure on defense. Once teams scouted us, they knew when he came in the game they'd better watch out for the press. And like all great characters, Leonard had a trademark saying. In huddles, in the locker room before the game, when you saw him in the hall or after school, he always said the same thing: "Let's go, baby. Let's get that ass."

12

I like the ones from Eastern Europe. Polish. Former Yugoslavia, Croatia. The Russians and the Latvians and the Lithuanians are not as good, they're a little dirty. I like the South Americans, too. If you can find an Argentinean, they're the best, though a lot of guys go for the Brazilians. The Bolivians and Colombians are more like peasants, like the Russians. But they're all better than Americans. There's nothing worse than an American stripper.

I make them come. That's my thing. They like it when they get on; it's always been that way. It's my cock. It's big and good. Two songs into it, I grab their hair or their throats. They're all the same when you go into them like that. They look at you at first, not wanting to break through the crust of their daily routine, not wanting to go into the real part, like a ballplayer practicing at three-quarter speed. But then I do something violent and it turns them on. That's not just true for strippers, by the way. I try to drive in to touch a part in the center. There's a place in there, inside them, that when you get to it they explode. Doesn't matter if you're in them or it's through the clothes. It's mental.

I pass so poorly with paper and types. . . . I must pass with the contact of bodies and souls.

American strippers don't understand. There is something disconnected about them, something protected and guarded and prohibited and inhibited. They try to make you spend more money. They're junkies, bipolar, incest victims. They're also lazy, avoidant, petty, and pure idiots.

The ones I like, like Polish girls or Argentineans, are tough but not worn out. They have it right. They toy with you and then press the back of their pussy against you so hard, you have no other choice but to come. They stop you from thinking.

I got hooked on strippers for a different reason from most. I wanted to finish, I won't lie about that. But I got *hooked* because I wanted to touch a woman, to feel up the rib cage to where the breast starts, the round of hip to the thigh. I wanted the contact more, the sense of touching the strange. It's like a food. They said those Romanian babies who didn't get any mothering just died if the nurses couldn't get to them. I believe that.

Strippers play games with eye contact when you get to a bar. They're nuts; they pretend it's a real flirtation, when it's all conjured. It's a mind-fuck. It's why guys get hooked. American strippers slap your hands away, even when you stay for a third song. No stripper from Honduras or the Czech Republic would ever do that. No stripper who was ever locked in a room and force-fucked by an apparatchik working on the ass-end of a vodka bottle would have that hang-up. That's what I brought home the last time: one from Honduras and one Czech. I pulled them from a club. They said they'd fuck me for three hundred each. I got them in bed and all I could think of was a third stripper I was sweet on who wasn't working that night. A Polish girl who I couldn't get out of my head. I couldn't finish a second round with the other two. I had to beat off on the Honduran's back looking at the Czech, thinking about the Pole on the pole.

13

A good body is a brick house. A really good body is a brick shithouse. A really, really good body to a great joke teller in a taproom is a brick red shithouse. It is all redbrick: Independence Hall, the Palestra, the facade of the Spectrum, the row homes on Osage Avenue, the sidewalks in Stuckley.

Independence Hall is a museum. It's a shell. A cemetery. Tourists come to see the set where they shot that movie with the guys from *The White Shadow* and *St. Elsewhere* as Jefferson and Adams. Or they come to see ghosts.

The rebuilt row homes at Osage and Sixty-Second—where MOVE had its compound—are empty. No one wants to put up with those ghosts. No one wants to live where those people lived.

The sidewalks of Stuckley must have been pretty once, when the clay was so good and the men worked so hard that sidewalks and even roads were made of red brick, before the ground-stone cement mixes took over, before macadam and concrete. When the bricklayers did everything. The guys from PennDOT say there's brick under every street this side of Jersey.

The earth's diurnal course.

Weeds run through the sidewalks everywhere around the city, and they are uneven. The ground has moved in two hundred years. It's moved more than the bricks have decayed, that's for sure. *Diurnal course.* That's Wordsworth, boy.

On January 6, 1974, when I was thirteen, as the sixties ended and the seventies started, the stars aligned. Richard Manuel, Fred Shero, and John

Africa were all in Philadelphia. The Band played with Bob Dylan at the Spectrum; the Flyers were resting before a road trip; and John Africa was living in West Philadelphia, recently resigned from the Powelton Village Housing Co-Op.

It's a principle of physics. Elements will try to join up, try to fight off the emptiness of being alone. Teams form, bands form, troupes form, atoms combine.

You don't appreciate William Penn unless you know the Puritans, too. No one remembers the names of the three women and one man who were hanged in 1660 and 1661 by the Massachusetts Bay crowd for trying to return to the colony after they were banished for blasphemy. Poor bastards couldn't take the cold winters and were freezing so bad they had to go back to the blank wooden pews and benches and the black and the white clothes full of perspiration and shit stains. They wanted back bad enough to eat the fire and listen to the brimstone and see the symbols instead of the meditative quiet they believed was right. Or at least more right, more right-feeling when it came to the Lord than the bile and tightassedness of the nuts who ran that place.

William Penn had been through that already, in England. He wanted to change things. He saw a chance to set up everything between New York and Baltimore as a place where you couldn't get hassled. No hanging of motherfuckers just because they saw the light differently.

The story is the Indians loved him because he beat them in footraces.

14

It's great having money. I can take my time with the paper in the mornings. Lets me see things like Wally Rafferty's funeral notice. It was at a church out in Bucks County and I sat in the back. He was single and sang in the church choir. He was probably gay judging from the makeup of the crowd. It was Unitarian or some such—they certainly didn't penalize him for having killed himself. The minister was kind and spoke of Wally's love of music and his companionship with his white husky, Spirit. I sat there watching Wally Rafferty's old mother bawl her eyes out and all I could think about was the ass of a stripper. It was all pretty sad.

I thought about all that had happened as I drove back, about little Wally, poor fucker. It all got to him. It all got to him. It all got to him. It all got to him.

I thought about the course I took at Lattimore called "Millionaires." It was a survey course about wealthy people across America, focused on what they had in common. The guy who taught it studied the data on rich people and made it pretty much incomprehensible, stretched enough for a semester's worth of lectures.

The bottom line was most people who are rich are rich because their father was rich. And everyone who is rich can trace it back to a guy who had an idea and started something. We learned that how rich they are today—in other words, how big it got—is a direct function of how much the original guy was in the right place at the right time. That much wasn't hard to figure out.

Nor was it hard to determine that I did not want to be an old man talking at restaurants about not having money and saying, "There's no money in that," and pissing all over everybody else's ideas. It made it easier that when I left college I had no one pushing me to get a job or to keep going to school. The power of no parent was an inverted power, stored energy. No one said you have to get with a firm, buy the house, or get the car. I had enough cash to get by every month. I got my diploma, which was a Dottie thing, so I was set. I moved back home and read books. There's something about having nothing, starting from nothing, that makes you more willing to lose it all.

I built an operation out of undercutting Walter Hudson. I had ten people working for me, which became fourteen, then twenty. I made sure that everyone was younger than I was, until the money got too complicated and I had to hire an accountant named Sammy Ferreter, an old-time Penwood guy. I also had to hire a lawyer, Harry Burke, an even older Penwood guy, to look after things.

I had a huge space in the industrial park outside Penwood with an open working floor and no dropped roof; all of the insides were exposed. I recruited the weirdest kids I could find from art schools, telling them they could draw all day. I knew they would love making up ads when their friends weren't watching. Especially for a paycheck. I realized I could take the money I was making as a middleman and invest it in a real advertising company. I knew I could make what the clients wanted and there was enough locally that the big agencies weren't covering. You just had to be smart. And I knew commercials—I watched so many of them.

For no particular reason other than being provocative, I named the company Disintegration, then I added my name, so it was Joe Knight Disintegration. JKD. We did funny, insurgent stuff. I could see patterns, which was an advantage. It enabled me to zig when everyone else was going to zag. So much was just below the surface, on the tip of the tongue. I started with radio and moved into TV. Video cameras made shooting stuff easy and I cut my teeth on cheesy local commercials. No production value necessary—guys talking to the camera, the kind of thing small-time entrepreneurs went crazy for. You need a big ego to start a business and there wasn't one of those guys alive who didn't want to be on TV. I told the CEO of a potato chip company to put a potato suit on and had a model with huge breasts play a pretzel. We made little bits of Styrofoam look like pretzel salt and—her idea—her jugs came through the holes perfectly.

It really took off with Eddie Sheehy. Once I got the idea to sell television campaigns, I needed somebody to take a chance. He was one of my first clients. He sold cars. He bought a shitload of classified ads, a few photo spots, even a magazine once or twice. But each time I saw Eddie I thought the same thing: he looked like Gilligan from *Gilligan's Island*. He was five six with a bowl haircut, even though he was pushing fifty. He looked a little like a monkey.

I told him, "Let me shoot one commercial and you do just what I say." I put him in the white shipmate's hat and a shirt just like Gilligan's with white pants, though I changed the shirt color to blue. I turned the brim of the hat up. I gave him his lines.

"Ahoy, mateys. I'm stuck on this island with all these beautiful new Chryslers and Plymouths and I can't get off until I sell them all. Rescue meeeee . . ." Then I threw a bucket of water at him.

"You're a fucking jerk-off," he said.

"Do another take, Eddie. I promise you you'll never stop selling cars. You'll be going to Florida year-round. Do it. Trust me."

There was enough in my memory that related to every other memory to convince me this was a big idea. The sixties were coherent in their polarity. There were reference points; the people might have been in chaos, but the context was not. The seventies were insane. No one had their bearings, there were no more sides. It was just images and symbols and icons and phenoms and meaningless, mindless, vacuous television personalities and characters hitting you across the head every moment of every day.

I sold that when clients asked for "New." I looked down the column of memory and retrieved a concept from youth to invert, subvert, revert, and advert. People my age were the target consumers, the ones whose attention brought with it five easy payments of thirty-nine ninety-five. I knew their symbols, their signs and signals. The soft fuzzy nostalgic places of memory. I put smiley faces all over shit. I did campaigns centered on every syndicated half-hour TV show since *I Love Lucy*.

The guys in town and in New York saw what I was doing out of my dickweed office in Penwood and told me it was time to come into town, to join the bigs. I said no, thinking about the "Millionaires." I buried myself in work. I didn't see anyone, barely talked to anyone outside my office, ate hoagies for lunch and cheesesteaks for dinner, and watched the end of whatever game was on before passing out. I had a couple of girls I could call when I wanted, so, all in all, life was groovy.

Things fell into my lap. Like when my friend called me from an agency that was owned by some French company in New York. "Quick, what would you do for a two C's in a K for P&G?"

"What?"

"You know, two cunts in a kitchen."

"Product?"

"Floor wax."

"Let me think . . ." He waited. "Do Alice bitching and moaning."

"Let me get a pencil. What does that mean?"

"You put a housekeeper who's lost her shit at a table. Six kids run in and out. She complains about the guy getting married to a broad with three more kids. Thank God the floor is waxed with this great fucking floor wax or she doesn't know what she would do."

"*The Brady Bunch.*"

"Yes."

"You're a genius. Could you guys do this?"

"Sure."

"Send me something."

I made Eddie a star in cars and set about doing the same in every other big local product line: electronics stores, furniture stores, jewelry marts, even lawyers. I put a guy in a wheelchair to advertise insurance; I dressed the mom of one of my graphic designers like Zsa Zsa Gabor in *Green Acres* to sell crap gold necklaces at the mall.

My friend in New York got me a crack at national commercials and I did the same thing. I put a private eye like Barnaby Jones—an old guy with a southern accent—in a funny spot about toilet paper. I had a

Partridge Family–like singing family ride around and sell underwear. It was like shooting fish in a barrel.

A friend of a friend knew a newspaper writer in New York. He heard about JKD and thought it was hooky—a new breed of advertising. He wrote for the *New York Times*. He came down and walked around for two days. I got him talking and it turned out that both his parents were dead, too. The article ran on a Sunday, the lead of the Business section with a picture of me in the wide-open office space inside.

There's nothing better for business in Philadelphia than being in the *New York Times*. It was only a matter of time. The stock market was hot and advertising companies were getting bought out like crazy. The big firms sent people to talk to me, managers of account teams who we were always beating for spots. They wanted me to join for a big salary and options. I told them I had nothing but options, that I didn't need any more options. Sometimes they laughed.

15

Since I was already out there, I stopped at a club near the airport. That's another great thing about having money: two hundred dollars means a lot more to a stripper than it does to me. It's dark in those places; when you go during the day your eyes need time to adjust. Sometimes I try to turn the waitresses out since they don't strip. I didn't watch the stage anymore; I was way past watching dancers show their junk up close, getting a snatch shot for a dollar like a drunken amateur. What I really did was meditate, quiet and alone, nice and isolated.

I don't want to admit how many days I found myself there. In the dark. Sitting by myself. Staring at the stage. It had become the only place I could go inside. It was a form of paralysis. But it was about the only place I could find quiet. It was the only place that distracted me completely.

In a way, I knew it was all over when I started going to those places. Married, separated, divorced, those are all just formalities. The real line was crossed once I went to a strip club alone. When you're in the state I was in, you know there's a moment, a look, an exchange, that will end it all if you follow it. Your legs are splayed open for life to be shoved up your ass and the crazy thing is you want it. So situated, the pressure of the opportunities gradually gets you. Each a door not entered; each a path not taken, a life not lived. It becomes too much. It becomes enough to throw away good night moments, enough to pass up all the lullabies you've got left. Then once you're gone, you're gone. You look up and you're at the free buffet at a titty bar. When I was a little kid, my uncle Artie gave me a Timex watch with a black band and a big face. Few things made me feel worse than the time I left Artie's watch at one of those places. I don't know when it was. I had gotten in the habit of taking that old Timex off before each lap dance after I had scratched a Brazilian with it. I realized I had left the watch in the VIP room just as I was about to get in the car. I went back inside to get it.

The guy at the window was also the DJ, turntables and microphone in front of him as he looked out to the horseshoe-shaped stage. He turned to the right to talk through a Plexiglas window like at a bank, or a gas station. A white piece of paper was taped in the upper left-hand corner: ADMISSION $6.

"Hey," I said, "did anybody turn in a watch? An old Timex?"

He had a dirty-blond ponytail. "Hold up," he said, indicating he was busy. He turned to the mike and suddenly he had a strip club radio voice. "Put your hands together, guys, for Anastasia. *Anastasia.* C'mon gentlemen, get your hands out of your pockets. And get ready, gentlemen, for the two-for-one coming up next. Pick your favorite lady here on the dance floor and get two fully nude private dances for the price of one. Next up, Di-vine. Give it up for this luscious lady, Di—vine. Two-for-one coming up next."

He turned back at me. "What did you say?"

"I lost a watch. I just left five minutes ago. Did anyone turn in a Timex? An old watch?"

"Nah, bro. I got nothing. You can ask the bartender."

I started to walk through the turnstile at the entrance. I almost flipped over the arm when it stopped me cold, not letting me pass.

The ponytailed guy tapped on the Plexiglas and pointed to the sign.

"Six bucks," he said.

16

Games at Glentop started at three. Scully picked the teams. It was a ritual, a pattern, a summit, a meeting. Practice. Elective practice. Getting Scully at church, Garrison and Phillip pulling in and throwing their gym bags down, Stokes's mom in a brown Datsun, with four big guys piling out. Herman usually got a ride from his dad. Sean Dunn jogged to Glentop from home in headphones.

Unlike Mike, who was always out drinking or doing something with the hardass Stuckley guys, Sean stayed at home a lot, hanging in their basement, which Mrs. Dunn had allowed him to make into a stereo room with shag carpet and beanbags, bookshelves and a stereo. He loved bands and records. He was my go-to guy for music. With Sean, I talked a lot about whether WYSP rocked harder than WMMR. Mike and Sean were both six four fully grown. Where Mike was like a gorilla, Sean was wiry and hit from outside—that was his game, shooting from places guys his size couldn't get. Sean was a quiet, soulful basketball player, a surprise, the kind of unscoutable sub every great team needs. He was a major part of the whole deal for us. Depending on what we needed, shooting or power, outside or inside, Sean was just as likely as Mike to be the first big guy off the bench for us.

Sean was the only other guy I grew up with who was really into music. He liked to talk about books, too. Books he had read, things he was thinking about. He was pretty different from Mike. Music wasn't like TV; music was an intentional choice. Sometimes I listened to certain kinds of music because of peer pressure. The burnouts and the heads went for hard rock—Led Zeppelin was big. Disco was out of the question. Only the brothers got away with anything like that. Springsteen was big. Real big. Bruuuuce. Sean and I went to the Spectrum to see him, getting a ride with a few Stuckley guys who smoked bowls all the way in and all the way home. Sean's car had an eight-track. Bob Dylan hadn't entered my frame of mind until Sean played me *Blood on the Tracks*. It seemed beyond me, something I had not risen to yet. Sean told me Dylan was in a bad car accident and after that he didn't do anything for a long time. I bought *Highway 61* and the one with the picture of him and his girlfriend on the cover because I liked how they looked, one of the things I wouldn't tell anybody, except I did tell Sean I bought those records. He said he had one but not the other, but I don't remember which.

I played the one with the girlfriend on the cover five times straight. Dottie got home and saw that I was in a spell. She sat down and listened, and said, because she was in the parlor, "Quite nice. Would you like a cup of tea?" And she went into the kitchen.

17

Mike Dunn was a man when the rest of us were kids. He got much bigger than Sean lifting weights in their garage. It said a lot that he was different from even his identical twin. The rest of us lived for the game, planned our day by it, never moved it. We weren't distracted by most other things. We watched football and baseball and talked about tits and getting hand jobs and all that stuff. But we were on a path; we weren't going to be deterred by any stray crap.

Mike Dunn was there because he liked it well enough. He didn't pretend there was anything else to it, a mercenary who didn't give away his heart. He wore army jackets and a John Deere baseball cap and he looked like he was coming off the farm when he got to Glentop. He hung out with older guys who were working, either at Scott Paper or at the refineries in Marcus Hook. During the summers he was with those guys—whichever ones weren't working for whatever reason—driving around drinking beer and smoking bowls. They went to the driving range at Clayton Park and hit golf balls at the highway, or sat in one of their parents' houses and got loaded.

But Mike showed up at Glentop. He played with a beery smell and glassy eyes, but none the worse for wear. The older guys, the real hard Stuckley guys, hung out on the grass, drank quarts, and watched, sometimes even getting up between games and shooting, their chained wallets hanging out and black boots scuffing the court. They shot like idiots, with two hands, and punched each other under the basket. It showed how good we were. Those guys—who did not go for sports, believe me—got sucked in. Scully went over and took swigs of beer from them between runs.

Mike walked onto a basketball court his own special way. Two steps in, he clenched his fists and brought his elbows out like wings, like he was doing a lat press. It was a rooster move. During the shootaround before games, he found someone under the boards and placed himself between that guy and the basket and gave him a shove with his forearm, as though boxing out. But he did it slow-motion. He was just getting contact, getting a touch. If you were the guy that Mike did that to, you felt good.

Over time we all started doing the same thing. That's basketball: when you see something good, you imitate it, you try to do it. Scully did it first. Mike was the only guy Scully looked up to, in some way I never figured out—a redneck way, like it kept up his reputation in Stuckley. Later Phillip and I did the rooster move, first to be like Mike, then out of habit. Garrison made it really funny when he banged into someone and he liked to do it to the black guys. He walked over before we started playing and gave a little push to Coverdale, who was only about six one but with a big thick body, huge guns, and a bulwark ass like Wes Unseld. Nobody, I mean nobody, fucked with Cove. The football coaches wanted him, but he played only hoops, stubborn as the bull he looked like.

18

I couldn't wait for Dottie to get done with work when I was little. Being with her made me happy and I missed her when she was gone. She took me to the playground in Stuckley Park and we went on the swings; she took me to the market and to the bank, where she talked to the drive-in tellers until someone yelled out of their car—half the time they knew her—"Hey Dottie, can you please get moving?"

The memories are clouded, but I do have a pretty clear sense of sitting with Artie in the Dodge Dart. She said she was too lonely being away from us all day and wanted us near, so she brought us to the post office.

She parked under a shady chestnut tree on Monroe Street, close to the A&P and its bathrooms, but far enough from the crowded sidewalks that no one would notice an old man and a five-year-old in a car all day. It wasn't so bad. Artie told me stories and we sang songs when he was awake, but he took medicine that knocked him out by mid-morning. Dottie started at nine, which on government time, Artie said, meant nine fifteen. She got a break at ten thirty, lunch at twelve, and another break at two thirty. By stretching five minutes on either side of her break, ten minutes either side of lunch, and with a little help from Paulette, she managed. It was better than quitting or worrying that Artie would lose track of me or something worse.

Getting to and from, Artie sat in the passenger seat and Dottie drove. When we parked, she bundled him up in a knit hat with a fuzzy ball on top and a matching scarf. They both liked junk like that: red scarves and hats and Rudolph pins with the red nose that lit up with the pull of a string. They put me in the backseat where I climbed and rolled and slept.

I found all the weird and subtle tactile sensations of an early-model 1960s American car: the chilly window against my face, a snowy cloud leaving my nostrils, going out, coming back, going out, coming back; the plasticky stick of my forehead against the grooves of Naugahyde seats; the warm safety of curling into a ball on the floor of the backseat, smelling the rug and feeling the rumbling center bump over the lifeline of the car, where the pipes carried gas, brake fluid, air, water, and exhaust.

Dottie never came back empty-handed. She brought oranges and pieced them to us section by section. One to Artie, one back to me, one to Artie, one back to me, telling us the developments within the Penwood branch of the United States Post Office. She brought crackers, white cellophane sleeves of saltines. I chomped them up while Artie ate them slowly. When I complained about dry mouth, he said, "You need to wet your whistle, boy." Dottie took me to the A&P, to the water fountain, and then into the ladies' room, until, toward the beginning of summer, when I told her I was way too big for that, and she said, "Oh, I see. Heavens," in that fancy English accent, and from then on she let me go on my own. She brought a white Styrofoam drinking cup for Artie and she filled it up before returning to the car. She handed him his next batch of pills, watched him swallow, and went back to work.

I realized much later that Artie was fading. I guess he had some insurance from the railroad, but it didn't really matter. I never knew; I just climbed up front on his big lap and played with his whiskery face and gigantic gummy bulb nose and stared into the pores of his cheeks and pulled at his hairy ears like he was a dog. He smelled like rubbing alcohol and butterscotch candy and a mature male. When it was the most cold, I got inside his overcoat and put my head against his flannel shirt. When I peeked inside the space between its buttons I saw his thermal underwear.

Before Artie went into the home, the parlor was used for his trains. They took up the whole room and were awesome. There were plastic bushes and bridges and a station house and a painted green hillside and a crossing with warning lights. He perched a couple of feet over the landscape as he watched his Lionel locomotive pull its way through the world he made. *What you build is best done with bricks.*

Artie had a record player he kept next to his train set. He loved Johnny Cash and Roger Miller. Days I came home before Dottie was back from the post office, or after she went to the restaurant, I always found Artie sitting with his trains.

Third boxcar, midnight train
Destination . . . Bangor, Maine.
Old worn out suits and shoes,
I don't pay no union dues.
I smoke old stogies I have found
Short, but not too big around
I'm a man of means by no means
King of the road.

He had Elvis's *Blue Hawaii* and a record by Marty Robbins called *Gunfighter Ballads and Trail Songs*. I loved "El Paso"—*"Out in the West Texas town of El Paso"*—the one about the guy catching his sweetheart just as he died. It was so sad. I grabbed the needle, set it right back in the groove, and played it over and over.

An old black-and-white photo of Artie and two other guys in matching shiny outfits hung in Dottie's closet. They were called the Inside Out Trio. She couldn't remember why. "Artie loved two things besides me and you," she said. "Trains and music."

It's blurry, but I remember sitting with him and the trains listening to records, the music in one continuous flow, like a long melody, a lullaby. I made them out later as songs, when I went back and studied his records. But I do remember him talking. He always talked about time. He told me to be on time. He gave me the cheap Timex watch, with the black band and big face. "It keeps good time," he said after he handed it to me. He was a Railroad Man.

Artie talked a different way than anybody else. He talked the way they sound in old-time records, the hard and scratchy 78s, with a little cry in his voice. He played me a song by Lead Belly asking the governor of Louisiana to let him out of jail. The governor heard it and let Lead Belly go. It was a great song.

He said to me, "Train is in a station but once, boy." His gray hair was really short, buzzed up high and tight. He sat on that stool and kind of dripped over the sides, like fluid. He worked off missed opportunities sitting there. "You make a record and then you go on. Train is in the station but once."

I was confused by it. I said to him, "Trains run every day, Uncle Artie. That's what you used to do, make them go on time."

"That's different. I'm talking about making your mark, boy. You got to make your mark."

When Dottie took the trains down, she didn't touch the record player and its little speakers. Artie's albums were all I had to begin with. The music is there when I think of Artie: constant. Jazzy, swingy, bluesy music. Background to Artie and his trains.

Don't let visual stuff fool you; music is the only narrative. The only question is what do you listen to when no one else is there.

19

Pinelli's had a bar shaped like a racetrack with a red leatherette rail. I got a busboy job when I turned fourteen. The bartenders, Norman and Lenny, rotated shifts, bet baseball, and did other things I didn't really catch. I worked Dottie's nights at first, then five, six shifts a week. I cleared dishes and wiped tables, put glasses behind the bar, changed soda canisters, and tapped kegs. The roast beef sandwiches were served wet or dry. If wet, the kaiser roll was sopped with gravy and melted provolone and sweet or hot peppers. Each table had one jar of mustard, one jar of ketchup, and one jar of hot peppers. The busboys stayed until the last table was gone and put the mustard and the ketchup and the peppers back into plastic industrial containers that went to the walk-ins. At least on Friday and Saturday there were two guys. And the cooks were usually drinking with the bartenders when we were done.

Everyday life is full of music, full of singers, especially growing up, especially at Pinelli's. People like Carol and Edmund and Pasquale. I could close my eyes at the end of the day and hear them talking and singing. Monologues, diatribes, and word songs. I can hear them talking and singing and saying stupid things, certain repetitive jokes. "Car-ol," "Ciao," "All right Joooooooey," "Paaas-quaaa-le," "It's all right, it's all right, it's all right."

I loved them all and they loved me. I was the only dependable busboy. I didn't know any better and I wasn't going to let Dottie down. There were a million secrets, and as I got older, I figured out the way the place worked. A young chef, Chris, gave Norman steaks and Norman gave me six-packs for Chris, which I put in a white bucket filled with ice. Chris left pieces of lobster and Budweisers for me in the walk-in and I picked up his dime bags of weed. It worked great. The dishwashers were out of the loop but we all needed them, so the guys fed me booze and food to get to them. It was before Mexicans.

Six girls worked on a busy night. There were about fifteen waitresses on the weekly schedule. Five of them, like Dottie, had worked at Pinelli's forever. Five or six more had been there a few years, and there were always a couple of new ones, young and usually sexy. Arnold Pinelli built the place and his son, Anthony, was the manager. Anthony was twenty-five and banged the new girls. "More of a guideline than a rule."

Edmund was a Jamaican cook who kept up a running, singing dia-logue with the waitresses: "Car-ol, where's my Car-ol?" Shit like that, sing-yelling at someone, Caribbean Sing Song of the Apple-Eaters. Carol hummed. Patty and Molly, sisters, worked the stations next to each other on Tuesdays, chatting over customers as they set food down. Pasquale said his own name randomly, kind of calling it out to himself and the waitresses, "Pas-quaa-le . . ." Call-and-response with the busboys: we saw him and said, "Paaas-quaa-le." As he reached for ice or opened a Michelob, he sang it back: "Paas-quaa-le."

Pasquale; Edmund; Carol humming; Anthony rattling his keys, pre-tending to work. He hit the floor for ten minutes and went back to a bar stool or his office, with the adding machine and the invoices, and smoked joints. The girls—and they were girls, even the hard ones, divorced with permanents, post-hysterectomy, men-loving, barhopping ladies—even called each other girls. "What other girls are working tonight?" "One of the girls from work told me." They chewed gum slowly, like a substitute for a long, slow grind. They wore black waitress pants and any blouse they wanted, invariably dark and satiny. The Italian ones wore gold necklaces with crosses or the Italian horn, that goddamn thing that looked like a hot pepper. The old ones were moms, the middle ones sisters, and the new ones fantasies.

The restaurant had three seating areas: four rows of booths split by two aisles in the front, back tables behind the bar, and a side area added on in the sixties called the porch. The waitresses governed their sections like warlords. I was like a shuttle diplomat. There were three bus stations: outside the kitchen, in the corner in the back, and at the front of the porch. In the bus stations were silverware, coffeemaker, coffee filters, coffeepots, silver bags of coffee for the coffeemaker, napkins, bus pans, salt and pepper, Parmesan cheese, sugar, and hot water.

The waitresses' pants were tight, making it obvious what kind of ass they had, my education in ass. I studied them all from six till two in the morning. There was a tight squeeze coming around the corner of the back bus station. When a waitress was facing it, making coffee or getting silver, I came around the corner and ever so slightly rubbed my cock against her cheeks. Up and over the first cheek, so soft, down into the divot, and over the other side. A deft prank; jerking-off material. As I got older and bigger, I got more aggressive. You can't teach that.

The walk-ins at Pinelli's were cool. There was a refrigerated one for beer, vegetables, milk and butter, big buckets of salad dressing, and premade soup. The other was a freezer for steaks and seafood and was locked. The refrigerator was open but you could latch it from the inside. It was the place for secret stuff—drinking beer and smoking joints—and, by the time I got to high school, the cooks were doing lines in there.

The waitresses tipped the bartenders out at 15 percent and us at 5. The bartenders were supposed to tip us, too, but that didn't happen. There were lots of money games, bets, bags of pot. I got more aggressive with the waitresses. I loved Cheryl, who wore the stretchy pants more over her hips than at her hips, and they showed off her heart-shaped ass. When I was drunk one night, I swung by and rubbed my cock across her cheeks a little harder than usual. It felt like clean air, like being at Joe Rockhead's house for the closed-circuit fight, with sandwiches and no broads, like being at the Pussy Show I hadn't been to yet. I heard her go: "Em." She looked at me but I was already off to grab some dishes. When it was safe, I looked back. She was searching for another waitress, looking quizzical, like she didn't know if I really would do that. I was shy and dreamed about their bodies. I liked to talk to them, get in their heads, find their strengths and weaknesses. We talked about finishing school. Most of them quit school early and wished they hadn't. They all smoked. The ones who had been there for a long time had grown kids. The middle group was more eclectic—a few had daughters, a few had no kids but were married, and most were divorced. The divorced ones went home with losers from the bar, which I never forgot. I held grudges. None of the young ones were married.

Anthony was a guinea with olive oil skin, like the Hollywood guy in *The Godfather* said. He really did have that skin, it wasn't a joke. He was almost a different color, like a Mexican. I used to sit with him out on the porch as he did numbers at the end of the night. He talked to me smoking a cigarette. He talked about ass. He said, "When are you going to lose that basketball? You can't fuck that thing." He said it when girls were around, and they laughed at me. "There's something better than that thing. It's called P-U-S-S-Y." I don't think he ever dribbled a ball in his life.

20

Due to budget cuts, Tom Harris taught both tenth-grade English and eleventh-grade history at Fallcrest. I came to be close to Mr. Harris, over time. He was the first person I could really talk to about books and music. I spent the first part of tenth grade staying quiet, being cool, but when we read *Hamlet* I came out of my shell.

He asked the class, "What's the most important line in the play?"

When they were all done with their, "*Neither a borrower or lender be . . . To thine own self be true*" bullshit, I raised my hand.

"*There's more in heaven and earth than dreamt of in your philosophy, Horatio,*" I said.

He told me to stay after class. When everyone had cleared out, he asked me, "What writers do you admire beyond Shakespeare?"

"I don't understand Shakespeare," I said.

"Well, tell me this. What do you think the play is about?"

"The guy can't make up his mind."

"Anything else?"

"He changes into a guy who can make up his mind."

He gestured at a chair in the front row. "Sit," he said.

I tried to direct the conversation to basketball, and he said, "No basketball. Talk to me about anything but basketball."

So I went into music. He said he understood Dylan but didn't know much about The Band. He had heard "The Night They Drove Old Dixie Down" and "The Weight." He thought they were a little hillbilly-ish for him. I told him he should listen to "Acadian Driftwood" because he'd like the story, that it was about people who had to leave their home in

Canada and go south, to New Orleans, where no one wanted them. He gave me the look I got from people who expected less.

"They were people no one wanted. Like trash," I said.

"You're a little young for Bob Dylan. But you don't seem too rebellious. Are you? Rebellious?"

"No. Not really. I think about it, about what he sings. But, honestly, I like the bands more. For the music."

"Do you play music?"

"No."

"Do you want to?"

"No. I have to concentrate on basketball."

"Well," he said, "keep doing what you're doing on the side. I think your mind is waking up. And it can take you a lot of places."

"I think my mind's been awake for a long time."

He thought about that. "Okay," he said.

Harris was tall. He had that crinkly kind of hair, like Lionel Barrymore or the guy who played Ashley Wilkes in *Gone with the Wind*. He was southern, from Charleston, or something. Maybe that was why he liked the story about the song. He asked me to tell him about where I lived and what my other classes were. I told him we were studying dreams in science class, and we were supposed to be writing about our most vivid one. I told him I was making up a dream to write about because the one that fit the assignment was too weird.

"What is it?" he said.

I told him that since I was a little kid I'd had this dream that kept coming back. Every woman in the world has a special butter inside their nose that is wildly desirable to men because men need it to live past fifty. Girls only have enough butter to give to one man and extracting the substance from inside their noses was an extremely painful process involving surgery. So men spent their whole lives trying to convince a woman to give them their nose butter. And the cruel reality was there was absolutely nothing in it for the woman but pain.

I can't explain it away as a symbolic sexual deal because I remember quite vividly that this was all in addition to sex—it was separate, apart.

People in the dream still had sex and babies and families—the whole butter decision was at another level. And it was a bad dream; I woke up panicked each time. I was so nervous about having to get some girl give me her butter. I couldn't imagine convincing anyone to do that. It seemed like such bullshit, the level of manipulation needed to make the case when it was all a lie.

But the attraction in the dreams was so strong. The need for that butter. Every male had it and I remember it being so superfragilistically enticing, the drive to get it, the secret creamy, off-white substance, its consistency lighter than mashed potatoes, more like whipped cream, like Cool Whip. It made girls so irresistible that you just wanted to be with them for the shot they might give it to you. It was worth anything.

He stared at me when I was finished. "That's quite a dream," he said. He didn't say anything for a while. Then he said, "It obviously means something, don't you think?"

"I guess so."

"But I don't understand it."

I felt embarrassed. Like I exposed myself. "Yeah, me either." My instinct was to go back at him. "I don't understand why you teach here."

"Why do you ask?"

"You don't seem like the other teachers. You should be a professor or something."

"It's hard to get teaching jobs at colleges right now" was all he said.

When he saw I had a copy of *Fear Strikes Out: The Jimmy Piersall Story*, the memoir of a baseball player who went crazy, he said he was impressed. Dottie gave it to me—she told me it was the only time she ever read a book and saw the movie.

"It's a little complicated, isn't it?" Harris said. "I mean, there are some very mature themes."

"He went nuts." I said. "So what?"

"He was courageous, I suppose."

"I don't believe a lot of it."

"No?" Harris said.

"Maybe not that I don't believe it. It's just a little made-up-seeming, you know? The guy blacked out for a whole season? I bet that made it easier to pretend he didn't know what happened."

"You mean convenient?"

"Yeah, convenient. It's always convenient in books, even in books that are supposed to be true."

Harris stoped and seemed to reflect on that. "It's a good point. Hard to like a work when it's too convenient. Hard to like something when it's inconsistent, too." He paused again. "Or someone."

21

L ife changed one day when the JKD years were in full swing and my accountant, Sammy, asked me, "Have you heard of Hubert Betours?"

"No."

"He wants you to meet him in Center City in two hours."

Betours was in the lounge at the Four Seasons having tea. He wore a beige suit and blue shirt, only Frenchmen can really pull that off. He was cologned, with his hair pulled back, but natural, didn't seem like anything was holding it.

"What are your grosses for this year?"

"About three million," Sammy said. Old pro, thumb on the scale. "We'll do four and a half, five next twelve months."

Like a movie, Betours said, "I like to fuck on the first date. Publicité will buy one hundred percent for ten million in stock. A little diligence and we close in thirty days."

I loved the way he said it: "A leetul dil-i-jenz . . ."

I said, "Why would you do this so fast like this?"

He said, "Good question. Same thing I would ask. I will tell you, no bullshit. I need two things: US presence and gross. I will make you show more EBITDA than you are now, aggregate several companies, and do a rollout in the next twenty-four months. You are not the only ones with a public stock market, no? If you don't accept my offer, I have two agencies in Chicago and one in San Francisco who will jump."

"Fifteen," I said. "And I only give you two years."

"Twelve million and no need to give us any time. We will throw in a consulting contract for you for a few years for—let's say half a million dollars, but no requirements. You can do what you wish."

I looked at Sammy. He said, "Don't look at me."

I said, "I need to make a call."

I walked to the hotel lobby, and then outside and stood still for a minute. The doorman was getting a cab for an old couple going to dinner. "When you need to come back, tell the driver to bring you right to Center City. Right in the middle. He'll know where we are." People say things are "surreal" but I don't think they know what that means. I think what they really mean is "unreal." That's how it felt: unreal. Like I was watching it on TV. It seemed fake, but the hotel, the doorman, the fancy lobby furniture, the art museum around the corner, the fact that it was going down in the city, where things like this happened every day, made me accept it as real—like pinching myself. Why not, I thought. It's a New World out there. Just like William Penn, just like Philadelphia. You make your fate. I deserved it.

When I walked back in, Betours was on his cell phone with his back to the door. Sammy sat there, not knowing whether to shit or go blind. Betours said, *"À bientôt"* into the receiver and ended the call.

He turned and faced me. We were both standing, I had my hands on my hips. "On this consulting deal, if I want to go around the world or something like that—do absolutely nothing, that's still okay?"

"But of course."

I stuck out my hand. "Feels weird, but you got a deal."

He gave me a firm, brisk shake. "Then it's done. Very good." After a few pleasantries and instructions to Sammy about what to do next, he was gone.

Sammy drove us back to Penwood in his Oldsmobile. I was pretty stunned. Sammy was giddy like a little kid. Like most old-timers, the ones who were raised in the Depression and went to World War II, he got a little nuts when modern amounts of money were thrown around. They want to be reserved, untrusting of it, skeptical. But they get so excited they can't help themselves. Their mood improves, their outlook gets breezy. We went to the piano bar at the Marriott on 202, the first place we could find once we got away from the city. It was as though until we got out of Philadelphia proper, Betours could still call off the deal.

Sammy said, "If there was ever a shot-and-a-beer time, this is it." We got pretty housed sitting there in overstuffed red velvet chairs drinking Michelob with V.O. chasers. From the time I'd met him, Sammy never tried to tell me what to do. I appreciated that about him. And in the buzz of that cheesed-out hotel cocktail lounge, he made me feel like I was Johnny Unitas and he was a guy in the huddle.

"You know, my old man hauled garbage for five dollars a week," Sammy said.

"I know, it's crazy."

"I'm proud of you, Joe."

22

i.

We needed rides everywhere: to practice, to summer league, to all-star tournaments. We needed rides back up to school on game nights at four thirty so we could catch the team bus. Everyone had a tight schedule, had to be picked up and dropped off, needed to grab rides, get other guys, leave cars, walk to cars, wait in the snow for moms and uncles and neighbors and friends. The first choice for driver was Dottie if we could get her. Since I lived near Scully, we were usually together. And we picked up Leonard a lot. Dottie drove when she didn't have to work, anywhere we wanted. I liked her to take me to meet the team bus on game nights because she was good luck. We always won anyway, but when Dottie dropped me off I was more likely to have a good game. As usual with Dot, she had a routine for game nights: she sat at the kitchen table and when I came out of my room in the shirt and tie Coach Casale required for away games, she said, "My, my, who's this handsome fella?"

Dottie wore a big button with my picture from the program. As we rode, I gave her the scouting report. She didn't have a clue what it meant, but it settled me. "Now which one is their good one? Which number am I looking for?" When I reminded her, "Oh, Phillip will stop that guy, honey" or "Chris is better than him," or "Well, he can't be better than David Stokes, I'll tell you that right now."

She was always entertaining. Dottie said my grandfather—her father—was a bricklayer. Shanty Irish, not lace-curtain Irish. She said she could watch him for hours as he raised a wall, layering mortar, maintaining level rows under the line. "The thing was like a knife in his hand."

When it came to the last brick in a line, he turned his trowel sideways and cut it by eye. "Perfect every time."

The other guys liked her to drive; a ride home was never just a ride home with Dottie. She couldn't drive past a diner if she had boys in the car. She said, "Get these guys French fries," when she walked in. Cokes, shakes, burgers. Leonard got tuna fish and had ice cream with me. Scully got grilled cheese and nothing else. He was sweet with Dottie—whatever I had against him, I couldn't deny that. Starting when we were very young— maybe seventh grade—she made a habit of keeping track of how many points he and I both had in every game. Afterward, or the next time she gave us a ride, she'd tell him. She'd say, "Seventeen, honey." Or, "You had twenty-two, how about that?" He always made her feel that she was his only trusted source for the info, like it wasn't in the books until she told him.

Dottie had little things like that with everyone. That's what she did, she made everyone feel special, especially me. Her 1963 four-door Dodge Dart was the most durable machine ever made. It was green with a brown faux-leather top. You could see it a half a mile away from a parking lot, or a friend's house, or the Scullys' front yard, or the drop-pickup circle at Fallcrest. When she got within eyesight, she waved as if she hadn't seen me in two years.

It wasn't just love; it was protection, too. When I was six, Dottie had to leave the Tuesday morning sort at the post office. There must have been thirty of us in my first-grade class, seven across and four or five deep, in very straight rows. The teacher gave us red notebooks with picture questions: which-cow-has-three-spots-and-which-has-two. I finished the first one in five minutes. She looked at me funny and gave me a blue workbook and I did the same thing. It was simple shit.

She told me to go to the principal's office. He called Dottie and that's when she had to leave the sort. They moved me from first grade to second. Dottie said it was because the first-grade teacher didn't want to find things for me to do for the next nine months. The second-grade teacher was named Betty Bass. Miss Bass. She didn't have any problem keeping me busy. She gave me books to read and when I sailed through them she gave me bigger books.

That was the pattern with every teacher: special assignments, on my own little deal. They gave me public school books. *The Red Badge of Courage* I read in third grade; *A Separate Peace* in fifth; *The Catcher in the Rye* in seventh. Dottie got into these books by John Jakes about the Revolutionary War and I picked them when I was bored. When she saw I had *The Bastard*, the librarian said, "What are you doing with that book?"

"I'm reading it."

"It's pretty grown up."

"It's pretty crazy. Like the raping of the wenches," I said.

"What grade are you in?"

"Fifth."

She told someone on me, but it blew over.

Sometimes the teachers asked me questions and I told them what was happening in the book. Some of them asked me what this or that meant—why the guy pushed the other guy out of the tree house—stuff like that. I said I didn't know if he did push him out of the tree, that I missed that. The teacher said he did, which was a shitty thing to say.

None of them saw the important thing. Neither the teachers nor Dottie understood that by putting me up in second grade they ensured that I would never make the starting five. That the effect of their conspiracy was to join me with the coincidence of talent in that age bracket, in that makeshift school district, in that hodgepodge township, in that county, at that time. That I would always play behind Scully. That I was part of the best team ever in the area, but that it didn't have to happen. I didn't have to have a lifetime of carrying Chris Scully's jock.

ii.

The second driver was Mrs. Scully. Her name was Eileen, maiden name O'Hare. She had short red hair. Mr. Scully was a cop, a soft-spoken guy who worked a lot. We didn't know what he was up to; Mrs. Scully made it seem like he was doing really important work, crime fighting. She was happy to sacrifice and practically raise her kids alone. She went to Mass every Sunday and made it her business to make sure the priests were happy, a concern she picked up from her mother, a device, a way to garner favor, the kind of plain sight corruption that plagues all parishes.

When I asked her what was wrong with Mrs. Scully, Dottie said, "Honey, sometimes in life you have to look at people and say: 'Maybe they're doing the best they can today.' You never know what someone is going through."

She drove a Ford station wagon. Eileen was an Irish mother; Chris was the end-all and be-all. I was in the picture as an element of Chris's life, a supporting role, a sidekick, the sitcom neighbor. But on any question on the issue of Chris Scully's domination over me, his vast superiority over me in all things of matter, of any currency of youth, Eileen Scully was there to correct it, to put me and the world back in line.

When I went to their house after school, she had peanut-buttered Ritz crackers waiting for him. Before we went out to the slab cement court put in by contractors as a favor to Mr. Scully, where Chris and I played Utah—a combination of one-on-one and foul shooting also called Thirty-One because it was played up to 31, or called Maul Ball if you added a player. She put them around the perimeter of the plate, with five in the middle in the same pattern as the five on a die. He ate them like crazy, never much else. She offered me juice or water but never soda and certainly never peanut-buttered Ritz crackers—those were Chris's domain, his special food, private between them.

She talked about everything as she drove. Local politics, gossip, the other mothers on the team, whom she feuded with constantly, as though she needed the distraction, or was jealous of the coherence that Chris brought to the team. She had her friends and her enemies and she switched them constantly, playing a game of her own making with no boundaries.

She was the kind that always made kids feel a little guilty about things. "You guys have it made, let me tell you." We got that kind of shit all the time when she was driving. "Enjoy it now, while you can." She saw her family as better than Stuckley and made it a point to let you know they were there because they got a huge house with a huge yard in 1960. The house *did* have a large, cool front yard, and like a southern house, it had columns and a front porch, bizarre for the town. It was located just at the border, as you drove into Stuckley. Everyone knew it, the Scully house.

She was a hypocrite, snuggling up to the black mothers at the games, railing against blacks in the car. Against welfare, same as all whites except Dottie or a guy like Casale, white folks who liked black people, she said, "Ron Scully is working his fingers to the bone when some lazy bum down in Chester collects welfare."

"Don't say that, Mom," said Chris.

"You're absolutely right, honey. Thank you for correcting me." She turned left. "But it's true, you need to see that."

Once I told her that Leonard's mom and dad worked hard and she said, "You have to learn something, Joseph. There's black folks and there's niggers. The Polks are black folks. I'm talking about lazy people who don't want to work, who just drink quarts of beer and shoot dope." She got going. "It started with slavery—they came up from the South, these blacks we have here now. They are country people, really. Southern blacks. That's the real problem, they belong back in Alabama and North Carolina, not on street corners in Penwood. Good Christ, you kids need to learn."

iii.

The third driver was Ervin. Because Leonard didn't come to Stuckley much—"Crazy ass Daniel Boone motherfuckers"—I went to his house.

Ervin piled us into his Cutlass 88 to take us to Glentop, or to take me back to Stuckley, or to summer league games, or wherever we were playing. Rides with Ervin, being anywhere with Ervin, actually, was special. He wore yellow knit shirts with short sleeves that barely held his biceps. He had a brown straw fedora and he smoked Kool King Filters. He always took his time, no matter what he was doing.

I was a little nervous the first time I visited their house since I had not been to a black home before. We walked to the house and his mom took his hand. "Come with me to pick up dinner. Joe, Leonard's dad will take you home." I stood in the doorway in my coat, looking around. It had the inside-a-house smell, not different from other inside-a-house smells. It smelled like coats and carpet, nothing bad. The furniture was normal, stuff on the walls, photographs of kids and weddings. They had a yellow couch with slipcovers.

Ervin said, "Sit down, man. Get comfortable."

He ran a building supply company out of a warehouse off Monroe Street. He was third-generation South Penwood. He sensed I was uneasy. "What's your hurry? You got schoolwork?"

"Yes, some. But I'm not in a hurry."

"All right. I'll be out in a minute. Would you like something to drink?"

"No thanks."

"All right."

In his car, he said, "Leonard says you're pretty good. And that must mean that *you really are pretty good* because Leonard don't say that." He laughed about Leonard. We came to a stop sign at exactly the same time as an old lady in a Buick to our left. Erv gave her a little wave with his left hand. "C'mon missus," he said. That's what he was like: he waved old ladies through stop signs, letting them go first.

"Leonard's awesome."

Erv looked like Wilson Pickett. He was a player himself. He was Penwood High's leading scorer in 1956, back when there was a Penwood High, before it was folded into Fallcrest. He went to the all-black Cheyney State Teachers College, and then went in the army. He went to Vietnam, that's all I knew. Erv wasn't a guy to tell you how hard it had all been for him. He didn't talk about politics, either.

We drove for a while in silence. "How you like living in Stuckley? Little different than over here."

"I come here with my aunt Dottie all the time. She works with Mrs. Polk."

"I know. I like Dottie. She's a nice lady."

We got to my house. When he was about to let me out, he said, "Okay, Joe Knight, here's the rule for my car: if I drive you somewhere, when you get out the car, you come over and give me a handshake before you go."

"Okay," I said. And I ran around to his side, where he had rolled his window down. I grabbed his hand and said, "Thank you for the ride, Mr. Polk."

He liked kids who were polite. "I'll see you soon, son."

If Erv liked you, you were in his life. He watched games closely. Leonard went to him at halftime to get special instructions. He didn't undermine anyone; coaches loved him, especially Casale, who always asked him for advice. Casale was smart like that. Erv and Casale talked all the time: before and after bus rides, as we warmed up, at halftime.

He dropped instructions from the window of his car, shaking hands and saying good-bye. Before a Boys Club championship game when I was on Rotary, he said, "You're going to be very excited tonight. Watch how hard you're holding on to the ball. Tendency is to hold the ball too tight. Messes your shot up—you pass it too hard, dribble the ball off your foot, all that. Be soft with the ball. You'll be all right."

23

The car phone rang as I left the strip club near the airport.

"Joe?"

"Who's this?"

"It's Ervin. Are you in a car? Did they give me the right number?"

"Ervin. God. How are you?"

"I'm good. Listen here: did you do something?"

"What do you mean?"

"When you sold that company and made us all that money?"

"Erv, what are you talking about?"

"They are sending some papers around about it. You better be careful, son. Something's going on. Leonard's at his sister's. Go talk to him."

I drove to Penwood. I had to ring the bell twice. One of Leonard's sister's kids answered the door and brought me into the kitchen.

"All Knight." Leonard was up in the doorway. "Hey, man." We did the bro-hug. "What up, boy?"

"Do you remember Wally Rafferty?"

He went into the fridge for two beers. Leonard became an administrative clerk at the courthouse. He ran the place: oversaw all court filings, case assignments, bail payments, security guards, and bailiffs. He worked in the courthouse since we got out of high school and was the highest-ranking non-judge or DA in the place.

"No."

"Killed himself. Went to his funeral last week."

"Did you know him?" he said.

"When we were kids. How's work?"

"Work's work. We got to talk." He reached inside his coat and put a legal envelope on the table. It was a subpoena from the United States Attorney's Office, Eastern District of Pennsylvania. "It's about JKD."

"Shit."

"Everybody's getting them. Stokes called me. Garrison, too."

"Fuck. I was just about to tell you that I went to see Scully this morning. He told me something was up, like it was a big secret. I didn't think it was going to be this fast."

Leonard's eyes got wide. "You went to see him today?"

"Yeah. Had breakfast at the diner."

"Joey, man, this is fucked-up." He shook his head. "That's what I wanted to tell you. He's the one behind this whole *gott*dammed thing." He stood up. "I got it from a good place."

"I believe it."

"You need to get yourself a lawyer."

"That's what Scully told me."

He shook his head again. "Scully." He pointed at me. "Need a smart Jew lawyer, son."

24

Practice started our senior year on October first. Casale prided himself on conditioning, so we had to run a mile for time the first day. He promised to make us all run it again if everyone didn't get in under six minutes. Scully made me join the cross-country team in the fall to get in shape, so he and I had run our asses off since September. When Casale blew the whistle, I took off and fell in right behind Scully. My goal was to run the mile in four forty-five. The other guys were in varying degrees of pain. Phillip, who was such a natural athlete, was the only one close to us. Phil didn't run cross-country, he just played ball every day and ran like a rabbit around the neighborhood.

At eight-eighty, we were on pace. I looked back and Mike was holding up well with Stokes, Leonard was in there, and the others were dragging. Scully yelled back at them to get moving. After three laps, it was Scully in first, ten feet ahead, and Phillip right behind me. I tried to push Chris as we hit the far turn on the last lap, but he gave me one of those looks and sprinted for the next thirty yards and broke me.

My chest was exploding and my thighs were on fire, but I felt pretty good because I knew by the splits I was coming in at four forty or so, which was pretty fucking fast for running in high tops. Then with one hundred yards to go, Phillip blew by me. Here I'd put Ben-Gay and liniment oil on my legs and run through the woods behind Scully for three months while Phillip was just jogging around his neighborhood, and he smoked me. I realized he was pulling up on Scully, too. With fifty left, they both sprinted—digging, gasping, basketball sneakers pounding the cinder track, blowing little misty streams out their noses, as they hit the line. I don't know if Phillip let him have it, but Scully won by two steps. The rest of the guys got in under six, so we stayed inside after that.

25

Redbrick buildings birthed the two most important documents in the last ten thousand years. By the time of the Revolution, Pennsylvania had three hundred thousand people. In 1776, Philadelphia had seven newspapers.

Penn was obsessed with the Great London Fire of 1666. He told his people to build in the middle of their lots. He would not have liked row homes. He wanted us to be free; no neighbors sticking their goddamned noses in to see your God.

He was a dipshit at business. He lost Pennsylvania in 1703 when he was swindled by his financial adviser. He managed to get thrown in debtors' prison. He fought over his right to the governorship for the rest of his life and he died penniless in 1718. His sons cheated the Lenape out of most of their lands.

Poor guy lost his ass on Philadelphia, the great love of his life. The thing that gets me is that, all told, William Penn was in America for a total of four years.

What are you going to invent? Liberty? Tolerance?

Today, the tour guides put on wigs and give memorized talks about ale and Ben Franklin's whores as stinking Belgians and Germans on holiday walk past discarded maps and popcorn boxes and thin waxed-paper soft pretzel wrappers blowing in the wind. Then the Belgians and Germans go back to the Quality Inn and the tour guides take off their wigs and go home to Pennsauken and Mount Airy to watch *Action News* and the Phillies before bed.

That's what it's like now. Makes me sick. It's like a stadium after the crowd leaves. Detritus. Everything broken. Symbionese Liberation Army–broken. Now gone to monetizing traffic; mortgage-backed securities; credit default swaps. O. J. Simpson–broken.

It's hard to follow William Penn's life. It's a big, long, weird story. But I know this: he was here for two years twice and he started the world.

II

BUILDINGS

Success is not the result of spontaneous combustion. First you have to set yourself on fire.

—Fred Shero

26

The second step was preparation of the brick. Once it was won, the spring clay was ready to be worked, kneaded with the hands and feet. It could be ground into powder or put into a soaking pit where it was mixed with water to get the right consistency for molding. The books say it was the hardest work of all, getting it ready like that.

Fred Shero was a bantam boxing champion in the Royal Canadian Navy during World War II. He played three seasons for the New York Rangers and then in the minors for a while. They called him "Freddy the Fog" because he was the only guy who could see the puck during a 1947 game in which the ice got steamy.

He finished his career as a player in 1957 with the Shawinigan Falls Cataracts, became their coach, and moved around hockey's lesser world, from places like Omaha to Rochester to St. Paul, for the next thirteen years. He was named head coach of the Philadelphia Flyers in 1971. That was not a major announcement.

We only started paying attention to hockey when the Flyers made the Stanley Cup semifinals in 1973. Mike Dunn was the first one into it; he began wearing Flyers T-shirts and banging guys like a hockey player. Scully and I followed. It got really big in Stuckley. We went to the Dunns' house and watched the games on Channel 29. The Flyers' captain was a little guy, Bobby Clarke, who did everything: scored, passed, gave orders, slashed the other players in the legs when the refs weren't looking. He was the leader through respect and tenacity and talent. Scully studied him.

The Flyers loved to fight. The Rangers and the Canadiens and the Bruins fans hated it, said it wasn't hockey. The Soviet Red Army team walked off the ice halfway through the first period of an exhibition game because Ed Van Impe cross-checked Valeri Kharlamov so hard the poor bastard collapsed on the ice. The Russian coach called the Flyers "a bunch of animals." What I don't think they realized is no one knew anything about hockey in Philadelphia. We learned it on the fly. Overnight, kids started talking about power plays and line changes and Bobby Orr being a pussy. The game was a novelty; the Flyers were a craze. Hockey was a mansport, appealing to a gray place and people who worked all goddamn day. The players from Montreal and St. Louis and Vancouver looked like tough dancers and their names sounded like music: "Maureese Richahrd, Alex Del-vekk-ee-o, Ee-von Corn-why-ay."

The Flyers didn't look like dancers and they didn't have musical names. They were Schultz and Saleski, MacLeish and Dornhoefer. They had nicknames like Moose, Big Bird, the Hound. Dave Schultz was the Hammer and he got into a fight every time he went on the ice. Every time. And it worked. The other teams were distracted by the fighting and the Flyers' skill players scored like crazy.

Behind it all was Shero. He wore tinted glasses and wrote motivational quotations on the blackboard before games. He had a system for aggressive play he called Shero's Commandments. He gave his players two laminated cards: one for their lockers and one for their wallets:

1) Never go offside on a three on two or two on one.

2) Never go backward in your own end except on a power play.

3) Never throw a puck out blindly from behind your opponent's net.

4) Never pass diagonally across ice in your own end unless 100% certain.

5) Wings on wings in neutral zone—unless intercepting a pass.

6) Second man go all the way in for a rebound.

We couldn't skate, had no ice and no pads. We bought street hockey sticks, balls, and nets. The Boys Club started a league for us and came up with goalie pads and masks. We ran with plastic-bladed sticks after the hard rubber orange ball and smashed into each other. We bought jerseys that had CLARKE or SCHULTZ or PARENT on the back, number 16 or 8 or 1. Mike Dunn even joined a real team and had to go to practice at midnight, the only time they could get the ice. We wanted the Stanley Cup more than anything—two years earlier, we didn't know what it was.

> 7) Defense with puck at opponents' blue line look at each teammate.
> 8) Wing in front of opponents' net must face puck and lean on stick.
> 9) Puck carrier over center with no room and no one to pass to must shoot puck.
> 10) No forward must ever turn his back on the puck.

Every guy on the Flyers roster was from someplace in Canada we never heard of. But the absurdity of it all didn't matter. Symbols and signs in 1974 were so out of whack, we didn't notice. At the Spectrum, the fans sang "Bernie in the Nets" to the tune of "Bennie and the Jets." We watched the games on black-and-white television, contests on frozen floors of municipal arenas in Buffalo and St. Louis and Toronto and Minneapolis. It didn't matter that the NHL was so fucked-up, Philadelphia was in the Western Division. It didn't matter that there were only three periods, not the symmetrical two halves or four quarters of normal sports.

> 11) No player must be more than two zones away from puck.
> 12) Never be outnumbered in defensive zone.
> 13) On delayed penalty puck carrier must look for extra man.
> 14) Be alert to time left on opponent's penalty.

Basketball was survival, oxygen, life. Hockey was fun. I knew everything: who was on each line, which goalies were hot, who was hurt on Boston. It was low scoring, like soccer, which no one played, or the girls' sports, field hockey or lacrosse. It was about position and pressure more than the free flow of basketball. It was about keeping it up till you broke through and put it in the net. That we understood: putting it in the net.

27

I am a tit man, I can't help it. I can be anywhere and if a girl bends over and I think I can see the nipple come out of the shirt, or even the dark part—the areola—come out over the bra, my eyes shoot there. Sometime it's not appropriate because the woman is too old or ugly or fat or young. No one would want to see those tits, but I stare anyway. I know some guys have a leg thing, that it's not just a cliché that there are leg men and tit men. I admit there's a lot of talk about the ass-leg combo. I see the ass-leg-combo-loving guys at the strip clubs. They couldn't care less about the tits.

Not me. I have the American fascination with tits. It's from *Hee Haw*, it's from *Playboy*, it's from the Farrah Fawcett poster, I don't know. It is something deep, scary. It is primal. I like the rest of them, but it all starts with the chest. I will even get into small breasts. They all get me. I know the girl with the best tits in any group, the way the guy from *The Bourne Identity* knew how to use explosives even though he had amnesia. I look at women and I take their shirts off in my mind, wondering if the bra is pushing them up. I love the ones who hide them, who have had giant tits that they didn't know what to do with since they were fourteen, the ones who you get in bed and you can't even talk when the shirt comes off, it's such a bonanza.

When I was growing up I did not realize how many had big tits. Those are the ones who really love me. There is a subliminal cerebral cortex connection between me and girls with big tits. They are as attracted to me as I am to them. They look at me in a different way. I see their eyes when they walk by. It's like we wear the same color lightbulbs over our heads. When I get among them, I am calm and steady.

Once I got in Janice's shirt, I did not stop. I felt her up in the car and in restaurants. She said she hated it, but she loved it—all women love it when you are hungry for them. Janice especially. In bed I went straight for them, assaulting the nipples with both hands, with kisses, with pinches.

It might be stupid to decide on a girl because she likes a song, or a band, but that's what happened. We stayed up all night a few times when it was new, drinking and doing coke, just a little, and playing records. She had taste. There are threshold issues with me. I wouldn't let a girl who didn't know the Beatles blow me. She passed. She knew Fleetwood Mac was just okay, for example, not like every other fucking girl. Janice was the real deal. She told me *Exile in Guyville* was a reply to *Exile on Main St.* She even knew where Sandy Row was.

I remember the night I went all-in. She made me dinner at her apartment and I went through her CDs while she cooked. We both loved The Band. She got quiet when I played *Tears of Rage*.

"It just shows you how much better they wrote songs then. It's so . . . I don't know, it's so sophisticated."

"Dylan wrote it."

"I know. But Richard sang it."

"I know."

I put it on again.

We carried you in our arms on Independence Day
And now you'd throw us all aside and put us all away
Oh, what dear daughter 'neath the sun could treat a father so?
To wait upon him hand and foot and always tell him "No."

"That's me and my dad," she said. "*To wait upon him, hand and foot and always tell him no.* That's our story. He thinks I am so stubborn, but I'm just like him. He used to make me meet him at the dining-room table every Saturday morning at seven—seven in the morning—to look at my schoolwork from the past week."

"Oh, man."

"Yah . . . till eighth grade, when I told him no more. We had this huuuuge fight. But I won. He moved on to my sister. Then she wouldn't do it past eighth grade, so for the past ten years he just sits at the table on Saturday mornings by himself."

"Christ."

"Ask my sister, it was insane. And you know what's funny? Every week now, I call him at seven in the morning on Saturdays to say hi. That's when I check in. Like it's some fucking ingrained pattern in my head. And he's always there."

We had inside jokes. The great private stuff of friends. We loved so many of the same things, Bertha, guilty pleasures like "Rocket Man," stuff like Taj Mahal, and the centrality of Dylan. We talked about how he filled our heads with pictures. "I don't know why he gets to me so much," I said.

"He lets you access your feelings, dumbass," she said. "That's your whole thing with music. It's obvious. You can't talk about how you feel."

She could call me on things. And I could do the same. Her mother was crazy for photographs—she was just the kind of person who was fascinated with them. When Janice and I went anywhere—like *any*where, even to Atlantic City, even to the Poconos—her mom would say to us in her Brooklyn accent, "Send me a picksha . . ." Janice would roll her eyes, and later complain that her mother never failed to ask for a picture. We debated why the request was so important. Its purpose, its origin, its meaning to her mother. We debated it as only kids who had grown up when we did could debate such a subject—we were both of a time when what was possible for daughters was impossible for their mothers. Janice said, at bottom, her mother was trying to rise above their conflicts and it was a plea for love; I maintained Janice should go easy, and rather think of it as an expression of love. Janice thought it was, "Please love me." I tried to explain it was a way of navigating that mother-daughter thicket by saying, "I love you so much. Send me something—a piece of you—that I can have always."

This little disagreement about her mother's true feelings started out as a real argument, but Janice and I agreed to disagree, and I can still see her laughing and us falling in love with each other the first time we held up a Polaroid camera for a prehistoric selfie on the boardwalk outside a soft-serve ice cream place at the Jersey shore. I found an envelope at a card store and scrawled her mother's address and put it in the mail.

The little incident stayed with us through all the hard times, and for a long, long while it was the secret button that couples have to shut down conflict. Whenever we had a fight, whenever Janice was mad and I didn't feel like dealing with it, I'd look at her really seriously and say, "Send me your picksha. . . ." It broke her up. It was her favorite thing, the way other couples save photo booth film or ashtrays from Bermuda. No matter how bad the argument, she lost her shit laughing every time. It was more than just a tension breaker, though. I never talked with her about it, but the reason it was funny was that it was me being passionate. And me being passionate was so weird, it was funny.

Send me your picture.

I came close with Janice, I really did. I came close to being a real guy. I wanted her picture, her to send me her picture. I just didn't make it.

I'll say this: we played no games. There was no pretending to be other people. After a few months, she said to me, "Let's say we're getting married, okay? Let's not go through the whole thing with the ring and all that. Let's just say it, okay?" She called her mother, who told her to think about it for a while. Ray didn't say anything.

I did the ring thing anyway a few weeks later—a diamond from the Jewelry Mart. I did it in the car with a bottle of champagne on our way to a party. She got excited like it was a complete surprise and they made a huge deal out of it at the party. At home, we had sex slowly because I thought it wouldn't be right to do it any other way.

We got married at the Ritz-Carlton. Her greatest act of diplomacy was telling Ray he was splitting it with me when the truth was his check didn't come close. The night before, Leonard and I were in a hotel room with a bunch of guys and he said to me, "Why are you getting married?"

"What do you mean?"

"Why? Tell me why. Give me your best reason."

I didn't have to think about it. "Because she loves me. I know that she will be like that always. I don't know what it is, but she loves me. I don't think I should miss that, right?"

"My man."

Never go backward in your own end except in a power play.

I didn't want to be alone. But more than that, more than anything, she came after me. And when she got me, she had great tits for me to hang on to. The bus was in the station and I went up the steps and said hi to the driver, take me anywhere you want to go. I didn't know what else to do. She was the wave that I was riding when the music stopped. There wasn't any word from above for her. I didn't have a long talk with anyone and I didn't ask her dad. I never wanted to write her a song. For a time—a fairly long time—I preferred being with her to being alone.

28

We played "The Lost Boy" every night for a while, missing it only when Dottie had to take extra shifts at Pinelli's, or we both fell asleep too tired. She fell asleep with me a lot. Much later, when I was thirteen, I had a bad panic attack. A death attack. I jumped out of my bed and ran with my hands up to my ears. I tried to distract myself to make the frenzy stop. I went to the refrigerator and stared at anything: a pickle jar, anything. But it didn't help. It came back and the thoughts grabbed me and wrenched me: "You're dead. It's me. It's me. It's me. It's real. It's real. It's real. I am going to die. It's me. It's real. I am going to die. I will be dead. In a box. I won't see Dottie. There is no heaven. They are pretending it is not real. It is real. It is real." I even took a pickle out of the jar, focusing on that pickle, something else. But it was shaking my head. I felt a turning in the deep part of my lower intestine. "Dead. Gone, no more. They pretend it's not true but it is. They are all going to die, too. They are lying."

Dottie didn't wake at first. She was exhausted. It wasn't one of her nights, but she took the shift of one of the girls with a kid in the hospital. She found me in the kitchen stamping my feet with my hands over my ears. Seeing her calmed me, but I was shaken—this was a bad one. She sat me down and went to the fridge, chatting just to make noise. She took two glasses and poured milk. She got the can of Hershey's, took off the yellow top, and turned it upside down to run out the triangular hole made with the can opener. It was empty but we had another can. She made a full indentation on one side, just a brief gash in the other, for aerodynamic purposes I never understood but followed for the rest of my life, putting the opener all the way through on one side and only a little dent on the other. The chocolate ran like blood through the milk, like a black tree root, splitting into veins cutting through skin, through earth of the milk, turning it first off-white, beige, then creamy brown, the perfect color, not too dark, spoiled by too much Christ's blood. The spoon stirred it, leaving marks of syrup untouched, oil deposits at the bottom of the ocean, black reminders of the parts that didn't mix. She gave me mine before making hers. She always did that, my aunt Dottie.

"Let's get you back in bed. I'll lie with you." When we were under the covers, she said, "Okay, 'The Lost Boy.' Ready for a story?" I was too old for it, but that didn't stop her. She looked at the ceiling and started speaking.

The Lost Boy couldn't go to sleep one night in the Stick House. He went outside and looked at the sky. It was black except for five stars. And then, just like that, a white light was on his face, like a spotlight, but not so bright. It made his body feel really nice. He wasn't sleepy or cranky or lonely anymore. He felt all his cares and worries go away.

He took a few steps and realized the light followed him. He ran three steps left, and it was on him. Then three steps right, same thing. He saw the light was leading him down a path away from the Stick House, so he followed, and soon he was twisting and turning through trees, up the hills, and over the little creeks in the Jungle Forest. He didn't worry about finding his way back; the light took all worry away. He was too big for worry, he felt too good to be scared.

He became tired and did not know if his legs could take him any farther, but he still pressed on, carried by the light. He saw something ahead. He ran through the last group of trees toward a giant glowing area getting bigger in front of him with every footstep.

He made it to the edge of the trees and found a beautiful open space the size of a circus, a huge pond to the left with grass growing all around. And to his right . . . there was a brand-new basketball court with all the top-notch stuff: socks and warm-up suits, sweatbands and different colored uniforms. Off to the sides there were bumper cars and burger stands and bookshops and record stores.

He stood there and looked at it all. He didn't know what he had done to deserve this. It was the greatest. The best. The most perfect place he had ever been. The light was still on him, still giving his mind and body such a lift. All of his sadness and worries were gone.

And he looked at the light and a voice said to him:

Such a wonderful feeling being too much for me alone, may it know no replacement in this life.

And, BANG, a thunderbolt hit beyond the pond and in an instant there were people everywhere. His mommy and daddy, his aunts and uncles and grandma and grandpa. And his friends, from home and from the forest. He walked over to the court and grabbed the sneakers he had always wanted. Candy and Ronnie were talking to Henry and his other friends from school. Horatio the Bear was there. They dressed in the new uniforms and socks and fancy warm-up suits. They were all so happy to be with each other. When the Lost Boy walked onto the court he looked to his left and to his right and saw all his friends. And they started to play and play and play—for as long as they wanted. The End.

29

The waitress from the Lenape Diner, the punctuator with the green check, was named Connie and she was cute like Cheryl Ladd, the replacement for Farrah Fawcett on *Charlie's Angels*. She went to Fallcrest—another one who went to Fallcrest—but I didn't remember her. She told me the names of the crowd she hung with in high school. I didn't tell her that those were the names of people I thought of, then and now, as anemic, semi-burned-out cannon fodder. The types you get at a high school like that: unspectacular, bluish-white modern American consumers.

She was of that, but not that. She had a teensy bit of something special, something that made me predatory, if nothing other than the Cheryl Ladd–ish business and the unit. She was sexy, even with the bad roots, and the two-tone thing at a certain angle was a turn-on. I told her to meet me at a business hotel near the airport. We drank wine at the bar, which was dark and felt secretive and romantic. The bartender was schooled in the ways of hotel bars, friendly, treating us like we were on a legitimate business meeting. No questions, no chitchat.

"What do you think of Chris? You know, Scully?"

"I don't know. It's like his office in the diner. He's a politician, you know?"

"Think he's a little full of it?"

She shrugged. "All those guys are the same. You know they're full of shit, but when you're with them it's fun. I think those kinds of guys, like Scully, they're usually sort of nice-looking, and they get all full of themselves and it goes from there. But you can't trust them. They're fucks."

"You think he's good-looking?"

"Sure."

She was in a rough patch, hence the Lenape Diner. She was getting past her second divorce. Number one was a local kid right after high school; that marriage went fast but had been enough to fuck her up good, stop her schooling, kill her ambition to do anything other than land a rich guy. This happened when she met a chiropractor at his office on Namans Creek Road—Al somebody or other. They had a kid and it sounded like it went pretty well until the guy started drinking and moved them to western Maryland and the wheels fell off.

I like hotel bars and then the move upstairs. I like it when there is the hint of a possibility that someone will see. I liked to make it exciting. It mattered less since I had moved out, but I still enjoyed the cheesiness of it, like it was an episode of *Love, American Style*. Like day-old wine. When the elevator doors shut, I was on her, grabbing her face with my hands and kissing her hard.

The room had that inevitable Revolutionary War ambience. Hotel Room Colonial, something you can only get in Philadelphia. But I knew she liked it, thought it fancy. I undressed her quickly, hurrying to get her big phony breasts out of the bra, her bottom half naked. I was still in my clothes but got my face between her legs, and she gasped until she grabbed the pillow to muffle her yells. Then she pushed me away because it was too sensitive, post-cumular. She pulled me up to her.

I got over her and kissed her hard again. I put my elbows gently on the tops of her shoulders, put my forearms next to each ear, timing the pace like an engine starting up, like a plane taking off, incrementally faster. I looked down and watched her face, watching her feel it inside. Its effect is like truth serum. They can't lie, they can't fake it. They can love me, hate my guts, or not even know me, but when I stick it in, the eyes close a little, the hard breathing starts, and they go. They just go.

Women can always come when they get on top, but the challenge is in delivering it to them on their backs. She was arching up into me within a few seconds and the yelling started again and I went faster, concentrating on getting my tip up inside as far as it goes, thinking about getting the

117

top of it against the top of her and then plunging down. As she got off she closed her eyes and looked to the side, avoiding my eyes. It felt like I put a hole in the hull of a ship and the oil was running out, down her legs.

I'm usually quiet afterward. I don't put the TV on or anything like that, and I don't say much.

"You must mean something to him," Connie said after a few minutes.

"Who?"

"Scully. He never eats with nobody."

Never eats with nobody. The bad grammar was the sign of a lower Dover County white. The drink-wudder and touch-your-farhead type. "He goes around and bullshits, but he always eats alone and reads the papers. He reads like four papers. We bring him coffee and juice, whatever. He eats peanut butter."

I said, "I know, it's weird."

She changed the subject. "So, you're not at home?" She knew it was prying. "Hey, believe me . . . I know what it's like." She rolled her eyes back and forth. She was trying to be cool. She was cool, actually. I can't really say anything bad about Connie. She sat up and looked at the room service menu.

"Yes, I'm not at home. I live in Center City in an apartment."

"How's that? Do you like it"

"It's great. I have a bedroom for my daughter. She likes to come over and have Chinese food."

Connie tilted her head and made a sound indicating she thought that was nice. Then she was back at it. "Can I ask you something?"

"Sure."

"Is everything okay with you?"

"What do you mean?"

"I don't know. You're all . . . like . . . intense." She was talking like she was my old friend now. "And that day in the diner you got into a fight with him. Scully. Am I right?"

"Yeah, kind of. I have a lot going on."

"The divorce?"

"Lots of things." I decided to answer because I liked fucking her. "I go way back with Scully. He brings a lot of things to the surface."

She nodded and went back to the menu. Without looking up, very quietly, as though she was talking to herself, she said, "I don't trust that guy."

"How well do you know him?"

She put the menu down and climbed on me, with the after-market front end grazing me on the way up. She kissed me, then headed back down to her business. The *Charlie's Angels* thing was good, I got to say.

30

All types came into Pinelli's to drink at the bar. There were lots of goombahs, Italians on the make. Stupid fucking guys in their mid-forties looking for tail. They wore leather jackets and cologne. The women they hit on were worn down with poodle hair, smoking long, brown, skinny cigarettes. Norman and Lenny both had their regulars, lots of couples coming out to eat and shoot the shit. What a night out: coming to Pinelli's, having a few drinks, and talking to a bartender. Lenny spent a whole baseball season betting against the Phillies when they were away because they had not finished with a winning record on the road for ten years. He figured over time he had to make out. The whole bar would be rooting for the Phillies and there was Lenny, hoping they'd blow it.

Casale came in one night before I went to high school. He was really happy to see me. He was with a guy named Dennis. Casale was Italian but Dennis was more of a guido—like a guy from his neighborhood in South Philly. When Casale got up to make a call, Dennis said, "Jimmy says you're a basketball player."

We talked about it. I told him I was saving to get new sneakers. He said, "Do you kids know about Jimmy Casale? Do you know how good he was?"

I said I didn't know anything.

"I still have no idea why he went to Canisius. He could have gone to Villanova or St. John's. They all wanted him. Do you know he played against the Olympic team when they were training for Montreal? Scrimmage game at the Palestra in the summer. He had twenty-eight. Guys were asking who the fuck he was."

There wasn't any bullshit with Casale; he wasn't trying to make up for something he lost. He was a guy on our side. He was tough. In the summers he came to Glentop just to play. He hit it from all over and made twisty, double-pump-leaning shots look easy. He had little chips in two of his teeth—one on either side, incongruous as though they were the products of at least two of many fights. He was thick in his body, a guy you want to be in jail with. He slapped you and put his forearms in your back. When he put his hands on you he left marks. He wasn't like a coach. He got bored at practice or waiting for a game to get over, like a kid. He had hair pushed back and long in the back. He also had a mustache. If some mustaches look like mustaches and some look like overgrown hair, his looked like overgrown hair. He said he went to Canisius instead of a big school because he liked the coach.

That he smacked and pushed and punched while he played had a big effect on us. Phillip got it first: Play harder. Slap it harder. Dribble harder. Take the fucking ball away from them with two hands. It's your ball. When it's loose, use your shoulders, bash your way in. It was like saying: This is for keeps, it's a scrap fight. Ninety-five percent of basketball games are won by the more aggressive team. It's true, check it out.

It wasn't easy playing on the same team as Chris Scully and Jeremy Garrison, the two best guards the school ever had, through some freak luck of the draw them being the same age. And it was hard for *them* to be on a team with Phillip Ford and Stokes—Phillip the All-American and Stokes a way better college prospect because of his size. And you rarely get a kid who was six ten like Herman. And it wasn't easy for Leonard or me or the Dunns or Cove—we all would have started somewhere else. But Casale made each of us feel right, and not in a pussy-ish way. With me, it started when I first got to high school, not long after he saw me at Pinelli's. He knew that I knew the deal. I was with Scully and Garrison. He found me in the hallway and said to meet him in the coaches' office after school.

"How's classes?"

"Fine."

Enough chitchat. "Chris Scully is a great player. I know you know that. And I've never seen a natural shooter like Garrison. And Phillip, well . . . Phillip is Phillip."

"And Stokes is Stokes and Leonard is Leonard," I said. "I know."

"So, where's that leave you?"

"I don't know."

"Well, let's take a shot at it together."

"Okay."

"One, you fight with them every day. I want you to be in Scully's face. Take him right up to the point of a fistfight. Run the B team for me. I will get you in the games; those guys will have off nights. And then you have to be ready. No excuses. You don't get to have a bad night."

I nodded.

"And number two, sit next to me on the bench. I need you to watch defenses and tell who's tired. I want you to talk to me. You got it?"

"Okay, Coach."

"You have tons of heart and an unbelievable brain, Joey. You have to use it and I'm going to help you do that. You can do anything you want when you get out of here, you know that, right? More than anyone." He tilted his head down and lifted his eyes up to make sure I saw his eyes. "Including Phillip. Including Scully. I know you know it, too. Am I right?"

My head was burning.

"All right, hit the bricks."

Casale did things a coach or a teacher shouldn't do. Springfield had a pretty boy named Neilson. He had blond feathered hair, socks way up high. He wore pookah shells when he wasn't playing. He could shoot and he was a cheap-shot artist. After he reached in a second time on Phillip with no whistle, Casale got pissed. "Get him off of him," he said to the ref. He reached again—a third time—and Casale turned up the corner of his lips, a sign that he was going to blow. When Neilson drifted by our bench, Casale said, "Watch the hands, faggot." The kid took a few steps before it registered. He shot a look back at our bench to see if that came from where he thought it came.

"You heard me," I said.

What we were not into was school pride. None of us gave a shit about that school. Fallcrest H.S. was built on eighty acres between Stuckley and Penwood with the developments to the west. It was a seventies creation: state senators found enough of a tax base to build a school and dilute their busing problem. The plan guaranteed a mixture of poor whites, poor blacks, rich whites, and not much in between. They floated a big bond and took the money and mixed red brick, cinder block, white pavement, tile floors, round industrial clocks, building-grade porcelain water fountains, metal lockers, plastic-polyurethane chair tops, drop ceilings, and fluorescent lighting and came up with a suitable, mindless name. Fallcrest. Stupid name. Oxymoron. With no other way to express frustration, kids rebelled against the surfaces. They spit on the water fountains, wiped snot on the cinder blocks, threw pencils into the drop ceilings, put gum on the floor, spray-painted the bricks, and ripped doors off of bathroom stalls. Blacks and whites fought. Kids smoked pot outside and took pills. The administration brought in security guards who stood around the cafeteria and hallways.

We were in the first generation of suburban high schools. The school had no identity, like Royal Brown and my mother in the ditch. Its DNA was left to the imagination of the yearbook staff and an adviser, an English teacher who didn't want to do it. They came up with a phony tradition and a weird, affected devotion to red and gold. They made up a school song, "The Alma Mater":

Hail to our alma mater, hail all hail!
Our voices rise in praise of thee
Enshrined in our hearts is the memory
Of the hopes and the dreams we share with thee.
Fallcrest salutes the red and gold
Fallcrest forever brave and bold
Thy name, in honor I behold
All hail, Fallcrest High.

Enshrined in our hearts is the memory. It didn't exist. It was a school by zones, put together to meet racial quotas and budget restraints. No more town high schools, no more walking to school—the brick and cement and gray-painted places looked like prisons but had plenty of ball field and open space. History, spirit, and tradition would grow like grass in the sodden yards of Hidden Hills. That's what they thought, that they could make the place seem less harsh, less likely to make you suicidal. To think there were people there who believed it.

Like I said, it didn't mean shit to us. We wanted to win. We wanted the season, the games, the crowds, the noise. We wanted to hit shots. We wanted that thing, the button, the click Brick is looking for. We wanted to play at the Palestra and make the first bucket and feel the streamers.

Growing up going to the Palestra, where there are three games a night and the place is packed, you learn that the way a team takes the court says it all. We practiced it. We worked on four-corner pass-and-go-behind drills and three-man weaves. We ran laps around the court, breaking into two lines at the half-court line on the way back—we thought of everything.

We settled on the right one. We stood at the locker-room door leading to the gym, Scully gave the fire-up and ended it with "One-two-three," and we all yelled, "Glentop." We lined up, shortest to tallest. I was first, Herman was last. From me to him was a steady rise of heads, like a bar graph of the stock market since 1929: flat at the beginning and getting really high at the end. Two balls, me and Scully each had one.

We busted out. I dribbled up the right sideline, turned left at half-court, got to the circle, slapped the Quaker with the palm of my right hand, kept my dribble in my left hand, and headed to the bucket on the left side. Scully did the same thing but went down the right, catching up with me so we were parallel. Garrison followed me, Leonard followed Scully, and so forth, forming two lines moving toward the basket. When we reached the hoop, we put it off the glass, throwing it high off the backboard. The next guy came and tapped it up for the next. The Dunns came second-to-last, side by side, and set up Herman and Stokes, and the end of the lines. In sync, they attacked the bucket. Herman went first, a split second ahead, snatching it and dunking it. Then Stokes came flying through, catching it and slamming it with both hands. Back-to-back jams. *Blam blam.* Take that, faggots. Let's rock.

The GMC B-Series school bus had six wheels, twelve rows, two seats to a row. The school district bought the buses new every five years and by our senior year they were just about done. The benches were coming loose and the pipes of the frames were busting through the foam padding underneath the green plasticky rubber covering. After we won an away game, the kids from the developments—Garrison, Phillip, Marlowe, and Beatty—rode home with their parents. The rest of us fell asleep on the bus.

We sat in the same seats every time. Scully had the last seat on the right. Stokes had the left. Leonard sat in front of Stokes, and Coverdale and Etheridge sat in front of him. Garrison and Herman were on the other side and the twins sat together for luck and by choice. Phillip didn't care; he sat with the guy he was talking to when he walked on or sometimes he sat way up front and looked out the window.

Casale sat in the first row, with the other coaches across from him. He liked to bring Scully up to talk. He called me when he was done with Scully. We kicked defenses around, covered what the other team might play, who matched up, when to press.

But most of the time, I rode in the back. Spending that much time sitting on a bus, you get to know people. Who gets nervous before a game, who's light. The loudmouths shut up, eventually, except Leonard.

Leonard was never not late, which worked for his ritual. He had to touch everyone, a whole production. After he came up the steps, he shook hands with Casale and he gave me a little whack on the back. He slapped hands with Scully, touched foreheads with Stokes, and took the knuckle of his right middle finger and baby-punched Herman where his biceps met his shoulder. Then he did this thing with Garrison where they put their toes together and put their hands up and wiggled their fingers, the tips touching. With everybody, he said, "Let's get that ass, boy."

Terry Beatty's grandfather died the day we played Ridley for the first-half championship. Casale said Beatty's father told him Terry was very close to his grandfather. Nobody cared very much. We talked about dying.

"I'm an atheist," I said.

"You mean agnostic?" said Stokes.

"No. I mean atheist. I don't believe in anything. None of it."

Stokes looked at me.

"Why not?"

"Because it's all just lies, Stokes. There's nothing out there. It's a bunch of bullshit. They just feed you lies. We're all full of all this stuff they feed us."

"So, we're just full of whatever we believe?"

"Yup. That's a way to say it."

It was newly night, the hour the red of the brake lights on the highway really jumps out. It was cold and gray and the bus was bumpy. The cars were dirty. A truck carrying mirrors passed us, showing our reflection: a yellow bus with green lines and a bunch of teenagers' heads looking out windows, back at the mirrors.

So high above the wall.
No forward must ever turn his back on the puck.
I got winter in my blood.

"Well, how you know you ain't just got a lot of atheist in you? I got whatever I got in me, you got whatever you got in you. Why someone always got to be wrong with you? You got it from somewhere, I got mine from somewhere. That's what it's like."

The Black Muslim movement had traction in South Penwood and Coverdale went to a few meetings. He started wearing a little kufi cap when he was in his street clothes. The first time he wore it, Mike Dunn said, "What the fuck is that?"

Coverdale wasn't a fun guy or anything; we never wanted to see him lose it. You had to call him "Henry." He didn't like Hank or Harry or any of that shit. He was left-handed, and he went deep in the corner to shoot, which was dumb because it took him out of rebounding position. But it was his thing, so nobody bothered him, not even Casale. We let him have his corner shot. We called him Cove, which rhymed with Dove, but he was not always peaceful. He regularly knocked guys on their asses. Cove was not smart, and he didn't like school. It embarrassed him. He was quiet, but, like Mike Dunn, he could get mean. He was coming out of his shell by then and basketball was good for him. No one anywhere wanted to see a black guy that strong start to turn.

Cove and I were friends. I was interested in the kufi cap. His father was long gone, a Vietnam guy, but enough of a memory that Cove liked army stuff. He looked at army magazines on the bus. He had three little sisters and his mom didn't work.

"What's that feel like?" I said, gesturing to my head, meaning his head, meaning the skullcap.

He blew out his lips. "Feels fine," he said. He pointed at Mike. "Why don't you ask fathead what that tractor hat feels like? Farmer Brown with his tractor hat. Nobody says, 'What's up with that hat?' to that mahfucker."

Phillip had a radar detector for dissension. He wandered into the conversation. "Cove, can I get one of those hats in red? It'll have to be smaller because I think your dome is bigger than mine."

Etheridge said, "Phil, you're a corny motherfucker."

Cove blew out his lips again. "I guess, if you want one." He looked at me, shook his head, and laughed. He rolled his eyes at Phillip. "The Hope."

There was a bookstore on State Street in Penwood, where they also had all kinds of meetings and poetry readings. It smelled like incense. I went there and talked to the guy who ran it. Guy's name was Binwah. He was bald and had a beard and wore a white caftan. I asked him what literature he had on the Black Muslim movement and he took me to the Religion section. He showed me a paperback copy of the *Koran* and another book called *Readings on Islam*, which I bought because I knew the Nation of Islam handed out copies of the *Koran*. I put it in Cove's locker in the team room. I didn't leave any note.

* * *

The summer of the Powelton Village shooting—the one Officer Jimmy Ramp was killed in—we were playing at Glentop when Mike Dunn said, "Leonard, you going to be Leonard Africa?" Herman, who didn't say much, said, "Mike, don't."

The fact that Herman spoke up made even Leonard, who didn't give a shit about anything Mike said, stop short. I took it to mean that Herman's parents supported the whole anti-oppression thing. Herman just grabbed a ball and went down to the other end and stuffed it, unable to express himself—the way big, quiet guys often can't.

Coverdale was also really quiet. I asked Stokes, "What's going on?"

"They're going to lynch those MOVE niggers, I know that."

"They should," said Mike.

"The fuck you know, Mike?" said Etheridge. "Cops shooting black people every day."

"C'mon. They killed a cop," said Phillip.

"So that means more?" said Leonard.

Scully said, "C'mon," and took the ball up. Mike was guarding Coverdale. As they walked up the court, Mike did his standard elbow swing and gave Cove a fake, slow-motion shove. Mock-serious, his way of moving on from the discussion.

Cove shook his head. He had to smile. "I'll fuck you up, Dunn." Mike made like a boxer, like the Notre Dame Leprechaun. Leonard ran by Mike from behind and swatted the top of his head. Not hard, just annoying. *Swaaat*. He kept running.

"Awwww yeah."

"C'mere, Leonard, you faggot," Mike said and went after him.

Leonard pretended he was going to do kung fu on him.

31

A few days before we were supposed to sign the deal, Betours called me. "We have an issue. American lawyers, they fuck it all up."

"What's the matter?"

"Ahh, they make it impossible. Special provisions, taxes, worse than in France. The kind of thing that always happen. They want me to kill the deal. They say it is impossible."

"Okay." I started to crash hard, feeling like a sucker. But I wanted him to think I could roll with it. I was used to guys trying to renegotiate the price, and I figured the big guns did it better than anyone, and now it was coming.

Then he surprised me. "I said it is unacceptable and now we have found a way. You know, Joe, in fact, it will be better for you. Here is what I propose. We run this through my subsidiary in the Bahamas. We will do a secondary offering and acquire JKD through a holding company which you will remain part of for six months with your own board of directors. You will need to get a board together. You can do that, *non?*"

"Uh, yeah. I should be able to do that. Can it be . . . ?"

"It can be anybody. Your mother, father, anybody. You build a little something in for them. It will all happen fast. *Rapide.* Your lawyers can take you through this kind of thing."

"What do I need other people for?"

"It is standard. The price—it can't all go to you. I am going to buy shares with you. It is how I've done probably half of these in Europe. The truth is I like these structures because it allows me to demonstrate my personal commitment to the sale."

"Ze truth is I like dese structures." That's the way he talked. He said the big words right but his accent showed up on "the" and "these."

"Okay, sounds okay. But the basic deal remains the same, right?"

"Yes."

"And how do I get my money?"

"It will be the same—in Publicité Rouge stock, which you can sell in ninety days. In fact, I will increase your stake. On this I insist. Because of the inconvenience. I am a man of my word, and I don't like delay. We will add a half million US dollars to the value of the deal. You can divide it around to your people."

"Well, that's cool of you, Hubert."

"Don't be stupid, I insist. In ninety days, you are in cash. Unless, of course, you want to roll it, to hang on to the PR stock. Which you should do, because it's going to be quite valuable someday."

I wanted to show I knew what I was doing. And I wanted the money.

"Well, obviously I have to talk to my guys."

"Yes, of course. But let me tell you something, Joe. A piece of advice. This is how it is done on the high level. You have no way of knowing, you are a young man. I will help you with dese things, as I said. I learned a long time ago to trust my gut, and you should, too. How do you say it, the train is in the station?"

Trains and stations. "I got it," I said. "Hubert, we're on the same team. That is something I value." I hung up.

I read somewhere that Betours disappeared two years ago in the Caribbean. Publicité Rouge cratered and one of the French conglomerates bought up the remains.

After we closed the deal, I had dinner with him twice when he came down from New York. We had a lot in common; he built a company from scratch, had one daughter, and liked to read. He told me about Jacques Derrida and how he was trying to deconstruct through business. I didn't understand that.

I did understand the rest. He was interested in my theory about recycling iconic images from the past to sell products. "I think this is a very big concept you have discovered." He liked to philosophize about business: "Americans felt the alienation that Europe felt after the war, but it comes out different. It is coming out American, no?"

He was one of the first Internet guys. At the restaurant at the Four Seasons he told me, "There is a great global change coming. Do you know what the worst sin of all is?"

I said I didn't know.

"Fear. You can never allow children to see you scared. Do you know what the worst sin in business is? Fear of change."

I took that in.

"The narrative of your country was originally religious persecution and exile. It became about political struggle—human bondage, *non*? And then about global ordering. Massive world wars and financial wreckage— redistribution of capital. After, with wealth and excessive leisure time meeting the American mass market, the narrative became dominated by entertainment. Reality gave way to radio and cinema. And much, much more important, television. With each step, the life is more commercial- ized, *tu sais*? Now, we are in the age of advertising, and it will be fueled to even greater heights by the Internet. The marriage of capitalism and the image. Profit and ideas. Whether l'Académie likes it or not, this is the main language of the world. You will see. You have been on to this, Joe Knight. I commend you." He raised his glass to me. "No one knows the rules anymore. But, you will see, advertising is the new narrative. Everything else is gone. It will move through new delivery systems. You will see. It will all be through the Internet."

My head was spinning from the booze and the money. Publicité Rouge had made seventeen acquisitions in the past year. I actually began to understand why he was buying me. Made sense and I was drunk.

After he called me with the tweak in the deal, I came up with the idea to cut in the guys from my team. I kept in touch with most of them and they all could use the money. Harry Burke said it was fine, I was free to give my money away. His only condition was that they all buy in. He was old school and he wanted to see any shares actually purchased, even if it was at a steep discount. They all had to come up with ten grand. And they had to let me sell them as a block when I punched out. In the end, I even lent the money to buy in to Leonard and Garrison, who was teaching and didn't want to borrow from his parents. I think he was going to the track pretty heavily, still hanging around with Stuey. And I talked Harry into letting me buy a share for Ervin and Paulette, getting their fifty grand out at the end of ninety days along with everyone else. The only one who didn't take me up on it was Scully.

I negotiated big raises and bonuses for my employees. Sammy got a nice payday. Harry was busy for half a year. When I got back from signing the papers, I took the whole office to O'Hanlon's and we drank from noon till two in the morning. The tab was thirty-six hundred and eighteen dollars. My lucky number, I told the waitress, a college girl. I told her my name was Joe. She picked up what had happened from one of my guys. I asked her to come home with me.

"Get the fuck out of here, Joe."

"Did you know Nixon was a Quaker?"

"Go to bed, Joe. You're a rich man now."

"Then you should come fuck me." And I tried to kiss her. Luckily, she was the cool kind, one of the ones who abides getting hit on by drunk guys. She just took it in stride.

"You're too old for me, silly."

32

When it was cold, I stepped inside the church at St. Ignatius to wait for Scully. I sat in the back and watched the six thirty Mass. There were always about ten people in the pews, mostly old ladies who sat in the front. There were two priests, Father Shea, the pastor who had been in Stuckley forever; and a young guy, Father Rossi. Father Shea went early Monday, Wednesday, and Saturday and Father Rossi took the rest.

The church was an old, gray, stone Gothic building with stained-glass windows. There was a cement stand that looked like a birdbath with holy water in the foyer, thirty rows of wooden pews, and a marble altar with the tapestry of Jesus behind it—the rug. Stage right was a pinewood podium from which priests gave homilies, nuns read John 2:23 at weddings, and someone at every funeral read "Though I pass through the valley of the shadow of death. . . ." I didn't like Rossi, he didn't seem like a priest to me, not yet thirty, with thick black Italian hair side-parted. He used to come out the side door before Scully had changed back into his normal clothes. He gave me a little smile and said, "You're going to be bigger than Christopher soon." Always the same line. I dribbled down the sidewalk to get away when I saw him coming.

I never told Scully, but I liked waiting in the back of the church when Father Shea said Mass. He spoke Latin. I loved the old ladies with their silver-cropped head backs staring at me, first sitting, then kneeling, then sitting, then standing, then kneeling again. Then walking down the middle to take the Eucharist, then going back to their spots and kneeling for a while and then sitting down again before standing before they left.

They were so into it, the ritual, the sacramental feeling, the supplicant things. They chanted back and forth with the priest:

"Senior exsisto vobis."
"Necnon vobis."
"Permissum nos tribuo him gratiae quod laus."
"Licet ut tribuo him gratiae quod laus."

Scully was on the side, anticipating the next cue. With Scully and Father Shea, it was like watching actors in a well-worn play. Chris rang the bell, brought him the wine, the bread, all the things he needed. It wasn't the same with Rossi. They didn't have the same feel for each other. The thing I never told anyone about happened in the dead of winter. I was late getting to the church. It was Friday, and as I walked through the parking lot, I passed Father Rossi rushing to his car. "Is it over, Father?"

"No, no. Father Shea said Mass for me today. I am on my way to the hospital."

I went to the side of the building, worried Scully was going to give me shit for being late. He wasn't there, so I walked to the entrance by the changing room off the side of the structure. The last of the old ladies was pulling out of the parking lot. I hardly ever went in there, because when I did, I felt like a dirty outsider in a Catholic sacred space. The church and the altar were more public, for guests as well as members. But the side vestibule was different, it seemed private. It was a human area, not covered by symbols.

The place seemed empty. I pushed down the bar to the big white door and entered. The door to the changing room was dark walnut like the rest of the walls and paneling, and the carpet was dark green. It swallowed the sound so completely, you couldn't hear footsteps. The door was cracked open and I heard whispers. I gave it a little nudge and peeked in.

Father Shea was seated, facing the corner, his back to the door. He was in a wooden chair with three posts. His robes were off, lying on the side of the room. He was in a white T-shirt and his black priest trousers were around his ankles. His bare white ass showed through the bars in the back of the chair. Scully's head was in his lap. He had changed out of his altar boy clothes and was in jeans and an inside-out Notre Dame sweatshirt. It rode up his back. The bumps of his spine were covered with the same bone-colored skin as the pastor's ass. Father Shea's head was back and his hands were on Scully's head, running back and forth through his curly brown hair.

I got out to the sidewalk and stood where I usually stood. Scully came out a few minutes later, stuffing his sneakers down the back of his pants. He zipped up his Eskimo coat and slapped the ball out of my hands.

"Ready to get your ass kicked?" he said. As we walked, we talked about Widener's 1-3-1 zone.

33

The green breakfast check from the Lenape Diner was in my faculty mailbox. Over my message he wrote: "Kennett Square Stables Sat. 8 a.m."

The main riding area was surrounded by a rectangle of stables and a paved walkway. There were benches every thirty feet for viewing. In the ring, Scully's three girls rode huge, expensive-looking horses, alternately walking, trotting, and galloping, depending on what the trainer in the middle yelled.

He was sitting on the closest bench with his arms stretched out, as though the girls were sitting on the bench with him and he had his arms around them. He had the papers next to him, folded up in fourths the way guys read them on the train. He watched me approach but didn't lower his arms or uncross his legs. I sat down.

"I told you the rack was fake."

I shook my head. "I got a thing for fake tits."

He didn't laugh, he just gave me the Scully smirk that was almost a laugh, a quick acknowledgment. He looked back at his daughters.

"Twenty-five grand a year, this place. But I figure it's worth it. Keeps them out of the malls and the clubs and the raves or whatever shit they do now as long as possible."

"Good idea." I watched the girls, too. "Another morning meeting. You're spoiling my sleep, man. I'm single." He didn't laugh. "What is it this time?"

Without looking at me, he said, "I have some info to give you."

Before he could get going, I said, "Listen, Chris, this thing . . ." I held up the green check from the diner. "It's not . . ."

He stopped me. "Yeah, what the fuck was that? The fuck do you *know*, Joey? What the fuck is that? What's with the note? You *know*? Kind of shit is that?"

"I know. I know that must seem weird." I leaned back and looked out. One of his girls, the biggest, she must have been thirteen, was starting to do the jumping course. "I don't know. I left you that because I just wanted you to know that I know what it's like. Where we're at, me and you. No one else has really done what you've done, but I get it. I know what you go through living with the stress day in and day out. The expectations. The stuff that comes with being successful, having money, whatever. We were arguing and you walked away and I knew I wouldn't be able to say what I meant."

He was trying to figure out if I was being serious. But, behind it, against his will, he showed a little relief.

"Look," I said, "We're friends, we grew up together, we're from the same place. I left you that because I wanted you to know that I know all that, I know everything. I know *you*. I was pissed about the Betours thing and I had a gut reaction to take it out on you personally. It was fast. I just wrote it. It was an in-the-moment thing. I've wanted to call you to explain, because I knew it must have seemed weird. But the main thing was I wanted to tell you that no matter what you become or I become, I know you and I know what you're going through. That's all." He took a long look at me and I was worried he wasn't buying it. Then he reached out his hand and we shook. All white this time. No brother stuff, we were past that now, it was not the seventies anymore, we didn't have pulled-up socks and long hair and sweatbands.

"Okay, man." He turned it back to my situation. "I'm worried about you, Joe. I worry about you." He lowered his head to make sure I was looking at him. "All right, now again, I'm sticking my fucking neck out telling you this, so understand that."

"I do."

"My guys in the US attorney's office are telling me it's bad for you. It's not just a squeeze—they want you."

"Why?" I felt panicky.

"They won't tell me. I tried. The most they will say is that it's 'inside your tent.'"

"Inside my tent? What's that? Like someone I know?"

"Yeah."

People where I come from say yeah in two syllables. The second is almost silent, the "ah" part. It resonates in the throat, hanging there like a curveball. He was back watching the ring. All three girls were in motion around the course, jumping and galloping.

"Are you fucking a lot? If you're banging Connie, I can only imagine what else you're doing."

I didn't say anything.

"You better watch where you stick it."

I thought about Connie, about Carolina, about Hondurans and Poles.

"That's where you start. You have no idea how much we get from ex-wives, ex-girlfriends, prostitutes. That'd be my guess."

I listened. "The other thing I would look at is whether you know anyone in trouble." He was staring at me. He hesitated because he knew this was sensitive. "I know you helped some people in the deal. Some of those guys—that's the other kind of person who would leap to mind here. Are any of the people you know in Penwood in trouble?"

"You mean that would turn on me?"

He shrugged and opened his hands.

"For what? What is any of this for? I didn't do anything, Chris." I threw my hands up. "Can't anyone fucking get that through their heads? *I didn't do anything.* I sold my company to the guy. Eight fucking years ago."

He shook his head. "I don't know, man. Inside your tent, that's what I'm hearing."

Exasperated, I said, "Well, I don't know what that means."

We sat there in silence watching one of his daughters ride. Without glancing at me he said, "And by the way, I need fifteen hundred bucks."

I was stunned. "Really?"

He laughed. "For the *school*, Joe. For Fallcrest. We're raising money to redo the court. The idea is we sell the old floor in sections—you know, cut the boards up into little pieces, like the size of a brick or something. Each piece of court is fifteen hundred. The money will pay for the new one."

"Okay," I said, relieved and embarrassed. "I'll send a check."

Motherfucker, I thought, as I drove away from Scully and his perfect little daughters at the stables. Now he had made everyone suspect in my eyes. Everyone could be someone out to get me, everyone I had ever known. I couldn't be sure it was someone in on the JKD sale, but I knew that would be the list I'd have to look at. But it could be anyone. I had to look everywhere. I punched the roof.

It was probably a woman. It had to be. I could never sort them. Had to be some rotten bitch. Some slot, some stinky gash who was mad at me. It didn't even have to be an obvious one, that's what made it even harder. It could be some stripper I had banged who looked at my mail. Or some old girlfriend who knew I had money now. It could be one from college, for all I knew. Women always suspected me. That's why I stayed away from them. Now somebody was getting me back. Getting me back for treating them like potato chip bags, taking the snack in the center and throwing the rest away.

Maybe not. It could always be one of the blacks. Face it, I thought, there's that back part of your mind that always suspects them, the part you don't say out loud, the part that gets nervous at the cash machine, in the elevator, in the hall. The part that's scared of the dark. Everybody's the same way, might as well admit it. Why not burn me, why not stick it to me? The past was the past, memories don't pay the bills, don't get you a plea deal. No black guys stay out of the way of the system completely; it's not built that way.

Or, shit, it could be one of the white guys. Either category of white guy—rich or poor. It could easily be someone from Stuckley, one of the trashy burnouts or drunks who knew something about me from the way back. Some Marlboro Red–smoking disgusting fucker getting me for the money I have. Or the other kind, one of the two-faced buttoned-downed Audi-driving whites. They fold like umbrellas, they cry like girls. They're weaker than everybody when it comes right down to it. They can't deal with their minds and their guilt and their fucking of the babysitter and each other's wives. One of them could easily be talking on me.

34

Fallcrest picked the Quaker as the school mascot. Outside of outside, replica of replica. We were the Quakers. "The fuck is a Quaker, anyway?" Mike Dunn said to me on the bus.

Sean overheard and got pissed.

"You don't know that, Mike? Freedom of religion? That stuff? Are you an idiot?"

"Like the Pilgrims, Mike," I said.

When I get tired of Scully and Mike, which was all the time, I hung with the black guys. Little Etheridge was great. He was about five eight and like lightning. He read comic books and drew pictures of *Ultraman*. He loved *Ultraman*, the crazy fucking Japanese show where a guy in a seriously weak superhero suit fights B-grade Godzillas. I got him talking about *Ultraman* once and he said to me, in all seriousness, "Do you think they could ever be a *Ultraman?*"

I told him, "Why not?"

He said, "Yeah, maybe." He left hopeful.

The other brothers picked on Etheridge because he was so little, but it was friendly. I remember sitting on the steps at the Boys Club in the summer with Leonard. We saw Etheridge rolling up from the corner of Sixth Street. As he approached, Leonard got a huge smile. He tilted his head up slightly, the way he did when he was going to sing or yell.

"Eff-ridge. You . . . ain't . . . got . . . no . . . bigga . . ."

Etheridge swung his hand down to me. "What up, Joe." Then he turned to Leonard, who grabbed his hand with a big looping clasp and continued with his greeting:

"But . . . you . . . *stiiiiill* . . . my . . . nigga."

Then they fell out. "Ahhh, heh heh ha." Laughing their asses off at nothing, just saying hi.

I don't know where green, red, and black sweatbands came from. "The Blood, the Earth, and the People," Leonard said.

He wore one at Glentop, and Mike Dunn said, "The fuck is that, Leonard?"

"It's what's up, Dunn, you tractor-head motherfucker. Come here and get some of this." He hit a jumper from twenty-five feet.

"Ciao," Stokes said after he let it go. That was a big thing with the brothers: saying "Ciao" to predict it was going in. That's what they said if someone else shot it. If they shot it themselves, they said, "Face." As in, "In your face." The rest of us copied it. "Face" and "Ciao," ringing up and down the court until the sun or the rain or the cold sent us off. White guys didn't say "Face" too much to black guys, except joking around. Leonard could say it to anyone. Phillip said it to Stokes to tease him. Scully said it to me all the time.

"Face, Joe. Punk."

We knew each other's funny side. Stokes was quiet, but he kept it light; he wasn't a brooding big guy. Stokes said, "All right, Joe," when he saw me. That's how they said hello, the black guys. "All right . . ." and then your name. When Phillip walked onto the bus, Stokes said, "Aaaaall right, Phillip." They were funny together: friends, mutual respect. Phillip said, "All right, *Stokes*. Move over."

They rode like that on the bus to St. Thomas Aquinas on a Sunday in early November 1978. Casale and the other coach were teammates in college and they cooked up an early season scrimmage. It was a big deal because we were two good teams who would not usually play each other—we were in the Dover County Public School Central and they were in the Philadelphia Catholic League. We couldn't even meet in the state playoffs.

A Sunday scrimmage was against the rules, but it was the only time that fit. We drove into an empty lot and walked into an empty school.

And an empty gym. It had wooden pullout bleachers like every other place, but these were massive. Green and white banners from past championships hung in the rafters, and a brand-new clock looked like the control panel of a rocket ship, with clicking numerals for the score and time—automated red and green lightbulbs inside rectangular squares. Lights and time and score. They ran out and did layup drills on the other end. They were big pale fuckers supposed to win the Catholic League South for the third year in a row. They had five football players on their roster who didn't join the squad for good till November, and then they only played three days a week till Thanksgiving, still in pads the rest of the week. They were physical. Teams like that didn't play their best till after the New Year when they finally got in basketball shape and stopped fouling out.

Casale and his buddy decided to play half-court so both teams could work on their sets. It was tense, with the players who were out of the play standing up close on the sidelines. They were tough, with a kid, Callahan, who had a full boat to St. John's. We hadn't seen a guard as big as him. Ten minutes into it, he split Scully and Garrison and drove down the middle. Stokes stepped up and rejected the shot, swatting it into the stands. We went nuts on the sidelines. They set up again and Casale said, "Time." He called Scully over and switched the defense to man-to-man. He put Mike Dunn in to guard Callahan.

Down on the box, Stokes set up next to his guy, a football player named Martin. Stokes was a little tired and bent over and held his shorts.

I know exactly what happened. It was the principle of the matter. Stokes's block was black to Martin. A white guy could never reject a shot like that. It offended Martin down to his boots that this boon was here at Aquinas on a Sunday blocking shots the way boons do. Big, thick, Catholic, Irish fucks from shit-brown brick houses with statues of Mary and faded pictures of Jesus with the soft dirty-blond hair and the nice trimmed beard and a halo with robin's-egg, watercolor backgrounds in Yeadon and Ridley and Conshohocken are loyal like the dumbest dogs:

obedient alcoholics sensitive to failure who grow up to do the White Man Shuffle in lousy union jobs, all their lives protecting the shiftier, smarter, better-looking pricks like Callahan. And this spade junglebunny came in here and did it to Callahan, too. That would not sit. Martin's lips moved.

Stokes stood up. No one else heard it, but I saw it from the sideline. He gave the guy a second chance. Martin smiled and pushed him and said, "You heard me, nigger."

They had another big load, Dooley, who was six eight, same thing, stupid yellow-toothed Mick, destined to drink and play softball and live in a row home and work in a hole in the ground or with a tie loosened selling home warranties or mattresses while holding two mortgages and five kids and Mass on Sunday. He sensed something and started over. Just in time to see Stokes's left hand smash into Martin's face, a straight fist on the button.

It was so brutal, it took a second for the sidelines to collapse on the lane. Dooley left Martin on the floor and headed toward Stokes. If Martin had been mad, Dooley was apeshit. Now it was on: a jig smoked his boy on their home court. Guys like Dooley and Martin loved to sit in bars and talk about kicking the shit out of spades and moolies. Now Dooley could be a hero and talk in bars forever.

He took a giant stride at Stokes, who did the same thing, ready to give it back. We ran in toward them, but there was time for them to go at it. Time, I thought, for Stokes to get really hurt by this asshole.

Stokes turned his palms up, lifted his arms slightly to the side, and stuck out his chest moving toward the goon. He spit out, the way black guys say it, "What's up? What's up motherfucker? You want some . . . ?"

Dooley lunged.

And a fist came across his jaw like a holy bolt of lightning. His nose crackled as cartilage bent and bone snapped and not-yet gin-blossomed capillaries burst and the skin broke open in two slits. It was Mike Dunn.

Before the pushing and shoving and extra elbows and arms around the necks, before the coaches settled them all down, before any of that, Stokes and Mike Dunn stood next to each other, looking down at the bleeding Dooley and Martin, saying but not speaking, "Come on. We're right here."

After a lot of noise and jostling, after "Fuck you up" and "Better not show your face in Penwood, son" and "Break your motherfucking neck, motherfucker," the coaches got both teams off the court. Casale looked over and drew his finger across his neck. The Aquinas coach nodded fast.

We got on the bus and Casale said, "Listen up." Everybody was quiet. "No one says a word about this, you understand? Not a word." Then, he couldn't help himself. "Good job." The next day at practice the principal, Jack Scott, walked into the gym. He motioned Casale over and they had a brief conversation.

Mr. Scott was, like Casale, not what you'd expect. He was a smooth cat but he was cool. He made you laugh and didn't sweat the small stuff. People loved that guy. He talked to the men teachers about chasing ass and the women teachers rolled their eyes but loved it. There was lots of fucking going on back then and he kind of watched over it all. You couldn't help but dig the guy. Black kids loved him because he didn't talk down to them, because he went to Penwood to hang out. He even drank in Penwood. Drank in Stuckley, too. One time, I was underage at MacAleer's when I saw Jack come in with a lady not his wife. Neither one of us was supposed to be there; neither spoke a goddamn word about it.

"Mike," said Casale, "come here."

Dunn ran over and Mr. Scott put his thumb and forefinger on the back of his neck and took him for a walk. They went down to the end of the gym, away from where we were. I saw Mike nodding. After a few minutes, Jack gave him a push and he came running back. Casale said, "Okay, let's run high-low with Stokes on the box and Sean up high. Run it from Jeremy's side."

I stood next to Casale on the sideline. "What'd he say?"

Out of the side of his mouth Casale said, "He told me the bishop from Aquinas called. They said they might call the cops on Dunn because their big kid is really messed up." On the court, Scully bounced it in low to Stokes. "Jack told him go ahead, because he'd call the editor of the *Inquirer* and say it was a racial attack."

"Why'd Jack have to talk to Mike?"

"He wanted to tell him to hit the cocksucker harder next time."

We relaxed and finished practice. In the team room, Mike said, "I thought he was gonna bust me."

Leonard was standing there. "No way, Mike," he said. "Jack Scott know what up."

35

I was late for the Annual Fund-Raiser and Dance for the Gladwynne Presbyterian Nursery School at the Gladwynne Performing Arts Space because it was the same night as the Friends of Chris Scully Dinner. Janice was on the fund-raising committee at the school and looked forward to the dance all year. Somebody spent a ton on the new building. It was all glass and wood beams with a massive performing "space" in the main hall and another "space" to have cocktail receptions on the side.

The main was spilling with tables full of glassware, flowers, and fancy rented plates. It was a nice night—an evening people plan for and there I was, going black. The parents were not particularly annoying; they did nothing wrong. They were just a bunch of yuppies and Main Liners. It seemed like so many of the moms didn't work. On those mornings when I dropped Tia off, they stood outside the school and talked with a capacity for minor detail I couldn't fathom or understand or take. It was like running a gauntlet as they tried to hook me into conversation: "Did you sign up for the Teacher Auction?" or "the Valentine's Day dance?" or "Did Janice get my message about Tuesday?" I felt nothing but pent-up sexual energy from them, probably because they didn't go around fucking each other's husbands, like in Raymond Carver or Updike. Or maybe they did, for all I know. But, no matter how good my mood was, even if I had nowhere to go, I didn't take the bait with any of them, acting like they were those bozos at the supermarket trying to get me to sign a petition against global warming. At the benefit dinner, they were all drunk. Dinner was not yet down and they were dancing. It might have been "Sexual Healing," but that might not be fair—my memory might have superimposed it on that scene. Janice was clapping her hands and dancing with her girlfriends in a circle. One of them tried to pull me onto the floor, but I said, "I got to go eat something." They were drunk at the table, too. It was a blowing-off-steam thing, a night when everyone was a little nervous and ready to let it out. The women truly did not get out enough. We'd become parents and didn't get to party much anymore. Larry, one of the guys, a regular guy—the guy I liked to talk to most, actually—sat with me.

"You have to hear this one. My buddy at work, one of my partners . . . he's an idiot, right?" Larry hit my arm, even though I was right next to him. "One of the secretaries, a nice kid, right, pretty hot, but not, like, the best ever, but pretty good. She sends out an e-mail saying she's in local theater in Yardley or some fucking place and they're doing a musical. Yadda yadda, but she says she's the lead and she's in a bathing suit in one part, so she says in the e-mail, 'Don't tease me in the office if you do come.'" He hit my arm again. There were probably two hundred people there. It was like a high school dance ten years later, twenty years later. It had the feeling of a reunion with some office party thrown in.

"So, my idiot partner sends me and two other guys an e-mail that says: 'I've got wood. Is that wrong?' But he double-clicks it. When you double-click an e-mail and send it on our system, it goes to *everybody in the office*." He grabbed my arm above the bicep and doubled over. Janice was enjoying herself, which only made me feel more distant. She got a feel for my mood and said, "Eat something. I'll get you some wine."

Earth's diurnal course.
Puck carrier over center with no room and no one to pass to must shoot puck in.
More, more, more . . . how do you like it, how do you like it, how do you like it . . . moremoremore . . . howdoyoulikeithowdoyoulikeit . . .

I went to the bathroom and I saw an old-fashioned school trash can. Almost all public restrooms these days have an aluminum side panel, where the paper towels come out of a slot at shoulder level and there is a trash hole right below for used paper towels. This men's room at the shiny new Performing Arts Space had the modern panel and the trash hole, of course, but there was also a classic indoor trash can, made out of that brownish steel, the dark brown tinny steel seen in public schools. Sort of greenish, too.

I made a ball with the paper towel after I dried my hands. I was ten feet away from the public school can. I nailed it. Dead center. I wet my hands, dried them, and made another ball. Short. I felt it coming. I did it again and again. If I make it, I will get into this tonight, normalize. Too much air, short. I will stay with Janice. I tried to miss and I did. I will stay with Janice. I tried to make it and I missed. There is life after this, after I die, I will know peace and my soul will go on.

The Gladwynne Presbyterian pastor, Steve, came in. He said hello and introduced himself and went to take a leak. Janice had mentioned how much she liked him, but I hadn't met him yet. He was younger than me, a chunky, friendly guy, brown hair. He was a comfortable guy who moved very easily. I didn't slow down with my paper towel shooting. I took another one from the sink. Steve washed his hands and watched me but didn't say anything. Only when he was done drying off did he really figure out what I was doing. He watched me follow through. I kept shooting but I stopped with the silent, internal stakes because I never did that when another person was present. That was private.

Some fathers came in and Pastor Steve made a break for it. I ignored the new guys. Larry came in and watched and started shooting with me. "Hey man, you're alone in the crowd." He was hammered and he wanted to bet a hundred bucks a shot. He missed three and I hit three and with that he was out three hundred bucks and it wasn't fun anymore. He hit me on the arm and headed out. I said, "Dude, forget the bet."

Outside, in the cocktail reception space, they played an old song written by Clarence Henry that I remember The Band doing. It was the only other lullaby I ever sang to Tia:

I ain't got no home
No place to roam
I ain't got a home

No place to roam
I'm a lonely boy
I ain't got a home

I looked at the front of the rim each time I let it go. I felt the front part of my eyelids at first. Then when I hit it solid, with good backspin, against the soft inside of the bucket, the whole underpart of my eye was wet.

Well, I got a voice
And I love to sing
I can sing like a bird
And I can sing like a frog
I'm a lonely boy
I ain't got a home.
Woo woo woo woo woo woo woo

My life is like a battleship. I built it from scratch, shined it, polished it, and kept all the bolts tight. When I left home, I let the boat go to rot. I began taking care of it again when I started the company. I got it back shipshape. I ran around with a wrench in my hand, tightening every bolt that got loose.

After the Betours deal, I let the ship go once more. I started not to care if things got loose or the beginnings of rust overcame an edge. With time it slipped away, Janice and Tia going with it. It's like I'm watching it on TV, the boat taking on water, nuts and bolts scuttling across the deck, fading into the sea. I can't get up to grab a wrench.

36

We played street hockey in the alleys between the redbrick houses of Stuckley, shooting at goals made of fence mesh and pipe. In the freezing weeks of winter when there was no snow to make things interesting, when it was just icy air and solid earth underfoot, we chased the modern oddity of the glow-orange hockey ball—pucks didn't work on stony surfaces—through the potholed streets, bashing each other with shoulders, legs, hips, and feet. In the spaces between junk parked cars and clotheslines, the back walls of structures built 50, 75, 150 years ago out of dried red clay absorbed thousands of mindless slap shots of teenagers fixated on a new and real Rollerball landed down in a world gone batshit anyway.

I was at the Dunns' for the sixth game of the '74 series against Boston. The Flyers led three games to two and could lock it up at the Spectrum. Fifteen people sat in the living room screaming at the TV, including Mrs. Dunn, who didn't really have any idea what the rules were. She liked the fights.

Bernie Parent was perfect and we won 1-0. Rick MacLeish scored on a wrist shot with five minutes to go in the first, and it was just running out the clock after that. When it was over we jumped up and down and watched the Flyers skate around with the Cup. We had so much energy, we didn't know what to do with ourselves. Mrs. Dunn said, "Just go outside with your hockey crap. You're going to knock the walls down."

We ran to the end of their driveway and stood by the mailboxes. The Dunns lived near the intersection of Stuckley Road, the street leading to CRI, so there was a pretty steady flow of cars. We had our hockey sticks. They were made from pinewood with beige hard plastic screw-on blades that we held above stove burners and then bent for the right curve. Mike's was practically hook-shaped; he basically melted the thing.

We lit some trash on fire and waved our sticks and banged the asphalt as the cars honked. Everyone had watched the game. We were the champs. Everyone knew.

37

Wendy had hair on her ass. A red-brown furry coat. It shocked me the first time I pulled her pants off. She had little hairs around her nipples, too. She was unapologetic. It hardly stopped me from putting my body all over her, trying to smother her, cover her totally, getting all over her with my mouth and hips and knees and feet and tongue. I liked to put my face flat on her anywhere: chest, stomach, side of her ribs. I liked to bury myself in her, take her strawberry hair around my face, press the place right below my eyes into her dark brown pussy hair, two shades darker than her hair, which left my nose and mouth in the soft, slick part giving way, leading finally to the hole, tongue in as far as it will go. I liked to taste it up in there, with my eyes covered, blinded by it, my mouth on its mouth, the lips pink and soaking for me, even when she said she didn't like me anymore, when the fucking was for memory.

College unleashed me on sex. The inhibitions of life up till then vanished like a little boy's Erector sets and X-ray glasses when I left Stuckley and its sadness. Wendy was the first I really hit a rhythm with, the first who I wanted all the time, like air, feeling like they had left me alone with a bottle of baby aspirin and I could eat as much of it as I wanted, not just one measly pill. Now I could slide into the drowning middle again after I was done, same as lighting one cigarette with the end of another. She liked me to wake her up pressed inside her thighs as she slept on her side. I fucked her five times one night. She fucked me back. It takes two to fuck five times in one night. All Knight long.

"You are so juvenile," Wendy said. "You're obsessed with sex. You know that, right?"

"I don't know that."

"Well, I know it. All guys are, but you're ridiculous. It's, like, in your head a different way."

"I'm obsessed with you, not sex."

"Oh, shuuut up. I'm not a moron, Joey. You're a predator." She grabbed me. "But it's okay. I like it."

There is no doubt my adult life started at college. Nothing gets you further at a school like Lattimore than being poor with no family. A yard or two grew between my experience and the story I told, but it was basically true: I was a knockdown kid from Stuckley who had overcome things the spoiled people of Lattimore had not. Lots of guys are wild at college, but it was more than that for me. I was on the road of not giving a fuck.

It worked best with chicks. There were a lot of kids from New York City and they were older-seeming, shiftier, more into drugs. I got my rap down with the Jewish girls. I was foreign to them, I didn't dress well. The jappier the better. It was vacation for them with me, safer than fucking a black guy.

I played basketball. It wasn't the same. The competition in high school was much tougher. Lattimore was Division III and bad Division III at that. I played because it was what I knew. We played other small colleges. I started the last few games of my freshman year, and then till I graduated. We never played in front of nine thousand like at the Palestra. The average crowd was fifty people, a total joke. We went all through upstate Pennsylvania and New York and into Massachusetts and Connecticut. We had a few nights in New York City. We even played in the Garden: against John Jay College at ten thirty in the morning. It was lame.

I rolled from girl to girl. I liked to get attached to them for a while, make them fall in love with me. I liked the ride. It was always the same: a brief chase, intense all-day sessions, sleeping together every night, a rough breakup. It could never sustain the weight of the acting. It was all acting: acting like I'd made it, acting like I was going somewhere, acting like an intellectual, acting like I was into politics, acting like husband and wife. Everybody acts in college.

I know what happened. There were dozens, but only a few didn't get thrown back. I found out through feedback. In college. Little things at first. Till I hit a few real sluts. A jiggly bag named Noel in one of the Gothic dorms—up a long stairway in a tower. She got on her hands and knees. "It's big, you know." A black chick, Andrea, the token in a sorority of blondes. She bled on my bed. There was Wendy, and then there was Mary Jo, and then there were a few random ones in the middle, strays, fat ones, ones I hit when I was drunk, artsy ones with hair under their arms, a thirty-year-old grad student, the one who liked it in the face, the first Chinese one.

After Wendy, I found Mary Jo Casey. My friend knew her from Brighton High School in Rochester. I met her in a pub, then I saw her in the library by herself. She liked music; I thought she liked me. I made a great move. When she went to the bathroom I left her a note:

Her and her boyfriend went to California,
Her and her boyfriend changed their tune
My best friend said, Now didn't I warn ya.
Brighton Girls are like the moon,
Brighton Girls are like the moon.

I don't know if it was growing up in Stuckley or what, but I had this feeling I would end up with an Irish girl. I felt there would be a freckle-faced one with brown eyes, a baby maker who would feel permanent, and one day she was there. She was an engineer, which was weird—I usually banged English majors, pre-law, business school, that kind of thing. Engineers were mostly Asians or Pakis or geeks.

Mary Jo was all dark brown hair and freckles, grass-green eyes, like Dottie said my mother had. She was little, which I liked. She flirted with me but held out, always going home to study at night. We went out for something to eat or I pretended to study with her. Then we'd walk home, through the snow, past the old Gothic buildings with flying buttresses, to her apartment she shared with five other girls, all dogs. We kissed for a while outside the door, stopping whenever one of her roommates came home or went out. She stopped me when I tried to grab her breasts and sent me off into the night, frosty and hard.

After a month she gave in. The impossibly girlie room smelled like peaches. It had two single beds, but with the roommate gone to Syracuse, I got her horizontal for the first time. She pushed me off and said, "Let me go to the bathroom." The water ran on for twenty minutes. She got cleaned like we were going to take pictures.

After the first week, I didn't like something. I didn't know much but I had studied *Penthouse* enough to know. "You never come?"

"I can't come," she said.

"Why not?"

"I don't know, I just can't."

When I asked her if she jerked off, she said, "That's disgusting."

I took the challenge. I got her going and guided her on top of me. I let her rock easy for five minutes, then I started arching my back into her and pulled her legs down and it happened. Her face went red and her eyes got watery and big. I pushed the flat of her back into me and she let out a little cry and kept going. I pushed her back and forth, wringing it all out of her, watching her go through it.

"That was it?" I said when she lay on me.

"That was it."

Mary Jo was smart. I talked to her about what it meant being Catholic. She said she liked the way it made her feel inside. She didn't have to take English and art history classes but she made As in them anyway. She followed things better than I did, and that was something because I was rolling through it all pretty easy.

Mary Jo had a thing for Flannery O'Connor and wrote a long paper on her and bought pointy glasses and told me in bed I was like some of the men in the stories, rough and distant.

"You like her because she was Catholic?" I said.

"I like her because she was so fucking cool. She was sure of herself."

"Don't you think it's all fake? Like a comic book?" She was naked and when I said that, she went over to her desk. Her back was small, stark white with the freckles of the really Irish. Scare-you-to-death white; Nicole-Kidman white. She got a book and climbed back in and pulled up the covers. She was always cold; it made her feel warm, she told me, to have me inside her. She found the page she wanted and read it, all about the Eucharist being more than a symbol and the rest of life being expendable.

"And you believe that?" I said.

"Inside I do. Don't you? You're a Catholic, right? Isn't that what you told me?"

"Half. Kind of. I don't know," I said. "What's the Holy Ghost?"

"Same as God."

"Like, what the fuck is that? A ghost? Come on."

She giggled. "Didn't you listen in church? That's the mystery, you bozo."

She liked me to play her music. I told her stories about my team, how we played. She tried to care but she didn't. It sounded like a story. Still, she hugged my neck and, Flannery O'Connor or no, she didn't ever want me to leave.

You must do these things. You must smell nice. You must make them laugh. You must make them come. Make them yell. Make them holler and yell and come and come till they can't come without you and then you can do whatever you want.

There's a very specific look people give you when you've done something crazy. Like out-of-control crazy. Their faces tell it all. It says, "I'm telling on you. I'm telling the whole world what you just did. I'm telling the whole world what you just did and the whole world is going to know you're crazy."

Mary Jo took my car on a Saturday night. She was three years younger than I was. I'd been with girls a lot since high school, no complaints, doing just fine, thanks. It was August and we were both at school for the summer. It was lonely and quiet. I was staying at our frat house on the third floor. She was supposed to take my car to see her mother and come back to stay over. She called and said she would be late. We had a keg of shitty beer, Schmidt's or Schlitz, in the basement and I kept going down and filling a plastic cup and going back up to my room. Up and down. Waiting for the phone to ring. It rang again around eleven and I heard music in the background. She said her sister wanted her to go to a bar and she put her sister on to prove it. I fell asleep around two, drunk. At seven thirty she woke me up with a kiss. I don't wake up well, I don't come out from the land of sleep, can't transition. There are brain chemicals or something that keep me in the other place, in dreamland.

"Where is my car?"

"It's here, it's down there." She pointed out the window and I saw the brown roof.

"Why did you leave me alone? Why did you do that?"

She turned around and walked out. She ignored me when I yelled to her to wait. I was waking everyone up but I didn't care. She started up the sidewalk, toward her dorm. I grabbed her elbow.

"Stop."

She swatted it away. "Get off me."

"Stop. Where were you? Where were you with my car?"

"I went to a party with my sister and slept at her house. Leave me alone."

I noticed she had no shoes on. "Where are your shoes?"

"I left them somewhere."

When she said that, I knew she was lying. I pictured her fucking a nameless, faceless guy, a long, lean guy with wavy hair. I started my left hand by my belt and brought it across my torso, ribs, up by my chest, and took the back of it across her face. A smack. Hit a girl.

38

We spent a half hour each day shooting fouls, another half hour without the ball, so insistent was Casale on defense as a focus. He was obsessed with our conditioning. We had to run four suicides in eight minutes, anyone not making it was done for the day, no more practice, and if you didn't practice, you couldn't play. We did shuffling drills, starting under the basket, to mid-court, back shuffling to the foul line as the next guy started, then moving to the foul line, moving to the right sideline, then back over to the left sideline, where we did ten push-ups and got back in line. Once three or four guys were in motion, it was all communication. "On your right," "Under, go under," "Up top, up top." We slapped the Quaker at half-court. It was beautiful when it got going, like music, *badadamp, bada, bada, dump, dump, bahda, bahda, bahda, dump, dump, dump.*

I'm the one who had to deal with Marlowe and Beatty all the time. I had to play on the same scrimmage team, show them where to go, all that. The statistical fluke of great players in our class meant there wasn't anyone who was any good in the grades behind us. No one good enough to play with us, anyway. Casale saw the handwriting on the wall, so he picked Marlowe and Beatty and put them on the team. We talked about them as a pair, never alone. They did everything together. They were both brainiacs, in the smart classes, taking calculus in eleventh grade. Out of the rest of us, only Herman was in the smart section, though a teacher who liked me, Mr. Harris, put me in a couple of their classes when I was a senior. The difference between the smart section kids and the rest of us was the way they worried about going to a good college. Marlowe's and

Beatty's parents were obsessed with sending them to college. They were into basketball for their applications.

Everyone else—maybe except Phillip and Herman—only thought of college as the next place to play. Tons of scouts came to our games. Phillip had been getting letters since eighth grade and Stokes started to get people looking at him as our senior season went on. Herman got a lot of interest because he was so big. Scully and Garrison got noticed by the scouts who came to see Phillip. Casale told me and Leonard he was going to kick our asses if we didn't play somewhere.

Marlowe was more extremely bad than Beatty. He was six four and a complete dodo bird. Casale chose him to play because he was the biggest of the bad crop, but he was goofy and robotic in his movements. Everything he did was thought out, creating the opposite of smooth. His parents had a dream that he could get into the Naval Academy. I asked Casale if that was realistic and he said, "It better not be or the country's in trouble."

Beatty was a smaller, more coordinated version of Marlowe. He played three man and Marlowe was, in theory, a power forward. Their mothers were friends. After the boys made the varsity, they decided they didn't want them to get their eyes knocked out. So two weeks into practice, Marlowe and Beatty showed up with goggles, the kind with the black elastic band around the back of the head. Kareem Abdul-Jabbar goggles.

When they walked out, Casale said, "What the hell are you two doing?"

Marlowe did the talking. "Coach, I know." He was embarrassed. "Our moms said we need to wear these. Do you want us to take them off? Should we tell them you don't want them?" Casale had seen Mrs. Marlowe and Mrs. Beatty in action. He was into women, always looking at skirts in a devilish but charming way, but he didn't really like women too much from everything I could see. "No," he said, "leave them on."

Leonard came into the team room, the special section of lockers set aside for the varsity basketball team. There were fourteen floor-to-ceiling steel cage lockers, much coveted among the athletes of the school. He was next to Stokes, his usual place. He looked at Coverdale. "Cove, you are an ashy motherfucker."

Leonard was into one-upmanship. Etheridge, Stokes, and Leonard had Afros, but Leonard's 'fro was always a couple of inches higher and rounder than the other guys'. He was way into the Super Fly thing and had lots of bell-bottoms and silky shirts. He walked around with a pick in his hair, strictly to attract the girls, part of his look.

The black guys did not like two things about personal hygiene: ashy legs and nappy hair. Ashiness came from dead skin on the legs, which we all have, but it is much more visible on black people. Nappy hair meant an Afro had not been properly picked. I used to grab Leonard's pick and examine it, feel in between the teeth. It was oily.

I studied things like that, bodily functions. I guess it's natural when you are young. The bodies and bodily habits of others. Their smells, their grooming, their sweaty stuff at the end of practice. Some guys were neat and kept their bodies clean, even perfumed. Others didn't care. Privacy was not a concern. There weren't even doors on the stalls. Before practice, Stokes, Phillip, and Sean took shits sitting right next to each other, talking the whole time.

Leonard was superclean, and he policed everybody else, especially the blacks.

"And your feet stink, too."

"Shut up, Leonard." Cove was naked, putting his jock on. We wore jockstraps under our shorts, nothing else. "Nappy-headed faggot."

"Nigger, your feet do stink," said Etheridge.

"They do," said Mike.

"Don't talk, Mike. You're the worst," said Phillip.

"Don't make me come over there and beat your superstar ass," Leonard said. "Because I will. In a second." Phillip responded by nailing him in the back with a roll of tape.

We gave each other a lot of shit about music. Marlowe and Beatty couldn't believe we liked Bob Dylan; they thought he sang like a dog. They loved Yes and Journey and Boston and Foreigner, guitars and hair. We debated Dylan's voice, the debate of all kids at all schools. Scully and Mike liked Led Zeppelin. Stokes and Leonard listened to Earth, Wind & Fire and the Commodores. Garrison and Phillip liked Steely

161

Dan. Leonard gave us all long lectures about music being the way to get sex.

We all lied about sex, but it was clear the black guys were getting ahead of the rest of us. Leonard and Etheridge liked to talk to Phillip, who was shy, about what he was doing.

"What's *wrong* with you, boy?" Etheridge said on the bus to Marple. "That girl is *throwing* it to you."

"I'm telling you," said Leonard, which was a phrase indicating agreement. "If that was me, that ass'd be worn out."

"Yeah, well . . . I have a plan," said Phillip.

"C'mon, now?" said Leonard. He moved in close. "Give it up."

Leonard cornered everybody and pried into their shit. He got all up in everybody's business. I'd look over on the bus and see him whispering to Phillip or Herman or even Marlowe. He was in on every guy's private love life; he asked who the latest target was, how far they'd gotten. He extracted what they liked to do sexually and gave authoritative advice on what to do next. He required updates; he kept a running tab of who got where with whom. He knew it all.

Sean Dunn liked easy, pothead, artsy girls and, like Leonard, he coached me on working those girls. Leonard was a general practitioner, Sean was a specialist. He told me, "You know what I say? 'I'm not into politics or any of those scenes. I'm not even that into sports. I'm about the music.' Try it out, bro, I'm telling you."

Stokes—who was clearly banging his girlfriend, getting constant sex, which was hard for me even to imagine—was like the old cowhand on the subject. Between Leonard and Stokes, we got nonstop bullshit about their conquests, how to do it, what to do.

What they hated above all other things was eating pussy. Sean let it slip that he liked to go down on his hippie girlfriends.

"What?" said Leonard.

"I like it, I do."

"You dirty-ass motherfucker."

"Seriously, what's wrong with it?" Sean liked to take Leonard on.

Etheridge got up from the seat next to Sean and walked over to Stokes's seat, like he could not be near him, like he could catch something. "Ahh, nah, nah," he said. He shook his head and moved his hand underneath his neck as he moved. "Uhn ugh."

"What?" said Sean. "I like it."

"Aww, nah," said Stokes.

"White boys eating pussy," said Leonard, like the old southern man on the porch. "Pussy-eating motherfuckers."

"You won't do it? Stokes, you never did it?"

Stokes gave him a ferocious look. "Never, ever." Then he turned his head and closed his eyes. "That's so nasty. Uhn ugh. No way."

Etheridge was thinking it through. "And you're eating that nasty hippie-ass pussy, huh, Sean? Those your girls, right? Flower child kind? Boy, are you crazy?"

"With that bush?" said Leonard. "That Woodstock pussy? You eating that, you dumbass?" He made his face all serious and lowered his head and looked up at Sean.

"Absolutely."

"Aww, nah." They screamed: Leonard, Coverdale, Stokes, Etheridge. They fell over each other. "Nah, nah."

39

The minister, Steve, was married to a woman called Cindy, who, just as her husband, was hard not to like. We were making dinner for them at our house. She was stuck talking to me as Janice and Steve held a sidebar about the church's construction steering committee—not its work so much as the members of the committee. Cindy knew I didn't come to church, and she wasn't judgmental. She had a face that was cleared of worry. I did not then as I do not now find it easy to talk at dinner parties, but she was so nice in a serene way that I could relax. After the obligatory talk about kids and schools and the hectic workloads of daily life, I poured us a second glass of wine.

"You must do this with near strangers every weekend," I said.

"Pretty much," Cindy said.

"Okay," I said. "How do we make it not boring?"

"I don't know. Let's talk about something not boring."

"Like?"

"Like what do you guys do when you're sick of each other?" She had a comfortable way of being inquisitive. Neither of us was flirting. She was easy.

We were situated around the counter in our kitchen, marble finishes, stainless steel stoves, Sub-Zero and wine refrigerators. One of the many conformist behaviors I had adopted was wine loving. Getting into wines seemed to me to be more or less a way to feel better about drinking, and I was all for it. I mastered matching the very basic wine-food combos. I was working on vineyards, trying to elevate past knowing what a Bordeaux was to knowing the difference among Bordeaux.

"Janice," I said, interrupting her conversation with Pastor Steve. "What do we do when we're sick of each other?"

She and Steve laughed, surprised but genuine.

"Irritated or fatigued?" Janice said.

"Let's go straight to irritated," Cindy said.

"We bicker," I said.

"Over small things, you mean?" Steve said.

"We do not," Janice said.

I didn't get it, nor did Steve, but Cindy did a spit take. "Nice!" she said, and toasted Janice with a lifted wineglass.

Steve said, "We do the usual thing. I try to get to the actual things we are doing to make each other feel angry, and Cindy wants to talk about how I make her feel." He smiled at her. "No, I'm kidding. That's terrible. The problem is that it's hard to make Cindy angry."

"Oh, that's not true," Cindy said. "But the big thing is not to stay angry."

"Joe stays angry," Janice said. With that they were all looking at me.

Cindy waded into it instead of changing the subject. "I know that feeling. I can stay pissed about something for weeks."

"Nah," I said, walking toward the fridge. "You're sweet to try to rescue me, but you don't have to." Then, "I'm going to open a bottle of white. Maybe we'll have some red with the pasta when Janice is ready."

I brought the bottle back to the counter. Everyone had stayed in the conversation, and there was surprising ease that facilitated candor. "To be angry, you have to have expectations that aren't being met. I gave up having expectations a long time ago."

"Oh bullshit, Joe," Janice said.

Steve, like his wife, leaned in, enjoying it. "Oh no, Joe? No expectations?"

"None," I said.

"Did you ever have expectations? You must have. You've accomplished a lot."

"I think I accomplished things because I didn't have expectations," I said. And I pulled the cork. "Not for a long, long time."

"Joe's an enigma, didn't you know that?" Janice said. I smiled to keep Steve and Cindy relaxed. Janice stayed playful. "I'm not kidding. It is impossible to figure out what he likes or doesn't like."

"Another good game," Cindy said. "What don't you like?"

"Suburbia."

"You're in a tough spot for that," Steve said. "What do you like?"

"America," I said. "The idea of America. I like Philadelphia, too. The history. Not what's going on now. But the freedom, all of that. I like to read, I guess."

"He's incredibly curious about what he likes," Janice said.

"That's just guys," Cindy said.

"And not so good about what I don't like," I said.

Steve tilted his head and said, "I think to be a minister you have to see the world through what you read." That washed over the other three of us. "Maybe? In part?"

"You're getting wasted," Cindy said.

40

On one of my last shifts at Pinelli's, after Dottie was gone, Cheryl said, "Meet me in the walk-in."

She didn't say it very nicely, so I got embarrassed. I thought she was going to talk to me about rubbing her, maybe that she had told Dottie. That was the one thing I couldn't take. She shut the latch behind me, pulled out a roach, lit it, and hit it. She gave it to me.

"I don't."

"C'mon. One time. I need to talk to you about something."

She held it to my mouth and I breathed it in. She finished it and put it out on the floor. She put her hands on her hips. "Got a girlfriend?"

"No."

"You better get one."

She was wearing a purple blouse. As happens with a nice ass, she had great tits. She approached me. "Do you think I don't notice it that you practically molest me when you walk by?" I felt my dick get hard.

"I'm sorry."

"You can't do that. You're in your own little world." She came closer and I thought she might slap me. "I want to see something." She reached for my belt, unhooked it, and shot her hand down my pants.

It was cold but she put her fingers around it perfectly. I was like a rock in a second. She dropped to her knees.

"I thought so," she said.

It was hot, her mouth. Soft, hot, and wet. She didn't give me long before she stood up. She turned around and lowered the stretchy pants I loved. The floor was made of black rubber panels that fitted together like pieces of a jigsaw puzzle. It was walked on, worn out, and just above it her ass was clean and white, more fleshy removed from its shaping fabric, but soft like a water balloon. I stared at the crack, the skin so pale I could see blue veins. She took a few steps over to a stack of beer cases and leaned. I followed and she put me in, wet and hot again but constricting. A vise. I went into her and I heard her make a noise, and then a louder noise. I was stunned with the velocity of the sex act and the cold and the beer and the pot. I could smell her, fishy and cloying, and she pushed back into me.

It was like the death dream, awakening from something abstract to the here and now, to the realization of death, to the red open pussy lips inside the ass in the air. I felt the same way as when I got up on water skis the first time: "Whoa, I'm here." She was yelling. It didn't last, but it went on long enough to do something to her, and I exploded into the hot mess. My head spun, I stood there.

She pulled up her pants and came over and put her mouth on me, still soft, hot, and wet, then her tongue, kissing me after it all went down, after I was inverted in the grown-up world. I tasted boxed red wine and menthol cigarettes. She pulled off me and reached down and pulled up my pants, buttoned them, zipped my fly, and buckled my buckle.

"Don't tell anyone," she said. She unlatched the door. "And stop acting like a pervert."

I got a letter in the mail. It was a standard white business envelope, from the post office. It said, "Joseph Knight," in blue ballpoint pen. A piece of notebook paper was folded inside:

Dear Joe,
I want to thnk you for the book titiled "Readings on Islam" I will like
reading it and havin discussens with you about it,
Sincerely,
Henry Coverdale, Jr.
"Cove" #45

* * *

Neither the *Bulletin* nor the *Inquirer* mentioned us in preseason polls and our local paper didn't pick us to win in our league. Casale put us in a Thanksgiving tournament in Abington with a few decent schools and Coatesville. Coatesville is a steel town thirty miles west of Philadelphia up there with Chester in being a rough place. The basketball team was all brothers and they didn't lose.

In the locker room, Casale sat us down. "You are as good as anybody. You can play with these guys. You know each other better than any team I've seen ever. I want you to stand up to them. They run, you run. Diamond and one press after every made bucket from the field or from the line. Do not let up. Let's go."

In every sport, be it football, baseball, soccer, whatever, when players take the field or the court or the pitch, they look at the other team. Guys will say they don't do it—that's horseshit. Every kid who's ever played looks to see how big the other guys are. When we looked down at Coatesville, we felt it. They came out of the locker room flying, big and fast. It was a big gym and our two hundred people who drove to Abington to see us were overwhelmed by the three thousand fans from Coatesville.

Scully said, "Stop looking at them. Run lines, let's go. Shoot some fouls."

Herman got fouled first trip down, missed one, made the second. We set up the press. They gave it to their point guard, Bixley, and he went right past everybody. Right by. When he got to the foul line he dished it to a monster named Jackson who jammed it. Then they set up *their* press. Herman took it out and he couldn't find anybody. Five seconds. Their ball. They ran a double screen for Bixley and he hit it from the baseline. Four to one, just like that.

Things got worse. Scully, who could usually bring a basketball up against anyone, was trapped by two and three guys at a time. Stokes was stunned when Jackson outjumped him. Phillip was cold, Herman was scared. Casale put Leonard and Sean in but they couldn't do anything.

Running with them was a disaster. They spanked us. Steals, traps, break-aways. They threw behind-the-back passes and lobbed it over us for jams. We set up nothing, never getting into our offense. It was over by halftime. Casale got in our faces in the locker room but it was no use. It was a blowout. Score: 96-63.

It was a long bus ride home. We thought we could go undefeated and we lost our very first game. Before we got off the bus, Casale called us together. It was dark and cold. "Look," he said. "I'm not going to tell you I'm happy because I'm not. I expect more out of you guys than what I saw tonight. Be ready when you come to practice tomorrow because it's going to be hard, I promise. And I want every single one of you to be ready to explain what happened out on that court tonight."

He said, "Bring it in," after layups and defense drills and we stood around the half-court circle. "Well, here we are. Who wants to go first? What happened?"

Scully said, "We got scared."

"True," said Casale. "Who else?"

Phillip said, "We didn't execute anything. No plays. No defenses. Nothing against the press. Nothing."

"Also true." Casale looked around. "All that's true. But the real reason is you punked out." He slammed the ball down. He pointed at Scully. "He's right: you were *scared*. You didn't step up to them and say: 'I'm here and I'm ready to play you, you son of a bitch.'"

He had the whistle behind his neck, the way he did when he felt like playing instead of coaching. "You guys have to decide: are you going to be a bunch of pansy-ass suburban faggots, or are you going to find something different inside yourselves? I am not—and I mean this—I am not going to stick around with a bunch of guys who are scared. Fuck that."

Stokes raised his hand.

"Go ahead," said Casale.

"We are a white high school."

Casale said, "What's that mean?"

"It means we shouldn't have run with them," Scully said.

Then Phillip spoke. "We can run, Coach. We can slow it down, we can do whatever. But run on the white schools. Run on Marple, run on Sun Valley. Don't run on Coatesville."

There was silence.

"Can't run on Coatesville," I said.

Casale got it.

41

You don't really coach T-ball as much as organize the chaos. Tia and her friends put ponytails through the backs of their caps—through the hole that isn't even supposed to be there. Though we were the Dodgers and had Dodger-blue shirts, hats, and socks, if I didn't pay attention, they showed up with pink socks.

I put them in positions in the field and pitched from one knee. I laughed with the other parents. Grandparents set up lawn chairs and watched. No one gets more out of T-ball than the grandparents. It's like Grandparent Heaven.

Ray was a pain in my ass. Janice was on my side with him no matter what happened and she knew I was on her side when it came to him, too. Ray made such emotional demands on everyone, especially Janice. Then it spilled over to me and made her sad. She just wanted her dad and her husband to be close, maybe give each other what they didn't have. A father, a son. Fathers and sons.

"You've come a long way," he said every time he'd been in the house for an hour. He never knew me as a kid, but he knew the history.

"That's him trying to be nice," she would tell me after he left, after the visits south from Rockland County, in the suburbs of New York City, where Janice O'Malley's parents lived. Janice's mom's family was from there and Ray moved up from Philadelphia. He was a stocky guy. He was stuck in the nineties, after raising kids in his twenties during the sixties, when everybody else was taking acid. He felt like he was always trying to catch up with the times, Janice told me. He went to law school at night and went on to work in the legal department of a big drug company in White Plains.

We had dinner at the Valley Forge Park Hyatt, in the dining room looking out. Ray was one of those guys who fancied himself a historian. "Self-taught," he said. There was a portrait over the fireplace of Washington on the boat. "Can you imagine what it was like for them?" He told me how great Ben Franklin was. We went to the Rose Tree Inn and had steaks. He told me about seeing Bob Cousy play at the War Memorial when he was a kid and about going to Army-Navy games at JFK.

"What kind of stuff do you handle at work?" I asked him.

"Oh, I do all kinds of stuff. I get involved in pretty much everything. Personnel claims, insurance, business disputes. Just about anything— except the drug patent issues. That stuff"—he backhanded the air—"that stuff is for the Poindexters. I stay away from that."

Poindexters. A Philadelphia kind of thing to say. His accent was extreme. He had that signature nasal sound. Years of cultural pounding have etched it in everyone: the Philadelphian as the working-class dummy. He had moved to the suburbs in New York, worked his ass off, become a kind of corporate lawyer, but he was a guy from Philly. It was all in the way he talked. The Eagles fan, the colloquialism-strewn diction. The implied ignorance, the slangy talk ridden with hoagie, dem, dese, and yous. The things about personal hygiene too close for civilized people.

"What's your big product? Do they have a blockbuster, or whatever? Like Prozac."

"Nah. We make knockoffs. Generics. Our guys really led the whole generic movement."

We looked at our steaks.

"Still doing good up there," he gestured at my head.

"Sorry?"

"You still got your hair."

"Oh, yeah."

He rubbed his bald spot. "Mine wore off a long time ago."

I couldn't really tell if he was trying or not. There was so much tough-guy stuff going on from both sides.

"Janice says you were a ballplayer."

"I played a lot of basketball."

"Yeah, I played football."

Back again to the food.

"What about now? You a sports fan?"

"You know, not much," I said.

"Aw, c'mon," he said. "Guy stops following sports, he gets dead inside."

After a second, I said, "Well, I mean, of course I'm a fan. I know who's who, who's in the playoffs. But it's not the same as I get older. Doesn't it seem, I don't know, silly sometimes? Pro sports at least? I like college basketball. But even that . . ." I drifted off. Unconfident.

He gave a grunt of agreement. More like I get your drift. Halfhearted agreement masking complete disagreement, possibly distrust. He was sizing me up.

"Who's your baseball team?"

"Anybody against the Yankees," I said.

"Oh boy. We're in trouble, me and you."

"What, you like the Yankees, Ray? You?"

"Janice never told you? I took her to Yankee Stadium all the time. She always went with me. It was our thing."

"Wow. No."

He thought that funny. I did, too.

"You'd think she'd have told you that."

He was weirdly pleased. He drank martinis and I kept up with him. The booze helped, and he asked what he really wanted to ask.

"Tell me about selling your company. That must have been some deal."

I went through the story, more or less. I told him in pieces; I left things out. I fashioned it at the right time like I was asking his advice. You can't tell a story without lies.

"Do you think I should have held on to it?"

"Depends on what you got." He was imitating the other lawyers and bankers he'd seen at luncheons and meetings. It breaks my heart when blue-collar guys go to college and law school at night so they can wear suits and go to nice restaurants and pretend to be big shots. It's playing dress up. Shuffling around. The White Man Shuffle. I hate the White Man Shuffle.

"Eight figures."

He whistled. "That's a good number. Hard to argue with that." He was blown away. Just like Sammy, just like all old guys when they hear about modern money. They want to tell you there are no shortcuts but they about pee their pants. Such a tell.

"What, the French guy just had money to burn, huh?"

"Right place, right time."

He should have been a father to me, I guess, but I couldn't do it. He was uneasy, like he didn't trust me. We went through the motions in the early years but never broke through the crust. We came close; I even felt like confiding in him when Janice was pregnant. I wanted to be taken in. But it faded. I preferred to pick my fathers for myself.

He surprised me at the business school two days after I moved out of the house. I got him in the car and drove to TGI Fridays and we sat in a dark booth in the middle of the afternoon. He told me he had a mind to wring my goddamn neck, I had responsibilities, I couldn't just walk away from things, who the hell did I think I was? I told him he wasn't my goddamned father, he should mind his own business, and, if he asked me, he was going to drive his other daughter away from him unless he stopped meddling in her life. And for what it's worth, I said, he should knock it the fuck off with Janice's sister, too, who was also about to lose her husband over his shit.

After the deal at TGI Fridays, it degenerated into an e-mail war. Since I had moved to the apartment and was feeling out from under his yoke, I gave it to him between the eyes.

Ray: Stop sending me e-mails. And stop berating Janice. I don't know what the hell you think you are accomplishing, but knock it the fuck off. You are not my father and do not tell me what to do or how to raise my daughter. If you keep this up, I will make sure you never see her. I hate to do that, but that is how out of control you are. So knock it off. I'm not telling you again—cut it the fuck out.
Joe

He let me have it with his response.

Dear Joe:

Here it is in your words you'll understand: Fuck you. I'm coming down there this weekend but before I do, I want to straighten you out on a few things. Your behavior is appalling. You will be older one day and you will realize that you have blown it all by acting like a spoiled child. You are completely unaware of the problems of the people in the world around you. This troubles me for my daughter and is unacceptable when I think of the issues it presents for Tia. Do you ever think of anyone but yourself?

Since you don't have anyone else to tell you this I will do it: shape up. Your behavior is not helping you. You are selfish and self-absorbed and think that just because you have a few bucks you can tell everyone what to do. The world doesn't work that way.

The truth is, Joe, that Janice and I never fought until she met you. Her mother and I did not like the idea when we were told, but we kept our mouths shut, leaving her to live her own life. We were all hopeful. In fact, there were a few times that Janice told me she wished I could be a father to you and that you were beginning to feel that way.

To tell you the truth, I never felt like getting that close to you. There is something about you that does not seem worth the time. You are inaccessible. That is your business. But when it comes to my daughter and grandchild, it is my business.

I hope you take these things into consideration as you look at yourself. And steer clear of me. The T-ball park is big—I will keep to the side.

I will do and say as I feel when it comes to my daughter. That is not for you. Oh, and fuck you, too. Say it to my face next time.

Sincerely, Ray

You can't win with your wife's father, unless you are a lucky fucker. It's not a good setup. One, girls pick bastardized versions of the old man, so that's weird. And, two, you're hitting it, which isn't cool. It's not like you can have a frank and open exchange of feelings about *that*.

That they drove all the way south for the weekend didn't matter, Janice told him, he still couldn't come to Tia's T-ball game. "Joe is the coach and the way things are he doesn't want you there."

"It's a big field. I will sit in the stands, for Christ's sake. It's a free goddamned country." Janice told me that's what he said. But she put her foot down. He didn't come. He didn't see Tia play T-ball because I didn't want him there. I won that one.

Car-ol. Where's my Car-ol?
Paaas-quaaa-le.
Aaaaallright, Joey.
It's all right. It's all right. It's all right.

The thing chasing me, the thing that was unthinkable, the thing that brought on the death attacks, did not come from where I expected. I was at the apartment on Locust Street when Janice called me. "So my father died." Ray had a heart attack at the office. He was dead by the time anyone found him.

God, I never thought the sonofabitch would die. He was always up my ass about being fat. He was thick but he was in great shape like a typical hardass. He watched what he ate, got up at five in the morning, and ran all the time. His parents were in their nineties. He made Tia run races with him at the park and he didn't let her win; he told Janice it was good for her to lose.

I drove up north with Janice and Tia, who read books in the back and didn't make a sound. It was pouring. Janice leaned against the window on her side and didn't say anything. We listened to the radio and when it was too staticky we listened to the rain. We stopped at a rest station off the Pennsylvania Turnpike. What a place: thousands of people going in to pee all day every day. I was done first and bought candy bars and bottled water and when I came out they were standing in the nondescript antechamber between the outer door and the inner door. The place without a name where you wipe your feet.

Janice was standing behind Tia with her hands on her shoulders facing me. Janice's eyes, those big brown beautiful eyes, were wet with rain. Her face dipped a few centimeters and the eyes came at me: scared, lonely, deserted. The eyes begged me to help, come back, look at me, look at us, now my father's dead but all I care about is you, Joe, please don't leave me, don't leave us, don't stay gone, oh Joe I'm not mad I'm just scared, baby, I thought you were in this with me and now my life is eroding and I am lost and wet like this turnpike piss station, will this bring you home, can you make it all better, can you just make us whole, because he's gone and you're gone and she is still just a kid and I am so utterly alone.

"How about a Milky Way, Goo Goo?" I held it out to Tia, who grabbed it fast. I held out a bottle of water to Janice. "Here."

She whispered, resigned and so sad. "Thanks."

We got in the car and pulled back onto the massively inhuman, concrete Pennsylvania Turnpike. Other than the completely building-grade, Property of the State of Pennsylvania Rest Sites positioned coldly every twenty-odd miles, there is not a diversion to be found on that beast. Even the raindrops are uniform. Jesus Christ, I thought, what of the things William Penn hath wrought. Think of the things that bear his name.

We rode in silence till I noticed that Tia was crying. She was in the middle of the backseat where I'd told her to sit so I could see her.

"What's the matter, honey?"

"Daddy, how come you don't want to live with us?"

The big black thing had finally come to get me. The scene at the O'Malley house was terrible. Janice, her brothers, her sister, her mom, they were all zombies. They were stunned and scared and popping Xanax to cope. I held Tia's hand as the priest talked at the funeral. "He loved his granddaughter more than anything." I never heard a priest talk like that, so informal, so not-in-the-liturgy. I felt like he was trying very specifically to make me feel bad. They all said it. Again and again and again. Dozens of red-faced cousins, ruddy-faced uncles, permed and fake-pearled aunts. Irish Catholics. The wake was brutal. Don't listen to what people tell you. It's not a big party when anyone dies.

I stayed with them for a few days and acted like a good husband and father, maybe sort of a son. The kind of son who never allowed the poor guy to see his granddaughter's T-ball game. I got the fuck out of there and went to my apartment. When I got back I sat on the couch and stayed there.

Never pass diagonally across your own end unless 100% certain.
I am the American Dream. Don't touch me, I'm beautiful.
The man I sent can make them.

42

It might've happened like this:

When I walked in the side door, Scully was looking into the dressing room. He was in the doorjamb with his back to the door. He was keeping lookout, but he couldn't see me because I was obscured by the outer door. Inside, past Scully, I saw the Rafferty kid with his face in Father Shea's lap. The priest's hands were on the top of his head, guiding it up and down the shaft of dark pink. I pulled back from the door. It was a picture inside a picture. Scully was looking back in the room, getting impatient. He didn't see me. I ran away.

I saw Wally Rafferty after that once in a while, when I came to meet Scully at the church. He was serious about his altar boy deal, especially compared to Scully, who treated it like a dishwashing shift, or mowing the grass, or social studies, or any of the things he had to do when he wasn't playing basketball. Scully got there right before Mass started and, when it was Father Rossi's service, he was out of there five minutes after it ended. I noticed it took much longer for him to get done when it was Father Shea's. Sometimes he even had to go over to the rectory with the old man and the other altar boy.

Two weeks after I saw the Wally Rafferty thing, I told Scully I didn't want to meet him at the church anymore. He said, "Fine," which was not like him, to let me change the way things went. "I told my mom I'm not doing it past Easter, anyway."

After the Wally Rafferty deal at the church, I didn't know what to do. Chris did not change; no noticeable change, at least. In the car, I said to Mrs. Scully, "Do you ever talk to Chris about being an altar boy?"

"Of course I do." She was in the front and looked at me in the rearview mirror. It was a wounded look, scared.

"Do you know what they do?"

"Do you want to become an altar boy? I could talk to Father Shea." She hesitated. "Would Dottie let you come to St. Ignatius? I always thought she wouldn't because of Artie."

"Oh no, thanks. I was just wondering if you pay attention to Chris's schedule and stuff."

"Of course."

"They act kind of weird sometimes. Do you know all the stuff they do in there?"

She turned from the front seat. "I know everything Chris does, Joseph. I'm his mother." Then, "I have no idea what you are talking about and I suggest you knock it off."

She went back to the wheel for a second, and then came back after me, out of the driver's seat, snatching my hair. She pulled it in a fist, jerking my head toward her. "Watch your goddamn mouth, you rotten little bastard." She pulled the hair back so my eyes looked at her. "No more. You shut your filthy little face."

"Okay, okay." She let me go and I fell back in my seat.

Chris got back in the car. "I'm hungry."

"You? Hungry?" She smiled at him. "That's new."

43

"Like 'Wrath' with no 'W,'" my lawyer, Eric, said, explaining his surname. He looked like an English professor. A scratchy beard didn't really cover his face. His tie was loosened and his feet were up.

All the guys—Leonard, Stokes, Garrison, Phillip, Herman, Etheridge, Mike, Sean, Marlowe, Beatty—had subpoenas. So did Ervin Polk and Coverdale's sister, Rolanda.

"Okay," he said. "You sold to Publicité Rouge for thirteen million dollars in stock."

"Right."

"And you gave a piece to nine guys. Who are they?"

"My basketball team. We were close."

"Your basketball team." He pursed his lips. "Huh." He said it in a short burst, not like he was humming. Like he was surprised, as in "Ah-ha."

"And you lent the money to buy the shares to four of them?"

"Right," I said. "They didn't have the money so I worked it out with the bank."

"And you sold out after a six-month lockup?"

"Right." I figured what was coming next. "They netted about two hundred thousand after they paid taxes."

"A great success," he said. "Why did you cut them in?"

"Because I wanted to. I don't have any family. I wasn't married yet."

"Chris Scully was on your team, too? And he didn't take it?"

"He said he couldn't."

He sensed hesitation. "And . . . ?"

"I've always thought he didn't have the front money and he was too embarrassed to let me lend it to him."

He put his feet up. "How much money do you have now?"

"I don't know. . . . I have a house that's worth a million-five and about six million with brokers. I'm getting divorced."

He reached for the subpoena and looked it over. "It could be nothing, it could be big trouble." Then he leaned forward. "From here on, you don't talk to anyone but me, do you understand? I am your only friend."

"Okay . . . but, let me ask *you* something." I was angry. "What the fuck? It was eight years ago. How can this be anything?"

"I don't know. You're in something. I don't know what it is yet."

44

First time I ever got drunk was at the Flyers Parade in 1976. I was wandering around Chestnut Street at five, looking for my buddies, trying to get to the train station. Two cops passed me on horses and one leaned down and smashed me across the shoulders with his billy club.

"Watch it, asshole," he said. There was trash everywhere.

The thing about Fred Shero was he was unique. He looked like a normal Canadian hockey coach, but he evolved into something great. Then it ended. He left the Flyers for the Rangers in 1978. It was just running out the clock after that. We stopped watching hockey. Some guys got excited again when they came back in the eighties, but it was gone for me. Shero died from stomach cancer in 1990, two days after Thanksgiving. The guy who read the news said, "Shero is remembered for dark eyeglasses and colorful quotes. He was sixty-five."

Think about 1974. The Flyers won the Cup. The Band's tour with Dylan was one of the seminal rock tours of all time. John Africa was not doing too much, no bombs or police fights that year, but it was coming, the stage was being set all over that city. I was thirteen. Nixon was going down. All in 1974. It was the very center of mayhem, if you ask me. That's when the stitching came off the ball. We went to high school in the wake of that mess. Fuck me.

III

CENTERS

Perhaps they could see the forests again from beneath the asphalt of the city, the cars rusting and returning to the earth, the sky-scrapers crumbling into piles of stone, and the choked and pol-luted creeks of what was now West Philadelphia running clear under the canopies of virgin green.

—Michael Boyette, *"Let It Burn!"*
The Philadelphia Tragedy

45

Step three was molding. Three is five down the middle. The brick molder was the main guy, working fourteen hours a day, taking clots of clay and putting it in the molds, scraping the extra from the top, lining it up. This was where it took shape, when the brick became a useful thing. A good brick molder could make five thousand bricks a day.

Next, the off-bearer moved the clay-filled mold from the table, stacking it to dry. Then he returned the empty mold where the brick molder—the three man—was still cranking, ready for more.

Vincent Leaphart was born on July 26, 1931, at Philadelphia General Hospital. He grew up in Mantua, a little neighborhood in West Philadelphia. He was drafted into the army and went to Korea. He got married in his minister's living room. He loved all animals and stepped over bugs on the sidewalk.

He changed his name to John Africa after he started MOVE. After years of conflict, on May 13, 1985, the Philadelphia police dropped a bomb made of C4 explosive on the roof of MOVE's home at 6221 Osage Avenue in West Philadelphia. John Africa and ten other MOVE members, including four children, died in the fire the bomb started.

In the early '70s, John Africa dictated a three-hundred-page manifesto, which became known as *The Guidelines*. He attracted followers and gradually MOVE and the city began to fight. MOVE members were mostly black, grew their hair out into dreadlocks, ate raw food, and had lots of dogs—all by-products of Africa's philosophical leanings. The

mayor of Philadelphia was Frank Rizzo, a big fat goon, a cartoon character, a former police chief who appealed to the people in town who were
more or less the same as the people in Stuckley, ready to blame blacks
for all their problems. MOVE's policies didn't make anything any easier.

It was probably inevitable—it was brewing for a while. In the summer of 1978, after a yearlong standoff, MOVE refused a court order to
leave its original home in Powelton Village, a hippieish part of the city.
MOVE members patrolled the house in military fatigues and had rifles
and shotguns. The police tried to remove them forcibly. They started
shooting and a cop named James J. Ramp was killed—Jimmy Ramp, the
one who had been in Korea with Mr. Scully.

*Come! I should like to hear you tell me what there is in yourself that is not
just as wonderful.*

Supporters of the police call it a fire; supporters of MOVE call it a bomb-
ing. Ramona Africa, one of the three to survive, said, "They put me in jail,
charged me with everything they did—charged me with possession of
explosives, arson, recklessly endangering other persons, risking a catastro-
phe, aggravated and simple assault." She was convicted of two of the twelve
charges and served seven years in jail. She was released in 1992.

In 1974, a chimpanzee got loose on the set of *The Mike Douglas Show*.
Stagehands handcuffed the poor thing to a chair where it was shot with
a tranquilizer gun. The next day, members of MOVE, whose political
actions till that time were limited to demonstrations at the Philadelphia
Zoo, marched into the studio and handcuffed the popular talk show
host to a chair. The incident ended without violence when Douglas,
ever smooth, talked his way out of it. There were no actions of any note
taken against MOVE.

*How do you like it . . . How do you like it . . . How do you like it?
More . . . More . . . More.*

All this freedom.

46

At two thirty a.m., only a few hours after we lost to Coatesville, Henry Coverdale Sr. walked into the South Penwood row home, where his ex-wife was sleeping with Henry and his two baby sisters, and shot each of them in the head with a Colt .45 revolver. After he had blown the youngest child's head off, he put the gun in his own mouth and fired. The only survivor was Rolanda, who was sleeping at a cousin's house.

He had been released three days earlier from a VA hospital in Newport News, Virginia, and rode buses and hitchhiked back home. The coroner's report stated there was evidence of seven different antipsychotic drugs in his system. He had a blood alcohol content of .21, which was attributed to a bottle of Wild Turkey purchased on Front Street after he got off the bus. Coach Wattle told us after school let out. Casale canceled practice, so we just sat in the team room. After twenty minutes, Scully left quickly and came right back. "Casale said it's okay if we want to move around. Let's shoot fouls. We can't just sit in here."

We grabbed balls out of the rack. We started asking questions, countless questions about details, the details you look for when something bad happens, as though facts are going to help you understand. I just went to the foul line and worked on my stroke. After a while, the other guys did the same.

Here's the deal about that team: we weren't into school spirit, we didn't play for our parents, and we weren't going to pretend that there was some greater meaning that winning a few more basketball games was going to give Cove's death. We put on suits and went to his funeral on Saturday and stood around his aunt's house. "Auhnt's house." Black people where I grew up said "auhnt" like the richest white people said "auhnt." Never fucking figured that out.

There were four caskets at the front of South Penwood A.M.E. The preacher said what every guy, white or black, says at those things: that the deceased are in a better place, that we who are still alive are the ones who are really fucked, and that we better get used to the fact that evil exists. Oh, and go win it for Cove. Of course.

The Fords and Garrisons were crisp and appropriate, all pearls, belts, and creases. They seemed even more alpine at stuff like that, very clean and healthy. Scully looked like he was in a Catholic school uniform and his mom was uglier than usual. Everybody from South Penwood wore their best clothes. Poor people in purple dresses and hats, necks and arms inside the black double-breasted or three-piece suits. The walls beneath the paint, the floors beneath the rugs, the dirt outside the building, all scraps, remnants, shit on the floor.

Dottie cried her eyes out at the service. Later, she sat on the couch talking with a couple of old ladies she knew from the post office. I walked out on the porch. I was sad and stunned and distracted. Ervin was there alone, smoking a cigarette.

"I knew him, you know."

"Who?"

"Coverdale. The father. We went into the service at the same time. I rode a bus with him to Fort Bragg in 1963, going back from Christmas."

"Was he crazy?"

"Nah. We both had little kids."

"What happened? What do you think?"

"Just talked about the army and the neighborhood. He was from Virginia."

"Why, Erv?"

He waited. "Life is very hard, Joe, when you got nothing. That's why you got your family"—he caught himself—"and your friends. That's why this team, what y'all put into it, is so important. Remember that."

"Okay."

"People are like pieces of string. Hold them apart and they are weak. They have to be weaved—woven. You understand me?"

I told him I did.

"Our lives and stories are like that. Like I said, interwoven."

"Interwoven."

". . . Guys got a game to get ready for." He was looking far away. "It's right for you boys . . . you should stop and say good-bye. But don't stay here. Stop, not a stay. You can't—cannot, cannot—stay in this grief. It's a waste of spirit."

47

I got Mr. Harris again as a teacher for eleventh-grade history. On Back to School Night he told Dottie that he had made sure I was in his class. He wore a suit every day and kept his hair short, and in 1977, those things were not common. People thought he was a hardass. I now understand that he was not so much a Republican as a libertarian. Harris was a good English teacher because he was so well read, but American history was his passion. And he used the fact that budget cuts kept not just the teachers but the administrators shorthanded to do whatever he wanted in class. He ignored the curriculum he was supposed to follow in order to teach us what he thought were the two most important things every kid needed to know: the framing of the America's system of government was awesome; and that after World War I everything, but everything, changed and nothing was ever going to be the same again, and that was the human race's fall from grace.

He took us on the standard field trips to Center City and Valley Forge, to the Bell and Independence Hall, to the battlefield at Brandy-wine. Rather than zone out and complain about how boring it all was, to not risk seeming interested and therefore uncool, I hung in there. There was something about Harris's storytelling—the depth of his knowledge about the strategies, rivalries, and forces that combined to bring about our world—that made it real to me.

Up till then, I had coasted, even in his English class. The work came easily: writing book reports, ticking off multiple-choice questions in classes like health, making coatracks in wood shop. Classifying clouds and soils. Looking at rocks and writing observations in workbooks: Paleozoic era, cleavage break. Equations with square roots and nth powers and the fun of figuring out the puzzles of algebraic word problems.

But from the first day of school, when he handed us copies of the first map of Philadelphia from 1656, his class was fantastic. Harris brought home for me that it all started here, in this place, on these streets, in this land. You could tell he *believed* it, that he *lived* it. Before I heard his lectures about William Penn and Franklin, about the guys no one knows about like John Dickinson and Caesar Rodney, about Jefferson and Washington, the Revolutionary War era was as inaccessible to me as the idea of wearing a wig. Gradually, though, as he told the stories, I realized those guys were badasses. Not just smart and writing about abstract concepts—Harris talked us through the Declaration of Independence with the care of a cop talking down a jumper—but fucking and fighting. Jefferson paying scandalmongers to write crazy shit about Hamilton; Franklin banging women left and right into his seventies. And all of this added up to me being free. No government telling me what job I had to have, no one forcing me into the army.

I have since learned the term "sense of place." I did not know it was what washed over me on those field trips. After eleventh grade, I had a lens: when I watched the news with all of its reporting about politicians in Washington, the war in Vietnam; when I watched TV shows about detectives in New York, cops in Los Angeles, wrestlers in Florida, cowboys named Ben and Hoss; when I heard disco music and Fleetwood Mac; and when I lay on the couch on Sundays to watch the Eagles, I knew it was all possible because of what went down in our town. All that freedom.

Harris taught us that World War I changed everything. It was the fall from grace of humankind as we know it. He talked about the modern weapons, modern writing, modern painting, and modern man that came afterward. We have lived in a wasteland since then. As with the founding, his passion and detail and fire got to me. The British soldiers in their tin hats, the fucking Germans. Harris felt that what is properly called the Great War was the key to understanding the world in which we live. The period since the printing press and Michelangelo and the French

Revolution and Whitman was the Enlightenment to Harris. The clash of civilizations in 1914 put an end to it. Seventeen million dead from fighting and disease, maps obsolete, rationalism unmoored.

He spent a lot of time on our country's brutal internal conflict about joining the war. He said you could sum up the history of the United States' foreign policy as a long series of decisions about whether to jump into bar fights. He tied the debate over joining the war back to the founding in Philadelphia. He had written his master's thesis on the topic. The point that got through to me is there are higher principles that eventually carry the day in America, and those principles can be traced back to Pennsylvania, to Philadelphia, to the place that Penn built.

Harris's personal connection to history—his ability to relate books and other artwork to the events of the past and in our lives—woke me up. He carried a curiosity about things that made me realize he had risen above schoolwork by making it more important than the everyday to his own happiness. He developed his own opinions based on his own reading, his own thinking. And he often—as often as possible, it seemed—tied it back to our own history, our place, this city of red bricks, of William Penn's tolerance-filled DNA that created this home for the tradition of passionate compromise necessary to let freedom ring. That's the first thing I think of when Harris flashes back to me.

The other, which I only recognized later as an unavoidable fact, was that, in life, events happen that shatter everything. Life before will be gone. And in the aftermath you exist as a changed person. You will almost certainly be darker, Harris used to say, and you will believe that less is possible. His opinion was that this is the natural arc of life, of humans, and the modern world, post–World War I. Things are more dire, less romantic. It is bleak. Harris said most good fiction since World War I is about alienation. His theory was that the only available relief was a belief in the principles of America. That we are the only source for a hopeful new world.

I believed him and still carry chunks of him with me now. I am stuck on the shattered part. I would take it further: I think once you get blown away, you don't want to risk the pain of being blown away again. I am an orphan. From that beginning of zero and the weakness of youth, I allowed myself to find hope. It was taken from me. I won't be fooled again.

It is like being on top of a giant steel ball, holding balance by keeping your weight steady and the ball from rolling. If you fall off, you go into an infinite world of flames. Imagine fifty doors of opportunity in a circle around the ball fifty feet away. Any step toward the enticing doors may get you closer, but the more blunt truth is that any step will cause peril. And when you fall you face the pain. It is avoidable if you simply don't buy in, if you stay where you are and do not get taken in by the enticing hope of a new world.

I feel lucky, kind of. I was born with the benefit of knowing zero. I fell off once, but, knowing the zero point, I was able to get back more easily. And you know more certainly that it was silly to have tried in the first place. The great love of Dottie, the hazy memory of a dreamer's fathering by Artie, and the perfect harmonic convergence of my basketball team convinced me when I was young to try to walk my steel ball forward. Those things caused me to shoot for the fifty doors through which something else exists; once I was shattered, though, I experienced the cold, hard truth that any step on the ball, in any direction, was stupid, futile. The truth is I did not step off the ball in marrying Janice, in fathering Tia, and I still haven't and won't. The only reasonable course, even if it hurts those two who offer me unconditional love, is to wait out the inevitable in my natural state of zero.

48

Casale scouted other teams in person when he could but had to rely on the info from the paper and a few other teachers he could get to run over to the other gyms on game nights. He could see the other teams early in the year, but when the season started, all league games were on the same nights. So when we played Haverford on a Tuesday, Springfield played at Radnor, and so on. At practice the subs from the bench had to prepare the starters by pretending to be the other team. Casale would write his scouting report on a yellow legal pad and on Saturdays and Wednesdays before practice we met in the team room and he wrote on the chalkboard.

Radnor

Flakey—5'10" lh—no shot, hustler, point of 1-3-1—JOE
O'Hara—6'0" rh—both sides 18 ft and in—LEONARD
Metcalfe—6'3" rh—strong side off. Temper—26 vs. LM—SEAN
Mobley—6'7" rh sht blocker; off rebounds—BEATTY
Deckner—6'10" rh; lp turnaround; no lh; FOUL TRBLE—MARLOWE

Since Marlowe and Beatty barely even knew how to play as themselves, they weren't much help. But the rest of us got into it. I am ambidextrous, so I was left-handed if my guy was left-handed, right if my guy was right. If he was a shooter, I was a shooter. In my mind's eye, I actually became the guy, like I was there on the Fallcrest court in Fallcrest's practice and I was Tim Flakey from Radnor. I didn't care who Scully or Garrison was; I wasn't limited to being Joe Knight. Even Phillip wasn't necessarily better than I was.

Because he wasn't a starter, Leonard had to play the scouting teams, too. He had to play the two man or the three man from the other team, sometimes both. When we were getting ready for Conestoga, Casale said, "Okay, Leonard, you're MacMillan. He can hit it from around the foul line and in, but not much outside that."

"What's he look like?"

"How the hell am I supposed to know what he looks like?" Casale said. "There's no pictures here, for crissakes, Leonard."

"All right. All right. I'll feel him out."

Casale looked at him, paused, thought better of whatever he was going to say. "Okay, let's get out there."

I walked the ball up and Leonard hung back next to me.

"MacMillan. Mack-Millan." He was thinking out loud. "Is he black or white?"

"Just play," I said. "What's it matter?"

"Biiig difference, boy. Big difference. I got to explain that difference to you?"

I waved him to get over to his spot on their offense.

"Okay," he said. "I'm playing him black. If he's white, it ain't my fault. Don't come crying to me if he's all clunky and shit. I don't want to hear it." He started to run up the court. He yelled back, "Don't want to hear it!"

He ran by Scully and yelled at him, "Don't want to hear it!"

Scully looked at me and put out his arms. "What's he saying?"

"Forget it."

I crushed my college boards, which surprised the shit out of everybody, except Dottie, who said, "Jolly good, honey," though I don't think she had any idea what the numbers on the little piece of paper meant.

I think Harris said something, because they switched me to the Academically Talented Program. I didn't know any of the kids in the classes. I wasn't ready for calculus, so they put me in precalculus, with Marlowe and Beatty and the other brainiacs in eleventh grade.

It was fine with me. I was okay with school. I was listening to tons of music—lots of Beatles but anything I could get my hands on. I let my hair get longer, which Dottie didn't mind, but they didn't like it much in Stuckley. I had a lot more homework for those classes. I bought a brown leather jacket and wore big collars. I didn't shave.

That I switched classes did not make Chris Scully happy. He retaliated by saying that being in smarter classes meant being with uglier girls. "You can probably get on Martha Taffy right away." He was still into his grades, I noticed. "You'll probably get shitty marks now, dumbass. You'll be against all those brains."

Mike was the same: "Why do you even let them do that to you? You don't have to, you know. It's civil rights. You should just say: 'No. I'm staying in my own damned class.'"

She read a lot of crap, Dottie. Romance novels and Harlequins. She said she liked the stories, imagining she was far away, that it took her mind off this or that. When I was little, I asked her what the stories were about. She shut her book and brought me in close and said, "This one is a love story." I giggled and she'd put her face on mine and if she had makeup on that day because she was on her way to Pinelli's, it rubbed off on me. She smelled like Jean Naté perfume and Aqua Net hair spray and the smell that Avon lipstick and cold cream makes.

She read real books more often as she got older. Artie usually slept when she visited so she had lots of time. She liked *Sermon on the Mount*.

She liked what she liked and kept her mind open—when she went to Mass it was to Holy Trinity in Penwood, not St. Ignatius right down the road. She listened to Artie talk about Eschatology, which he did even when he went senile, and I think she was into it, but for his sake more than her own. After Artie went to Woodlawn Acres, she asked me to go to church with her once in a while. I never did.

Artie went to California once a year to visit his teacher. He left in a Ford pickup truck after the Fourth of July and returned in the beginning of August. He was tan, rested, and more nuts than ever when he got back.

He talked about having good thoughts and moving the clouds. He asked me where I was going every time I left the house. He pestered Dottie to tell him the route she planned to take before she drove anywhere. She told me later it was because he wanted to make sure we were safe. He moved the clouds and the cars around so we'd be okay.

He wouldn't see doctors because the Eschatology deal was to heal yourself. I think now he avoided the home an extra five years that way—there's no doubt he drove way longer than he should have.

"I've had two Prince Charmings, most girls only ever get one, and that's if they're lucky," Dottie said at Farrell's on my eleventh birthday. "First I had Artie and now I have you." The bill came to the table. Dottie grabbed a sour candy and talked to the girl at the register. That was a given with Dottie: nobody at a cash register escaped a few minutes with her. "How are you making out with this weather? This is a nice place. Do they treat you well? They better."

This all embarrassed and bored me so I slunk out into the hallway. I loved ice cream and I was back in a few days. I ordered a hot fudge sundae, the dessert of a rich man, with a glass of water. The waitress in the striped shirt with buttons gave me the check and then she had to run over to the other side to sing the Farrell's song because some mom at a birthday party ordered the thirty-six-dollar Farrell's Zoo Sundae. I walked by the cashier without stopping. Dine-and-dashed for an ice cream sundae. I did it two or three times a month. Kept it to a hot fudge sundae—never real food or anything like that.

I didn't have money to get hot fudge sundaes as a little kid. Dottie worked two jobs and volunteered at the facility for retired nuns at Holy Trinity. And then Artie went into Woodlawn Acres, so she never stopped going to nursing homes, like a lot of the ladies where I grew up. There wasn't a lot of free change. For lunch she made me peanut butter and jelly on Wonder bread and put a Tastykake apple pie in the brown bag for something sweet.

49

"It's complicated and it's simple," Eric said. "But the bottom line is you're in pretty substantial shit."

"Can you give me the simple?"

"Yes. In a nutshell, Betours got his company to issue sixty-five million dollars in preferred stock for US acquisitions. Greedy French businessmen. Did you ever deal with any other French guys besides Betours?"

"No."

"Yeah, well I have. They're greedy. They don't get enough attention for that. Anyway, these guys believed Betours was going to build US advertising assets, combine them with other European and Asian assets, and come out of it with a spin-off consulting and marketing company called"—he reached for his pad—"Rouge Monde de Publicité. They thought they would take it public in France or maybe the German NASDAQ, which was hot back then. They had bankers telling them to value it at two to three hundred million dollars."

"He kind of told me that. He told me to hold on to my stock because it was going to be worth shitloads."

"Right. They always say that. Scumbag. Okay, I have that he paid you thirteen million in stock for JKD and six months later bought another little company in Newport Beach, California. But on your deal he talked you into the 'secondary offering.'"

"Yeah?"

"Well, it was total bullshit. He ran everything through a subsidiary company he controlled. After he bought your company and the Newport

Beach company, he told the Publicité Rouge board that he spent fifty-two million euros on the acquisitions. He put the real Publicité Rouge stock in, paid it out to the acquisition targets, like you, and kept the spread. You still ended up with real stock and you punched out and never knew the difference. And you sold for the rest of your group by proxy. Some of them you put on the board of directors—Ervin Polk, Leonard Polk, and Phillip Ford."

"Correct. They all got out and resigned from the board. They made a hundred grand each. I think I kept two hundred and fifty thousand dollars of the subsidiary stock to deem committed to the company, I think Betours might have asked me to do that. It never went anywhere. I think it's worthless now."

"It's *definitely* worthless now, schmuck. Forget that." He shook his head at me. "You were a patsy, my boy. This guy, Betours. He's something. The fucking French board was so happy, they gave him a bonus. They apparently thought he was showing restraint and saving part of the war chest. Some of them were probably in on it. Anyway, he spread ten million around in various operational ways and he laundered the remaining twenty-five million to himself through the subsidiary and various Bahamian partnerships."

"Who would believe he spent fifty-five million on two small ad agencies?"

"He was paying three accounting firms a million dollars a year in fees. Each. Those assholes would have confirmed he bought the Republic of Singapore for a cheesesteak and a bottle of Bordeaux. Five accountants have been arrested in the last two years. That's how the feds do it. They're flipping those guys. It's all been very quiet. Southern District New York stuff. Even if they don't catch Betours, they get the accountants, maybe a few lawyers. In the long run, it's a deterrent. Keeps the lawyers and accountants honest. At least that's what they think."

"So, he used me in a fraud. What did I do? Why am I in trouble?"

"The government's theory is that you assisted him. They have the baseball bats out."

"How did I assist him?"

"That's easy. Let me ask you a question, Joe. And I want you to think before you answer it. The day you went to the closing at Bain Brothers, do you remember that?"

"Of course. I was going to get thirteen million dollars, Eric. Of course I remember."

"How long were you signing documents?"

"A long time, like half an hour."

"Do you have any idea what you signed?"

"I don't know . . . acquisition agreement, employment agreement, stock stuff, bank stuff."

"Who was your lawyer?"

"Harry."

"The fuck you think Harry knew about doing a deal like that?"

"He was my lawyer, I don't know. He's like eighty. I couldn't fire him. He's like a guardian."

"There's your answer."

"What, Harry did something?"

"No, Joe. Harry didn't know what the fuck he was doing. You had a country doctor doing a heart transplant."

So there it was. Eric was my rabbi. His success was built on delivering news like this and then making the best of it.

"What about the other guys? What the hell did they do wrong?"

"Well, it's not clear they are going to charge them yet. They are scaring them—it's called 'freezing' the witness. And they are isolating you. They don't want them helping you. And they are setting them up to flip in exchange for testifying against you."

"For what? I just got them money, for Christ's sake."

"That's the theory: you did all of that to look good. You gave them all a piece to make yourself look like a good guy because you knew it was a dirty deal, and they were all in on it. At least that's what they can hit you with. It's definitely enough to scare your boys into talking."

"To say what?"

"That they had no idea what you were doing. That you approached them and even offered to lend them the money. Basically, that you were all alone."

From the West down to the East.

"What a load of shit."

He let me sit there and think about it for a second, then he came around the side of his desk, grabbed a straight-backed chair from the other side of the room, and came real close to me, putting the back of the chair in front and sitting in it backward, his hands draped in front.

"Okay, my boy, we've come to the point where I have to ask you a simple question: is there anything you are not telling me? Before you answer it, I need to advise you of the following.

"If it turns out at a subsequent point that in answering this question you held something back, that is, if later you tell me that you didn't tell me something, no matter how inconsequential it may seem now, there will be no more you and me. I will resign on the spot, you will forfeit all fees paid to me to date, any sums outstanding will become due and payable immediately, and I will be done with you. This has been my policy for thirty years and I never deviate from it, no matter how much I come to like you personally. Other lawyers don't do this but I do. It's the way I work."

I nodded. I realized I was getting a speech. I did not know what I had done to bring it on at this point. Some "tell" set him off. Something in the secret recesses of his expert criminal defending mind, a secret of the trade, the mystery of Eric Rath, made him want to give me this talk now.

"So, Joe, is there anything about this that you are not telling me?"

I thought of the long-lost lonely years, of Stuckley in my youth, of old gray churches and rooms inside churches and Wally Rafferty and Scully. I thought of my aunt Dottie and uncle Artie, of my dead mom and dad. I thought of where I'd come from and Mrs. Scully and peanut butter crackers and the science of last things. I thought of the Palestra and its redbrick atmosphere. I thought of long walks in the freezing rain to play basketball. To just play basketball.

"There are a lot of women by the side of the road."

"That's okay. We'll work through that. Anything else?"

"No, Eric. I've told you the whole fucking thing."

50

There's a famous story about Willie Mays rounding second in the World Series with his cap flying off. He hit a triple with the bases loaded and everyone on the field was moving. Some say it's the greatest baseball moment of all time, where one player saw it all, one player in complete control. He was dead smack in the middle of the diamond and driving every part of the game. He controlled every axis of space and time.

I ain't no Willie Mays, but I did have a moment against Lower Merion, one time when it all came together and I felt that thing. Scully had turned his ankle right after the tip so I was in earlier than usual. A guy from the other team was shooting a foul shot. I was at half-court where guards hang out at free throw time. We don't usually line up in the lane. When the ball left the kid's hand, I could see it was a brick left, and I started to move diagonally, to the wing between the bucket and the sideline. Stokes pulled the board and I was three steps toward him by the time he landed. He hit me with the outlet pass. I caught it at the top of the key, moving right to left as facing that basket. I turned up court, not losing a step, starting the break. Stokes followed his pass and filled on the left side. Garrison, born-cherry-picking bastard, was already up court, and he filled right. Two guys back on D, we had the numbers, a three-on-two break.

It has been long ago deduced that the optimum way to run the three-on-two is for the ball handler to stop at the foul line while the two wings head toward the basket. One defender has to stop the ball, and the other guy can't cover both sides. Hit the open man and you score.

Everything I'd ever done in basketball led to that instant. Running the break for a point guard is like breathing. It's math and logic; it's geometry, a game of triangles. I went into my zone, inside, as though the rest of the game was in slow motion. I saw what was going to happen like I was in the West Stands at the Palestra. I crossed half-court and I was Willie, in the dead center, in full stride, in full control of the game, blowing by the other guys, who were just statues, because I was in flow and they were in counterflow, and flow always beats counterflow.

I pushed through, straight at the cup, toward the middle of the foul line. Garrison flew at the bucket on my right, Stokes on the left. The up-defender came to the foul line to stop me. I dipped one half step to the right and looked at Garrison. The guy in the back took it hook, line and sinker. I snapped a perfect behind-the-back bullet pass to the wide-open Stokes busting down the left side. Pure Cousy, pure Ernie D., pure Clyde. Pure Magic. Stokes caught without breaking stride and jammed it the fuck home.

We ended up dusting Lower Merion by twenty-six. It was like stretching our legs. We all got in the game and Leonard, in particular, played well, scoring sixteen. On the way back we were sitting against the windows in the bus and we started talking about ice hockey. Sean and I talked about the Flyers-Rangers game the night before.

Leonard said, "You know, I was watching that, too. I didn't have anything else to do and I said, 'What the fuck, I'll watch this shit for a while.'"

Sean and I adjusted in our seats.

"So, I'm watching, and the goalie gets it and he goes behind his net and leaves it there."

"Right," said Sean. "So a defenseman can come get it." The other guys stopped to listen.

"That's right, I can see that." Until this point, Leonard's legs were stretched out across the bed of his seat with his back to the window. Now he swung them onto the floor. "I'm watching, and one cat circles by the goalie and he doesn't take the puck . . . he just keeps going. Then the next guy comes . . . and he does take it, and he goes up the ice."

Sean and I looked at each other. "Yeah?" I said.

"That's when it hit me: these motherfuckers have *plays. They run plays.* All their shit is *planned out.*"

"Well, yeah, Leonard," said Sean.

"What did you think?" I said.

"I don't know. Those guys are always beating the fuck out of each other. I thought that's why y'all watched it. I thought they all just put on those pads and said, 'Let's chase this fucking puck around.'"

In the laughter, Phillip said, "Wait a minute. Leonard, you thought it was all, like, a free-for-all?"

"Yup."

We were dying. "Like a big game of Kill the Carrier?" I said.

"That's right. You know, white people are crazy. I don't know what those Dudley Do-Right motherfuckers do."

51

I didn't know what to do after I left Scully at the stables. I tried to calm down for a few days. I knew I had to look into Coverdale's sister. Other than the waitress, she was the obvious one. Couldn't be any of the guys or Ervin. It just couldn't.

So I went to Leonard.

"I don't know, the waitress, maybe?" I said. "It freaked me out that Scully knew about it."

"You talked to her?"

"That's the thing, man. I've been calling her and calling her. No answer, nothing. So I went to the diner and they said she moved to Ohio."

He dismissed it. "What could she know? You just met her. Even if she's a spy or whatever nonsense you're talking, she don't know about the deal or anything from back then."

"I know."

"You need to calm down."

"I know."

"Tell me again where it's at."

"Scully makes me come meet him and he tells me I'm in trouble for the sale that happened eight years ago. Then you guys get subpoenas. I hire the lawyer, Eric. He confirms they are investigating me. The feds. Scully tells me it's someone I know but he doesn't know who. I'm trying to figure out who it is."

"So, we try to figure out who it is. Start naming names."

"How's Etheridge?" He was in the army or the Marines, I knew that. "Last I saw him, he just got back from Germany."

"Can't get work. Spends all day drinking."

I looked out the window. "He's much older now, with hat on drinking wine ..."

"What?"

"Song. Never mind. What is Rolanda up to? Cove's sister?"

"She a nurse. At Riddle."

"How's she doing?"

He studied me. "She's all right. I mean, I guess so. She lives on Second Street."

"It's just Eric says I should figure out what everyone who was in the deal is doing these days."

There wasn't any hesitation. "Lemma call her and we'll go talk." He talked like Ervin. Matter-of-fact. He grabbed the phone book. Without looking at me, he said, "So the lawyer thinks some nigger flipped on you?"

I tried to respond in kind, like always. "We know someone did."

52

Lattimore was 150 years old, with an arts quad full of vast Gothic gray stone buildings, a place for fantasy. Everything was old—I joined a fraternity that was turning ninety. It had composite pictures of all the guys dating back to the twenties. I stared at them for hours. They had F. Scott Fitzgerald collars and straw hats and bow ties. There was nothing as weird and funny to me as pissing on all of that tradition. I learned the word "nihilist" and thought that's what we were. Someone stole a sorority composite picture and we burned it on our porch.

School was easy for me. I lived in a triple room with Stoney and Gilchrist. Stoney's real name was Rossiter and he was from Upstate New York. He got his name for obvious reasons. Gil was from Jersey. I came home early from the bars one night because I had to finish a paper for modern American history. The guys were in the class, too, and they were waiting for me. They hadn't started their papers.

"What are you doing?" I said.

"We're dead," said Gil. The books from the class were lying around the room. We all shared them, saving money for beer.

"I still got to finish my own," I said.

"C'mon, man," said Stoney. He was sitting on a beanbag and had a bong next to him. "Help us out, Jo-bob."

"Show me the questions again." Gil handed me a piece of paper.

1. *"Harry S. Truman's form of liberalism sowed the seeds of America's decline in the remainder of the twentieth century." Comment.*

> *2. Discuss the political, international, economic, and social bases for your answer to #1.*

"Doesn't even make sense," I said. I remembered looking at the question before. "It's either an answer or a comment."

Gilchrist threw his hands out wide. "That's the same thing I said!" Stoney held a lighter to his bong. "Put that down," I said. I held the exam where they could both see. "Okay, look. First, you do an introduction where you say the statement is right—they always want you to do that. That's how these professors are—they're all writing some book and the class is just about the book." I hit it with the back of my hand. "Then, look. He organizes the answer for you. You guys are not morons. You can do this. Make the four parts of the question the outline of your paper."

Blank stares.

I grabbed a pen and began to write. "After the introduction, there's four parts, right? Political is section one, International is section two . . . get it?"

"Aahh," said Stoney.

"Yeah, but then what?" said Gilchrist. "What do we write?"

I pointed around the floor. "Just look at the books. Look at the stuff I highlighted—you know, copy the shit in and put it in quotes and repeat it in your own words. Put something about England in the international section, McCarthy in the political . . . like that."

"What's 'social'?" said Gilchrist.

"Like Vietnam," said Stoney.

"That's international, fucknuts," said Gilchrist.

"No, man. Hippies." He handed him the bong. "Think about it."

I shook my head and went to my side of the room. "Just make sure you both don't copy the same sections."

We drank all day in the TV room in the basement and played euchre, a five-card bidding game. We put grain alcohol in trash cans and mixed it with Kool-Aid. We gave it to girls who passed out and sometimes threw up on themselves as they slept it off in bedrooms nicknamed The Cave and The Barn and The Sportsmen's Lounge. We did coke when we could afford it and without any guilt—it was before Len Bias died.

The best thing was the robes. We had ceremonial outfits handed down over the ages. They were purple and white with gold trim. There was a special one for the Grand Sage, which was red around the collar. They were supposed to be locked up during the year and only come out for Initiation Ceremony in the spring, which was meant to be an almost religious rite. It has become so bastardized over the years that all we did was lock the pledges in the third-floor bathroom for two days before bringing them out one by one. We blindfolded them and pretended we were throwing them into a fire, and then they were spun around at the last second and told to pray. On the ground, they got smashed with a paddle and that was it. They were in.

But we used the robes all year long. Guys wore them when we had happy hours. For a while, you got to wear the red collar if you got laid the night before. Then whoever fucked the fattest girl got to wear it. Then it was the ugliest, then after that there was no reason. We took mushrooms and ran around campus in the middle of the night. I liked to climb on statues with no underwear—free-balling it in just the robes of Sigma Pi.

53

That nigger Mumia Abu-Jamal says, "MOVE is a family of revolutionaries, founded in Philadelphia in the late sixties/early seventies, who oppose all that this system represents. . . . To them, this system was a death system involved in a death style. To them, everything this system radiated was poison—from its technological waste to its destruction of the earth, to its destruction of the air and water, to its destruction of the very genetic pool of human life and animal life and all life."

This, about the city that Penn built.

Penn told the people to build in the middle of the lots. He would not like row homes, the ones you see everywhere in Philadelphia.

A greene country towne which would never be burnt, and always be wholesome.

"Let it burn," the police and firemen said. And they let sixty-one houses burn.

54

Rolanda Coverdale was thick bodied like Henry, her face was that black black, African black, and she had gold hoop earrings. She was just off work, still in whites. The inside of the house had bookshelves and narrow ebony African statues, the ones with long limbs, the females with cone-shaped breasts. There were all sorts of framed photos of two boys, one a high school graduation photo from Fallcrest, a big thick kid strangled by a tie under a black mortarboard with a red-and-gold tassel.

Back when the deal went down she had thanked me profusely with a long letter. She told me she would use the money to send her boys to college. I never followed up with her, something that trailed me like the ache of an easy chore not done, like vitamins not taken. I told myself it was because I didn't want to play savior, the white sugar daddy beneficiary, coming to take a victory lap in a Gregory Peck white suit and black-rimmed glasses. But the real reason was I didn't want to get involved. I was too busy with myself. I felt good about it and wanted, ultimately, to leave it at that.

She was nervous. Leonard made small talk.

"What's Harold doin'?"

"Oh, God knows," she said. She was soft-spoken and smiled when Leonard reminded her of Harold, whoever he was. She was very dignified. I felt terrible. "What can I do for you gentlemen?"

"Well, thanks for seeing us."

"Oh please. It's good to see you. I've been meaning to write you a letter about the boys and telling you how they've been and all . . ."

"No, that's fine," I said. "I've been meaning to come by myself." Then after a second, I asked, "Are they good?"

"Great. Bobby's supposed to get home in a minute. Maybe you'll see him."

Leonard saw that I was awkward and said, "Listen, we need to know if anyone has come by to talk to you or anything like that."

"You mean," she nodded at me, "about y'all?" Rolanda considered Leonard a part of the JKD deal because he was the one who explained everything to her. I didn't blame Leonard if he took a little credit, it would have been only natural. It would have been only Leonard. I wondered if she had been hot enough eight years ago for him to take a crack at her. That kind of stuff a white guy can't know: the stuff between black women and black men, the attraction, the sex, the power relationship. Sex drive and secrets. Lots of big talk. They almost taunt each other, really. But somewhere there's acquiescence.

"Yeah," he said.

"No." Her eyes darted from him to me and back. "Other than when they gave me those papers. When I called you all. Is that what you mean?"

"No, no," said Leonard. "My dad's been talking to you about that, right?"

"Yes. He said I should talk to Mr. Coleman, and I have spoken to him. Tell you the truth, I called him when you said y'all wanted to see me."

"Listen, Rolanda," I said. "We—I—probably shouldn't even be here. But, I am in trouble for some reason I can't figure out. I asked Leonard if we could come see you because . . . well, because I am just trying to find out what they are going to say I did wrong and who . . ." I stopped.

She figured it out. "And who is talking to the police?" She looked at Leonard. He nodded. Her face dropped and her eyes looked at her wall, light brown, clean, immaculate wall. She looked back at me hard.

"Well, it isn't me. I would hope you wouldn't think that."

"No, no. Of course," I said.

She was tearing up. "I am grateful to you guys for what you did. I would never talk to anyone."

"Don't trip," Leonard. "We know. We just running things down. Like private eyes, you know what I'm sayin'? We Starsky and Hutch. Which one are you?" he asked me.

The door opened and Bobby came in. It took my breath away. He was the image of Cove. He looked at us suspiciously.

"Say hello to Mr. Knight and Mr. Polk."

"Man," said Leonard. "You getting big, boy." Bobby smiled a little at Leonard. I shook his meaty hand. His hair was shaved close to his scalp. I thought of Cove, how he never grew an Afro like the other guys. About his kufi cap, about MOVE, about what it must be like for this kid.

"Get the trash from the kitchen and take it out," she said to him. He left. Rolanda turned back to us and said, "I don't understand all of this—Leonard, I never really knew what the hell went on back in the day when you got me the money. I always just assumed it was a gift from God. Maybe Henry and my sisters were getting it to me somehow."

"I know," said Leonard.

"Now I got a lawyer and he's telling me I might have to go to the grand jury and what not." She hesitated. "I'm very confused."

I nodded.

"But I will tell you this," she said. "If somebody diming you, it ain't me."

55

Janice is not to blame. Our married life pre-Tia wasn't very long. We bought a new house in Gladwynne, a refurbished barn on an acre with stone chimneys and a long driveway and a study where I set up a computer and desk and thought of projects for my new career as a teacher. We took trips to St. Maarten and Jamaica and I took her to Paris over the New Year's holiday, when it was freezing. We walked around Montmartre and shopped and drank coffee and talked about not needing the rat race of America.

Janice told me she was pregnant a week before our second anniversary. I didn't read any books about what to expect when you're expecting. I didn't feel like I could learn anything in some book about raising a kid. I still don't. I listened to all of the crap you get from anyone who has kids. When I meet a pregnant woman, I make it a point not to tell her anything. If it's a guy with a pregnant wife, I tell him, "You'll be fine. People have been making babies for a long, long time."

There was this one lady, on a plane, once, when I was going to Boston. She asked me if I had kids and I said one was on the way. "Enjoy it now," she said. That usually pisses me off, when people feel the need to give you the unsolicited long lens, the wisdom of their years. But she surprised me by sparing me the lecture. She got totally cool all of a sudden, like a friend, a real friend, somebody who talks to you in a normal way. "Here's the deal: You haven't lived till you have kids. That's all I will say. You haven't lived. Everything else is bullshit."

We had Tia on a scalding hot day in August. Tia O'Malley Knight. We wanted a name that would stand out among all the bullshit names Main Line people give their kids, and also remembered Dottie and Janice's parents. She had one dimple like me and the rest of her was her mom.

Maybe I'm just a callous sonofabitch, but the truth is I didn't burst out crying when Tia came out. And I can't say it was the happiest moment of my life, like all those faggots at the dinner parties say. I was too stunned by the violence of it. I kept thinking of *Blue Lagoon* when that guy says to Brooke Shields, "Why did you have a baby?" It got real too fast. The abstraction of the womb, the fat tummy, the hands around the stomach in the maternity dress in the car with her head to the side daydreaming and watching the trees go by on one of the country roads no one thinks of as Philadelphia, it was gone, right before my eyes, as the hair of the head and then the shoulders pushed through, a skinny pink cartilage and marrow mess, eyes blind with gook all over her, blood and shit and urine and embryonic fluid and water and plasma and Pitocin and God knows what else left behind on that cloth, that hospital cloth, that blue-gray hospital cloth. Women tell other women, "Don't let him watch, because once you do it's not the same." It's true but it's not what they think. It's not the loose, stretched-out pussy, the Paradise Lost, the no more hair-pulling-fucking for fear that Junior will come in. It's not the Mom jeans or the are you finished yet, then hurry up and come. You should know it's true. I came for you, for you, I came for you.

It was more primal. It was that I was not ready for the expansion of the horizon or the vertical and lateral tearing. I could not take the stretching and the burning and the screaming. I did not cry with love because I was thinking only of how loud it was and how fast it was happening. I don't know what you call it when there are shrieks and metal being inserted into the flesh and a person shitting on a table with human fluids running out, but I call it war or something like that.

It all went away, of course, when Tia was in a yellow onesie and scrubbed and patted with powder and gentle shampoo and oils and ointments. The fear from the moment never went away for me, but the later moments, with Tia, at least, helped me wear the responsibility. I recovered a little of what I'd lost; I thought I could be a real guy. I went to the first appointments with the pediatrician and saw the first shots, inoculations against the world. I carried the bassinet and I did feedings in the middle of the night. I could get her to sleep by singing, like magic.

As she got older, my favorite time with Tia was after Janice said her good nights, after she was done with the face washing, teeth and hair brushing. After the princess pajamas went on and she and Janice had their own good-bye, their own snuggle good night. Then I got in bed with her and we read or she said, "Snuggle me this way," and turned her back and I put my arms around her and smelled her hair and that's when I sang, real low, real soft,

You are my sunshine,
My only sunshine.
You make me happy
When skies are gray
You'll never know dear
How much I love you.
Please don't take
My sunshine away.

"Hap-py" and "Skies are gray" are the parts where my voice cracked if I sang fast or too loud. But I found that if I did it just above a whisper, like singing just above a talking voice, it sounded okay. I remembered this from Johnny Carson, who said he couldn't sing a note. But before he left the air, he sang with Bette Midler. She started singing his favorite song and he joined in. He simply softened, slowed down, and sang it just above his talking voice. It was beautiful. I sang like that to Tia.

Every night she said, "Daddy, will you lay with me?" Each time it was a fresh question, like she expected me to say no. Once, Tia had a new pink blanket. She wasn't used to its dimensions yet. It was huge and the way it covered her made her smile with her eyes closed. It's that moment I think about now. I miss all of those moments with my little girl, my flesh and blood, who is not ash, who is my only hope. The one who makes me smile when I think of her because there is some ignition of life in my center when she enters my mind's eye. Not an apparition or a vision. Those big round and brown beautiful eyes.

"I'm going to sleep like this." She held the blanket over her head with her arms stretched out straight. She was under it like a tent.

"You have to get to sleep, it's late."

"Okay. But I don't want you to leave."

"I'm not leaving, hunnybunny." I squeezed her.

"Okay, here's what I will do. I'll put it up like a tent but I will try to sleep. I'll hold my hand outside." She put her little hand on the outside of the corner she was holding up closest to me. "If I have one finger up, that means I'm still awake and you should talk to me."

"Okay."

"If I have two fingers up that means I'm asleep and you can go."

56

The season moved quickly. We kicked everyone's ass. We were fun to watch. The school was on fire for us. Phillip was a superstar, but all five starters were great. Leonard was a beast off the bench and Mike, Sean, and Cove all were playing well. They repainted the lane and the lines and the fans started throwing red and gold streamers after the first bucket, like they do at the Palestra. The *Daily Times* ran a photo of the starting five plus Leonard all with their hands on a ball. The caption said, "All for One and One for All at Fallcrest."

Our gym held about two thousand and it was almost full when we played Haverford. Scully stole it on their first possession, made the layup, and we pressed. It was 6-0 within a minute and they called time-out. Garrison knocked three down by the end of the first quarter and we didn't look back. We were up by twenty going into the fourth for the fifth game in a row. I was in with Leonard, Sean, Mike, and Coverdale. With four minutes left, Casale turned to Marlowe and Beatty and said, "Okay, you two, get Sean and Mike." They came bounding in from the table like a couple of golden retrievers with goggles.

The crowd loved them. I was worried at first because you could actually hear people laughing. When I crossed half-court, I hit Leonard on the wing and he swung it back to me. I looked at Cove on the other wing but flipped to Marlowe inside instead. He had pinned his guy nicely and had inside position, but he wasn't ready and the pass nailed him in the head. His goggles went up around his eyes. The Haverford point guard grabbed it and started up court. Marlowe chased him with the goggles all cockeyed on his face. The gym went crazy. I looked over and the guys on the bench were standing and laughing and clapping.

A few days later I knew something was wrong when Garrison's dad walked out of the gym with Lou Scott. He was red-faced, more than usual. He wore corduroy pants, the ones with the thick cords that WASPy people wear. He was crisp, alpine. He said things like, "Get in there, Jeremy," and "Shoot it." Mr. Garrison liked me. He wore tortoiseshell glasses. I wondered if that meant anything about hiding. He didn't speak to many people, but he talked to me. It wasn't that he was mean. He asked me where I was going to college and I told him I was looking at Lattimore. "Good school," he said. But he was hesitant. "Lots of Jews, you know."

Garrison had been caught playing hooky at the Brandywine Race-track on a Tuesday afternoon with Stuey. One of Garrison's dad's clients was there with a bunch of other businessmen on some outing. Jeremy knew he was busted as soon as he saw the guy. He stayed with Stuey through the fifth race. Garrison's dad, Lou, and Casale decided on a five-game suspension.

Leonard started against Marple because Garrison was suspended. We still dogged them, even without Jeremy. When you broke it down, Leonard really was almost as good as Jeremy, better in some ways. Better on defense, definitely. My normal job was to rest Scully, so with Garrison out, I rested Leonard, which meant Scully and I were in the game together, which didn't happen much. We trapped their point guard twice in a row and took the ball from him. When I made the layup after the second steal, Scully slapped hands with me and said, "Yeeeeah, buddy. Good job."

The suspension didn't hold. Garrison was only out of the starting lineup for two more games. I knew Casale was hedging his bets because he let Garrison get dressed to play even though he was suspended. Once it was a little bit close the second time we played Ridley, Casale got him back in there—so much for five games—and he stepped up and drilled three jumpers. That was it. Casale said to me, "Maybe I'll give him twenty bucks for the next time he goes to Brandywine."

Casale put Marlowe and Beatty in with three minutes to go in a blowout against Chichester. I got it to Marlowe around the box and he got whacked and the ref called it. He went to the line. Before he took the ball, Beatty came over, waited a second for effect, and then they pointed at each other. The idiots had planned a little show for the crowd. Marlowe got the ball from the ref and drained the foul shot. Beatty came over and they did the pointing number again. Marlowe hit the second. The crowd went crazy.

Then Beatty got fouled. They did the same little routine. Beatty made the foul shot. As Marlowe came up to do it again, a guy, a geek nine rows behind the scorer's table, stood up, "Soul Patrol!" It was parody, ironic, a send-up of their whiteness. Beatty hit the second. The place went wild. On the other side of the court the black section was lit up. A chant began: "Soul Pa-trol, Soul Pa-trol, Soul Pa-trol. . . ."

I spun the guard at half-court and picked his pocket. There were only a few seconds left, so I didn't take it all the way in, looking for Marlowe. "Soul Pa-trol, Soul Pa-trol." I scooped the ball underhand and laid it out in front of him. He ran it down and made the layup.

The next game, kids from Marlowe's and Beatty's class took a bed-sheet and spray-painted "SOUL PATROL." They wore white T-shirts and goggles. They began chanting for Marlowe and Beatty in the second quarter, but everyone knew they wouldn't get in unless it was a blowout. It kept the crowd interested as we beat the piss out of everybody.

57

Pastor Steve was waiting for me on the track at the DoveCo Community College football field. He was making like he was stretching, standing with legs crossed, and bent at the waist with his fingertips not reaching his toes. He wasn't trying too hard. He didn't have a fancy track outfit—just gray sweatpants with a few paint stains on them and an old T-shirt. He had on running shoes that could have been mine, less splashy than likely to be splashed through a puddle.

"Welcome to my office," he said.

He asked me to come join him on his nightly exercise walk. It was when Janice and I were just about done. The facilities at DoveCo were new and impressive. The track was spongy and its lane lines were crisp—I still get a tactile rush when I see professional sports surfaces, the groomed grass of a football field, a fresh batters' box on baseball dirt, waxy, sneaker-squealing hardwood. New tracks are an underreported improvement since my childhood when we ran on cinders and ground-up gravel. It was a deep color, redder than a brown leather basketball and more orange than Philadelphia brick.

"So this is how you do it," I said. "You walk and they talk?"

"You figured me out. I get so fat if I don't do this. The older folks like to talk in the office, though."

"Sure," I said. "But this is good."

"I'm a terrible golfer. You must golf."

"No, not really."

Relieved, he said, "Doesn't it suck?"

I laughed. "I know."

"Want to start?"

"Sure."

We stayed in the outer lane, so we wouldn't get in the way of the kids who were running.

"I never asked you how you like teaching," he said. "Do you get anything out of it?"

"Honestly, it's just something to do."

"Do you think about going back into business?"

"I don't know. I made a killing in another time—I might as well be an expert on making men's hats for all the good my experience would do me now."

"That's the great thing about my job. There's still a demand." He moved at a nice pace. "I'm sure you could adapt to something new, no?"

"Nah. I worked in a very analog world. I like to say that I did local ads and TV commercials in a culture of warmed-over nostalgia still oriented in a solar system of limited information, conformity, and the prominence of men. My company, I don't know, I looked at it like an old-fashioned business—I tried to make more money than I lost. It turned out that was valuable in this gigantic transition that is still sweeping over us all. I couldn't do anything now. I don't recognize this world."

"What do you teach, then?"

"I teach them how to start a company. You know, the intuitive things that someone doesn't really have to teach them, but that's a lot of what business school is. Filing for a d/b/a or an LLC. Opening a bank account. Hiring people, getting an accountant. Figuring out what to do for yourself and what to pay someone else to do. I throw in a little—very little—shit about advertising. Stories about the old days. War stories." We were under the big scoreboard at the far end zone. "I gotta tell you, teaching for me is limited to that. Give them a few useful tips and tell them stories and stare at them. They're aggressive kids. They will fill in meaning for themselves. It's like that Peter Sellers movie."

He looked at me. The goalpost was behind him, yellow bars shooting up into the air. "*Being There*?"

"That's it."

"Love that movie."

We started into the turn back toward the grandstands.

"Yeah, I just say things and"—I snapped my fingers—"there they go."

He laughed. "You're kind of depressed, I think."

"Yeah, I am."

"Listen," he said, "I've beaten around the bush, but I think this is the part of the show when I finally ask you what your thoughts are about it."

"What's 'it'? My marriage?"

"I was thinking God." He lifted his hands up and pointed to himself. "You know? My turf."

"Oh yeah, God."

"I know you have a view. Don't tell me you don't."

"Well," I said, "I never knew my parents. My aunt raised me, and she was Catholic, but she didn't make me go to church. I did once in a while to make her happy."

"But you're not drawn back?"

"No," I said. "I'm glad Janice has gotten into it with you. Didn't ever think she'd become a Protestant, though. I guess you never know."

"We get a lot of transfer business," he said. "My read is that, more and more, I don't think it is easy to buy the idea that the wine is really blood."

"Her old man is not happy."

"Yeah, they're usually not."

It was sunset. Steve was showing sweat under his neck and in the armpits.

"I'm thinking about trying to be a Quaker," I said.

He considered this. "Interesting. That could be good for you." Two girls were playing catch with lacrosse sticks, cradling the ball six or seven times before throwing it back. The one closer to us had braces with bright yellow rubber bands. "Do they still wear kilts when they play their games?"

"I think they do," I said. "Do you want to ask me about Janice? About splitting up?"

"If you want to talk about it." I didn't say anything. "Look, I'm going to say the standard thing: Do you want to see a therapist? Do you want to talk to me together, the three of us?"

After a few strides, I said, "Steve, I just think I'm done."

"Why?"

"The truth is, I've been faking it the whole time."

"Do you really feel that way?"

"It's tough to explain. It's . . . I don't think I'm broken. I think I'm not able to do it. Like, I don't know . . . like the same way I can't fly, or something. And I tried once. Like, jumped off a roof and got all smashed up. After that you don't make the mistake of trying to fly again."

"I get it."

"Everything is different, and you know you were kidding yourself when you climbed the ladder the first time. That's what it's like. I know better. And the fucking truth is I knew better. Excuse my language."

He kept his gaze ahead, listening but not reacting, other than a small nod, which was barely more than the rhythm his head was lightly bobbing as we walked. "It has something to do with not having parents. And something to do with losing my aunt."

"Why do you want to try to be a Quaker, if you see it as bleak as you do? You're looking for something."

"No. I think it's practical. Maybe I'm wrong. I think they know the limits of faith. 'Row to shore' and all that."

"Yeah," he said. "Well, look"—he paused to look at the grandstand, and changed the subject—"you want to do the stairs?"

I shrugged.

"Yeah," he said. "Forget that. There's no need to be fanatics, right?"

"Right."

"Okay, one more lap?"

"Sure."

We began walking again.

"What were you going to say?" I said.

"Yeah, look, all I was going to say was if you're done, you're done. People get divorced."

I nodded.

"You have to prepare for the aftermath and take care of your responsibilities, that's all. Make sure Tia is okay. Janice, too. Whatever your spiritual issues are, keep them separate. You don't have to believe in God to get married and you don't have to give up God to get divorced, even with kids. Maybe you'll feel differently as you get older."

"Sounds right, except for the last part. I don't think it's going to change. It's a full stop."

58

By mid-February, we could clinch the Central League by beating Conestoga at home. We had won fifteen in a row. Scouts were at every game, and each of the starters plus Leonard was being chased by recruiters. We were packing twenty-eight hundred people into our gym, a nightmare place for other teams to play. The noise was insane. Girls screamed at Phillip. I told him he was one of the Beatles.

The black kids stomped their feet like it was a revival. They did call-and-response cheers. White people did not understand. "Sar-dines . . . uh huh . . . and pork and beans." They repeated it, clapping, till Kenny Mosely stood up and sang, "Sardines on my plate, 'cause I can't afford no steak."

Conestoga didn't have anyone who could stay within a hundred miles of Stokes. When he got it going on, there wasn't much any high school kid anywhere could do. We were up four in the second quarter when we made a turnaround from the low post. He noticed something as everyone headed the other way; he played possum for a step, looking out of the corner of his eye at their guard, starting back for the inbounds pass.

After a bucket, we are conditioned to look away from the ball. It's from TV. When a basket is made during a televised game, the camera cuts to the guy who scored. It happens on the court, too: players start back the other way and attention leaves the ball for a microsecond. Stokes moved at that moment and made a quick steal, a smooth larceny. Before the guy—MacMillan, actually, who *was* white and slow, after all—could catch it, Stokes tipped it away, toward the foul line, where it bounced quietly, like a pretty girl standing alone on the dance floor.

He corralled it with his right hand and transferred it to his left in an instant. One dribble and then took two strides. One, two. With his left leg lifted, he planted on the right, the rock cradled in his left arm like his little brother in a headlock, and he split his legs in the air like a gymnast on the balance beam. He extended, the ball crooked back behind his head as he flew toward the hole. The tip of his left elbow was six feet four inches from the toe of his right shoe, parallel in the air to the baseline, forty-six inches from court to body. He flew. It was flight. I saw it.

It all contracted in an instant. His legs scissored back together, the right arm came down as the left thundered through, and his center overcame the basket. He made a big "O" with his mouth and shouted from his very middle, the bottom of the diaphragm, the center of his core, playing a game, *the* game, the one that he was meant to play, precisely because he could do things like this, things of grace and surprise. He said, "AAAAAAAAAH."

A photograph from that moment hung in the trophy cabinet at the entrance of Fallcrest High School for the next twenty-four years, until a construction project moved it to a cardboard box in a storage closet near the maintenance room. In the background of the photograph, a tenth-grader—who lived on the block next to Phillip Ford and said hi to Phillip whenever he saw him and told people that Phillip was such a cool guy because he always said hi right back—was coming out of his bleacher seat, his eyes widening, his arms shooting out of their sockets, as Stokes smashed the ball through the cylinder.

They never got closer than eight. With a minute and a half left, the nerds started working on the "Soul Patrol" chant. Everyone watched Casale, who left the starters in as it wound down under a minute. Phillip got fouled.

Leonard grabbed my arm. "Want to see this place go off?"

I was dying to get in the game and didn't really acknowledge him. I stared at Casale to let him know I wanted to get in. Leonard shoved something in my hand. It was a pair of goggles like Marlowe and Beatty wore. He had a pair in his hands, too.

"What, *wear* these?"

"Wait till we get out there."

Phillip made the first one and put us up by nine. It was safe. The chant was taking over the whole building: "SOUL PATROL, SOUL PATROL, SOUL PATROL . . ." Casale turned to the bench and said, "Okay, Joe, Leonard, Marlowe, Beatty, go ahead. Get everybody but Phillip."

We ran to the scorer's table to check in. Marlowe and Beatty put their goggles on. We went on the floor and the crowd went berserk. Scully, Stokes, Garrison, and Herman were coming out of their last home game. The clock was stopped. It took a few minutes to get us in, because the scorer, who had a good sense of drama, sent us one by one, hitting the buzzer each time. The refs let us have the celebration and the fans loved it. We slapped and grabbed and hugged the starters as they passed us on their way to the bench, where they were bear-hugged by Casale.

Since Phillip was on the line, he didn't come out. That's when Leonard Polk had his finest moment. He had an extra pair of goggles for Phillip. Before the refs could settle everyone down for the second shot, Leonard went to Phillip and slipped him the glasses. He motioned toward me. Phillip understood right away. With twenty-eight hundred people hanging from the rafters, he put the basketball down on the floor, took out the goggles, and strapped them on his head. Leonard and I did the same thing at half-court. Phillip kept the ball on the floor and started clapping, slowly turning and applauding the crowd. He did a full circle like that. Then he bounced it three times and swished it.

The place lost its shit, stomping and pointing and yelling and throwing cups of Coke in the air. The guys in geek section, the heart of the Soul Patrol movement, hyperventilated. Casale stood at the scorer's table with his hands on his hips, not knowing exactly what to do. Scully and Stokes came over and grabbed him. They were laughing so hard, Casale gave up being mad and just started smiling.

They brought it up and missed and Marlowe grabbed the rebound. I came and got it and walked it up. We had about twenty seconds. I handled it out front and waited for Phillip to come through on the left side. I planned to hit him for one last jumper, one last basket for Phillip Ford,

All-American. Beatty set a screen and Phillip got it with six seconds left. He squared up, but he didn't shoot. He dribbled back toward me and gave Leonard a nod. Leonard read it and floated out to the wing. Phillip took a hard step toward the goal, forcing the defense to collapse, and flipped it to Leonard, now open twenty feet from the bucket.

Leonard lifted up and let it go. He was a collage of goggles and perfect Afro and skinny-ass frame, a crazy chocolate inchworm going into the sky. It hit the center of the basket, splashing cord, nothing, as they say, but net. You couldn't have written it.

59

Janice set the old house up as a petting zoo for Tia's second birthday party. Two guys—a sketchy-looking farmer from Horsham and his scrawny son—came with a trailer full of lambs and calves. The animals were put inside wire fences with hay all over the grass for the droppings.

I never saw Janice happier. She had a bandanna wrapped as a do-rag. Her blue-black hair against the navy cloth was like the Union army in the nighttime. She bounced from child to mother to child, bringing baby pigs to little boys and wine and beer to the parents. And she seemed to touch everything that came out of the trailer. You can tell a lot about a woman by her ease with animals. Janice was in the moment. She was from the earth and the middle and the sky.

Tia had so much Dottie in her, that was the thing. There's a photo from that day. Janice is holding a bunny up to Tia, who is standing transfixed. I took it, that photo, and when I look at it it's all there for me. My three girls. Past, present, and future. Tia so like Dottie: pudgy little body, thin brown hair with the eggshell beret, old-fashioned party dress, blue to match Mommy's long-sleeved T-shirt, the kind found in the clean, sleek stores in the good malls. Janice delighted and in love with the day. Tia the brand-new face with Irish eyes.

I took it because it jumped at me, but I didn't know till I looked at it developed. Tia stood with her two hands in front of her, chest level, bent with fingers forward, the way Dottie did when she was talking in the A&P, or collecting a one-dollar bet on the Phillies from a janitor or the postman. It was my whole life in that picture. Dottie and Tia and Janice in the middle. They are all girlie girls, my girls. That's my kind. My kind of girl.

But when I look at it, I also feel shitty in part because it is the only one—the only photo of Tia's childhood I have kept. I guess everyone takes photos and videos, but, at least when it comes to keeping records of children, women are the custodians more than men. I know why this is—I know it factually, mathematically, like a done proof. I can't speak for the future—the world of wallet-size school photos and Plexiglas picture frames on desks is almost certainly gone—but in my lifetime, women have collected children's images more than men. It is because it hurts less. When I go to the house and look around at the dozens of photos Janice has spread on mantels and shelves and bookcases, in all sizes and variations of print and frame, I see a lovely family smiling back. Janice is good enough to keep me in the pictures, not cutting or Photoshopping me out. I crawl inside the cliché of the divorced father. I look at Tia smiling in third grade, in soccer uniform, at a Phillies game, at the zoo, with Ray and Grandma, in Disneyworld. I am there in front of the Eiffel Tower, on the sky deck of the Empire State Building, with her on my chest at three months, holding her up to stand on fat little legs at the beach. And when I look at each picture, I only remember being not happy. I only remember feeling stuck, irritable, grouchy. I remember from all those years, all those photos, only anxiety and impatience, discomfort and unease. Moments before each still was captured, I was either complaining or counting the moments till the next thing—whatever it could have been, dinner, a taxicab back to the hotel, the merciful last out of the last inning—would relieve me. I knew for me that I could never be the keeper of these photos because they only mean pain. All this freedom and success have only translated into not being able to look at baby pictures, grade school wallet keepers, graduation cap and gown fulfillment photos. Janice and women like her have to organize those things. I can be terribly lazy but this is not that—this is pain.

I love Tia, believe me. I called her Goo Goo until, at the apartment on the first weekend I had her alone, she told me she was too old for that. It reminded me of when she was three and I was getting her dressed. I put her little white socks on and was preparing the little white-buckled shoes when she protested.

"No." She held her feet out from the bed and pointed at the toes. "No."

"What?"

She lifted her toes up again. "No, Daddy."

The little inseam of the socks was only halfway across the line of her toes. The socks weren't on totally right. I adjusted them and reached for the shoes.

"No!"

She spurted tears of rage. They still weren't right. I had to take them off and put them on again for the inseam to be just so.

There was an implication in it. That I was not serious, that I was correctable. There was the impression that only her mommy could do it right, that I was more than silly. That when it came to serious stuff, I was the child. You can't tell me that wasn't from Janice. When I felt shit like that I wanted to leave, to be by myself. Say the names: Janice, Tia, Joe. Which one sounds different? I felt like they didn't need me anyway, and as it went on it would only get worse, till I was this wandering oaf in my own house, doing battle with the Matron and her lieutenant, and the nannies and housekeepers, a weird eunuch in the convent.

Tia got bigger and Janice got bored. You can't keep a person like Janice in that job, the Mom/Housewife job. She was devoted, but the other moms drove her bananas. She went through nannies, never deciding whether she really wanted one or not. She harassed the guys who worked on the house. And gradually she became one of them: one of those precise, severe bitches exacting from other understimulated, exacting mothers the specifics of how, when, and where things were to be done. I went further inside, no help whatsoever.

We tried to stem the tide. I bought an even bigger house on Penn's Meade Farm Road in Dartwynne. We still got along and we loved Tia like crazy. But it went cold. She knew it, I knew it, and she knew I knew it. It was like gravity. Her hair got shorter, her ass got fatter, and I drifted away. People always say they're best friends. "She's my best friend,"

They say, with an Internet dating service commercial look. I loved Janice in some ways—appreciated her sometimes, felt sorry for her at others. But that's not love. What we had wouldn't be adorable to watch in a commercial.

Construction guys came all day long, seven days a week, for a year. I don't know when it was, about halfway through probably, on a Saturday. Two electricians were in the bedroom and I was lying on the couch in the living room. Tia was coloring across the room, deep in the carpet. I looked at her. I knew at that moment.

It was like the blackest coal, blue-black coal, took over my insides, like my rib cage became petrified rock. I thought, I am a scumbag and I am going to leave her. Alone like I was alone. I can't believe it. I . . .

This hour I tell things in confidence, I might not tell everybody but I will tell you . . .

And you know you gotta go,
On that train from Dublin up to Sandy Row.

"What kind of person wants to be alone?" That's what Janice asked me when I told her I was out. "What kind of asshole doesn't want to be with his kid?"

I told Tia: *You are my sunshine, my only sunshine, you make me happy, when skies are gray, you'll never know dear, how much I love you, Please don't take my sunshine away.*

Knight Out.

60

During the JKD years—the Disintegration years, I like to say—I drank with Mike at the Southpaw Tavern in Penwood when I wasn't working. He was a janitor at Habbersett's, the place where they make scrapple. It's a combination of every part of the pig that is unthinkable: balls, nails, colon, snout, penis, nipples, hoof, heart, liver, anus. Scrapple comes in a package in plastic wrap and gets cooked on a griddle. You eat it with ketchup.

He blew any money he made on the usual bullshit: trips to Atlantic City, betting games, drinking. I lent him money to buy a condo, which he did at the wrong time, ending up way upside down. Then he was just an unemployed, depressed, drunken Irish guy in the Reagan recession. He went to college at Shippensburg but dropped out under bad circumstances. Four drunken morons from his fraternity pulled a train on a girl from Erie visiting for the weekend. Mike was with them. He told me he blacked out and couldn't remember if he tagged in or not. "I guess I did," was all he said.

He got arrested, the whole deal. One of the guys was from Upper Darby and had an old man who owned a diner—they're all Greeks over there. The father gave a lawyer twenty-five thousand bucks in cash and after about a year of bullshit they all got off with probation. Mike brought me with him to see the kid's old man, who had driven up to Shippensburg and bailed them out. His name was Stavros. He came out of the kitchen and gave Mike a hug. He called him Michael through a thick Greek voice. It was a father's hug. It shot through me, this immigrant and protective and forgiving kindness of a stranger.

When JKD got big—before I sold it but after we were doing well—I put five grand in an envelope and drove to Upper Darby. I gave it to the girl behind the counter before Stavros got in for the day.

"You want to know the key to life?" Mike said at the Southpaw.

"Shoot."

"Never tell anyone what you really think."

61

"**Y**ou have no idea how many younger guys with lots of money I'm seeing get in trouble," said Eric.

"Like criminal trouble?"

"Criminal, SEC, civil suits. Everything."

He liked me to come to his office at the end of the day so we could talk. He was lonely; his kids were away at school and his wife was a busy environmental lawyer. I got the feeling she represented bug companies, like the oil companies, and she wasn't around much. "Different worlds of dirt," he said.

He reflected when we talked. He was resigned to a world without pity. "We all thought we were changing the world when I was a kid—all the clichéd stuff you read about, it's true. But it's exaggerated. I enjoyed the cases. I'm not much of a crusader anymore. Life takes the crusade out of you."

"You're back from the Crusades."

"Yup. I represent rich people in trouble. I won a few cases down here and now they come to me from all over." He looked over his glasses, smiling. "But mostly from New York. That's where they keep the money."

"Right."

"I still like the fight." I felt sorry for him. "I guess I'm interested in the whole issue of imposing rules."

"And you think it's different now?"

"It's a scary time, bubs. It's magic time for too many of these guys—they are inventing their own rules. I represent the layer underneath the famous people—there are a shitload of people making less than a billion but more than anyone needs. And some of them did dumb things. When you see the size of the money, you understand." He looked at me. "Well, shit, you would understand. Look, people in this country never made fifty, sixty million in one pop before. Especially not when they were under thirty. It hasn't happened in all of human history."

"People can't handle it?"

"Almost no one. It's got to be bad, all this money. Like fertility drugs. Not natural. Can't be good. Anyway, in business, it used to be that big money—even the amount you got—was ground out over the course of a life. And then only by a few very, very ruthless people—most of whom already had a lot of money. But they did it under a system, more or less."

"But there have been booms before."

"Not like this. This is bankers fucking around. Not just stockbrokers and snake oil salesmen—this is the real money guys. There's never been this kind of ability to extract so much from the well. Wall Street is just a big laboratory, dear boy. Those guys might as well have lab coats on. They're sorcerers. All they do is look for newer and better formulas. The markets have been gamed by these fuckers. And some young guys are getting really rich. And most of them can't handle it." He twirled his glasses in a circle. "Plus, people want to nail them. I haven't seen it yet where the money that goes to one of those guys doesn't come out in a very painful way. Emotionally, physically—they get sick. Spiritually, most of all . . . but you don't want to hear me go on about that."

"So I'm typical?"

"Well, not really. You're earlier and you're smaller. Your money is not that big. I'm sure you'll make it back—if you decide you want to. And you're in Philadelphia. Most of my cases are in New York and California. I've been to San Francisco six times since the summer—I could have an office out there. But with all the old money down there you'd be surprised how much trouble people can get into without leaving Philly."

He looked out the window. We could see City Hall. In the old days, the lawyers who controlled the city wouldn't allow anything higher than the top of William Penn. They broke the rule and the sports teams didn't win anymore. It's all about sports in this town. It's all a game; it's come to that. Walt Whitman picking through dead bodies on the ground, watching *Rollerball* and the Eagles. The Phillies finally won when Comcast stuck a figurine at the top of its building so Billy Penn's cap would once again be the highest thing there was. A figurine.

"The trouble starts after the money comes," he said. "It's the damnedest thing: guys make all this money under a system—I'm talking six or seven hundred million dollars in half a career. And they start making their own rules. Like the money makes them magic. They're in fairy-tale land." He swept a crumb off his desk and said, "If you really want to know, that's the problem—that's my concern for my kids. Wide-scale self-deception. No one has a life anymore. People think their story is more important than their life."

62

Thing about Ervin was he still wore the yellow double-knit short-sleeve that showed off his arms. This was fitting because he was always the same guy. I found him at the house by himself, something soft in the background, Charlie Parker maybe. He had a TV tray out and he was looking at a ball game, like Hyman Roth from that scene in *The Godfather* when he says if the money's on the table, I know I have a partner, and if it's not, I know I won't. Very calm. The house was the same, immaculate but lived in, graying and dustied a little, like Erv and Paulette, by the sheer passage of time.

He went right to it. "What's going on, man?"

"What has Leonard told you?"

"He told me you're in deep water."

"I am."

"Give it to me. From the beginning."

I told him the story. He knew about Betours, obviously. I'm sure he still had every cent I steered his way in a savings account at the Penwood branch of Penn Federal. While he was always a good man, the passage of time only made him shrewder; he was a better version of himself. The carpet was worn by people, like me, coming for advice. And you knew by the time he got to the end of life, he would have more money than anybody, outfoxing everyone. I told him about Scully.

"Inside your tent?"

"That's what he said they said."

I told him about going with Leonard to see Rolanda.

"What your lawyer say? How's he see the case?"

"He doesn't say much. He definitely doesn't say don't worry about it, I'll tell you that."

He gave a little grunt. "Well, I don't know, Joe, I haven't been in a tent since the army." He grabbed a napkin from the TV tray and wiped his mouth. "Maybe Leonard and his friends been doing some camping I don't know about."

I felt like an asshole. "Damn, you're right." I was an idiot. "You know . . . this whole thing . . . I'm going paranoid. It's probably not anyone. I shouldn't be . . ."

"Oh no, it's someone. You can bet on that."

"Huh?"

"Someone is definitely out to get you. For sure. I been around long enough to tell you that. You got that part right."

"You think so?"

"Know so."

"So what do I do?"

Just then, Paulette came into the room. "Joe, come here."

She took me out of the living room and into the hallway leading to the bedrooms. The walls were filled with the framed picture collages she loved. Dozens of photos fitted inside circles and squares in picture frames, lots more just fastened to corkboards. Shelves ran down the hall at waist level and held even more. There must have been thirty of them—graduation caps over Afros, football uniforms, little girls in tutus, Ervin in wide lapels, old ladies who looked like they were 120. She led me to a bulletin board–sized collection at the end of the hall.

"Look at this."

In the bottom right-hand corner there I was. My school picture. I was nine or ten, a hole in my smile from missing teeth.

"Look at that," I said. It was all I could say.

"Dottie gave me one every year. Me and her had school pictures of all you little rats by our sorting table." She gave a little laugh of memory.

"She always made me give her one of the five-by-eights of Leonard—you know, one of the bigger ones. Every day she had Leonard's big butt smile right in her face. She said, 'He's so cute.' You know Dottie." She shook her head. "I said, 'Girl, I'm gonna bring him over and make him stay wich you. Then you'll see how cute he is.'"

We stared at all the pictures. "Don't know where the rest are," she said.

I went back in and sat with Erv. We watched the game.

At halftime, he said, "I don't really know what to tell you. All I can say is whatever it is, I will help you if I can."

"Thanks, Erv."

"Play it out a little. And listen to that lawyer. Every dumbass I ever known went to jail thinks he had a bad lawyer. Ain't the lawyers. It's the dumbass got himself in that position to begin with."

"Okay."

"Most times, anyway." He gave a backhand to the air. "Play it out. You know, see the court."

It was a stupid cheer: "Be . . . aggressive . . . be aggressive . . . b-e-a-g-g-r-e-s-s-i-v-e . . . be aggressive." They did it during the first time-out of each game. It was sexual to me. If you are not aggressive you get nowhere in business, you probably get frustrated in life, and you get nowhere in basketball. The red underwear they wore under their cheerleader skirts were called bloomers. Not a bloomer, bloomers. Plural, like a *pair* of underwear. It's like they are protecting what's under there. You remember things like that.

Set my compass north, I got winter in my blood.

Being aggressive is not something you can teach. For my money, it comes from being poor. Some rich guys have it, but that's usually from being really fucked-up or losing all their money or both.

The one exception I've ever seen was our team. No rules like that applied. It was our world. I don't know if players know players. I kind of think you find a team, a connection, a crew, a partner or two. It can work but it can't last.

I understand the large hearts of heroes, the courage of present times and all times.

63

I was drinking in Center City with an account guy from Saatchi, down from New York. The bartender was Italian. "How come you don't see any MOVE members around here?"

"I give up."

"Because they get bombed at home."

When a brick chips, you can see that it was once clay. When it's old, it is not so much that it is chipped as it is curved—the curvature of time. The edges round, because brick disintegrates slowly. The better the brick, the slower the disintegration. The less it erodes.

In the end, they blew those dirty, loudmouthed motherfuckers away. They burned their asses to the ground.

IV
ENDINGS

No motion has she now, no force;
She neither hears nor sees;
Rolled round in earth's diurnal course.
With rocks, and stones, and trees.

—Wm. Wordsworth

64

The next step was drying the brick. They stacked them with clappers and dressers to keep them straight. After four blistering-ass hot summer days the bricks were dry enough to be put end to end. In a few weeks they could fire them up.

The one thing you know for shitsure is music is the most important. The Holy Ghost only made sense to me once I saw it as music: the motor oil, the money flow, the cartilage, and the sound track. Music is the heart of relationships and the soul of life. I got winter in my blood. They named themselves The Band. They were Dylan's band, The Dead's band, and lots of other people's band until they just became The Band. I don't know why a bunch of guys from Canada told the only American music. It's the kind of thing that was never explained to me, not by Dottie or Ervin or Casale or Harris. Artie might have told me but he got Alzheimer's.

Richard Manuel was the Holy Ghost on that squad. No one else would have pulled it off. They met in their late teens and played backup for Ronnie Hawkins and the Hawks, starting in 1961, the year I was born, the year my parents got killed. The thing about those guys was they all sang. They were together until Thanksgiving night, 1976—the Last Waltz, in San Francisco. I bought *Music from Big Pink* with tip money on a Sunday morning when I was fourteen. Richard's voice is the first thing you hear on the record in "Tears of Rage," Janice's song. He sings solo again on the last song.

Kevin Morris

They say everything can be replaced,
Yet every distance is not near.
So I remember every face
Of every man who put me here.

You had to be there to know how fucked-up disco really was. And not just that, there was all the one-hit inanity. "Billy Don't Be a Hero" and "Rock the Boat." Cheese everywhere, dripping off bell-bottoms and black-light posters. Me and Sean knew it.

We stayed in our zone of music. I still do.

I see my light come shining
From the west unto the east.
Any day now, any day now,
I shall be released.

It must mean escaping, or coming home from the war, or coming home to die. I know it means something. It must mean getting the hell home.

65

My last dinner with Betours was after the closing in New York. He took me to a Japanese place in the East Village and we ate sushi and drank hot and cold sake. At the end he said, "Ready for a little ad-venture, *mon ami?*"

"Sure."

"We are partners now, *non?*"

His driver took us downtown. I get confused below a certain point in the city, so I didn't know where we were. The car stopped in the middle of a block and we went into an old building. The house to the left had boards on the windows. Betours and I entered and were met with loud and thumping English dance music. At the end of a long set of stairs was a little oak room where people huddled over drinks. There was a bartender in the corner of the room—it was a real bar, like a speakeasy.

"This is a cool place," I said.

He asked me if vodka was okay. We were at the table only long enough for him to pound the drink. He motioned me to the back of the room and I followed him through a little dark connecting tunnel.

The other side was smoky, with reddish light, and it was hard to see. I looked down and to my right two people were fucking in a thick leather club chair. The woman was lashing the guy in the back with something that looked like a wire brush. Another guy walked by me naked from the neck down, only a leather hood. He looked like Mr. Wrestling II from *Wrestling from Florida*.

"Excuse me," said Betours. He walked away.

"You freaky motherfucker . . ." I said to myself.

I moved to the wall. My vision adjusted. It was full-on; everyone was in some state of nudity. The men were older, fat business types. The girls were hot and hard, they must have been paid for. One came up to me and said, "Kamikaze?"

The music was blaring and there wasn't much talking. I was already hammered but I slammed it down. She said, "One more, with me this time?"

She looked like the younger daughter on *One Day at a Time*. She had to yell in my ear. "Hubie said I should take care of you. Make sure you don't get lost."

"Great."

She took out a plastic thing the size of a kid's portable pencil sharpener and put it in her nose. She gave it to me and I hit it.

"You want rough?"

"What?"

She pointed to the guy getting fucked and beaten.

I put my hands up. "Not me."

We watched and then she grabbed my arm and pulled me, past the commotion, through a curtain to another section. Three more hostesses— one white, one black, one Latin—stood smoking. There was a big booth-like thing in the corner that looked like the confessional box from St. Ignatius. The *One Day at a Time* girl whispered to the others, and they giggled like I was Richie Cunningham and we were at Arnold's Drive-In on *Happy Days*. They put out their cigarettes and kept talking as they disappeared into the booth.

"Go ahead," said the *One Day at a Time* girl.

"What?"

"Go over there."

I went over to the confessional. It was made of dark wood. There were carved pictures of naked ladies.

"It's from the olden days," she said, like a lady at an antique show. It had three square openings, each the size of a baseball card. She grabbed at my crotch and got me hard. "Go ahead." I unzipped and put it into one of the holes.

The craftsmen who made that thing had thought it through—there was a wooden bar overhead to hold as you were getting serviced. First it was definitely a mouth. I started to close my eyes, like I would for a regular blow job, before I realized that was unnecessary. Then a different mouth, then hands, then I was inside something. I looked at the *One Day at a Time* girl and I couldn't remember if her name was Julie or Sam. The sister was Julie? She had the same juicy little unit as the one on TV. I reached for her and she let me. I felt her chest and kissed her and then I put her against the walnut pane. Inside the booth, I felt buttocks grinding into me slow at first, then thrusting hard. The other two had their tongues in the action. I turned the little sister around, face against the confessional, and got my fingers in. It was The Cure, that was the music, and Barbara, that was the little sister, and now Barbara was leaning against an antique, handcrafted glory hole in a speakeasy on the Lower East Side of Manhattan. I put another finger in and pulled her hair with my free hand, while I fucked one inside the confessional in the ass, and numbers two and three licked my balls. I kept at it till I brought them all off, inside and out, wet and screaming their heads out, almost busting that booth to bits.

66

I found myself getting up in the morning and driving around all day like Maria in *Play It as It Lays*. I loved that book, so fucking bleak. She calls queers "faggots." Love that. Seems so recent to have done that. I got onto 95 South, took it to Ridley Park, where I got off near the malls. I drove around endlessly, killing time, trying not to go there. I went to malls and spent forty-five minutes looking for the perfect parking spot. I wandered around looking for ATMs so I could bring cash to strip clubs.

I felt like every man in America knew exactly what happened to that guy in New York, the governor who got caught fucking whores. When the TV pundits talked and talked about what a douche bag he was, we all just sat there. But we knew. Inside we were thinking: shit, I'm forty-five—or fifty-five, or sixty-five—and every young girl I saw had her mouth on my cock or my cock in her ass until I woke up and someone was talking to me and I didn't know where I was. I got sad wondering what the fuck happened to me. I was past fifty and bringing strippers home two at a time. They were all so crazy. I got addicted to their pain, to their trapped lives. They all had someone touch them somewhere they didn't want to be touched. They dealt with it by letting everyone touch that place now. It was ripped away so why not depower it? Give it to everybody. Sell the fucker. Forget things, make like what was there was gone, that that day had passed, that ship had sailed. That it was gone. Just the soft pretzel wrappers and masked wrestlers. It's those trash can fires that the Italians and the brothers hung around in the old days. Gone.

Not that they were not practical. They could make so much more money stripping that they could never go back to the regular world. They were whores. They knew it and it occasionally troubled them. But they also knew they couldn't be receptionists or hygienists. Ask a stripper and she'll tell you it's a waste of time to go to school and bust her ass to make forty-five thousand a year answering the phone and getting tee times for a management consultant in a twelve-by-twelve box with a view of Logan's Circle, getting chatted up by messengers and IT guys until she goes with the girls to Harrigan's or Bennigan's or Whateverthefuckigan's for happy hour and she says fuck it and takes Rodney the paralegal home and bangs his brains in just for the sake of it, finding she's hornier than she realized, really letting Rodney have it, only to get to work the next day hungover and see Rodney in the lobby or in the hallway and he either ignores her, or maybe he's sweet and says hi but then he doesn't come around anymore and she has to tell the one in the cubicle next to her what happened and then it's out all over the office.

It wasn't always like that for me. I didn't use to have this self-loathing bullshit. After high school, I went on such a tear. I didn't care about anything. What I started at Lattimore I perfected when I moved home and got into business. No one could touch me. The girls I banged were so unbelievably smoking hot. I was in the perfect slot, could hit on anything. College girls are all over the place in Philadelphia. At twenty-five, twenty-six, it was on.

I met one from Haverford College, when she got back from a semester in France. I saw her at a Starbucks the summer before she left. She sent me letters in blue ballpoint pen on airmail envelopes with observant detail combined with stupid girl-shit. Like,

> *I spend my days at the Louvre—there's really so much to see—I haven't yet worked my way through the Renaissance—tellement pour voir!!!! And as for you, mister, I miss you I miss you I miss you!!!!*

She was stick-thin with tits like cantaloupes. The day she got back I met her for happy hour. We went back to her apartment after two vodkas with cranberry. She pulled her shirt off on top of me and I turned on my side so I wouldn't bust my bolt. I had pulled down some pussy in my lifetime, but this was stunning. I was actually passive, caught in the headlights a bit.

I didn't push things but she kept going. I heard Leonard in my ear: "She's *goot* to *go* . . ." I loved it from the bottom, but I usually took the first one from the top; it's like driving, or serving when you take them out to play tennis, or going first in miniature golf so they aren't embarrassed when they put it over the goddamn fence or in the pond. It always seemed like the thing to do. She put it in and leaned back, putting me right up high. It did the trick, a thought since France, a settled score. Me for her. Made her yell.

Even that didn't really make me feel any different—that was how it went for me back then. I had that mojo. I didn't care. That's what was taken from me when I got married. That's what you lose. You are banging girls every night and there is no end in sight. You think that that Adam stuff is bullshit. You think that there is no return necessary, that the community part of the Christ myth doesn't matter. I thought I could sell advertising forever and that I was unstoppable. That *they* would always *need me* to give them the Monster. I thought *they* all would always *need me* to put it in and lean back, way back, into the wetness, long and strong, way up high to that spot where they explode.

I was wrong. Way fucking-A wrong. It changes. I have more yesterdays than tomorrows. I play the game more in my head—with these memories—than I do on the court. Pathetic loser talking about the girls he fucked in college. I was better when I just watched TV and stuck to the facts. I was better when I was separate from the magic, separate from the story.

67

My uncle Artie said a lot of things when we sat in the Dodge on Monroe Street. He spoke in long monologues. And he talked as he looked at the trains. He was telling me his story; telling me what he could before he went.

"Some things you learn as you grow up, and some things you just know. You wake up one day and you know them. Someone asks you a question and you know it. There's book smart and then there's the things that are in your blood, boy. Like the path of the train, over the creeks, past the rocks. Like the stones on the side of the tracks. 'With rocks, and stones, and trees.' That's Wordsworth, boy. That's how you remember that. Those words have worth."

68

"**Y**our boys are lawyering up," Eric said over the phone. "Arthur Craft just called me. He has . . . Ford, Marlowe, Garrison, and LeFeber. Does that sound right? That they'd join together?"

"I don't know."

"He told me Chris Scully got him into it. He is still rounding up a few more. Where are my notes . . . yeah, here it is. He's pompous, Arthur. Stick up his ass. I think he went to Princeton. I hate Princeton." He mocked Arthur's voice: " 'I've been referred by Chris Scully.' " He knew that I was being quiet. He paused. "Let me guess."

"It's all the white guys," I said.

"Yeah, these things can go that way. Wait, I wrote something else down . . . oh, yeah, they can't find one guy. Bates? Badey?"

"Terry Beatty?"

"Yeah, that's it. They can't find him. Arthur said they think he went crazy or something." I always lumped Marlowe and Beatty together, but they turned out very different. Marlowe really did get into the Naval Academy, which was a big deal. He went to work for some company when he got out, Raytheon or Monsanto or something like that. He was psyched when I called him about the Publicité Rouge deal. He sent me a check in no time flat.

Beatty went to a little school in Ohio, which I thought was weird at the time. I saw him a few times over the years, mostly during the holidays, but we were out of touch. I couldn't find him when I was making the deal, so I talked to his dad, who was way into it. He said that Terry was overseas on a trip. He said he worried about him—he hadn't been the same since his grandfather died. That was the day Stokes told me on the bus that I was full of *something*. Mr. Beatty wrote a check for Terry so he could be in on the deal. I was glad about that.

69

The dean of the business school called to tell me they were discontinuing the class. "It's a different time, Joe," he said. "Don't take it personally. You know I would back you up. Christ's sake, now I have to find someone to explain CDOs and someone to teach SEC crap. You don't want to know."

70

We moved through the playoffs and after we spanked Springfield at a neutral gym, the third time we beat them that season, we were one game away from the Palestra. Bad news was we had to beat Coatesville to get to the championship.

This time we practiced for Coatesville differently. Casale wasn't going to make the same mistakes. We put in a delay game, using Leonard as a third guard and pulling Herman out. Scully, Garrison, and Leonard were given a three-man-weave set and told to kill time out around half-court. "Don't even look for forward motion past the top of the key until we hold it for thirty seconds," said Casale. His goal was to keep them under forty points. "Do that and I guarantee you we win."

The night of the second Coatesville game, the team bus was quiet as we all sat for the ride. Leonard got on the bus late, as usual. We looked at him. The air was thick with nerves. His expression was so serious; I thought something was wrong. Then he stomped his foot, held his hands up on either side of his head, snapped his fingers loud, and sang: "She's a briiiick . . . HOUSE." Etheridge chimed in. "She's mighty, mighty, just letting it all hang out." We sang it with them. The white guys, too.

The game was at Penn Charter High School, which had a new eight-thousand-seat arena for big games. It was sold out. It felt like the whole town of Coatesville was there an hour before tip-off. For a big game like that, we took the court early—about forty-five minutes before game time, to shoot awhile, before returning to the locker room for our last set of instructions. Casale pulled us in when he saw we were tight with all those people there, booing us as we did our early shooting drills. "Look

261

around," he said. "I mean it. Everybody look around this place, all around." We did small standing circles and looked at the arena. The booing got louder. Leonard smiled and waved to the crowd. Casale said, "You can't pretend the crowd isn't here. Take them in as part of the court. Absorb it. Bring this noise into your body." He gave us a second and he said, "Now close your eyes. This noise is like the air you are breathing; it is constant. It is not going to change. It will get louder and louder. The better you play, the louder it will get. They expect to win, these people, and when you take away something people expect, they get angry. This crowd is going to get angry tonight. Be ready. Reacting to a crowd is like a fear—it's in your head. Fear is the strongest force on Earth. You guys have each other. When you hear the crowd, look at Phillip, look at Stokes. They will be right there. Remember your teammates. If you get bothered by the noise, you look at Chris Scully. He will be right there. He is not going to let you lose. You are better than them. You are at home. Look at the front of the rim when you shoot the ball. Go back to your lines."

In the locker room we were loose. Coach Wattle came in with new warm-up shirts with our names on the back. They were totally cool, a big Quaker on the front. Leonard sang to himself. Phillip smiled and went to us one by one and put his hands on our shoulders and stared in our eyes.

A tunnel led to the court and at six fifty, we sprinted out. Our fans were at the other end. Three dribbles out of the archway and we felt the collective weight of the eyeballs hit us. The sound was a huge wave, and the hairs on my arms stood up. I felt like I could jump over the backboard.

But then a small object hit me in the head, right above the temple. Something thrown at me from the stands; it stung. I put my hand to my head and looked around the floor. Etheridge was looking at the back of his arm; something hit him, too.

We kept running our drills. I saw a quarter hit the ground in front of me. "Jesus Christ," I said, "they're throwing at us." I picked up the quarter, as well as a penny under the basket. No one else noticed and Etheridge was back to his warm-ups. Then Phillip got nailed between the shoulder blades.

"Ow. What the hell is that?"

I picked up the quarter that hit him. The noise was deafening because Coatesville was coming out of the tunnel for warm-ups. I said to Phillip, "I think they're throwing quarters at us." Then the screw top of a Miller Lite whizzed by.

Casale was on the bench reading his notes. It was so loud, he didn't see or hear anything over where we were warming up. I ran to show him. "You gotta be fucking kidding me," he said. "C'mon." And he grabbed my arm and we walked back over to our guys. "In the locker room, now." Everyone was shocked—the game was supposed to start in nine minutes. It was a cardinal sin to change routine. But the guys saw he was furious about something, so we ran off the court. In the tunnel, I said, "They're throwing quarters and beer caps at us."

"*That's* what that was," said Etheridge. We sat down in the locker room and Mr. Wattle checked my head for blood.

One of the refs came in to see what was up. "Out there," Casale said, pointing to the hallway. They walked into Penn Charter's A wing, with its beige lockers and cinder-block walls.

Inside, we heard everything.

"What's the matter?" said the ref.

"What do you mean, 'What's the matter?'" Casale said. "What's the fucking matter?" We heard his fist smash a locker.

"Jimmy, calm down. The kids . . ."

"These people are fucking animals! Here, Tommy, do you want to go get a fucking hot dog?" There was a pinging sound of coins spraying against the walls. "There must be four bucks in quarters there. They're gonna kill one of my kids. You want that?" He smashed the locker again.

We heard the muffled sound of the PA system. "Attention. The throwing of any debris of any kind is strictly prohibited. Anyone violating this rule will be removed by the state police. Attention, the throwing . . ."

It was like putting blood in the water. Eight thousand people stomping the aluminum push-out stands and screaming at full volume. After three announcements, it didn't get any quieter. The refs came back in the locker room.

"We have to get you guys out there," said the younger ref.

"We're not doing it," said Casale. "I'm not putting these kids out there."

"Jimmy, listen to me," said the older ref. "C'mere."

This time, they just went to the other side of the locker room where we couldn't see them. But we still heard though the wall.

"Look," the older ref said, "I understand. But listen to me . . . I'm worried about what happens to all of us if we *don't* put you guys out there. I mean, these people are nuts. I'm not sure we can get out of here, if you know what I mean."

After a minute, Casale came back to where we were sitting. He said, "I don't know what to do, guys."

Scully said, "Let's go, Coach. We don't care. Let's go warm up."

We walked down the tunnel. Phillip pushed his way past the smaller guys and came up on my left.

"Give me the ball," he said. "Hold back till I hit half-court, then follow me."

When we got to the edge of the tunnel, Phillip walked through the path to the court. The Coatesville crowd saw him first and started to boo. He went deliberately slow, dribbling and walking the ball until it was clear to our fans that he was walking the team onto the court. Seeing this, our crowd rocketed to their feet and went nuts. He kept walking.

"What's he doing?" said Etheridge, next to me.

"Watch," I said.

Around the three-quarter court line, the near foul line on the opposite end of the court from our basket, he stopped and stood there dribbling. The whole place became focused on him. The booing became thunderous, and our people tried to match it. The place was off the hook. The noise built and built and built.

After thirty seconds or so, when the backboards were about to shatter from the noise, he started walking, dribbling. Then he broke into a little jog, then he went faster, till he was at full speed. When he got halfway, I followed onto the court, all the guys behind me, into the lights and the colors and the flying quarters and beer caps and streamers, running past the Coatesville maniacs, toward our people who were on their feet screaming.

Ahead of us, Phillip ran alone. Alone like an astronaut, like a pioneer, he went right at it, cool as Steve McQueen. He pulled up from thirty-two feet out, four feet outside the top of the key. At the top of his jump, his right arm perfectly straight, with a dead flick of the wrist, he let it go, a patented Phillip Ford jumper, right into the teeth of the anger, into the mouth of the madness. The moms and dads and teachers and neighbors and kids from school realized just what the hell he was doing. He was a fucking hero. This would be talked about forever. The ball sailed from his hands as he floated down. And as he stood there in his follow-through, just like they teach it to you when you are seven, hand bent at the wrist, pointed at the rim, it splashed through. Dead center perfect. Swish. Phillip Ford. The Hope.

Our crowd went crazy. Right behind him, we went into our tap drill and Stokes and Herman brought it in with slams. The Penwood section went off: "That's the way, uh huh, uh huh, I like it, uh huh uh huh. That's the way, uh huh, uh huh, I like it, uh huh, uh huh." Pandemonium kept up in the stands as we ran the rest of our warm-up drills. I looked at Leonard and he moved his head back and forth, like a rooster, like Mick Jagger. I did it, too.

We were down 8-2 after a minute. They had a big guy, Randolph, who really came on during the season, and a six-three shooting guard named Jeron Dixon who was hurt and didn't play the first game. So they were even tougher. Bixley stole it from Garrison in the backcourt and broke away. After an offensive foul on Phillip, Casale called time-out.

"Slow it down. Forget the score. Remember: If they score less than forty, we win. That's all you have to worry about. A minute each time before we shoot." He put Herman in for Leonard.

Scully said, "Clear out for me up top."

When they brought it up, Randolph pinned Herman inside a little too obviously and was called for an offensive foul. Scully walked it down, and this time, instead of staying with him, Garrison went to the corner on the left side. Stokes, Herman, and Phillip all set up down low. Scully dribbled standing still. Twenty seconds, then thirty. The Coatesville crowd started to boo. After a minute, Scully cleared everyone away from the right side and busted the guy down the middle, stopping and burying it from twelve feet.

That settled us, but they hit jumpers the next two times down. We didn't get within eight for the rest of the first half, which ended with them up 24-16. We had slowed it down, but they were in control. When they ran a double screen for Dixon at the start of the third quarter and he hit it from the baseline, Casale tensed up next to me. Their fans were going through the roof, still feeling a little bottled up from the low score, but more confident as time elapsed.

Scully stuck to Casale's orders to take time off the clock. Herman had the night of his life. He grabbed three offensive boards in the third quarter, all leading to buckets. Casale had an instinct to put Mike Dunn on Randolph and it worked. Phillip began to come on. Coatesville's coach told the *Bulletin* that Phillip was the only one they were worried about. In that third quarter he showed that to be a worthwhile concern, because our boy Phil busted out with ten straight points. They never saw a white boy take it to the cup like *that*. They called time-out. They put Dixon on him. Phillip took him right down the middle and banked it to make it 33-30.

Dixon missed off a double screen, but the opposite forward, one of the endless string of monsters on their bench, tapped it in. Now it was 35-30. Panic started settling in on our side. Our fans began to think about getting out of the parking lot, conceding that this one was over, that we had lost by twenty-six in the first game of the season and this showed we were much better, that you couldn't beat a team like Coatesville where it was all blacks and all they did was play basketball, that this group of kids were a hell of a team and it had been a fun year but it had to end somewhere. It had been a good run. "It's a good lesson." I knew that was coming.

But I believed I would play in the Palestra. It was the way I felt about life: work hard, follow the rules, avoid illusions, stick to facts, and you will prevail.

We traded a few buckets and it was 39-34 with a minute and thirty-eight seconds left when Leonard came out of nowhere to pick off Dixon's pass across the top of the key. He laid it in and Scully and Garrison stayed up with him to press. Bixley caught it in the corner and Chris and Jeremy trapped him. He picked up his dribble and our guys were on him, all slap hands and arms stretched. Bixley tried to pass it to Randolph, who was coming back to give him a screen. Surprised, Bixley bounced the ball off Randolph's shoulder into the hands of Phillip Ford, who saw it coming like Larry Bird against Detroit in the Boston Garden. Phil took it in stride, dribbled once, and stroked it home from just inside the top of the key.

Score, 39-38, forty-six seconds left. They got it to Dixon in the frontcourt, and he tried to take some time off. Scully was in his face and turned him. Jeremy Garrison, that awesome, sneaky little fucker, was right there and smacked it out of his hand. It spun out toward the sideline and Scully gathered it in. We had the ball with twenty-one seconds left. Chris called time when he crossed half-court.

Casale designed a play. Scully took the inbounds pass and brought it up the right side. He penetrated the middle, causing their front right guard to sag in to help. This freed Garrison on the wing and Scully hit him. Garrison pump-faked, making the forward who had come out to get him jump by, allowing Garrison to flip it with his left hand to Phillip, waiting at the corner of the foul line. Phillip put it on the ground once and their center came at him from the left and Randolph came at him from under the basket. Phillip left his feet, but Randolph and the center were going to swat him, so he tucked, causing them to pass him in the air. When Phil came out the other side, still in the air, he found Stokes open at the foul line on the other side of the lane. Stokes caught it, reverse-pivoted, and let go his twelve-foot turnaround fade-away, the "Carolina" shot, the shot we wanted. The crowd stared as it flew at the basket. All of our work, all of our dreams of squeezing something real out of this world flying with it, three seconds, two seconds. It hit the inside curve of the rim and bounced straight out back at Stokes. The Coatesville side started to exhale, thinking they survived, thinking it's a win, that's all that counts, just one more step. And then Herman, minding his spot down low, lying in wait, just where he was supposed to be, jumped out of his size 14 sneakers, caught the ball with two hands, ten inches outside the rim, and, in the air, in one motion, softly guided it back above the bucket and let go. It fell through. The buzzer rang.

71

I've worked in the sugar fields up from New Orleans
It was ever green up until the floods
You could call it an omen
Points ya where you're goin'
Set my compass north
I got winter in my blood.

There is always America. We are all forced from the South to the North and the North to the South. Pennsylvanians mind the middle, the first guy on the north side of the tug-of-war rope. We fight our way back up and are the firewall when we are home. We are the keystone. We have birth fathers and mothers taken away. We have others foisted upon us. We find others still. But there is always America.

I do not want to die penniless in jail, rot away in Jersey, or hang myself on the road. I am lost. Lost and alone. I don't want this. Even in the center, I want never to be burned.

72

I didn't answer my phone for a couple days after getting back from the funeral in Rockland County. I dreamed I sent an e-mail to my father and he wrote back. I asked him to help me. And, since it was a dream, I asked why he was up responding to e-mail so late at night.

> *Bottom line, people write to me late at night because they know I'm up . . . and I don't make a single judgment . . . we are all together in this . . . so all that's left is a little comfort and a song line that gets you and a good smoke and drink . . . and the children . . . always the children . . . so now you are on the horns of massive guilt because there wasn't any closure with Janice's father . . . or maybe with me . . . or what happened with Dottie, what you did . . . well, I absolve you dear-hearted one . . . these are all life scripts and people have to deal with each other in lifetime . . . you can forgive him or anyone for being who they are . . . and them you . . . life is a stop and not a stay . . . that's just it in a nutshell . . . JK Sr.*

I couldn't believe he called me "dear-hearted one." I didn't know that he *really was* like Chad Everett, part on the side, kind and good-smelling, now older. I imagined him with strong arms and a tanned face, a ladies' man, a rascal, a good guy down deep. I wished we had gone fishing, even if only once. Fact was, he just hit a tree, poor guy. Unlucky coming out of the Lobster Pot. Could have been me and him in this life.

73

Some girls remind you of bands and some girls remind you of songs. Janice O'Malley was a song. As real as a song, that was the problem. A distant song, an old song. A song that was my favorite because it was so true, so encapsulating of what I was feeling. I loved that song. What the fuck happened?

Maybe it's the call to reality it makes. Anymore, I like my songs dreamy. I like to be Acadian Driftwood. *Try to raise a family, end up the enemy, over what went down on the plains of Abraham.* The Janice O'Malley song calls me back, where I don't want to be, to the here and now, over what went down on the plains of Abraham. To the detritus, the wrestlers unmasked, the shit on the ground. To the place of death.

Kids are funny. The night after the fund-raiser, Tia said, "Sing me the other one, Daddy. The orphan one you sing me. *I'm a lonely frog,* you know."

It was the song that had me crying only an hour before. I said, "Close your eyes." I sang it low for her. Low Levon Helm.

I ain't got a girl . . .
I ain't got a son . . .
I ain't got no kin . . .
I ain't got no one . . .
I'm a lonely frog . . .
I ain't got a home . . .

Woo–woo–woo–woo–woo–woo–woo–woo

"All you got is your family."

"Enjoy it now." Enjoy it now!

If I hear another person say either of these things one more time, I swear to Christ I am going to blow my head off.

I can barely feel it that Ray is gone. I think of Janice with him and I feel something, but then I go dead.

I can't feel it that I am with Tia one-seventh of the time. Two nights over fourteen days. Two nights at the apartment. I try to see her during the week. I go to games and dances and talent shows. But it doesn't get above one-seventh of the time. That's 14 percent. And I can't feel a fucking thing. Can't feel that I'm not with my best girl.

Janice said, "Tia wanted you to see her story." I was at the house, picking her up for my Wednesday court-ordered custody. "She's proud of it."

The orange construction paper had a Letter to Parents on it. The kids conceived, drafted, corrected, and published a story. Tia's had a blue Magic Marker picture of three four-legged animals. Inside, the story was on manila paper, solid lines with dashes in the middle.

Once a horse named Pedro was walking to his friend named Chopper. Pedro saw an elephant stuck in the mud. He went over to the elephant and asked, "Do you need help?" The elephant said, "Yes, please," and he tried to help him. But he couldn't pull him out. So he asked his friend Chopper to help him. They both pulled and got him out. The elephant said, "Thank you." Then they all played hopscotch.

I looked up at Janice. We didn't say anything.

74

Eric's voice was throaty. "I spoke to David Saunders. He's a prick, but I have him talking. He says that he has made very good progress with Arthur Craft. Arthur says his guys will give the government the testimony it needs. Saunders says he's ready to go to trial against you, but for me he will try to resolve it."

"Great. What does he want?"

"Well, hold on. There's another interesting thing. Do you know Cawley Coleman?"

"No."

"He's a lawyer in Penwood. Black guy. He called me today and he's got the others. Everybody except the crazy one, Beatty."

"The black guys."

"Exactly. He said there's an old man who is in charge. Ervin Polk. They're all listening to him." He listed Cawley Coleman's clients: "Ervin Polk, Leonard Polk—that's the son?"

"Yes."

"David Stokes, Etheridge Butcher, and Rolanda Coverdale, that's the sister of the guy who got shot?"

"Right."

"There you have it." He made another of his clicking noises, the one that meant, "Of course."

"Why would it go down this way? You're not surprised?"

"Nope. Not at all. You got to love it. The black guys in the drug cases—they will fuck each other in a second. But stuff like this, they never cooperate. When there are blacks who work for a living—you know, the real guys—they'll never help the government. Coleman is great at this. He will stonewall them forever."

"Amazing."

"Always. Anywhere around Philadelphia. It's in the blood. I call it 'Frank Rizzo Revenge.'"

"I can't talk to any of them?"

"Absolutely not."

"I can't talk to Leonard?"

"Nope. Now that they have Coleman, you talk through me and him. I can give Coleman a message and he might pass it along."

"Can he tell them I said thanks?"

"Yeah, I'll get that through."

75

There were days I got in the car and drove toward Penwood with no plan. I usually ended up in the strip mall near Trader Joe's. When worse came to worst, when I had been through a long cup of coffee at the Coffee Bean, through an individual-sized pizza at Uno's, I went to the market and wandered around the aisles. I looked at products, a regression to my mercenary days as an ad junkie, a fucked-up trip down memory lane. To my time as Trader Joe. Traitor Joe, Trade Or Joe. I missed the height of the organic market. Boy, I would have kicked the shit out of that. Right up my alley—the portrayal of things as original. Everything is new and improved. It's like cheating. Cheating in a game that's about cheating; or being uncouth and crass within a thing that is by definition uncouth and crass. Less fat, more taste, a sense that it is getting better, not eroding. Replicating, reinventing. Coke bottles have redemption value. Redemption value.

Bottled water was my favorite. I'd look at the Evians and Arrowheads, the Glaciers and the Aquas and the Fresh Penn Mountain Water. It's the triumph of advertising, the mecca of marketing. It's *water*, for crissakes. It's the epitome of salesmanship—who can best sell the most generic thing of all? It's like being on the foul line when no one else is around, when everyone is cleared from the lane. A pure test. I could have killed it.

I thought about getting back in, but it was gone. I just didn't have it in me anymore. I realized it was Saturday by the longer lines at left turn signals and the kids not in school. I parked in the lot and as I was headed in, a minivan pulled next to me. A guy in a tie-dyed shirt hung his head at the window. He had a huge pair of shades and I couldn't see who it was.

275

"Hey brothaaaa . . . what's happening?"

I squinted. It was Sean. I grinned. "Heeey man."

Sean kept the qualities that made him lovable into adulthood. I looked inside the van and there were six teenage girls in soccer jerseys.

"What's up, dude? How is it?" He talked like a Deadhead. He had gotten even groovier over the years. He was, as always, a great mix of a Stuckley guy and an art major. He had four daughters. He'd become a carpenter and built a little construction company, which was a great thing for a semi-stoner like Sean. His wife was a total ballbuster who ran everything for him. I'm pretty sure the JKD money helped them but they would have been successful without it. He turned the radio down and turned back to the girls. "Hey. Cool out. I'm talking." He waited a second and it quieted down. "Thank you."

We caught up on the general stuff: his wife; which kid was how old; who he'd seen from the old days. You don't really keep up with old friends, you see some of them once in a while and get their version of where everyone is in their lives. Some people are carriers—the ones who spread that information and put their spin on it, that way the carriers get a weird kind of control. Scully was a carrier as he got older. So was Leonard. None of the rest of us were. Sean dodged around the Janice-of-it-all as only an old buddy would or could.

"How's Mike?" I said.

"You know, he's really good. I think he's finally in decent shape. He's working with us and he has a big house that we're doing. All by himself, I gave the whole thing to him. He's totally in charge."

"That's great. I've been trying to reach him. Can't track him down."

"Huh. I'm sure he's just busy." There was a pause. "I'll tell him you're looking for him. Hey, I got to get these kids to a game in East Jabip somewhere."

"Okay, Sean-O."

"Okay, Joey-Boy."

We clasped hands in the brother shake. As he drove away, he looked back and said, "I'm going to see Jakob Dylan next week at the Wachovia."

The Spectrum was renamed the CoreStates Spectrum, then First Union Spectrum in 1998, and now it was named after another bank, Wachovia. "C'mon . . . dude. I'll drive. We'll take this craft right here." He hit the side of the minivan.

I laughed. "Yeah, man. I'm in. Call me."

76

Mike called me a few days later and, since it was Mike, I suggested we meet in a bar. I made sure it was a less local place than he would pick because I didn't want to run into any idiots from high school. I told him anywhere in Springfield and to my surprise he chose Ford & Fitzroy's, a restaurant with a full bar and cloth napkins.

I forget sometimes how big we all were. I'm six foot and Mike is even bigger, six four. People notice him when he comes in a bar. Sean was right. He was doing better. He even looked okay, wearing a blue button-down with khakis. "What'd you, get dressed up?" I said.

We shot the shit for a while. I asked him about working with Sean and his wife, and he said, "I should have been doing this the whole time. It's great." He ticked off his other options. "I can't make it in an office, I don't want to work in a restaurant, and I'm not cut out to sell, like. insurance or whatever. That leaves construction. So Sean is doing real good, so why the fuck not, right?"

The guy sitting next to us had half a bag on, hitting his third Scotch and soda since we got there. He watched us. We ignored him.

"Can I ask you something, bro?" I said.

"Sure."

"Has anyone tried to get you to talk about me? You know, cops? Like, feds? They're telling me that someone I know is giving them information that is going to be used against me."

"What, you think it's me?" He started to get up. "No, Joe, I'm not ratting on you if that's what you think."

"Of course not, Mike. C'mon, fucker. Knock that shit off." I sat him down. We both stared straight ahead at the bar. "They're after me, man. It's no joke."

He was quiet, deciding if he was going to stay.

Just then, the Scotch-and-soda guy started talking to us, having reached that point where the booze overcomes inhibition. Whatever kept him quiet to that point was at bay.

"You guys from Springfield?"

He was older, well dressed, working on a cigarette. Red-gray hair, with a red face. He swiveled his bar stool—which was shaped like a chair—so he was facing us as we looked forward. I turned and faced him, happy for the distraction. Mike was in the middle.

"No," I said.

Mike, not Mr. Chitchat by any stretch, was glad for the distraction, too, apparently, because he pointed at his drink and said, "Drinking the good stuff. Means it was a rough day."

"You have no idea." Then he said, "Are you guys Irish?"

"Yeah," said Mike.

"Pretty much," I said. "I have some other stuff rolling around but mostly Black Irish."

"Me, too." He leaned forward, taking the cue that he could get into a story. "So, I'm in counseling with my old lady, right? And the shrink, it's a woman, she starts analyzing me, of course."

"Of course," I said.

"So I said something and she says, 'Well, you're Irish.' And I said, 'What the hell does that matter?' And she says, 'Irish are the worst psychiatric patients you can possible have. One: you are the most stubborn people on the face of the earth.'"

"Right," Mike said.

"'And two, you all are utterly convinced that you're completely fucked.'"

We laughed and he backed up in his chair, proud of the story. "No hope," he said, making a safe sign like an umpire. We grinned and went back at our drinks. He looked for the bartender. "Jimmy, set us up."

He went to the bathroom and Mike came back to our conversation. "What are you going to do?"

"I don't know. Do you . . ."

"What?"

We were a long way from Stuckley. "Do you think Scully would do this to me?"

He chomped on his ice. "So now it's Scully?" He shook his head. "Course not. What's wrong with you?"

I didn't say anything.

"Joe. You've done great. You're a fucking millionaire. Personally, I don't know how you did it and I never understood what you were doing to begin with. I was way fucking happy to get that money even though I blew it. Says a lot about a guy, what you did." He leaned into me. "But, whatever you got going on here, it's gonna be hard for any of us to help."

"I know," I said. "I'm sorry."

He was really in my face now. "You know when I was in all that trouble, in college?" I nodded. "You helped me and I'll never forget it. And you didn't judge me. But, fuck me, Joe, what are you doing here, going around like some undercover cop? You know that'll last about two seconds around here." He sat back in his chair and before the Scotch-and-soda guy sat down where he could hear, Mike drew a series of breaths, took a couple of pulls on his beer, and said, "It's probably some skank you fucked."

77

The woman said she wanted to meet me and that it would only take twenty minutes. All she would tell me is that it was about Arthur Ventresca.

It was raining and she said to look for a red raincoat. I met her at the Starbucks on Chestnut Street, near my apartment. She was ten minutes late and I saw her from a table in the corner, away from all the laptops, away from all the ladies talking right in each other's faces like war buddies. She apologized for being late, saying that it was slow getting there from Thirtieth Street. She came up from Baltimore. She seemed in her late fifties, though I get those things wrong. She was the kind of lady who wears a red coat. Glazed with rainwater. A white turtleneck underneath.

Yet I swear I see my reflection somewhere so high above the wall.

I got a coffee and she got a hot black tea that she soothed with milk and sugar. "I'll cut to the chase since I'm sure you're wondering who this crazy lady is who called you out of the blue."

She was nervous, so I tried to be kind. "Sure thing."

"Your aunt Dorothy, Dorothy Knight Ventresca, was married to a man named Arthur Ventresca, right?"

My stomach seized.

"That's right, my uncle Artie."

"Arthur Ventresca was my father. Did you know that he had come from Baltimore?"

Dottie met Artie on the train. He'd left a wife in Baltimore.

It was crossed off, that part, never spoken about. In all the years, I never looked at that piece. I never thought of his earlier life.

"I Googled you and found your information and that's how I tracked you down," she said. "I know this must be kind of a shock. Is it a shock?"

"Very much so."

"You didn't know he had a family in Baltimore?"

"I knew he came from there, but I never thought he had kids."

"Oh yes, me and two brothers. He left us all. Just left on a Wednesday and never came back."

"Oh God. I never knew. Are . . . is your mom still alive?"

"No, she's been gone for ten years." She sniffed, starting to cry. "Only one of my brothers is alive. Al. My other brother, Cliff, died in his thirties. It was very sad. Al doesn't really care about what happened to our father, but I guess I just got to a point where I wanted to find out some things." She looked at her tea. "Is he . . . I mean, is he alive?"

I lied because I was scared. "Oh God. No, he died twelve years ago. Stomach cancer." Carolyn Taylor, that was her name. She married a guy named Taylor and she lived in Rockville, Maryland. She and her husband had two boys in high school. I asked her if there was anything I could do for her.

"No, not at all. I just wanted to see you." She hesitated a second. "And I guess I wanted to see that his leaving meant something. You know, that he helped someone."

"I'm not sure I understand."

"Well, he walked out on us so I can never forgive him. And your aunt Dottie took him from us, so I feel the same way about her." I had never heard a negative word about Dottie in my life, so it was as though this sweet woman with childhood-shattering secrets at a Starbucks had taken a red-hot poker from under the table and was poised to either use it or throw it away. "But, I guess all of that let them take care of you. So I wanted to see you. To see that it meant something."

In that moment I realized she was Artie's daughter and of course she had nothing but music at the center of her soul. "I'm sorry, Carolyn," I said, "I really am."

"It's not your fault, honey. It's not *our* fault." She was the kind of lady who said honey all the time, like Dottie. "I'm glad I met you. So much depends upon the little things." She was crying, but she tried to make the best of it. "Who knows, maybe we can make a fresh start." All I could get her was a few of those brown recycled napkins, the shitty kind that don't even absorb spilled coffee or tea.

78

"**Y**our boy Beatty, he's like the Unabomber," said Eric when I walked in his office. "They think he is in Wyoming but this came from North Carolina. I don't know how the fuck he sent it from there. Here." He handed me a letter.

Dear Mr. Eric Rath, ATTORNEY
DEAR SIR:

I am informed you are the attorney for Mr. JOSEPH KNIGHT. I ask you, esquire, to kindly forward the below letter to the harassing UNITED STATES GOVERNMENT AGENTS who are invading my PRIVACY. I ask that you protect any indication unintentionally given by this communication and that you deliver it inm tact. I would like you to also give MR. Joseph Knight my kindest regards and pass along to him that I support any of his efforts and that he may hereby exercise a PROXY of defending his rights through and CIVIL LIBERTY I may have on this situation. You will kindly advise.
Signed by and sincerely,
Terrence I. Beatty
[Included Letter:]
Dear Assistant U.S. Attorney DAVID P> SAUNDERS
Dear Sirs:
Regarding: Beatty, Terrence I., Subpoena Duces Tecum Erroneously and Fallaciously Mailed, Case No. EDPA 08-4956969
The United States GOVERNMENT, by and through and in proper

*persona acting by your behalf, has now for the sixteenth time attempted
too contact me by improper means under the First, Fourth, Fifth, Eighth
and Ninth Amendments to the United States Constitution. In regarding
Publicite Rouge and Joseph Knight Case No. EDPA 08-4956969 is your
reference hereby made.*

*NOTICE IS HEREBY GIVEN that I have no intention of respond-
ing in any way at law or at equity to your FUCKING SUBPOENA
which is a violation of the UNITED STATES CONSTITUTION,
AMENDMENTS ONE, FOUR, FIVE, NINE and FOURTEEN
on grounds that it is a complete INVASION OF PRIVACY of the person
and of the corpus intellectuality of the recipient, BEATTY, Terrence I.*

*NOTICE IS HEREBY GIVEN that under the UNITED STATE
CONSTITUTION, ARTICLE ONE< ARTICLE THREE and
AMENDMENTS FOUR AND FOURTEEN , you are hereby
ordered to cease and desist of such unlawful contact and that the under-
signed Beatty, Terrence I. does hereby invoke and institute the FIFTH
AMENDMENT RIGHT OF SELF PROTECTION guaranteed and
protected under the UNITED STATES CONSTIOTUION.*

*AND FURTHERMORE, said subpoenas can be taken by you, Assistant
Attorney General SAUNDERS and SHOVED RIGHT UP YOUR
ASS.*

Signed by and sincerely,
Terrence I. Beatty

"He's done you an enormous favor by going crazy," Eric said. "Were you
good friends?"

"We were boys together," I said.

"I like that. Hang in there, bubby. This might work out."

79

The Palestra was set for Friday night, one week after the Coatesville game. They had a pep rally for us in the gym at Fallcrest on Thursday. Jack Scott did his usual thing introducing us, and the kids ate it up. Phillip and Scully gave little speeches. Phillip said we wanted to win it for all of the people who believed in us. Scully thanked the coaches and the parents and the fans. Stokes got up. We agreed Stokes would be the one to do it.

"Like everybody knows, Henry Coverdale Jr., our teammate, died this week. We'd like to have a moment of silence for him." Then Stokes said, "I know Cove would want us to go win at the Palestra and that's what we're going to do."

The next day, the day of the game, we all wore ties to school. It was what I imagined a wedding day would be like. Everywhere kids wished me good luck. I went home on the regular after-school bus, which was weird. As it went down Middletown Road, through the intersection at Five Points past the Burger King, BrightSpot Cleaners, and Hoy's Flower Shop, I thought how far we were away from the lights. I was so excited, I didn't know if I could keep it together. I thought of how unreal it was that the guys from my reality would be in front of the outside world, the world of record, the world beyond our bubble, that we could play on that floor, where poetry and the music of basketball centered. It was the closest I was to grateful for the chance to live since the accident of my birth.

Dottie got off early to be with me. I had to be back at school by five for the team bus. The game was at eight, the second part of a double-header. We were playing Norristown. They were good but not as good as Coatesville. They had a few guys who were tough, but nobody big. Their high-scorer, Roberts, was six four, and Tolly Collins was a point guard who matched up well with Scully. They also had an All-American quarterback who played basketball for fun. He was huge, like six five, 210 pounds. He was going to play football for USC. Mike Dunn pretended to be him on the scout team. They were so worried about him getting hurt, we didn't even know if the guy would play. Casale kept teasing Dunn, "Mike, maybe Mike Hartman will give you his autograph."

Dottie was beyond excited for me. She took every game day seriously, but on the day we went to the Palestra, she was quiet as a monk. She laid my uniform out for me, staying silent so I could concentrate, only talking if I talked to her. She gave me a Hallmark card she bought at the pharmacy, with two roses on the front. Inside it said:

For your special day,
I only want to say:
I love you through and through;
Good luck, good luck to YOU!!!

I stood the card on my bureau, same way I did with her birthday cards— kept them for a week or so, till they disappeared, never thrown directly into the garbage, maybe slipped inside a drawer or a notebook, only to fade away indirectly, no betrayal intended, no intent to harm the feelings, just what boys do. There were dozens, maybe hundreds, of those cards: they came on birthdays, holidays, St. Patrick's Day, Valentine's Day, cards for Easter and Christmas and Thanksgiving, once or twice a year a card for just being me. Then there were notes, little notes saying, "I love you!" once saying, "Don't be lonely, you're my one and only!" She had my little school picture from every grade. She had several of Leonard's, too. As she got older, she left me long letters with big billowy handwriting, the sentences taking up large spaces until she saw she was running out of room, then she squished all the words together, crammed her thoughts down to fit as much as possible on a page, always ending with "love love love you!"

There was never an Aunt Dottie Day. Or an Uncle Artie Day. Except their birthdays. On Mother's Day and Father's Day, Dottie took me to the twin graves up behind St. Ignatius. Dottie never said anything on Mother's Day and it never crossed my mind to get her a card.

I put my uniform and warm-ups into my gym bag the same way I put my uniform and warm-ups into my gym bag every game. Reverse order of how I put things on. Warm-up top, bottoms, jersey, shorts, two pair of socks, Converse leather Dr. J's. Since it was the Palestra, I had to wear a coat and tie. I only owned two pairs of dress pants, two dress shirts, and two ties. I had just worn my good set to the Coatesville game. But Dottie had them ready again because she knew I thought they were lucky. I was dressed by four and stared at the clock.

I thought of all the games I'd gone to see and all the teams. Casale loved and copied the two-three matchup zone the great Penn teams played. Matchup zone. It's genius—it's not anywhere else in sports. It's an oxymoron; not man not zone. If you're smart enough to change on the fly, you can be both, neither, simultaneously. An invisible cord connects players, allows them to double down, collapse on the baseline, trap out front as the offense tries to penetrate, swing it, or post up. It confuses and frustrates the merely two-dimensional, the merely gifted, the playground guys. It is at another level, a roped-off place where only players can live and only players who have lived with each other win.

I zipped my bag, walked out in the hallway, and said, "Dot, we got to go. I can't stand it. I'll be early." She didn't answer, so I repeated it loudly toward her bedroom. She must have been still in the bathroom.

I waited on the couch. I was working myself. I ran through the other great teams. Michael Brooks at La Salle, Corky Calhoun at Penn. The guards at St. Joe's, Temple's one-three-one trap, Villanova's zone busters. I thought of the students coming in the cold night air down to the Penn campus and sanctifying themselves in the crowd and the heat and the streamers before going out to get drunk and laid. This night was more than just getting somewhere, it was peeking around the corner at a future. A future where, if you followed the rules and worked hard, you could be somebody.

At four thirty, I walked toward the bathroom and said, "Dot, come on, let's go!" The door was closed and I knocked. No answer. I started to panic. I opened the door.

She was sitting on the toilet with her slacks and panties at her knees. Her head was slumped down, like a drunk old man in the park. I spoke her name, stared at her, tried to wake her, and nothing. She was gray. I felt time and space collide. I didn't want to move. I reached down and felt her cheek and it was cold. When I put my head to her mouth I heard nothing. My stomach started to contract; bile came up in my throat; the grinding feeling hit my intestines.

All I could do was lift her off the toilet and try to get her pants up. I wrestled her onto the cold, rotten linoleum floor, which, no matter how much she cleaned it, she couldn't hold off its elemental decomposition, and after enough time, she couldn't stop it from curling at the corners and turning rusty brown, like a cigarette burn. She collapsed down in front of the stand-up shower, no life in her spine. I fell with her and we lay on the clean, dirty floor. I said out loud, "What time is it?" I got her big bottom covered up and she fell on top of me, a sack of blood and bone. I sat there. My pants started to get wet from something running out of her. I tried to remember Artie by staying on time. I had his Timex. I looked at it. I looked at it. I looked at it. I looked at it.

It was four forty. I knew Casale wouldn't leave till ten after five and it took twenty minutes to get to school. I laid her on the floor. I took the shower mat and rolled it up into a tube and put it under my aunt Dottie's head, closed the door, got my gym bag and her keys, and drove to Fallcrest to meet the bus.

At the corner of Middletown Road and 352, Stuey pulled up next to me. He rolled down his window. I barely knew him.

He said, "Nervous?"

I shook my head no.

"I got you guys by eight." He drove away.

80

"I heard you laughing across the store. I left you alone with her to go get a running bra," Janice said. She picked the restaurant but didn't like the table, so we moved. "I left you by the elevator, with the carriage. You couldn't see me. You were dirty. Your hair was stringy, the way it gets when you are dirty like that. And you had on a gray T-shirt with holes in it. I loved that shirt. You're such a *guy*." She was crying now. "I was across the escalator and I could see you with her. I needed the bra because she was six months and I was finally losing weight."

"C'mon, stop."

"You had your face in the carriage. You were nuzzling her and then pulling away and then nuzzling her and then pulling away. Tia laughed so hard. I heard her all the way across Niketown."

"Why are you doing this?"

"That's what you are walking away from. You want to leave her? The rest of her life she will be looking for you. All men will abandon her, that is what she will think. She will think it's her fault. Trust me."

"It's not true."

"It *is* true." She grabbed my hand. "We've had a bad time. Okay. It's hard. Blame it on me, I'm fat, whatever. But you can't just quit and run away."

"Bullshit, Janice. It's the same for you. You don't want to be with me, either. You're just not as lonely."

"What are you going to do? Is this because you want to fuck other girls? That's it, isn't it? You want to get laid, right? Go get laid. I don't care."

"I can't take it." I looked around the restaurant. "It's a bad cliché. It's all a bad cliché. Everything. I'm coming apart."

"You need to be at home with your family. How much money do you think you have, anyway? It won't last that long, dude. Do you think you have, like, rich people's kind of money? You don't. And you *like* money. You won't like not having money, trust me. You'll have to go out and get a real job again. Can you even get a real job? Could you even do a real job?"

"All fair questions."

"What about me?" She teared again. "What about how you're treating me? I'm your *wife*. What am I supposed to do? I *left* my job, Joey. What do I do now, go sell houses? Try to get on the guest list at Aronominck Golf Club? Find some old guy with a dead wife and go to Virginia every other weekend? While you take Tia?" She really cried. "You want that for me?"

"I'm not treating you badly."

"Ha." She took a drink of wine. "Ha!" she shook her head. "You are being selfish. You are feeling sorry for yourself and trying to protect against something that isn't there. You are untreated, I've told you that a million times. You're driven by fear."

"I've tried."

"You have not tried." She was mad now. "What the fuck is this, like, 'I'm no good for you, Janice'? Why don't you save that one. Try the 'I'm an ungrateful piece of shit who has no appreciation for what the world and . . . whatever, God . . . has brought me. I can't be grateful for what I have.' Is that it, a blend of those two excuses?"

"Kind of."

"That's just getting off the hook. That's like saying, 'I don't blame you for getting mad.' Utter bullshit."

"All right. How about this, Janice, How about it doesn't work between us. How about: you're not having sex, either." She didn't say anything and immediately I felt bad. "That's not the whole thing. I'm sorry."

"It doesn't help, I know."

"It doesn't help either of us."

Now we were both quiet.

"I don't know," I said. "I won't make you guys happy. I won't."

"You're broken?"

"Yes. No, I mean, whatever I am, it's permanent."

"Don't you see how ridiculous that is? There are ways to fix yourself if you are broken. There are ways to find gratitude if you don't have any. That's the beauty of progress." She said "progress" in a sarcastic way, even though she was serious about it, one of those idiomatic moments of conversation, when complicated emotions are running. "There's no reason you can't do that. You have discipline in so many other areas. But you don't try for me and Tia. You don't evolve."

"It's not about *evolving*," I said. "Don't give me that, evolving. You make it sound like some goddamned caterpillar to butterfly thing."

"What is it, then?"

I looked away. Then hard at her. "It's erosion, Janice. Changing in some gradual linear fashion is a fantasy, but you are welcome to it. Life erodes till there is nothing left. It's not something to be grateful for. Till we're just particles. There, I said it."

"Okay, so what? You want to be by yourself so you can sit and think about eroding all the time."

"Maybe. And I don't think you should have to, or want to, be with me. This was a mistake. I can't explain it."

"What about Tia?"

"Tia is your baby, Janice. I can't separate the two of you. I'm not going to fight that. You two decide if she should ever come be with me and when. I will go by whatever you say."

"You won't even fight me for Tia? Don't you love her? You're that big a piece of shit?"

"Of course I love her. That doesn't mean I see the world any different. Differently. Or that because I love her, this was a mistake, or I am making a mistake now."

"I love how you say *it was a mistake*—that our whole life since we got married has been a mistake—instead of something that doesn't work anymore. That's really nice, Joe. Now you're being really honest." Again, we sat there not saying anything. The waiter seemed not to want to come near us; only the busboy was tough enough to enter the hostility of our company. He poured water without flinching.

81

The difference is the lights. On the court, the white light was supreme. I realized that my whole life I had played in darkness. When I made the cut at half-court and slapped the *P*, I was in white-hot beams. We were in a stage play in front of every friend, teacher, parent, girl who we stared at, tried to feel or finger in borrowed cars, every guy from the hoagie shop who said, "I'm going to go watch those guys if they go to the Palestra." There were kids from vo-tech who were only at school from nine to eleven, when they were bused to a place that looked even more like a jail than Fallcrest, with drafting tables, iron shards, and welding equipment. Those guys came to the Palestra. Those guys.

The place is a big quadrangle and it has bleachers like the bleachers at Fallcrest except the bleachers at the Palestra go up to the sky. I could see their faces: the friends, parents, teachers, hoagie shop guys, vo-tech guys, girls, when I looked up. Phillip was behind me in the layup line and said, "It's not a big deal. It's just a big, old loud place." But then he laughed, as though all bets were off.. "But, Joey, this is the hottest gym I've ever seen. The hype is real. Place is on fire. It's made for one thing only. It's on fire."

Fire. Feel it.

Scully shook Tolly Collins and dished it to Stokes and it felt like we could've been back at Glentop. We were solid till Garrison picked up a third foul with four minutes left in the first half. Casale told me to go in, and as I ran by him he said, "Hold up." He held my shirt and was in my ear. "Just another night. Nothing special. I played here fifteen times. You probably will play here fifteen more times before you're done. There is nothing about this place that should change you."

*   *   *

He was not wrong. I did my job, I ran the plays, I stopped my guy. I made one great pass to Herman.

No one noticed Dottie wasn't there, the place was so big. Our fans could not get organized. Her absence was absorbed by everyone's confusion, the context of the event, and the arena being larger than and different from what we were used to. You couldn't hear in that place. The walls were farther away, the cavern was truly a cavern. Our people were small.

Collins fouled me driving up the right side as time went out in the half. Stupid foul by him because I wasn't going to do anything. We were in the penalty, so the ref cleared everyone off the court. I took the line and he tossed it to me. "Okay, one-and-one. Ball's dead on any rebound."

The Norristown guys stood at their bench, waiting to go in for halftime. Our guys stood at half-court. Phillip said, "C'mon Joey. Knock them in."

"Remember, ball's dead."

There may be a time when all time and memory stop, when God enters the room. Or there may be no such thing. That was the moment when the ideas of death and fear and how deeply earthly stinking bloody evil it is possible for it to all be run together for me. I held the ball and felt the eyes. So many people wondering what I could do, focused on me, concerned about me. Half of them rooting for me and the other half rooting against me.

Sometimes I think about the guys from vo-tech and them being focused on me in that moment. That there might have been burnouts there from my school who hated jocks and sports and conformity and preppiness and wholesomeness and anything clean shocks me down through the base of my sack: that inside they were still kids and they got caught up rooting for us and drove all the way into town to watch us. Even yet, sometimes I think they were kind.

You know if it's going in.

The ball felt very small. I dribbled three times, bent my knees to remind myself to bend my knees, cocked it right below my eye line, matched the center of the upward semicircle of its circumference with the front of the rim, touched it to the in-between part of my upper lip and nose. "Put it against your mustache," coaches said. I pressed my right elbow in to remind myself to keep my right elbow in. I let it go. Net.

The ref gave it to me again. "Here we go, one more. Ball's dead after you shoot it." I was alone again. I nailed it. Leonard ran up.

"Yea, boy." He slapped my hand. "That's what I'm talking about."

We didn't get to have a real locker room. They gave us an equipment closet under the stands. We went back in there at halftime. We were up by eight. Casale told us to keep it going, two more quarters and we had it. I was okay until he said, "Really good job, Joey. Way to be there."

That pricked the membrane. The jig was up, the rocket could not stay in space anymore. I had no center. I was alone. The two quarters left were the two quarters of my life; I couldn't live in the third, couldn't stop the fourth. The time on the clock would come and go and then I would be done. The scoreboard would be put away for the night. I could not look up.

In the morning I help pick up the dead and lay them in rows in the barn.

I made a noise, scared and urgent. My team thought it was excitement. They loved it; they fed on it. Scully clapped and said, "Let's get psyched, let's take it to them."

The third quarter went by in a daze; the music was gone.

They say that every man must fall.

Garrison missed two open jumpers. Herman got tired, choking in the big game. "Pussy," Scully said to him during a time-out. Leonard came in and made a few plays, but it was not enough. It wasn't that we blew it. We were rolled by Mike Hartman. He took the game over even though it wasn't even his goddamn sport. He went, as the brothers said, off. He didn't miss, rising to it the way someone who has been a mother goes to a baby crying in the park, the way a person who once had to sell apples will pick up a penny. He scored twenty-two by the end of the third quarter. He jammed it on a break-away to put them up by nine with three minutes left. Casale called time. I thought about walking out, but I didn't know where to go.

It wasn't fair. Mike Hartman was a football player. I'm sure he had his boys, his group that he played with; I'm sure he was one of the guys, a person, a high school kid, like Phillip. But this guy was a product. He was in the test phase, R and D. He would be polished and prototyped and premarketed and sold to the NFL and spit out as cornflakes, as Pepsi, as motor oil, as oatmeal.

After the time-out, Phillip went to work and chipped it to four with a jumper and then a steal and three-point play. Leonard made another steal, carried it across half-court, and got it to Scully, who cleared out the right side. Collins slapped him, putting him on the line. Everyone breathed a little. Scully on the line. Mr. Ice. He could cut it to two. They called time-out.

The guys who were in sat on the bench and the rest of us stood. The crowd made a loud piercing buzz and Casale yelled instructions. Then, imperceptibly, it happened. Scully looked at me and I saw what no one else could see. I didn't recognize it at first. Then I realized what it was and it caught hold of me. He was petrified. Like he was undressed and scared, vulnerable like when he was on the lookout for Father Shea. He looked back at Casale in an instant, pretending he didn't see me.

But this wasn't a fantasy league; this was the best it was ever going to be for us. The fantasy escaped. See, that's what sports are; that's what sports do. That's why they don't matter. You accept the rules—the way you accept a genie in a bottle as a housewife—but the rules are wrong.

Scully bricked it. Not even close. One of those shots that hits the deep right arc of the back rim and bounces straight out in the reverse angle. Same kind Herman put back in against Coatesville. Straight to Mike Hartman, who was immediately clobbered by Mike Dunn. Foul. Hartman made both. That was it.

* * *

In the end, there we were, having found the game at an elementary school playground between Stuckley and the developments. We figured ourselves out, then matched those abilities with the interpretive science and tactics of a composer and came out a team that could bring forth something holy. We followed the rules of our universe. We accepted it all and lived under its rubric. We should have won. And, in the end, it was all to get smoked by a jughead quarterback so fucking good he made all that work, all that magic, feel like bullshit not worth half a bag of piss.

We changed as Casale said a few words, which we knew meant nothing. Now I moved slower than everybody else, not wanting to leave. No one cried; I didn't cry. A janitor stood at the doorway anxious to wrap it up, another night. Phillip dressed quickest of all. He zipped up his bag and walked toward the door and stopped and said, "Let's get out of here."

The whole team rode the bus back. The parents were back at Fallcrest to meet us, to lick our wounds, to taste our sores, and to tell us it was okay. They applauded when we walked off. Garrison and Phillip and Scully and the twins said they were going to a party. The black guys were doing something over in Penwood. Professor LeFeber and his wife asked me to join them for a bite at a diner nearby, which was really goddamn nice, it really was. I said I had to go home.

It was dark when I walked in and I went to the bathroom. She was waiting there for me, like I knew she'd be. My girl. Dead on the floor.

They put her in a room with three other patients, but it was a formality. A nurse pulled the curtain around the gurney. The doctor came out and said, "Yeah, there's nothing. I'm sorry. It's a heart attack, massive arteriosclerosis. Don't see it much in women, but it happens. She's your aunt?"

"Yes."

"Is there anyone else to talk to? Is she married? Kids?"

"It's just me."

"Ah jeez. Tough one." He made a click sound with his tongue, the sound that means too bad. "Okay, I'm sorry. Let's get you out front where they'll take care of you."

We walked out into the hallway and a nurse took me to the station, where another nurse told me to follow her. They left me in a little office, a standard thing with two chairs in front of a desk with pens in a coffee mug and framed pictures of a wedding day and little kids in school uniforms. I started to cry. I cried by myself till the lady came in and gave me a box of tissues. Her name was Millie. She did the deaths. She was dressed like a nurse but a little more officey: the glasses on a string and scrub pants and a shirt like scrubs but not the same color. Flowers. What nurses who don't give a shit about wearing scrubs anymore wear. She was a big soft lady who ate pain. She must have been there all the time in that office with people who just had someone die. She absorbed it, like it went in through her chubby, spongy arms and into her intestines and later she dumped it out in a hospital bin with bedpans, dirty needles, and bloody gauze.

She filled out the forms and asked me to sign a few things. I said there wasn't anyone I wanted to call and I didn't need anything to eat. The light was bright, fluorescent, fake, and intrusive. I wanted it to be dark, I wanted to be in a cave or a hole. Millie had to go in and out because she had other work to do. I don't know what she was waiting for but she wasn't letting me go, the same way the cops hold people in cells. The time they let you go seems so arbitrary. There's no clock on those things. You sit there, never knowing how they are deciding when you've had enough, when you are ready to be let out.

She walked in and said, "There's someone here for you."

Behind her was Ervin. He turned sideways to get past, and came and grabbed me up out of the chair and pulled me in tight. "It's all right. It's all right. It's all right." That's what he said to me.

82

The truth is, regardless of what I've said, Fred Shero, Richard Manuel of The Band, and John Africa were not all in Philadelphia on January 6, 1974. It didn't happen. It doesn't make the date any less important, it's just not true that they were together. Or that their convergence is to blame for that time period signaling the bottom of civilization. Can't blame them.

The Flyers went on the road. They were on their way to Minnesota, where Bobby Clarke tied it at three in the third, and then to Montreal, where Jimmy Watson and Yvan Cournoyer went off for high sticking in the first period.

What is true is that Richard Manuel hanged himself on March 4, 1986, in his hotel room in Winter Park, Florida. His friends said he was doing fine, everyone thought he was okay. They couldn't really understand why he did it. I think I know why he did it. He was not with his full team— they argued too much, were tired of it, got old, watched it pass. He was playing covers of songs they wrote twenty years ago.

No matter how much time goes by, it's Richard's voice that always gets me:

Standing next to me in this lonely crowd,
Is a man who swears he's not to blame.
All day long I hear him shouting so loud,
Crying out that he was framed.

I see my light come shining
From the west unto the east.
Any day now, any day now,
I shall be released.

The most important principle is music because that is what is left of us when you take the natural world away. After we disintegrate. You will know this when the chair is kicked out from under you in Winter Park, Florida; in the ashes on Osage Avenue; in a ditch outside Gettysburg; wrapped around a tree by the Lobster Pot; getting dressed in an equipment room at the Palestra; or when you are lying dead on the dirty linoleum floor. You will know all that is left is the music, the way you played, the way you sang. You will know where the other guys will be. You will know you are better together. You will know this when you are carrying the Cup around the ice, when you see your reflection in a place so high above the wall, and when all around you there are dead bodies on the field. You will hear freedom, and you will sing its song. You will hear America, and you will know that music is best.

V
REMNANTS

It is not to diffuse you that you were born of your mother and father—it is to identify you,
It is not that you should be undecided, but that you should be decided;
Something long preparing and formless is arrived and formed in you,
You are thenceforth secure, whatever comes and goes.

—Walt Whitman, *Leaves of Grass*

83

The fifth, and final, step was firing, or burning, the brick. Burning bricks.

They knew from the old country that just putting bricks in the fire didn't work. Bricks had to be baked in the kiln. They built kilns by trial and error, lots of people got blown up, lots of motherfuckers got smoked.

When not fired enough, bricks crumble under a load. Like people. A red brick that is burned too much becomes vitrified, fragile. They didn't have thermometers back then. They had to do it by feel. Bad brick disintegrates. But feel it they did. They knew how to make brick that would last.

The Walt Whitman Bridge connects Philadelphia and New Jersey, a suspension expanse with seven twelve-foot-wide lanes. It was voted "Most Beautiful Structure of Steel" in 1957 by the American Institute of Steel Construction. It runs across the Delaware River from Gloucester, just outside Camden, to South Philadelphia.

The Archdiocese of Camden opposed naming the bridge after a homosexual. It is hard to believe there was anyone who wasn't opposed, hard to believe that in 1957 they named a bridge from Philadelphia to the Pine Barrens after old Walt Whitman, wandering minstrel, purveyor of smut of the expanding mind, lover of boys, singer of songs.

The Delaware is a cold and gray-black river, not inviting on its best day. The Walt Whitman is a shitty old bridge now. It begins and ends in concrete and metal and lighted directional signs with orange pylons and E-ZPass readers. Oil refineries and tankers and rusting boats and equipment are all that can be seen on the shores. Traffic is bad. The bridge tries to transcend the river, the reality below. No one speaks of its beauty because it is thoroughly modern, well beyond nature. It is the remains, the detritus. It runs outside the city. All it does is leave, because when all is said and done, there is Whitman, picking through the battlefield, sifting through the littered remains, never caring for Philadelphia.

84

L ife turned its page. We all tried to play in college. Phillip played four years at Delaware, but he didn't grow. He only played in five games his senior year. Stokes tried to play for La Salle but he got cut.

Leonard blew out his knee playing at Cheyney. In the middle of the Betours mess, I went out drinking with him. I was dating a Chinese girl at the time. She liked to go out to brunch. "She's a brunch-eating motherfucker, huh?" He was still getting the dirt. "Tell me something good," he said, like the old days. When I gave him details, he closed his eyes and stomped his feet. A lesser motion than when we were kids, but the same Leonard.

We drove home in his car. He sat behind the wheel and said, "You know, it's all fucked up. We had all this stuff to go through."

"I know."

"At least white people got shit like the Flyers." He turned to me and smiled. "We got shit like MOVE. That's what it means to be black. The shit you get is like MOVE when the white kids get ice hockey and Nixon. Diabolical-ass politicians and dumb motherfuckers skating around."

"What do you think?" I said. "Do you think that waitress fucked me over? The one that moved away?"

"Nah, man. Look here." He was sure. "Sometimes people just move to Ohio."

Phillip went to work for his father-in-law's used-car dealership during the recession in '83. He had a lot of drama with women, but he stayed married to a girl from high school named Lucy Eccles. The old man died and Phillip took it over. We did some business, but he was pretty conservative with ads. He didn't pump any money into Eccles Motors. I felt like Phillip didn't want to get too personally identified with things. Being a star was tough on Phil—he had an instinct to run away for the rest of his life, it seemed to me. That explained the women.

He was one hell of a golfer. He took me to his club, Spring Hollow. It was littered, as the guy says, with the wrecks of former basketball stars. John Donaly, the Ridley guy of flicked elbow fame, was a member. "He's still bitter," Phil said. "And he got fat as hell."

Phil's buddies were nice guys, tanned Main Liners, the kind that are happy as hell to be outside all day. No Jews or blacks at Spring Hollow. Phillip didn't like that topic. "They're working on that." he would say. We played with an old guy named Whitey who was the greatest player ever to come from his town, Mechanics Grove, near Lancaster.

It wasn't very fair of me, but I hated them. I hated their carpeted locker room, their men's lounge where some fucking old guy told me to take my hat off when Phillip left me alone at the table with a bowl of pretzels.

I got up and drifted around the bar. There were old black-and-white photos on the walls—club champs, shots of guys from the early days of the club in knickers and early-time golf clothes. A picture of Bobby Jones when he came there in the thirties. Lots of the old-line Philadelphia money. There were also pictures of the suntanned golfers of the sixties and seventies. I stopped by a picture of Joe Namath surrounded by thirty hale and hearty members. They were posing all around Joe and smiling their asses off.

"I was there," said Whitey. He and Phillip had walked up behind me and were looking at it, too.

"No kidding?" said Phil.

"Yup. Never forget it. He played a round and then we had a big banquet, just members and Joe. He gave the funniest after-dinner speech I ever heard."

"C'mon?"

"God's honest truth." He hit Phillip gently with the back of his hand, readying a story. "He gets up and he says, 'Okay, gentlemen, tonight I'm here to talk about the Four Needs of Modern Man.'"

Phillip was beaming, waiting for it.

"'The Four Needs of Modern Man are as follows. One: Food.'"

Phil said, "Okay."

"'Two: Shelter.'"

We nodded.

"'Three: Pussy.'"

Phillip cracked up. I smiled. Whitey grabbed Phillip's elbow for the punch line.

"And Four: . . . *Strange* Pussy.'"

With that, they both doubled over, loving the joke and Joe Namath. I laughed, too.

But I still hated the place, never wanted to belong there, even when Phil offered to sponsor me. It didn't help that I can't golf. I don't have the concentration. Case in point was the day we played with Whitey. "I can't figure it out," Phil said on sixteen. "You were tough. You never flaked. You should be good at golf."

"I'm different now. We all are. Except maybe you."

Whitey crushed one down the middle and I changed the subject with Phil. "Do you think you can tell when you see a kid who is a great player? I mean, do you think you recognize a kid like that right away, in a split second? You know, because you were so good? Do you think you have some kind of bond the rest of the world will never know?"

He looked at Whitey and raised his eyebrows, as in. "What do you think?" Whitey didn't say anything.

Phil gave me the All-American smile. "Never thought about it, Joey."

"Let me ask you this, then: When you're on the course and you absolutely smash one, doesn't matter, a drive or a fairway wood or even a putt and it just works dead, solid, perfect. When you hit that perfect shot, how do you feel?"

Phil grinned, and I knew I had him. "It makes me feel young again, Joey, what do you expect I'm gonna say? We had it good when we were younger—a bunch of guys who came out of nowhere and found each other, won championships, stayed loyal to each other, probably the best years of our lives—except for hotshots like you and Scully. That was some great stuff, we should hang more."

We finished up and all said our good-byes in the parking lot. There was a playground across the street and we could see kids playing a pickup game.

Phillip walked Whitey toward his car. "See ya later, pal," Phillip said.

The older man shook his hand and said, "So long, Ace."

85

Eric arranged for me to be processed quickly late on a Friday. I was home in a few hours. It wasn't really big news, and it came out on Saturday: page 3 of the *Inquirer*'s business section. They had a picture of me, a publicity shot from eight years ago, on page 5 of the *Daily Times*.

Janice called. "Joe, what's going on? You were arrested? You don't tell me? I can't even pick Tia up at school."

"I'm sorry. I'm sorry I didn't call. Eric decided to let them do it today. I can't talk to you. They can ask you about anything I say. They will ask you about anything I say."

"Oh my God. Oh my *God*. What the hell did you do? I can't talk to you? What am I supposed to tell Tia? What the hell am I supposed to do? Do I have to get a lawyer? I am freaking out. What the fuck did you do?"

"Janice, I can't talk. I'm sorry. Don't call anymore. They'll look at the records. I will come see you tomorrow. And I'm fine, in case you were wondering."

I didn't go.

I called my voice mail. Beep. "Joe, it's Eric. Listen, come to my office at five today. Saunders finally sent the discovery. I've got to show you something."

When I walked in he jumped right up, and I knew it was bad because he was being a touch nicer to me than usual. Just a shade, the way people are when something has happened to you and you don't know it yet and they are about to give you bad news. I'm very used to that. He held up a disc, like a DVD. "Can you believe it? They turn evidence over like this? They send shit like this nowadays. I can remember when videocassettes were the big deal. It was, like, a revolution." He put it in and pulled out the remote. He gestured at the chair in front of it. "Sit down, bub. Now, let me see if I can work this fucking thing."

He got the menu screen on the TV monitor. The graphics made me shitless with fear. It was so modern, professional. So far advanced. A big official seal: an eagle, a crest, something vaguely Pennsylvanian, like a silhouette of Independence Hall. "Eastern District of Pennsylvania, US Attorney's Office."

Eric gave a big sigh. "All right. Here goes."

The thing started and I saw Ray sitting at a table. A guy who looked like a plainclothes cop was putting a microphone on him. Someone said, "Let's begin. State your name."

"Raymond Michael O'Malley."

The invisible questioner identified the date and time. He didn't say where they were. "Mr. O'Malley, you've come here today to give a statement, is that correct?"

"Yes."

"And the record will reflect you are doing this voluntarily, correct?"

"Yes."

"Okay, please proceed."

"As I told the investigator, I have approached you folks because of the information I have about Joe Knight and the sale of his company . . . to a French company called Publicité Rouge and the fellow, Francois Betours."

Ray's face was gray, his cheeks were sucked in, there were dark circles under his eyes. He was angry, but it didn't show; he was collected, as though he'd practiced it a million times. My brain fuzzed over and he and the questioner started to drone through his relationship with me. I looked at Eric.

"You're shitting me."

Eric nodded at the screen. "Just watch."

Ray continued. "I just want you people to know what I know. I don't know if it was on the up-and-up or not, but I want you to know what I know and I don't want my daughter or my family caught up in anything."

I said to Eric, "Can they do this? I mean . . . He doesn't even have Betours's name right."

"Watch. We'll get into it."

"On several occasions, Joe as said to me that he was worried about the way he did the sale of his company. He told me the Frenchman he dealt with was . . . well, he said he knew the guy was involved in criminal behavior."

"Can you give us more detail about what Mr. Knight told you?"

"Yes. He said he was very worried about the shell company and the secondary offering, I believe that's the proper term?" He looked at the questioner, but he must have gotten a signal from that guy not to ask him, that it was all being recorded, to remember the camera. He looked back at the camera. "Joe said he knew the secondary offering was illegal and was very worried that he would get in trouble for it—and that he'd gotten his friends into it somehow and that they would, you know, get in the soup for it, too."

He tried to talk in the official language of cops and trials, which we all do when we are in any situation involving crime or the government. Another thing from TV. More of the White Man Shuffle. He came off as trying to sound smart, like he was trying to talk like Perry Mason or Jack Webb.

"Anything else, Mr. O'Malley?"

"Yes. He also told my daughter this on numerous occasions. He has trouble sleeping and is on antianxiety medication. He is worried he was going to get himself and all of his friends implicated in something. Naturally, my daughter is worried about herself and my granddaughter. So am I. But she is reluctant to talk about it, for obvious reasons."

It was short. Only eight minutes long. Eric picked up the remote and froze it.

"He's lying. He's fucking lying!" I said.

"Calm down."

Then I got quiet. "He lied."

"Okay. Take it easy."

I said nothing. Ray's face was sure. It gave off the feeling of hey I'm just being a good citizen and this guy's up to something. But there was the vengeance of the betrayed, of all the things I'd done. It was the black fear coming after me. It was the dark overhang of my life, the tragic rearing up. This was where it was always heading, where we have been heading forever. Justice for the heir who approaches, the old not giving the center away. He would be goddamned if I was going to get away with doing something like this. Not to his daughter and granddaughter. He was taking care of his family. He didn't care if he was ratting. I was foreign and he was there to stop me.

You can't block a guy like that from the T-ball field and expect nothing to happen.

86

At Dottie's funeral, everyone offered to take me home, even the Marlowes and the Beattys. All of the guys stood with me when we put her in the ground. They each tried to say something to me. Stokes came up with his mom. "She's with Jesus, now, honey. You let me know if you want to come stay with me and David."

Little Etheridge, of all people, is the one I remember most from that day. He was just a guy I grew up with. He was headed to a job at the shipyard or a furniture maker. Maybe to the service where he might get his ass blown away, or sent to Germany. It struck me as I stood there that there were two kinds of guys: the kind like Garrison and Mike, who thought everyone and everything was already rigged and had everything planned out—certain and cynical, like the guy in a story who weighed out the future and decided it was worth only half a try—and those like Phillip and Little Etheridge, natural inventors and believers in their own ability to make a change happen with their bodies or their minds, whether with a basketball or *Ultraman*. Little Etheridge stood with me for a while after everyone left. He didn't say anything. He looked me in the eye a couple of times, then stared back down at the ground. "It's pitiful," he said at one point. Then he said nothing again.

Finally, I said, "Thanks, man."

Mrs. Scully made it clear that I was coming with them. She helped me with everything, the coffin, the burial, all of it. When it was all done we walked into their big drafty house and she said, "You'll go up next to Aunt Mary." I forgot they had her up there. She was Mr. Scully's mother's sister.

Scully's father—Officer Scully—was sitting in the dining room reading the paper, still wearing his black suit. He and I had never spoken much. He wasn't around often and when he was, he didn't talk. He smoked cigars and read the papers for all I could see. I thanked him for everything.

He put the paper down and looked at me from over his reading glasses. I was pretty out of it and tired of sympathy, but he was not sending me warm vibes.

"Now you start being a man, Joe."

He went back to the paper. He was a fucking hardass, that guy.

There were two single beds in Aunt Mary's room, and Mrs. Scully pointed me to the open one. It was what I thought Ireland was like: sad and dark, with cheap antiques and stained beds and framed pictures of the saints. The pillows were the gray-and-white-striped kind you see everywhere from prisons to hospitals; the sheets and blanket were old and stiff, a bit worn after years of being hung from clotheslines. "You two can keep each other company." She tried to make it seem hospitable, even normal. I thanked her. I was too drained to say anything. But even so, there was a roguishness coming on me, not the Roger Miller kind. Maybe not the Joe Knight Sr. kind, either.

The old lady was ninety-six and faded in and out. They kept a washbasin by her feet, and every few hours Mrs. Scully came up and helped her go to the bathroom or cleaned her. Sometimes the stink woke me up.

"Jesus is my noble king, I am his humble bride," she said while she sat in the chair, waiting for Mrs. Scully to change the soiled sheets.

I slept there for a few weeks. She moaned in the dark. The first night, I went to check on her. She was scared. "Who's that?"

"It's me. I'm Joe Knight. I'm Chris's friend. You know, I'm staying here with you."

"Oh."

"Are you okay? Do you want me to get Mrs. Scully . . . Eileen?"

"No, no dear."

We went back to bed and after twenty minutes the moaning started again. I did nothing. I lay there. I thought of Dottie. She was all they had given me and now I didn't have her and I was in a room with a dying old lady with not one, not two, but three crucifixes on the wall.

When I got an erection, I worried about Aunt Mary hearing me. I jerked off easily at first, and she didn't stir. Gradually, I was doing it full throttle. I blew a load into Mrs. Scully's bleached sheets every night.

87

I was back in school by Monday after the funeral. I saw Stokes and Phillip talking in the hallway.

"Casale quit," said Philip. "He got a job with a pharmaceutical company."

"He waited till we were done," said Stokes.

Awards banquets were at the Log Cabin, a big restaurant and wedding hall on Baltimore Pike. It was full of players, parents, coaches, teachers, and other people from the school. We wore coats and ties and sat at round tables. The bread and butter were out when we sat down, the butter divided into one-and-a-quarter-inch-square pads between a strong bonded paper back and waxed paper on the front. BUTTER was printed on the waxed paper repeatedly, back and forth in patterns, up and down the square.

We each got trophies for being Central League Champs and District One Runner-Up. There were special awards: Stokes for Best Defensive Player, Herman for Most Improved. Garrison got the Sportsmanship Award, which was just a way to get him a trophy because the rest of the starting five got trophies. Scully and Phillip were Co-MVPs. Phillip thanked his parents and teammates. Scully did the same and gave a really nice speech about the assistant coaches and Casale. He also talked about Cove and mentioned Dottie. All the moms cried. "Everyone loved Dottie and Henry," he said.

Lou Scott announced a five-hundred-dollar gift to Cove's family from the Kiwanis Club, thanked all the parents and players, and introduced Casale.

Casale was uncomfortable. "I know I don't have to tell most of you this, but I will anyways for the ones who don't know it. It is a miracle to me that these kids were born in the same year in the same school district. They started playing together, on their own, without anyone telling them to, when they were twelve, thirteen years old. They drove, walked, got rides, hitchhiked, I don't know what else . . . to get to that little court in spring, summer, and winter. They played every day. They worked with each other, challenged each other, and made each other great. They made themselves better." He stumbled and looked down. "I have been playing and coaching the game of basketball all my life. Besides Marie and Flora, it's really the only thing I have." Then he stared at the audience and said it just above a whisper: "*I have never . . . never . . . seen anything like these guys.*" It was quiet for a while. He got his voice back. "To all of you, to their parents, their teachers, their friends, I want to say congratulations. We could all go another forty years without seeing a team like this . . . and we won't see it again." The crowd stood up and clapped.

"Now, if you'll excuse me, I want to address the rest of this to the players." He looked down from the little stage. "I'm going to be blunt. I want to say a few things that you might not expect to hear, but you guys know me, I have to say it like it is."

He cleared his throat. "Guys, as you all know, I will be leaving coaching and teaching in a month. I'm going to take a job in business. I want you to hear why I'm doing it from me, in front of everybody. I am doing it for my family. Teachers and coaches don't make a lot of money and my wife and I have decided that this is what I need to do.

"Now, this is the hard part. I want you guys to know that the game of basketball is not everything in life. I have watched you almost every day for the past five years. The way I see it, you have all—all of you—been drawn to basketball as a way to understand things. I know this because it is what I did—I've even done it into my thirties, I love it so much. I know how much the playing of the game means, how much putting your shoes on and running out to the court means. I know you have a desire to win—I know how much that means, *what* that means to you.

"But what I want to leave you with is that there is more to life than basketball. I know a lot of you guys are going to go and try to play in college. And I would never bet against any of you doing anything. But if you do—or as you do—think about this: you can also do other things. Play for the rest of your life, but make it a game. Thank you for all you've given me and God bless."

The school sent me to a counselor, and Harris checked in on me. I changed. I worked for a landscaper, cutting grass and getting high. I moved back into our apartment and, except for a few calls and a once-a-month visit from a social worker, I was on my own.

I didn't want anyone to make it a big deal. The other guys from the team were going off to school and their families were dealing with their own feelings. Ervin came to talk to me. He asked me how I was doing for money and he looked around the place. He asked me to sit down on the couch.

"Listen, son, I just want to tell you this: You always got a place with us. You can always call me and I will answer the phone and tell you what I think."

I told him thanks and I appreciated everything.

"I'm a tell you this straight, Joe. You can't drift. I know what you do. You drift. You're what they call a loner. Can't let that happen. Being alone is a stop and not a stay, you understand?"

I told him I did.

"You're good in the heart, I knew it since you was a kid. Don't let yourself down. That's all I got to say."

Artie lived at Woodlawn Acres for a long, long time. Longer than anyone could imagine, long enough that I literally forgot he was there sometimes. When Dottie died, I had to go tell him. I went down Middletown Road, past the Pines Tavern and the bushes and the hay grass on the side of the road, past Habbersett's and past the Franklin Mint, till I got to the big redbrick building. Nurses clogged the parking lot jimmer-jammering between shifts in the cold, freezing rain.

They brought him out to see me in a wheelchair. He had a pajama top on with a blanket at his waist. He was gaunt and gone. He still had thick glasses but the eyes in the back were shot. He didn't talk; he made noises like a baby. I insisted on telling him before the funeral. I wanted to let him come.

Ervin came with me under protest. "Don't do it. Leave that man where he is. He's not there anymore, son. It's okay to leave him be."

But I wouldn't listen.

We were in front of Artie; old, decrepit, Alzheimered Artie. He had a medic behind him pushing the chair, a heavily built black man. His name was David Solomon. "David Solomon?" I said. "That's your name?" He ignored me.

"Artie?" he said. "This man here to see you. He's your nephew—he's your boy." Artie strained to look at my face. It didn't matter.

"Uncle Artie, it's Joe. Hi, Artie." I shook his arm to say hello. "You're getting skinny, man." Then I got down in front of him. "Uncle Artie, we have to tell you something." He looked down at me and he smiled. For the first time I saw that he had no teeth. His dentures were not in that morning. Maybe they didn't ever put them in anymore.

"I have some bad news—awful news, bud." He made a squeamish noise, and he looked pained. "Uncle Artie, Aunt Dottie is dead. She died yesterday at home." His head bobbled, it fell back, and he closed his eyes, nothing but black olive pits now. He knew what I said and you could see it pierce him the way a bolt is put into steel by a large machine. Not even the rotting stink of the people in the tiled room could hide it; not even David Solomon could shield it. Through the fog of deteriorating brain mass the message came and his mouth opened up and let out no sound, just a hole with no teeth and the non-noise of a person in a shell, dying and alone.

Artie died that day but his shell lived for a long time, his Last Days not coming for years. The cemetery where Dottie was buried is off St. Agnes's main property, down a few miles. It is old now, and the graves are run-down. They don't clean up and pieces of paper blow across the grass. I went there on one of the last, empty days before I went to jail.

It was rocky; there was not much grass. Even the weeds were sparse, an aging graveyard filled with the corpses of Catholics from the diaspora of Irish in the nineteenth century. It wasn't flat like a military graveyard. It turned and rolled with little hills, small ups and downs.

88

We had to go to the federal offices on Chestnut Street. We went into a conference room on the twelfth floor. It was actually pretty nice—not as *Barney Miller* as I expected. There were four of them: Saunders, who was young; another lawyer, even younger; a thick detective with Brylcreem-ed hair and a mustache; and Scully, who lifted his head a little and smiled. Seeing the court. Chris Scully.

"Okay," said Saunders, "let's get started. District Attorney Scully has been kind enough to get involved and I want to thank him for his help. Now, I know he and Mr. Knight are old acquaintances, and that this is a little unusual. But we are here to discuss some possible resolution."

"All right, let's cut through it. If I may, Dave?" said Scully.

"Sure."

"Eric, since we are informal, do you mind if I address Joe directly?"

"That's fine," said Eric.

Scully looked at me. "This is hard."

I said, "I know, just go ahead."

"I am here because I want to help. This is a nightmare for me: a group of people I love are in a mess. We have to work this out before it gets out of control—or even more out of control."

"I agree."

"All right. I've talked to these guys," motioning at Saunders and the kid, "and we have it to a place where it is all in your hands. But first, you have to understand something, Joey: they are ready to go on some people who you don't want to see them go on. I imagine you don't want to see Ervin Polk involved in this anymore."

I nodded.

"Me, either." He swallowed. "Buddy, there's no version of this where you don't do some time, that's the bottom line."

"You've got to be shitting me," said Eric, forward in his chair, on his toes. A different Eric: game-time Eric. "We came here for this?"

Scully held up his hands, "Listen, Eric, I came here . . ."

"Why *did* you come here? Why the fuck are you in this? I can't figure that out."

Scully snapped. "Because I grew up with these guys." Scully, down to the bone. "Let me ask *you* something, since you're asking a personal question. Did you ever belong to a group of guys who meant everything to you? I was never in the service—I don't know what that is like. But the closest thing I ever had was these guys. Do you know what that feels like?"

"No, I wasn't on a basketball team." Eric was sarcastic. "I was a boxer, actually, Chris. Jews were boxers when I was a kid. You may not know that. They might not have taught you that at Villanova."

"Great, I bet you were tough," said Scully. Real rooster stuff. Then, he broke. His voice cracked. "I don't want to see this go any further, dammit." He smacked his hand on the table. "Not any further!"

Eric looked at Saunders, completely quiet, unmoved. "David, do you have an offer for me? Or are we going to jerk each other off for a while?"

"Why don't we get everyone out of here except me and you and Chris."

I went into the hallway with Dick Butkus and the kid prosecutor. They sneaked looks at me, both chewing gum. I knew they spent the last few months going through everything about me and now here I was, in front of them. They made whispery comments and laughed. A faggot and a moosehead. The kid had the same wing tips as Scully. They clicked on the marble floor.

"I won my fantasy league."

"No money, right?" said the cop, pretending to be serious. They laughed.

Eric came out. "Come with me. We're going to get a cup of coffee."

Saunders and Scully were behind him. Scully looked at me, like he was the only one that knew me, like we were in front of a group of strangers and he would meet me back at his house, where his mom had peanut butter crackers. I nodded. "Chris."

"See you in a little while," he said. "Let's try to get this behind us. Talk to Eric."

89

Eric knew a diner around the corner. "Is this where you bring all the girls before you nail them?" I said.

"That's good. You're good."

He ordered coffee and I asked for water. I was ready to shit my pants anyway and didn't need any coffee.

"You're lucky you're not a Jew," he said. "It's like a bad Jew joke. Did you hear the one about the Jewish plea bargain?"

"Tell me."

"Well, my boy, the good news is you can get everybody out of this: Ervin, Leonard, Rolanda Coverdale, all the guys. The bad news is you have to give them all your money and do three months."

Jail. And no money. "Eric, I can't go to jail."

"Just listen. It's better than you think. Technically, the sentence is six months to two years, but we have an understanding that they'll walk you out within ninety days. And it's even better: Scully's convinced Saunders to go to the judge to let you serve it in his jail. Dover County. Trust me, that's a lot better. I'm good with that part."

"What about Janice and Tia?"

"I think I swung that. You have to pay a four-million-dollar fine to the feds and one million to the state. That leaves a million in a trust for Tia."

"Janice?"

"Janice gets the house."

"What about my Uncle Artie in the home?"

"It's one of Scully's hospitals. He guarantees lifetime care."

I blew wind out of my mouth, "So, in three months I'm out and broke."

"Exactly. In three months you're out and broke. Fresh start. We will keep it out of the papers—nobody cares anyway, trust me. And in six months no one will remember."

"I'll just be back to square one."

He squinted at me. "You'll just be back to square one?" He was frustrated. He let it sit. "Let me ask you something."

"Shoot."

"Do you really think you didn't do anything wrong? Honest question."

"What do you mean?"

"Well, here we are at moment-of-truth time. It's time to fuck, fight, or play marbles."

"I understand."

"In your heart, do you believe you were completely innocent—that you didn't know that somehow, somewhere you were screwing somebody? A French shareholder, somebody? That someone wasn't getting fucked over?"

I didn't say anything.

"I'll say this, you're pretty inscrutable."

"That's what they tell me."

"There is a time in every case where it gets to this. My clients—no one likes to be compared to others, but there are important similarities— do not use guns, don't kill people, and so on. They are all in a jam of essentially the same nature. I call it the *Mr. Ed Problem*. What do you think the *Mr. Ed Problem* is?"

"No idea."

"It's that horses don't fucking talk, Joe. Everyone starts believing all of this shit they are involved in, even when it doesn't make sense. That guy Betours was completely and utterly full of shit and you should have known it. You bought his bullshit. All that talk about shell companies and the power of the Internet. You can't throw watermelons out of skyscrapers and think they will fly. You can't just sign some papers with some French lawyers and expect that someone somewhere isn't going to come after you. It's the same everywhere—Silicon Valley, Wall Street. It's like gravity. There's too much hocus-pocus. The rules are always going to come back on you."

"But . . . I didn't know . . ."

"That's the heart of it. You didn't? You didn't know something was weird?"

I said nothing.

"You didn't know? Are you going to get up on that stand and tell people you were tricked?"

He let that sink in. He scratched his beard. "I don't know." He looked at the counter, at the stainless-steel shelves sticking out from wallpaper with rusty edges from cigarette smoke. "Listen, I'll fight it for you." He added it up. "I like the case enough to tell you we can fight it. I like you. I like the blacks holding out and I like the crazy guy. The tape is bullshit. Scully obviously doesn't want this, so there's something there I can fuck around with . . ." He made a clicking noise. This one I didn't recognize.

"But?"

"But they're going to give those people—your friends—a really hard time. And we will still probably lose. Then they take all you money, bankrupt you forever, and you get six to eight years."

We sat there.

"What would you do?"

"I can't tell you what to do, bub."

"You've been here before. Tell me what to do."

"I can't do that."

"C'mon, man. I don't have anyone to ask."

He stared at me. "It won't be as your lawyer if I tell you."

"I know."

"Take it. It's only money."

90

In 1974, I was not the only kid who felt sorry for Nixon. I watched the hearings with Dottie when they replayed them at night. I loved the voice votes, the roll calls. There was a guy named Hutchinson, who was the third out of four old white men called at the beginning. He always voted for Nixon, which meant voting no.

"Mister Hutch-in-son . . ."

"*No!*"

He yelled it, like his vote counted for more, the louder he was. He was pissed off. He was faceless, part of the old gray establishment being ripped down. Like the other cops, the ones with no names, on *Dragnet*. I cared only about basketball, but you couldn't avoid Watergate, like you couldn't avoid death. You had to deal with it, make peace with it on some level. It was oppressive and needed an answer. Fucking guys like Hutchinson, fighting off the beginning of the end, favoring the creation of detritus.

Let me see you tell me your story without lies. Let me see you admit you felt sorry for Nixon. He was a Quaker. How do you square him? He was the president but he was so lonely. He was such a *victim*. Jeez-us, he was a victim. He probably deserved it, Dottie said, but she couldn't help feeling bad for him. She was happy that I felt a little sorry for him. She was happy when I was nice in any way.

Later, when I realized what had happened, what he did, I didn't feel that way anymore. It was the perfect bottom. We've lived in that pissed pool since. Goddamn monkey men, goddamn Charlton-Heston-*Planet-of-the-Apes* monkey-men, finding Statue of Liberty heads sticking out of the dirt.

We were playing at Glentop the day he resigned. A TV was on in the auditorium and they called outside to let us know. "He's about to resign to the country. You kids might want to watch this."

Scully and Mike Dunn showed no interest. Sean Dunn started walking toward the school and I went with him. Leonard came, too.

"C'mon," said Scully. "We can't play now."

"Just play threes or something," said Sean.

The box was set up on a brown-metal AV stand with a black plastic mat. Kids and grown-ups wore summer clothes.

"What happened?" said a younger teacher, hippieish with granny glasses. "What made him finally give in?"

"They told him he was on his own," said the woman standing next to me. "He's at the end of the line. He belongs in jail."

Then he came on. She was right. He was alone.

91

After Eric made the deal, I drove to Fallcrest on a Saturday morning. I knew they'd be walking out, on their way to lunch at the diner, like they did every week. Scully was the old-timer, still bringing the ball up, king of the court. The floor was the brand-new product of the fundraiser Scully had told me about at the stables—I never did get around to sending him the money for that. I watched from the doorway as they finished. At 11-11, he isolated the right side. The kid guarding him was at least ten years younger, a cousin, I think, of Etheridge Butcher. The Penwood guys had lots of cousins. And cousins of cousins.

Scully used his left as his pivot and did the jab step, stutter step with his right, drove by the kid, went up, and as the weak side big guy gave help, he tucked down, as always, went under him, and laid it in.

I hung outside the doorway. One of them, probably a cop, saw me. Scully walked out and saw me, too. He got it in a second and didn't flinch.

"It's all right, Tommy," he said to the cop. He motioned me back to the gym. "Let's go in here."

I followed him.

"How are you making out?"

"How do you think I'm making out, Chris? I'm going to jail next week."

"Yeah, I know. But we got you with us. And I'm going to walk you through as soon as it calms down. I promise. And you'll get a fresh start. Get on with your life."

"Do you ever shut it off?"

He cocked his head. "What?"

"Do you ever stop with the bullshit? You phony fucking politician? Why don't you just cut the fucking shit? For once. It's just me and you. I know you. You got it. You won."

"What are you talking about? Am I hearing this right? Let's start over. You should be saying, 'Thanks, man. I know you stuck your neck out for me. I know you got me and my friends and their families out of a mess that I created.' That's what you should be saying, you dumb fuck."

He was in my face. I pushed him back. He stopped.

I yelled at him. "You don't get it. I know, Scully. I *know*. I went to Wally Rafferty's funeral a few months ago. Remember him? Remember that kid? He killed himself. He took a bottle of pills and killed himself. Did you know that?"

He looked confused. "Of course I know that." He opened his hands in front of me, like he just got called for a foul he did not commit. "I was an altar boy with him, for Christ's sake. He had a lot of problems." He backed up. "What's *that* have to do with anything?"

"Oh, please."

"Does this have to do with that fucking note you handed me at the diner? I still can't figure that out."

I didn't say anything.

"Look, Joe. You're under a lot of stress. I realize that you were probably under a lot of stress that day we had breakfast, so I wrote it off. Then this all happened."

It was too much. "Stop. Stop it." I wasn't letting him get away with it. "It won't work. I saw you, Scully. I *saw you*. When we were kids, when I used to wait for you at St. Ignatius. I saw you suck his cock. The priest. And I saw worse. I saw you standing lookout while Wally had to suck that old man's cock. How could you do that, man?"

"What? Who?"

"Don't try to bullshit me, Scully. I *know* you. I even tried to tell your mother and she ignored me. That's how fucked-up you are. That's how deep it is."

"I don't know what you are talking about."

"The priest! Father Shea. You don't think anyone saw?"

"What?"

"What is it like? What's it like to live with that? Did you send Wally flowers? Did you say to your wife, 'Aww, that's too bad? I knew that guy. I used to stand guard while the priest fucked him in the ass'?"

Scully was still holding his hands up. "What are you saying, that Father Shea molested me? And Wally Rafferty?" He laughed at me in disbelief.

"I'm sure it wasn't only him," I said. "Wait, let me think. . . . Is that your excuse? That he was fucking you, too? That it was better to stand lookout than get fucked or have to suck his cock? Did you have to suck his cock first?"

"Oh my God," he said. "You are really fucked-up, you know that?"

"Don't lie to me. Don't you . . . fucking . . . lie to me."

I swung at him. I got a little of his chin, but he got his hands up. We wrestled to the ground. He punched me hard in the ribs and I lost my wind. He got me in a headlock and took me to the ground.

"You crazy fuck. What is wrong with you?" He lost it; the Scully temper was full on. "You stupid, crazy fuck." He had me pinned down. "Are you done? Are you done?"

He saw that I wasn't going to fight anymore, but he held me there.

"The fucking priest was *old*, you idiot!" He lifted my pinned wrists and slammed them down. "He had a *bag*! He had half his colon removed, for fuck's sake. He was an old man! We had to help him. It was part of the job." He was spitting as he yelled. "He had to get fixed up, his pants fixed up, right after the service in that room back there. Whoever was younger had to help him with it—the older one stood guard at the door so no one would walk in on him, none of the ladies. He didn't want to be seen like that." He got up. "You fucking sick-minded fuck. He was an *old man*! Did you go all these years thinking that?"

I was stunned. "You're making it up. What about Wally?"

"I don't know what happened to Wally, Joey! Shit happens to people, how do know what happened to Wally Rafferty? He was weird. He was gay and he killed himself. That's all I know. You think I have special information or something? I heard it just like you heard it."

"I don't believe you."

"You know what. *That's* your problem. Everybody only ever wanted to help you, you asshole. My family did everything for you. I had to drag your ass everywhere. My mother did anything she could for you."

"Oh, yeah, right."

"And you want to know what? I know some things, too. And the shit I know isn't fantasy. It's not made up."

"Yeah, like what?"

"My old man was a cop, Joe. Do you remember that? Huh?"

"What's that supposed to mean?"

"I know some things." He stopped. "I know some things about you. But I let them go. We all let them go."

"Like what?" The hairs on my arm started to tingle. My stomach turned sour.

"I'm not going to say."

"Because it's bullshit. Because you don't know anything about me. You're just a fucking politician, Scully. A politician since the jump. You watched out for priests doing little kids so you wouldn't get fucked yourself. On the road to something big. Still going places, right? What's it going to be, what are you running for next? Couldn't let this thing that I knew get out, right? So you had to take me down. Had to get me so I didn't have it over on you, right?"

"You are completely out of your mind. . . . That's what you think, isn't it? That's what you really think."

"It's the truth."

"The *truth*? That's the truth? I'll tell you the truth: you left your Aunt Dottie dead on the bathroom floor while you went to play a basketball game. Like she was a piece of trash. That's the truth."

"What?"

"Yeah, you did. *My dad was a cop!*" he screamed. "*Remember?* They all knew. They knew she had been dead for a while when she got to the hospital. My dad and his partner figured it out. They knew you didn't want to miss the game. They felt sorry for you. My mom told me the whole thing. We all felt sorry for you."

We sat huffing and puffing from the fight, the feel of the floor and the lights so familiar. I could hear the sneaker squeaks and see floor dust on the sideline. Memories swirled around. Legs, shouts. Me and Scully. Back where we started.

After a time, I said, "All this because of my fucking father-in-law. Fucking guy."

"Huh?" Scully pushed to his feet. He bent over, like he was catching his breath during a foul shot. He muttered, "I don't believe it." He stood up over me. "You think this is all because of your father-in-law?"

"Yeah. Of course."

He laughed. "They didn't care about that, man. Saunders told me early on he knew he couldn't use that statement. That was never the thing." He started walking to the door and shook his head. He didn't even turn back to look at me. "You did this to yourself, Joe."

92

Whitman was an editor, printer, typesetter, and columnist. He was a nurse during the Civil War. He went throughout the country, with a long spell as a clerk for the federal government, before he settled in Jersey. He released the first edition of *Leaves of Grass* in 1855. He lived in Camden for the last nineteen years of his life, dying on March 26, 1892. He kept working on the book till the end, not afraid to rerelease a changed version every couple of years. It kept being reborn.

For my money, the iconography is wrong. Everything is named after Franklin, who came from Boston and preferred France. Nor do I care for the other big names, like Doctor J, from Roosevelt, New York. He didn't grow up or stay here, either.

It was all redbrick. It's all redbrick shithouse now.

In the morning I help pick up the dead and lay them in rows in the barn. Objection. Lack of foundation.

93

The *I Dream of Jeannie* bottle was in a cabinet at the Penn's Meade Farm Road house. I picked it up when Janice wasn't home, in effect stealing my mother's remnants from myself. There were some papers with it: the death certificate for Jane Doe and a receipt from the funeral parlor.

It wasn't hard to re-create the death certificate. I had a graphics program and found an electric typewriter at the library near Tia's school. I got into it, actually. Once I had the layout and typed the info in the form, I distressed the paper, another thing you can learn on the Internet. I baked it between two aluminum sheets and then rolled some clay over it with a rolling pin. It had a gray complexion by the time I was done. Not brown like the Declaration of Independence, or the walls in Eric's diner, or the linoleum on Dottie's floor. It didn't look anything like the original Jane Doe death certificate, but it looked old enough.

I have fancy stationery cards. Three-by-five, beige, very high-quality paper, almost like cardboard. It was a gift from Janice. I don't send many notes, so I still had plenty of it.

Joe Knight

Dear Carolyn
It was a pleasure meeting you, even if the circumstances were difficult.
I appreciate your courage in seeking me out and I am glad you did it.
I am enclosing Artie's ashes. I know that he disappointed you enough to fill
a lifetime. I can't explain him. He was a puzzle. To me he was looking for
something and I now think that something was you and your brothers.

I apologize if this is wrong, but in some small way, I hope your having this might get you to a better place. I have a daughter, and I can imagine what he and you both felt.

It's a try. For what it is worth, Artie was a very kind to me. But you should know he was not my father, didn't want to be. I am certain he never replaced you. I think of him just as my friend. And although I miss him and my aunt Dottie still so very much, I want my friend to be with his family.

My best to you, Joe.

At the Penwood post office, I put the note and the urn in a breadbox-size brown box. I bought some of those Styrofoam peanuts to keep it from breaking. I put the phony death certificate for Arthur Ventresca, deceased 1997, in the box and mailed it.

94

I went back to my apartment and sat on the couch. Its leather was wearying. Soon it would be no good. When I couldn't stand it anymore, at dusk, I took the elevator down and headed out the front of the building. It was starting to rain.

I turned north and there was Janice. She was sitting on a stoop. She'd been crying. She looked like she'd been crying for days. She'd lost weight, her eyelids were black. Her face was shaking. She saw me and stood up.

She was so sad, it shook the dead off me. She mouthed the words, "I'm ... so ... sorry." The things we do to each other. We are playing with dynamite in this life. The bullets are real, and I've left them all crying. We erode away in a box of space and time. The greats were greats because they were real, they set themselves on fire. The real guys sang songs. I prayed for the glint between old and young, when players knew players. I wanted to be real.

I gave a weak smile and walked to her. The things we do. So much under the bridge. I reached down and pulled her in and she buried her face in my chest, sobbing. "Shhh," I said. "It's okay, it's okay."

I felt her hair and held the back of her head close. Some girls remind you of all the songs in the world. I whispered into her ear: "Send me your picksha ..."

Janice O'Malley smiled and cried. She hugged me hard and I hugged her back. After a time, she let me go. I wiped her tears and we talked. She wanted to stay but I told her I had to be alone. I left her there on the stoop, wet with rain.

95

I left Center City in my running stuff and headed to Penn's Landing. I liked going down by the river on my last few days of freedom. At the main entrance, I went left along the shoreline, navigating cars, vendors, and people on foot. I ended up facing the statue honoring Penn's return in 1703—the famous one in the skyline of the city. I sat on the bench and looked at him. And it came over me. I began running back toward Center City.

A greene country town which will never be burnt, and always wholesome.

I ran to Chestnut. A Quaker meeting was settling inside an old brownstone at Fourteenth Street.

Funny, the Quakers are the only ones who still possess spiritual places where we can mainline William Penn, and the soul, spirit, and tenacity that set this place up. The Religious Society of Friends. Originators of the profundity of Philadelphia. Outside the city, you don't run into Quakers much. People just think of motor oil and oatmeal. People think that smiling red-cheeked guy in the three-cornered hat on the oatmeal box is William Penn. I think of growing up, of *I Dream of Jeannie* and potato chips, of the Palestra. I think of red bricks.

Several hundred people sat on benches, some with their eyes closed. The center of it. Not the Bell, or Rocky Balboa, or a cheesesteak, or Independence Hall, or the *Bicentennial Minute*. Here, closer contact with God, with the Quakers. No signs, no symbols, no robes, no cloaks. No crown or cross. *No Cross, No Crown.* Unfettered access to those not of the material world. Pursuit of the center—like Rome—the errand of a fool. The American center could only have been here, where they dropped roots, built with brick, and communed with a modern God.

Nixon was a Quaker. I was too young then to understand what the guy did, and to this day I feel sympathy for him. I still think things never got worse than 1974. It was the bottom. So much fell apart, so much burned, so much left to be burned. Nixon got his ass burned down to the ground.

But we grew like flowers after that, me and my friends, my team. At least for a few years. Like strong iron flowers, like those flowers that grow out in the middle of the country where all there seems to be is dirt. But that was before Dottie died; before we, too, got burned down at the Palestra.

After that we were weeds, like grass. Weeds grow, grass grows. I grew, but nothing for me was like the life I had known in the seventies. Nothing has been the same for me. Nothing has been the same for anyone.

96

The members of the Quaker congregation were still. The service was quiet. The speakers who rose were expectedly ecumenical. There was a sort of sense to it all—of it all making sense, at least in a human way—which was heavy with me. It did not seem divine, it seemed that I was in a familiar place. This was not an epiphany; I am not now, nor have I ever been a Daedalus.

It was rather the effect of the quiet meshed with voices talking in turn about God. Amid all this freedom, all here in Philadelphia. I was ready to protect the place and its sense of decorum the moment I took my seat, as unearned as that feeling may have been. It was as simple and overdone a feeling of manhood as keeping a punk away from an old lady. The meetinghouse was a place for the barely dormant side of my rage to locate itself. I looked up and down the rows for any homeless people or street assholes disrespecting things, much in the way we had acted taking shifts looking for members of other fraternities crashing any of our parties in college. Certainly, no one had asked me to assign myself such a role. I pulled it together and listened.

A man rose, ramrod straight and Sunday-suited, spectacles atop a two-bump Protestant nose. He said he was a tenth-generation Friend, was happy to see all those he knew, as well as any newcomers to the meeting. He said he taught literature now at a local college. He began to speak in the same sort of comforting, yet dissonantly invincible tone of those who had preceded him. As he began, I realized I missed so much about the few stretches of time when I had felt at home—with Artie and

Dottie, for a while with Janice and Tia, and now, even in my self-loathing, above the city in the apartment on Locust Street.

The schoolteacher began, "Poetry is much on my mind today, I find, and, as usual, I am thinking this Sunday of old Walt Whitman. You may know, Friends, Whitman was not much on Philadelphia. But like the heart is to the body, as we have learned in this meetinghouse over the past three centuries, our home here has needed to be passed through often. I am moved today to speak of the poet, to celebrate him in relation to the Lord, though I doubt very much his spirit deigns to ask for it or requires it for a boost.

"Many of you have heard me express before that I think of Whitman as the one who freed us—all of us—from the carcass of an old world the Lord wanted us to discard and therefrom emerge. And, similarly, you know that when we pay our holy respect to our founders, of this city, this society, and this country, we should remember that just as our Constitution brought us forward as free individuals, Whitman's celebrations and ruminations, set down in such unconventional and daring ways, brought the American imagination through to a new terrain of freedom. And through the worst of times—disease, starvation, poverty, bitter ethnic division, and our war to save the Union—he recorded America unflinchingly. In my heart I believe that because of Walt Whitman, you and I are free—*free*—to speak and write and paint and express ourselves with a signature new voice, where before there had been no such freedom of artistic or personal communion with our native lands, of our native selves."

He had a sharp head of white hair, and he looked throughout the building with an intensity that did not equal his speaking voice. He was not preaching. It was true, one could see, he was simply a schoolteacher. He put a hand in his right pocket, as strong public speakers often do at a penultimate moment—as they are about to wrap up, when they know they are bringing it home.

"Whitman wrote that America has a perpetual rite of transformation that is maintained by its spirit—an invincible force, as he says, which 'is fittest for its days.' By this I believe he meant modern—as in that not lost in past symbols nor in the human usurpation of God's will. This American spirit is always on guard to transform—indeed, Whitman said it watches at the threshold of the door. It has enough courage to be prepared for transformation when necessary—and in fact he defines what we are perpetually on the lookout for. We seek, Walt Whitman said, 'a stalwart and well-shaped heir who approaches.'"

His hands clasped with gentle emotion. I felt for the first time what so inspired the nonconformist and holy people William Penn brought to this land of freedom.

"That is, we have the ability to allow the current to be transferred to the new, just as a parent's love and holiness descend to its child, we are blessed with a readiness to be modern, with all the challenges and problems that state of nature entails."

He paused for the last time.

"So, today I'd like to end by sharing that as I think of my responsibilities in this physical world—to my family, my community, my country, my history—it often feels overwhelming amid all the freedom we are blessed by. But I am always—always—bolstered by the feeling that we enjoy the inherent blessing bestowed by the Lord and expressed so well by the poet. And, so, Friends, I pray we may honor each other, and that we may feel as though we are all in his loving arms. God bless you."

He sat down slowly, hands clasped at his midsection under his seersucker blazer.

97

The morning I was set to go to jail, four days after my scuffle with Scully, there was a thump at my apartment door. When I opened it, a brown package the size of a shoe box lay in the hall. It had no markings, wasn't sent by UPS or FedEx. The guys at the front had not called up to tell me I had a delivery. The package just had my name on it in block letters in black marker, nothing else.

I took it inside and sat at my dining-room table. I tore it open and something covered with bubble wrap fell out. Inside was a piece of wood, a section of a board. One side was lacquered, like it came from a lane in a bowling alley. But this wood was at the end of its days; it was worn and full of scratches and black markings that all but buried the grain below the treated surface. I felt little indentations and looked closely. I realized it had been engraved.

FALLCREST SENIOR HIGH SCHOOL BASKETBALL
COURT 1960–2010

I put my fingers in the indentations of the letters. It was one small piece of our court, a wooden brick of that old beaten floor. A note fell out of the box. It was written in black marker, same as my name on the outside of the package.

Joe: You should have this. I'll come see you first chance. L

I held the little piece of hardwood. I wondered which part of the floor it came from, how many times I had stepped on it, or whether there was a place on that court I had never been. To that last bit, I decided the answer was no way.

I drove to the internment gate of the Graterford state prison. Eric had called and offered a ride, but I didn't want anyone to see me, so I went alone. I parked in a long-term parking lot and took a shuttle bus to the processing center. So, in the end, I drove myself to jail. It was like checking into the hospital. They took my name, made me wait. They found my file and a guard came to get me.

Eric and I had talked about trying to gauge the first day. We couldn't tell from the assistant US attorney's office or Scully's office where they were going to put me. If they took me down to the general population and put me out in one of the wings, I was in for it, the whole nightmare.

There was a chance, and Eric was pressing his contacts at the jail for this, they would hold me in the few cells reserved for transfers and court appearances. That's what we were aiming for. Eric said I had it pretty much guaranteed till I went to see Scully. His guy at the jail stopped calling him back after that. "You might have fucked that one up, bub," he said.

They put me in a temp cell by myself. Bed, aluminum toilet, bookshelf. Five or six cells on the row. Eric told me it was the easiest place I'd see. I had to wait.

I was all Chris Scully's now, if I hadn't been before. I was all-in. A Friend of Chris Scully for sure. He controlled my liberty; he controlled whether I would get the shit kicked out of me; he controlled whether I'd be anally raped by animals with HIV. I could be out after serving five or six nights in a transfer cell, or I could be in for two years, extended by time you get for what you do in order to stay alive once there. Fight: thirty days. Complain: you get hassled in the yard and you miss curfew. You start racking up time.

It all started to crash down; the sheaths of ice ran down the frontal lobe of my brain. My intestines locked; I had chest pain; I got the chilly sweats you get with the flu. I was on a bench. Inside. Alone. In a cell. Ungrateful for all that freedom.

The end of the line.

No one knew when I would get out. No answers from the magistrates, the warlords, the tribal chieftains, the ward leaders, the Home Office, the Bureau of Prisons, the Department of Prisons, the US attorney's office, the office of the Honorable Chris J. Scully, district attorney. I could be on that bench for five minutes, five hours, five days, five months, or five years. Five chapters, five players, five stories, five redbrick columns at the Palestra. I did not feel the rule of law applied to that bench, I only felt crushed by the manhood of custody, of physical possession. The law, jammed up and in.

98

Her face appears in the mind's eye, not like an apparition or a vision, but vivid in my imagination. Nineteen, short hair, spiked up, a tattoo on her shoulder blade but not her neck, a proud, defiant mess. She wears black Converse high tops and carries poster board for an art project. Mad and excited, arguing with three out of every five she meets in the course of a day. I look closely at her and my brain gets the neuron shot bringing relief from the anxiety that's ravaged me all my life. With every pulse, every surge, every constricting blood vessel, I see more fully that I am seeing her as she will be, and as she will be, she will be fine. She will be fine. She is little but with her chin toward the world, headed for heartbreaks, weirdness, and danger; but also for good things, better things. I need only see her and I can tell that she is my wondrous and beautiful little girl. I will not lie dead in a ditch on the way to Gettysburg. She will be okay because I will be with her and love her as deeply as the sky, without condition, without cause. I can see her. I can see her as she is. I can see her as only I can see her. She may not love me; she may feel that undeserved. But I will not orphan her. She will be my child all the days of my life.

99

Whitman left New York in December 1862 when he read in the *New York Tribune* that his brother George was wounded outside Fredericksburg. On the way, he was robbed in Philadelphia. He made it to D.C. to help take care of the boys. I see Whitman the nurse. He's picking through the bodies, helping the doctors with the ones worth saving, holding up the ones who needed arms and legs cut off.

Nasty, burning, rotten battlefields. He walked around looking for live ones, no buggering on his mind then. Gestating the American song. But Ray and descendants like him, like me, for the most part, did not ask of him, "Can you imagine what it was like?" Not for Whitman. Washington, yes; Hamilton, yes. Whitman no. I'd love to meet the people—the civic people, the real Americans, the art lovers and literature buffs, the learned and dedicated people who fought in 1957 to name a bridge spanning from Philadelphia to Camden after Walt Whitman. Those were some stone-hard people taken for granted by some and underestimated by all the rest. Pennsylvanians.

So, it is not an accident, at least not to me, that you find Whitman with one of Philadelphia's main arteries named after him. He was the one who told us to connect. He knew this language that was emerging from farms and demolished towns, filled with jimsonweed, dandelion, muscadine, nightshade, goldenrod, maple trees and honeysuckle; knew that reeds of straw and indeed blades of grass would continually generate well-shaped heirs, and that slowly a line would form of song-singers, poets, and painters fittest for their days. With all that has come before us

Kevin Morris

in this beautiful and deadly land, he knew we faced a complicated future. Aware that his quarry was centuries, knew the true new world—the one started by William Penn and others—was beginning. It would exist with a new language and consciousness—*American*—amid the chaos of the freedom it has taken thousands of years to claim. Let Freedom Ring.

100

Like in the movies, but more real, it's a cinder-block cell with an aluminum toilet. It's not as though there's a door or a curtain; they watch you go if they want. I can't play basketball anymore. I couldn't keep a fantasy team if they let me.

I'm stuck, left with Penn in jail for being a Quaker, searching for the New World, coming here, finding it, building it. Left with ideas of Pennsylvanians, cold weather–ready people who built the brick buildings. Winning, preparing, molding, drying, and firing the clay. Left with Whitman, wandering around after the battles, hopeful for the stalwart and well-shaped heir who approaches, hopeful for the American song. I wanted to sing songs, to be the one sent to make it, to be the fittest for my days. And then it died. The thing built with brick. It was busted up in a million pieces by 1974. That song will not sing anymore.

At the Palestra, that first bucket that brings down the streamers was made long ago, leaving the popcorn boxes and the soft pretzel wrappers littering the stands, while the cigarette butts and empty wrestling masks boil in the deep stench of trash trucks stopping and starting down Locust Street.

A guard came to the door of my cell.

"Knight?"

I stood up.

"Didn't see you there for a second. Looks like it's a stop and not a stay."

Acknowledgments

I want to thank Morgan Entrekin for all of his guidance, support, and friendship. Many, many thanks to Allison Malecha and everyone at Grove Atlantic, as well. A very special thank you to Nikole Sullivan for taking care of everything with professionalism and grace. I owe a huge debt of gratitude to my agent, Jane von Mehren, for her patience, dedication, and savvy, and am similarly indebted to my good friends Alex Kohner, Annett Wolf, and Lindsay Wineberg for looking after me. My heartfelt thanks to my friend, Glenn Altschuler, who has been so generous since the day I met him thirty-five years ago, for countless hours of invaluable help and encouragement. It is difficult to express my full gratitude to my dear friend Eric Roth, because I can't thank him enough for the stories, the great books, the lunches, the ballgames, and the simple lessons about writing that are within plain sight. But I can thank him for his guidance and artistic advice in connection with this project from wire to wire.

I am grateful to my friends and colleagues who have provided inspiration and assistance in the course of making this book: Kevin Yorn, Phil Stutz, David Krintzman, Matt Stone, Angela Howard, Todd Rubenstein, Jim Gavin, Trey Parker, Stuart Liner, James Frey, Gus Van Sant, Jim Axelrod, Matthew McConaughey, Karen Green, the late David Carr, Robb Bindler, Stefan Nachuk, Dee Dee DeBartlo, Miles Metcoff, Anne-Marie Flustleby, Melodie Moore, Debra Greenfield, Gavin O'Connor, Anne Garefino, Betsy Walters, John Walters, Sydney Holland, Blaine Lourd, Dan Loose, Denise Klein, Matt Hudson, Pete Yorn, the late Herman Goldblatt, and everyone at MYBLKRK&G.

And, finally, thank you with my full heart and soul to Rocky, Dulcie, and Gaby for the love, understanding, and support they have provided throughout the writing of this novel.